PLATO'S

APOLOGY OF SOCRATES AND CRITO

AND A PART OF THE

PHAEDO

WITH INTRODUCTION, COMMENTARY, AND CRITICAL
APPENDIX

BY

REV. C. L. KITCHEL, M.A.

INSTRUCTOR IN GREEK IN YALE UNIVERSITY

NEW YORK ·:· CINCINNATI ·:· CHICAGO
AMERICAN BOOK COMPANY

PREFACE

In the following work the object everywhere kept in view has been to present the person of Socrates so clearly that the student may not fail to see what manner of man he was and why his influence was so decided upon his own time and upon succeeding ages.

To this end a part of the narrative portion of the *Phaedo* has been added to the *Apology* and *Crito* (so often given together without that addition) in order that the story may not lack its climax and catastrophe. The account of how nobly Socrates bore himself in his trial and under temptation to escape from prison needs to be supplemented by the picture of the serenity and courage with which he drank the fatal hemlock, that so the fair capital may be placed upon the stately column and the moral scope and splendor of the man be fully exhibited. The wrong which is done to the *Phaedo* in so mutilating it is more than atoned for by what is thus added to our view of the character of Socrates.

In the Dialogues contained in this volume the moral qualities of Socrates appear in their highest manifestation, as also some hint is given of his intellectual method; but the man is exhibited here at the great crisis of his experience, and but for a short time, so that we see only vaguely what the main work of his life was and still less clearly what was the intellectual process by virtue of which he made an epoch in philosophy. In the Introduction the attempt is made to state briefly what his life was devoted to doing, and what it was in his conversation which was intellectually so important and influential.

The outline of the argument prefixed to the notes on each chapter is intended chiefly as a suggestion that it is of the first importance that the student be led to search out and express clearly for himself the play and progress of the thought as it develops.

The dramatic form which Plato has given to his report of these conversations has been indicated by notes at the proper points. The form is very likely more regular and artistic than that actually employed by Socrates, but it has preserved for us the vital fact that skillful conversation was the method by which the great master brought himself to bear both intellectually and morally upon his followers. It has seemed worth while also in this way to emphasize the exquisite literary form in which the poet-philosopher has preserved to us these discourses.

The text is based upon that of Wohlrab in his revision of Hermann, as given in the Teubner text edition, of which the first volume is dated 1886; but the punctuation has been changed, especially in the removing of many commas before relatives and interrogative and declarative particles, and in a different use of quotation marks. Where the text has been otherwise altered, attention has been called to the fact in the Appendix.

The commentary has drawn freely from many sources, but is most largely indebted to Cron, while the general estimate of Socrates has been influenced more by Zeller than by any other authority.

The editor cannot sufficiently express his obligation to the friends and associates who have encouraged and generously aided him in this work. He especially desires to acknowledge the very valuable corrections and suggestions which Prof. M. W. Humphreys has kindly allowed him to make use of.

NEW HAVEN, 1898.

CONTENTS

INTRODUCTION

———•◇•———

PLATO

1. Life of Plato. — Plato, the son of Aristo and Perictione, was born in Athens, probably in May, 427 B.C.[1] He was of noble descent, Codrus, the last king of Athens, being claimed as an ancestor on his father's side, while his mother was of the family of Solon. About the age of twenty he became a disciple of Socrates. Before that time he is said to have devoted himself to athletics and poetry, and to have composed a complete dramatic tetralogy, which he was intending to bring out but committed to the flames when he met with Socrates and had his attention diverted to the field of philosophy. Plato took no active part in public affairs. If he had any such ambition circumstances were not favorable. His voice was thin, the name of his relative Critias, one of the Thirty Tyrants, was abhorred, and the condemnation of Socrates by the ruling democracy had filled him with grief and indignation. He determined, therefore, to devote his life to thought and teaching. After the tragic death of his master in 399 B.C., Plato, for the time embittered against Athens, went

———

[1] Diogenes Laertius (in the third century of our era), III. 2, cites Apollodorus (who died 129 B.C.) as saying that Plato was born Ol. 88, on the 7th of Thargelion = 427, May 29th (in that year, it is computed). This coincides with what Diogenes Laertius also tells us, III. 6, that Hermodorus, a pupil of Plato, says that Plato was twenty-eight years old when, after the death of Socrates in 399, he went to Megara. In Diog. Laert. III. 2, Hermippus (200 B.C.) is cited as saying that Plato died in Ol. 108, 1 = 348–347, eighty-one years of age. See Steinhart's *Platos Leben* (being Vol. 9 of *Platons Sämmtliche Werke übersetzt von H. Müller*), pp. 32–65 and 234–238, and Zeller's *Plato and the Older Academy* (Eng. Trans. of 1876), chap. I., note 2.

to Megara, and thence to Egypt, perhaps by way of Cyrene. Later, probably after a sojourn in Athens, we find him in Italy and in Sicily,[1] where he incurred the displeasure of the elder Dionysius, by whose direction it is said Plato was sold as a slave in Aegina. Ransomed by a friend, he returned to Athens about 387 B.C., and began to teach philosophy in the Academy, a gymnasium in the northern suburb of the city. Twenty years later, in 368 B.C., at the instance of Dion, his friend and the brother-in-law of the elder Dionysius, Plato visited Sicily a second time, hoping to win over the younger Dionysius to philosophy and his political beliefs, in which, however, he was disappointed. In 361 B.C. Plato made a third unavailing journey to Syracuse in the interest of Dion, whom Dionysius had banished and deprived of his property. After this he devoted himself exclusively to philosophy and teaching until he died, in 347 B.C., in his eighty-first year. Among his pupils were Aristotle and Phocion.

2. **Writings.** — All the writings of Plato known to antiquity, thirty-six in number, if the Epistles are reckoned as one, have been preserved to us. In them we see how profoundly he had been influenced by his master. All of his compositions except the Epistles are in dialogue form, as Socrates taught, and in all of the Dialogues except the Laws Socrates leads the conversation. Plato's object at first was to reproduce the personality and continue the method of his great master. While we cannot know positively, the opinion seems to prevail that he composed none of his Dialogues while Socrates was still living. The *Apology*, it is generally agreed, must have been written immediately after the trial, — the *Crito* after a longer interval. The *Phaedo* is referred to a later period, when the ideas peculiar to Plato had become developed.

[1] The seventh of Plato's Epistles, in which the journeys to Syracuse are recounted, though probably not genuine, was doubtless written by one who had learned the facts, perhaps from Speusippus, the nephew of Plato, who accompanied him on his third journey to Sicily. See Steinhart's *Platos Leben*, p. 12.

3. Literary Form. — The form of Plato's works is dramatic. They are not only dialogues (some direct, in the very words of the speakers, like the *Crito*, others narrated, like the *Phaedo*),[1] but they are, many of them, constructed throughout on the lines of tragedy which Aristotle prescribes.[2] After a prologue introducing the characters and the beginning of the action, which is a discussion (not a mythic plot as in tragedy), we have several members or parts of the dialogue, corresponding to the ἐπεισόδια in a Greek play, in which a complication (δέσις) and unravelling (λύσις) are developed. These members are sometimes separated, and often enlivened, by traces of something like the dramatic chorus, the whole ending with a distinct epilogue.[3] This dramatic quality is the natural result of Socrates' dialectic method, with which Plato had been greatly impressed, of the dramatic spirit with which, owing to the plays of the great dramatists, the Athenian people at this time were saturated, and of the poetic and literary endowment of Plato himself. The problem Plato had to solve was to unite the dramatic with the argumentative in the development of his theses, giving rise thus to what may be called the dialectic or argumentative drama.

Aristophanes of Byzantium (200 B.C.), the grammarian and critic of Alexandria, because of the dramatic form of the Dialogues, arranged some of them in trilogies, as if they were really tragedies. Later, in the first century of our era, Thrasyllus, the traveling companion of Augustus and the tutor of Tiberius, divided all the Dialogues into tetralogies, grouping together about the closing scenes of Socrates' life the *Euthyphro*, *Apology*, *Crito*, and *Phaedo*.[4]

4. Contents. — In the *Apology* and the *Crito*, written soon after Socrates died, while Plato was still under the more immediate

---

[1] See R. Hirzel's *Der Dialog*, pp. 174–271.

[2] *Poetics*, VI. and XVIII.

[3] See Thiersch's *Ueber die dramatische Natur der Platonischen Dialoge* in *Abhandlungen der baierischen Akademie*, 1837.

[4] Diog. Laert. III. 56–62, and Grote's *Plato*, chap. IV.

influence of his master, we have given to us with substantial accuracy the person of Socrates, his method, and his teaching; even in the dramatic portions of the *Phaedo*, although this Dialogue was written later, the spirit and character of Socrates are still portrayed vividly. This is what we should naturally expect, especially in the *Apology*. Immediately after Socrates' death loyalty to his memory would have forbidden Plato to offer anything but a correct representation of him to the many surviving admirers and pupils.[1] This presumption is sustained by the *Memorabilia* of Xenophon, in which we have substantially the same Socrates as in the earlier dialogues of Plato.[2] The difference between the two representations arises from the fact that Xenophon, being a practical man and no philosopher, did not appreciate or report the more ideal and philosophic sides of his master, as Plato did. Just so in the synoptic gospels we have pretty exact and literal reports of the deeds and words of Jesus, while their profounder significance is only indicated. In the gospel of John, however, while we have essentially the same Jesus both in person and in teaching as in *Matthew*, *Mark*, and *Luke*, the spirit and the significance of the Master's life and doctrine are developed much more profoundly. To arrive, through Plato and Xenophon, at what Socrates really was, we have no better criterion than Schleiermacher's two questions: What *may* Socrates have been in addition to what Xenophon reports without gainsaying the character and maxims which Xenophon distinctly assigns him? and, What *must* Socrates have been to call for and to justify such a description of him as is given in the Dialogues of Plato?[3]

As the years went on after the death of Socrates, although Plato's experience widened and his ideas developed, nevertheless he retained the intellectual method and the conversational form

---

[1] See Grote's *Plato*, chap. VII., and Grote's *History of Greece*, chap. LXVIII.

[2] See Zeller's *Socrates and the Socratic Schools* (Eng. Trans. of 1885), p. 182 ff.

[3] See Schleiermacher's *Werke*, III. 2, 293, and Zeller's *Socrates and the Socratic Schools*, p. 100.

which his master had used, and so, perhaps, justified to his own mind his representing Socrates as the chief speaker in nearly all that he wrote.

We are led thus to inquire as to the person, work, and results of the work of Socrates.

SOCRATES

HIS PERSON AND TRAITS

5. Life of Socrates. — Socrates, son of a sculptor Sophroniscus and a midwife Phaenarete, was born at Athens not later than 469 B.C., — perhaps a year or two earlier.[1] The son followed for a while the occupation of his father, and Pausanias says that in his time, the second century of our era, a group of the Graces, supposed to be the work of Socrates, was still to be seen at the entrance to the Acropolis. His wife Xanthippe,[2] whom he probably did not marry until he was about fifty years old,[3] was of a violent temper, which has become proverbial. By her he had three sons.[4] The incidents in his life as known to us were few. He served as a hoplite at Potidaea, 432 B.C., and, in the Peloponnesian war, at Delium, 424 B.C., and Amphipolis, 422 B.C.[5] In 406 B.C. he was a member of the Senate.[6] Early in 399 B.C., he

---

[1] The year of Socrates' death is ascertained from Diog. Laert. II. 44, who cites Apollodorus as saying that he died Ol. 95, 1 = 399. The time of the trial was, probably, at the end of the month Anthesterion (February, nearly), or the beginning of Elaphebolion (March, nearly), rather than in the second half of the month Thargelion (May, nearly), as some compute. The Delian festival seems to have been held at the end of winter. See C. Robert in *Hermes*, XXI. pp. 161 ff. Socrates was executed thirty days later (Xen. *Mem.* IV. 8, 2). At that time he was seventy years old (*Apol.* 17 D, and *Crito*, 52 E), so that he was born not later than 469 B.C., or, if πλείω ἑβδομήκοντα be read in *Apol.* 17 D, we should have to go back a year or two earlier. See Zeller's *Socrates and the Socratic Schools*, chap. III. note 1, and H. Diels in *Rhein. Mus.* XXXI. (1876), pp. 1–54.

[2] *Phaedo*, 60 A.

[3] Zeller's *Socrates and the Socratic Schools*, p. 62, note 3.

[4] *Apol.* 34 D.

[5] *Apol.* 28 E.

[6] *Apol.* 32 B.

was condemned to death by a jury of his fellow-citizens, and a month later drank the poison hemlock and died.[1]

6. Personal Appearance. — His personal appearance was not pleasing. In Xenophon's *Symposium*,[2] facetiously contending with the beautiful youth Critobulus as to personal charms, Socrates admits that his eyes project like a crab's, his nostrils are upturned like an ape's, and his lips are thick, but he claims that there is a practical advantage in each of these features. In the *Theaetetus*[3] his snub nose and prominent eyes are again referred to ; while in Plato's *Symposium*[4] Alcibiades is made to say that Socrates has a face like Marsyas the satyr, and again that he resembles the ugly carved figures of Silenus.

7. Early Training. — Like other Athenian youth, Socrates was early instructed in literature ($\mu o\upsilon\sigma\iota\kappa\acute{\eta}$) and gymnastics,[5] but his eager and active mind went on continually to make acquisitions from all sources.

It was a liberal education to live in the Athens of his day. He was born when the Confederacy of Delos was not yet a decade old, and his growth was coincident with the growth of the Athenian empire. Simonides did not die till after Socrates was born, while Pindar was living till he was nearly thirty. Of the great tragic poets, Aeschylus produced his Orestean trilogy when Socrates was about twelve ; Sophocles and Euripides were his contemporaries. He listened all his life to the competitions of these and many other great dramatists in the Dionysiac contests, and doubtless heard himself caricatured in the *Clouds*, the comedy of Aristophanes. The age of Pericles (460–430) falls into the very middle of his life. He must have watched the building of the long walls from Athens to the Piraeus ; he may have practiced his art in the workshop of Phidias ; he saw the Parthenon arise under the direction of Ictinus. Herodotus and Thucydides produced their immortal histories in his manhood and old age. He had intercourse with

[1] *Phaedo*, 117 and 118.
[2] Chap. V.
[3] 143 E.   [4] 215 A.
[5] *Crito*, 50 D.

the great sophists Protagoras, Gorgias, and others, with whom it would appear he often tried conclusions. It was in constant contact with such prominent and gifted men that Socrates developed.

8. Mental Characteristics. — But his mind was too vigorous and independent to be entirely shaped by its surroundings. It remained always unique. One trait of it was its great activity. Knowledge was the fundamental thing with Socrates, because in his view the virtues were essentially forms of knowledge, and for more knowledge he was continually seeking; the quest for it he unites with his great mission of testing men in obedience to the oracle of the god.[1]

Another trait of his mind was concentration. This is illustrated by the story Alcibiades tells of him in the *Symposium*.[2] On the expedition to Potidaea, one morning he fell to thinking about some problem he could not solve, and he would not give up, but stood fixed in thought all that day and the following night until the sun rose next morning, when he went his way.

One other mental characteristic was practical common sense. However exalted his conclusions at last may be, they all start from the most simple and commonplace beginnings. His discourses at first sight appeared ridiculous or rude, treating, as they often did, of " beasts of burden, smiths, tailors, and tanners — always repeating the same thing in the same words."[3] But this habit was practically most valuable. It was the basis of that logical induction which Socrates was the first to employ, by virtue of which he must be regarded as the originator of the scientific method. This same common sense lies also at the root of the humor and the irony which abounded in his conversation and made it so effective.

9. Moral Traits. — But though his body and mind were not conventionally elegant they were robust and healthy, and his moral nature had perfect control of them. His powers of endurance were wonderful. In military service he withstood fatigue

[1] *Apol.* 22 B.   [2] 220.   [3] *Symposium*, 221.

and hardships, was indifferent to heat and cold, and went barefoot in all seasons, even in the winter campaign in Thrace.[1]

He practiced temperance and self-denial to an extraordinary degree. "To want nothing," he said, "is divine." His clothing was homely, and the same in winter as in summer.[1] His diet was simple, yet he was no ascetic ; at a banquet with friends, he was the life of the feast, and could drink more wine without intoxication than any of his companions.[2] In like manner, though genial and attached to his friends, he was superior to the temptations of lust in what would seem at that time to have been its most insidious form, as is shown by his ignoring the solicitations of Alcibiades.[3]

His physical courage was remarkable. When Alcibiades was wounded in the fight at Potidaea, Socrates would not leave him, but rescued him and his arms, and deserved the prize of valor offered by the generals, but insisted it should be given to Alcibiades. At Delium, in the flight of the army, he walked off as coolly as though in the streets of Athens, and by his presence of mind and intrepidity saved himself and his companion.[4]

But his moral courage was quite as marked as his physical. The ridicule and obloquy of his fellow-citizens did not make him flinch, even when they culminated in threats and indictment. After the battle of Arginusae (406 B.C.) he refused to accede to the proposal that the fate of the eight surviving generals should be decided by a single vote of the ecclesia, although orators and populace cried out against him, and threatened him with imprisonment. Neither would he obey the command of the Thirty Tyrants, in their reign of terror, to go and bring their victim Leon from Salamis, though he refused at the peril of his life.[5]

But nowhere is this moral intrepidity shown more clearly than in his *Apology*, where he will not sacrifice his sincerity,[6] nor depart

---

[1] *Symposium*, 220 B.
[2] *Symposium*, 214 A.
[3] *Symposium*, 219 C, D.
[4] *Symposium*, 220 E and 221.
[5] *Apol.* 32.
[6] *Apol.* 17 A and 40 A.

one step from the path of duty,[1] nor do an ignoble deed to please his judges,[2] although by yielding even a little probably he could have saved his life.

10. Religious Belief. — In his religious convictions, Socrates was partly the child of the age in which he lived and partly superior to it. He acknowledged and worshiped the gods in which the city believed.[3] He offered prayer to the sun,[4] the greater part of his life was spent in obedience, as he claimed,[5] to the order of Apollo in the oracular response given to Chaerephon at Delphi ; and in the very moment of death he bids his friends sacrifice a cock to Aesculapius[6] in token that at length all is well with him. He believed in supernatural intervention as did most Athenians of his time. Prominent among such interventions which he himself experienced was his $\Delta\alpha\iota\mu\acute{o}\nu\iota o\nu$.[7] Socrates ascribed to a divine source that voice which from childhood came to him, frequently preventing him from doing what he was about to do, but never urging him on.[8] This was not the voice, as we term it, of conscience. That voice, also, Socrates heard and obeyed, and it often prevented him from certain courses of action, as, for instance, from consenting to the illegal trial of the generals of the battle of Arginusae, or from going to bring Leon from Salamis,[9] or from escaping from prison at the instigation of Crito.[10] But this voice of conscience he did not call $\theta\epsilon\iota\acute{o}\nu$ $\tau\iota$ $\kappa\alpha\grave{\iota}$ $\delta\alpha\iota\mu\acute{o}\nu\iota o\nu$. The monitions of the divine voice, unlike conscience, referred only to future actions, and did not approve or condemn the past ; they regarded exclusively the consequences of actions and not their moral quality ;[11] and they were given only in cases where his unaided natural judgment seemed unable to decide. It was because, under doubtful circumstances, he could

[1] *Apol.* 29 D.
[2] *Apol.* 34 C.
[3] *Apol.* 35 D.
[4] *Symposium,* 220 D.
[5] *Apol.* 23 B.
[6] *Phaedo,* 118.

[7] See Riddell's *Apology of Plato,* Appendix A.
[8] *Apol.* 31 C, D.
[9] *Apol.* 32.
[10] *Crito,* 46 B.
[11] *Apol.* 40 B, C.

not himself see what course to pursue that a clear intimation coming to him, as if a voice spoke in the ear of his spirit, seemed to be supernatural. From the human side we should call it "an unanalyzed process of reasoning." His natural instinct, quickened by apprehension, intuitively reached the adverse conclusion. The part of the process which he could not analyze he regarded as supernatural. It is no objection to this explanation that the divine influence came to Socrates while he was yet a child.[1] The intuitions and apprehensions of childhood are often more acute than those of maturity. And the voice would not urge to any action,[1] for the subtile intuitions favorable to any action do not resist the will, but quietly coincide with it, and so make no sign.

But Socrates, although involved in the polytheism of his times, under the influence doubtless of the nature-philosophers who had preceded him, as well as by the process of his own reflection, had arrived at the conception of One Supreme God, of whom the many deities were instruments. Contemplating the external world, he distinguishes the creator and ruler of it from the other gods,[2] and considers that He is related to the universe as the soul of man is to his body, everywhere pervading, controlling, and caring for it. Do not imagine, he says,[3] that your soul can think about things here and things in Egypt and in Sicily, but that the thought of God is not capable of caring for all things at the same time. To such a supreme and all-wise God it is that Socrates refers more than once in his *Apology*. To Him he yields immediate and implicit obedience.[4] His guidance he will accept wherever it may lead, even unto death.[5]

THE WORK OF SOCRATES

11. His Work as a Reformer and Philosopher. — The work of Socrates was that of a reformer, and as such he is to be regarded.

---

[1] *Apol.* 31 D.
[2] Xen. *Mem.* IV. 3, 13.
[3] Xen. *Mem.* I. 4, 17.

[4] *Apol.* 30 A.
[5] *Apol.* 19 A, 35 D, 42 A, and *Crito*, 54 E.

He was not primarily a philosopher in the modern sense. He did not seek to arrive at truth for its own sake alone, nor to draw up a philosophical system. His aim was mainly practical. There were great evils existing in men and society about him. To those evils he was particularly sensitive, owing to the peculiar quality of his intellectual and moral nature. For those evils he was persuaded that he had the only and sufficient remedy.[1] The application of that remedy in order to overcome those evils was the work of his life. His great aim was to make men care, not so much for their bodies, or money, or office, as for righteousness, and virtue, and the things of the soul.[2]

But though he was not a philosopher primarily, in the means which he used he was one. His method of reforming men was by an intellectual process with and upon them which he termed philosophizing.[3] He spent his time among his fellow-citizens, in the constant and public quest of truth, with them and for their good. He was convinced that so only could he do his part in counteracting the evils in men and society about him.

12. Moral Condition of Athens. — The evils which Socrates found prevalent among the Athenians were deep seated. In the *Apology* they appear most prominently in the form of self-conceit. Men, everywhere in the city, thought they knew the greatest things, when really they knew nothing.[4] This apparently harmless foible Socrates recognized as a symptom of a fatal malady, namely, the exaltation of the individual above truth and above right. He saw that a general skepticism, like a dry rot, was laying hold of society. There was no real knowledge or virtue, men claimed ; whatever each man chose to believe or do was right. The ancient gods were being dethroned, and practical atheism was spreading. The old standards of morality were vanishing, and a capricious selfishness ruled in their stead. As a result, injustice, cruelty, and distrust prevailed in both private and public life.

[1] *Apol.* 30 E.
[2] *Apol.* 30 A, B, and 36 C.
[3] *Apol.* 28 E and 29 D.
[4] *Apol.* 21 and 22.

KITCHEL'S PLATO — 2

Alcibiades and Critias may be taken as typical men of the times, the former the brilliant but unprincipled demagogue, the latter the most arbitrary and cruel of the oligarchs.

For this evil condition of things we may note two great causes. The first was the speculations of the philosophers.

13. The Earlier Philosophers.[1] — Greek philosophy, beginning with Thales and developed by Pythagoras, Heraclītus, Empedocles, Anaxagoras, and their followers, had been an attempt to account for the origin of things on a physical basis. Because their knowledge of the external world was so limited, the systems which these devised were in the main but idle speculation, and had rendered philosophy discredited and futile. One great result, however, they had attained. Through the conception of cosmic energy they had arrived at the idea of Deity back of and over the gods of Olympus. But thereby they had shaken the belief of the people in the ancient divinities. Anaxagoras, for instance, taught that the sun was stone and the moon earth,[2] and that supreme over all things was the all-wise and all-powerful essence, mind. Anaxagoras was exiled as an atheist, in spite of the influence of his friend Pericles, and the belief in one supreme Deity found little acceptance. Yet for all that, the old gods were becoming neglected and forsaken. Along with them also went faith in the existence of any gods at all. Such is generally the case in passing from an antiquated to a new and more adequate theology. But along with faith in the old gods went, in large degree, the high and severe morality of the heroic age.

14. The Sophists.[3] — But a second cause of the evil condition of things was the influence of the sophists. The name was given to a set of men, mostly foreigners, who came to Athens as instructors of youth.[4] As a result of the increased wealth and power of

---

[1] See Grote's *Plato*, chaps. I. and II., and Zeller's *Presocratic Philosophy* (Eng. Trans. of 1881).

[2] *Apol.* 26 D.

[3] See Grote's *History*, chap. LXVII., and Zeller's *Presocratic Philosophy*, (Eng. Trans. of 1881), sect. III.

[4] *Apol.* 19 E.

the city, young men needed instruction as to how to care for their property, and to be able to argue and speak so as to defend themselves, if need be, in court, or to come before the ecclesia to advocate or oppose any measure in debate. Such ability was the more important because in the pure democracy of Athens paid advocates were not allowed, and because the way to distinction and influence lay in the power to work upon the people in the harangues of the ecclesia. In the absence of high schools and universities, to meet this want the sophists arose. Their method was to receive as pupils the young men who sought them, agreeing to instruct them in their sophistic arts and taking therefor a sum of money.[1] In teaching their pupils thus to think and to speak, they necessarily had to do with rhetoric and philosophy. Of these sophists some of the most prominent were in the main good and able men, such as Protagoras of Abdēra, in Thrace, (480–411), the first who called himself a sophist and taught for pay, — who made more money, Plato says, than Phidias and ten other sculptors.[2] Another noted sophist was Gorgias of Leontini, in Sicily, who came on an embassy to Athens in 427 B.C., and acquired great celebrity as a teacher of rhetoric. Prodicus of Ceos and Hippias of Elis and many others might be mentioned.

15. **Their Influence.** — In philosophy, the sophists took a great step in advance. It was evident that the old field was for the time exhausted. So few facts were known about the external universe that all thought about it was mere baseless speculation. There remained, however, to be explored the field of man, the true and fruitful sphere of philosophy. To this field the general demand for education also invited, and into it the sophists entered, thus bringing philosophy out from the retirement of the schools and applying it to practical life. In so doing they debased it. For one thing, they subordinated truth to triumph in argument. Calling in rhetoric to their aid, they taught their pupils how to make the worse appear the better reason in order to mis-

[1] *Apol.* 19 E.   [2] *Meno,* 91 D.

lead a jury or deceive the populace. Florid and specious argumentation took the place of honest investigation, and discussion degenerated into controversy.

But even more serious harm had been done to philosophy by the sophists. Under their influence it had become skeptical. Accepting as their belief the teaching of Anaxagoras, that mind is supreme, they developed the doctrine that "man is the measure of all things," as Pythagoras expressed it. This they interpreted, not in the broad and correct sense that the reason of man properly guarded is the only arbiter of truth. Instead, they taught a bald individualism. The notion or impression of the individual man was the truth for him and the law of his action. If that were so, there was no real knowledge and no fixed standard of right and wrong. Skepticism took the place of belief, and selfishness of moral obligation.

Under these influences, character and society rapidly deteriorated. Yet at the same time, and just by reason of this perverted philosophy, the Athenians seemed to themselves to be especially intelligent, and while they knew nothing aright, thought they knew the greatest things perfectly. Socrates saw underneath this self-conceit the atheism and skepticism of which it was but a symptom.

16. Other Causes. — For this decline in faith and morals an abundant opportunity had been offered in the wealth and luxury which had come to Athens as a result of the Persian war and the growth of the Athenian empire out of the confederacy of Delos ; and in the party strife and passion which had been fomented in a city exasperated by its reverses in the Peloponnesian war and by the rise and expulsion of the Thirty Tyrants. One other influence deepened and diffused this conceit of knowledge. It was the pure democracy of the Athenian government, the natural tendency of which was to encourage the worthless and ignorant. The most incompetent men, because of the share they had in the government of the city, were led to feel that they were equal in wisdom to the wisest, even in the greatest matters.[1] Such a state of things was a very hothouse of incompetence and conceit.

17. The Socratic Not-knowing. — Against this conceit of knowledge which he found about him on all sides, Socrates opposed his claim of not-knowing.[2] The Delphic oracle given to Chaerephon concerning him he found to be true in this respect : he was wiser than other men in that while they thought they knew and did not, he did not know and thought that he did not.[2] His pressing of this claim, since it excited odium against him,[3] is especially prominent in the *Apology*. But, like the self-conceit with which it was adroitly chosen to contend, his not-knowing was only an indication of a deeper condition. It implied that he had an idea of real knowledge, compared with which the first notion or impression of the individual is mere ignorance. Neither he nor any other man could truly know, while they rested satisfied with their own conceit. They must recognize their ignorance, as the first step, and then go on to acquire real knowledge by patiently finding out and carefully testing the opinions of others. He thus asserted that sound knowledge is no man's possession to begin with, but must be acquired by long investigation and comparison. So regarded, Socrates' claim of ignorance is seen to be not insincere or merely ironical, though it had the effect of irony. It was, in his view, the fundamental attitude of mind in all who would be truly wise. It was put forward with consummate tact because it at once rebuked the conceit of his opponents, and exhibited the chief feature of his own method by which he hoped to reform them.

This not-knowing of Socrates was the direct opposite of the sophistic skepticism. The main article in his creed was that real knowledge can be attained, and that by such knowledge alone could men be made better. Everywhere Socrates claims that knowledge gives the power to do right, that if men know what is right they will do it ; that knowledge and virtue are identical.

[1] *Apol.* 22 D.   [3] *Apol.* 21 E.
[2] *Apol.* 21 D.

This doctrine, merely hinted at in the *Apology*,[1] is in several of the dialogues amply developed. The understanding of what is good in reference to different classes of facts constitutes courage, justice, and every virtue. It was this conviction of his which incited Socrates to go on and show men the way to attain to real knowledge.

18. Real Knowledge Attainable. — But Socrates not only believed that if men knew, they would do right ; he also was convinced that he had the method of arriving at real knowledge, and that he could teach it to men, and so save them and the state. This was the secret of his courage and of his influence.

We have seen that the sophists and all preceding philosophers had relied on the notions and impressions of the individual without subjecting them to critical examination and comparison. As a result, all real knowledge was, to them, impossible ; philosophy had become discredited and futile, and caprice and license had taken the place of moral obligation. Socrates saw the remedy. This poison of individual skepticism must be counteracted by sure knowledge and positive morality. These could be attained only through exact general conceptions derived by induction through the arduous process of dialectic. The formation of exact conceptions in this patient and laborious manner was the essence of the work of Socrates' life. This was " the sword of the Spirit," having which in his grasp he was not afraid to go forth against the ignorance and sin of his age.

19. The Process. — The process by which Socrates arrived at exact general conceptions through which real knowledge was to be attained was by induction. He would begin with familiar instances in which by universal consent the general principle was involved, and from them would infer that the same was true in the less familiar case in hand. Instances of such induction are, in the *Apology* (20 A, B) : since it is a good thing for the farmers to take trainers for colts and steers, so it must also be for parents to

[1] *Apol.* 25 E.

take instructors for their children. Or in the *Crito* (47 B; 48 A): since in developing the body the athlete regards the opinion only of his physician and trainer, so in seeking the welfare of the soul we must regard only the commands of the physician and overseer of the soul, namely, the truth. By thus deriving his fundamental principles from such well-known and perfectly evident instances, Socrates laid himself open to the charge of always talking about common or ignoble subjects, but he also laid a sure and solid foundation for his conclusions.

But induction must not only start from the commonest notions, it must also be conducted under constant criticism and definition so that all error may be eliminated. As a consequence, truth must be sought not alone, but in company. The co-operation of many minds must be obtained. The view proposed must be re-garded from every side, and challenged and limited and criticised with the greatest severity, until at last a general conception is reached to which no exception can be taken. This will be real knowledge.

In the *Apology*, the persistency with which Socrates goes to all sorts and sets of men in Athens to establish the truth of the oracle, and in the *Crito* the manifold and varied discussion by which he proves to Crito that it is never right to retaliate, illustrate his method. This prolonged conversational and critical process of investigating a subject, much as a besieging army approaches a fortified city by mines and parallels and assaults of every sort on every side, received the name of *dialectic*.

20. The Object. — The object of this dialectic was to correct the vicious way in which others thought. It was not only for his own sake, it was even more to impress and reform others, that Socrates was working. By the dialogue the master at once in-volved the disciple in the investigation, by first eliciting from him an opinion and then subjecting it to a rigid and prolonged cross-examination. The pupil was straightway confronted with his error, self-confidence was checked, and individual opinion was supplemented by many-sided observation and criticism. The mind of the master at every step was brought to bear on the pupil, who was thus provoked and stimulated to think for himself. No better method has ever been devised for influencing and instructing men than this, which ever since has been called the Socratic method.

Sometimes by these discussions the truth would be attained and sometimes not, so difficult is it to reach. In several of the Dialogues of Plato, Socrates is represented as arriving at no conclusion in his search. Such are those which Thrasyllus terms [1] tentative (πειραστικοί). Others are headed obstetric (μαιευτικοί), in which the truth is brought to light as by the aid of a midwife.

21. Manner of Life of Socrates. — The manner, then, of Socrates' life, as it appears in its ultimate form in the *Apology* and the Dialogues elsewhere, is that of continual conversation with men, in which his effort is to renovate them intellectually and so morally, by inculcating in them correct methods of thought.

In order to converse with men he had to go where they were, — in the morning to the gymnasia or palaestrae, where young men were assembled, later in the day to the market place when it was crowded, among the tables where goods were sold or money changed,[2] to the shops of working men with whom he was fond of talking, to gatherings of friends, and all public places. He did not, like the sophists, teach particular companies of young men for a stipulated fee, but he conversed openly with all who would listen, for the love of it, to benefit them.[3] Some interesting theme for discussion would be suggested by the occasion. Upon this, some one present would be led to express an opinion which, on examination, would be found to be incorrect or vague, which would lead to another modified statement, which in turn would have to be defined or amended. Finally Socrates, by proper inferences from self-evident premises, would either arrive at the

---

[1] See Grote's *Plato*, chap. IV.
[2] *Apol.* 17 C.
[3] *Apol.* 33 A, B.

true conclusion or would show that they could not rightly determine the matter. In this process Socrates displayed a wonderful resource and adroitness, by his acuteness and persistence and irony and wit at once provoking and delighting his listeners. In wisdom and knowledge also, as well as in dialectic skill, he is represented as easily surpassing his most able opponents. No honest and ingenuous man could engage in such talks without distrusting his old shiftlessness and skepticism and being inspired with belief in and love of the truth, and that, too, in practical directions which involved conduct and character.

22. Its Development Natural. — We may believe that this mode of life started naturally from small beginnings. At first Socrates was a sculptor working in his father's shop, but he had an active mind and a strong moral sense. These qualities led him to converse with men at every opportunity. In these talks the ignorance and conceit of his fellow-citizens were thrust upon him, and the desire to make them better began to burn in his soul. He found as he went on that he was admirably equipped for the task. He saw clearly what the trouble was, and felt that in his own mode of thought and life he had the remedy. He developed a wonderful skill in discourse and took great delight in the task of examining men. He had an infinite patience and persistence which opposition and failure could not overcome. His moral earnestness would not let him rest while he saw things so wrong about him. His unselfish spirit made him willing to neglect his own proper interests and ambitions, and labor with his fellow-men, going to them "as a father or an elder brother," and forbade him to take money for the service or to ask it, so leaving him in his old age in poverty.[1] At the same time, all along, owing to a religious nature particularly sensitive, he was called, he asserts, to the work by the Divine will in every possible way, by the visions and oracles referred to in *Apology*, 33 C, and so urged on to give more and more time to this activity. Plato represents him in the *Charmides*[2] as fairly

---

[1] *Apol.* 31 B, C.   [2] 153 B.

embarked upon it at the time of the battle at Potidaea (432 B.C.), when he was about forty years old. Aristophanes in the *Clouds*, which was given in 423 B.C., caricatures him as already a well-known personage,[1] and mentions no shop, no stone-cutting in the φροντιστήριον. But that up to this time he had entirely abandoned his workshop we should hardly suppose. We may perhaps reason that the practical and acute Xanthippe would hardly have consented to marry him when he had already given up work and become in her eyes a confirmed idler, and that he, easy going as he was in worldly matters, would not have been willing to incur the duties and responsibilities of marriage under such circumstances. Judging from the age of his children at the time of his trial,[2] his marriage could not have been earlier than 420 B.C., when he was fifty years old. Not long after that time, then, we may imagine that Chaerephon received the response from the oracle at Delphi,[3] after which Socrates says that he devoted himself entirely to the task of examining his fellow-men.[4]

THE RESULTS OF THE WORK OF SOCRATES

23. Devoted Followers. — The natural result of such a decided personality acting so vigorously and continually upon all about him was very marked. He excited widespread antagonism, as we shall see later, but he also gained the admiration and devotion of many of the most gifted and best of the Athenians, particularly of the young men. They gathered about him, attracted by the piquancy of his conversation, and while they were delighted at the discomfiture of his opponents,[5] they were powerfully influenced themselves for good. Alcibiades is made to testify to this in the *Symposium*.[6] The *Memorabilia* shows how Xenophon was impressed. A considerable company of friends who followed and conversed with him appears in the various Dialogues of Plato.

---

[1] *Apol.* 19 C.
[2] *Apol.* 34 D.
[3] *Apol.* 21 A.

[4] *Apol.* 23 B and 30 A.
[5] *Apol.* 23 C.
[6] 215 D; 216 C.

In his trial, though the attack upon him had been bitter and his defense had been aggravating, the minority which voted in his favor was a very large one.[1] But in Plato himself we have the most complete witness to the power of Socrates. Plato was a poet and a philosopher himself of the very highest rank, than whose the world has few greater names to show, yet he was so completely overmastered by his master Socrates that to a great degree he effaced himself in his writings and devoted his life to perpetuating his view of the person who had affected him so profoundly.

24. Moral Influence. — In Plato we have clearly exhibited the twofold nature of the influence which Socrates exerted. It was deeply intellectual, but his immediate followers were still more powerfully influenced by his character and spirit. What was most prominent about him was a strenuous and delightful personality, thoroughly devoted to noble ends. This Plato does not fail to recognize everywhere. Earnest reformer though Socrates was, a vein of playful humor, often in the form of irony, was frequently present in his discourse. In argument his fertility and dexterity amazed and delighted his friends and discomfited his opponents. Dealing at one moment with subjects common or even ignoble, as his theme led him on he became serious and profound, or rose to the loftiest heights of poetic eloquence. Without pretense or Pharisaism, in some respects even open to criticism when tried by our standards, the nobility and self-devotion of his life shine out everywhere. The charm of his personal character exalted and intensified the impression which his wisdom and wit produced, so that we may not wonder that Plato was so affected by him. Through Plato this moral and personal influence of Socrates has passed on down through all the generations since, working its ennobling work. No other witness to the truth who has sealed his testimony with his blood has had a wider influence, except the divine Jesus of Nazareth.

[1] *Apol.* 36 A.

25. Intellectual Method. — But quite as marked and even more permanent was the intellectual influence which Socrates exerted. From Socrates a new period begins in Greek philosophy. This was not alone because of the field in which he exercised his activity. He did, indeed, bring philosophy down from external nature and make man his chief subject, which was a notable step in advance. But still more, Socrates exerted a great influence on thought and philosophy, because he exhibited for the first time the true method of scientific thinking. Previous to him the ideas of philosophers had been impressions and speculations rather than well-grounded thought. Socrates did for philosophy what Thucydides did for history : he made it scientific in that he based it upon its true foundations. Aristotle's statement is correct when he says[1] that the great merit of Socrates consists in the formation of conceptions (τὸ ὁρίζεσθαι καθόλου) and induction (ἐπαγωγή). It is true he did not devise and write down philosophical treatises ; he merely conversed with men, but in those conversations he was constantly exhibiting these methods. He never would accept the impression of the individual as the basis of real knowledge. Continually he went back to what was generally admitted, and by inference therefrom established his conclusions under constant criticism, limitation, and definition invited from every side. Knowledge thus established he held was real knowledge. To us this is old and commonplace, but to Socrates and his contemporaries it was original and wonderful, for the art of conscious thinking was being learned in the world for the first time.

Plato had the genius to see what was new and extraordinary in the method of his master. This method he devoted himself to reproducing, and he recognized Socrates himself as the author of his intellectual life. Through Plato, Aristotle was developed. Zeno, the father of the Stoics, derived his inspiration from the disciples of Socrates. So Socrates must be regarded as the beginner of a new period in Greek philosophy.

[1] *Metaphysics*, XIII. 4, p. 1078.

26. His Opponents. — But Socrates had not only devoted followers; his mode of life and conversation naturally excited dislike and opposition. This he tells us in the first part of his defense. As early as 423 B.C., when the *Clouds* of Aristophanes appeared, he was a subject for caricaturè. His singular personal appearance, and his zeal in his peculiar practice of philosophy, had already made him a marked character. Aristophanes erroneously represented him as a physicist or natural philosopher, and so made him liable in popular thought to the suspicion of atheism.[1] He was so like both natural philosopher and sophist, that the distrust and odium popularly felt toward them were visited upon him also.[2] But up to that time it would appear that he was the object of ridicule rather than of dislike. He was regarded as persistent and eccentric,[3] but not yet as distinctly obnoxious. A little later, when the response of the Delphic oracle to Chaerephon[4] had led him to devote himself continuously and more zealously to the examining of his fellow-citizens, he more and more incurred their hostility.[5] Those whose ignorance and self-conceit he thus exposed, many of them hated him. Year after year he persisted in this " public, notorious, and exasperating discourse." Many of his youthful followers imitated him,[6] and by *their* lack of tact made *him* still more obnoxious. So a great mass of distrust and dislike accumulated. In the spring of 399 B.C. this opposition took the form of a legal prosecution. His accusers were Meletus, Anytus, and Lyco.[7] Of Meletus, who acted as spokesman, we know only that in the *Euthyphro*[8] he is described as a young man little known ; that Socrates treats him slightingly all through his defense, and that he acted in behalf of the poets,[7] from which it has been inferred that he was himself a poet or the son of a poet of the same name. Of Lyco we know nothing, except that he appears in behalf of the orators.[7]

---

[1] *Apol.* 18 C.
[2] *Apol.* 18 B.
[3] *Apol.* 20 C.
[4] *Apol.* 21 A.

[5] *Apol.* 28 A.
[6] *Apol.* 23 C.
[7] *Apol.* 23 E.
[8] 2 B.

Perhaps he was a professional speech-maker, and he may have pre-
pared the speech which Meletus delivered.   Anytus was a man of
wealth, a tanner by trade, and a prominent leader of the democracy, just then especially influential because he had been active
with Thrasybulus in driving out the Thirty Tyrants.   He is represented in the *Meno* [1] as narrow-minded, a hater of the sophists,
and as enraged at Socrates for suggesting the sending of a young
man to them to be taught.   Xenophon tells us [2] that Anytus had
become incensed because Socrates tried to dissuade him from
bringing up his son, a youth of promise, as a leather dealer.   It
is in Anytus probably that we find embodied the motives which at
this particular time led to this prosecution of Socrates.

27. The Charge. — The charge preferred is stated only in gen-
eral terms ($\pi\omega\varsigma\ \ddot{\omega}\delta\epsilon$) in the *Apology*.[3]   Xenophon gives it more
exactly : "Socrates violates the laws inasmuch as he does not
believe in the gods which the city believes in, but introduces
other and new divinities ; he also violates the laws by corrupting the youth."   The first part of the charge, involving impiety
($\dot{\alpha}\sigma\acute{\epsilon}\beta\epsilon\iota\alpha$), brought the case under the jurisdiction of the $\ddot{\alpha}\rho\chi\omega\nu$
$\beta\alpha\sigma\iota\lambda\epsilon\acute{\nu}\varsigma$.[4]   The second part of the charge, that he corrupted the
youth, contained the real substance of the attack, but was covered
by no law.   Under the Thirty, Critias and Charicles, in settling
what the laws should be, "introduced a clause forbidding any one
to teach the art of disputation, expressly to annoy Socrates," and
later warned him against holding further discourses with the
young.[5]   Such an arbitrary law had disappeared with the Thirty,
but charges of impiety were not infrequently brought at Athens,[6]
and in this way his accusers could get Socrates before the
court.

28. The Court. — The jury [7] consisted probably of 501 Athenian

[1] 90 and 91.
[2] Xen. *Apol.* 29.
[3] *Apol.* 24 B.
[4] Meier und Schömann, *Der Attische Process, neu bearbeitet von*

H. Lipsius, Berlin, 1883-87, pp. 366
ff.
[5] Xen. *Mem.* I. 2, 33.
[6] *Der Attische Process,* p. 370.
[7] *Der Attische Process,* pp. 145-171.

citizens over thirty years of age. Jury service was theoretically one of the duties of every citizen at Athens, but the number had been limited in practice to 6000 in all, chosen yearly, 600 from each tribe. These were divided into 10 sections of 500 each, leaving 1000 as a reserve, from which substitutes were taken in case regular jurors were necessarily absent. In more important cases two, three, four, and on one occasion that we know of, five sections sat together, giving juries of from 1001 to 2501 in number. In lesser cases the jury was 401, or sometimes only 201. The odd man was put in so that there might not be a tie vote.

Before entering on the duties of their office, the jurors took an oath[1] that they would vote "according to the laws and decrees of the Athenian people," and not on account of favor or enmity (οὔτε χάριτος ἕνεκα οὔτ' ἔχθρας). On a court day each one of the sections was assigned by lot to one of the court rooms, where the magistrate before whom the preliminary proceedings in any case had been held was present to preside. The parties to the suit were summoned by the herald, and when they appeared, after some kind of religious ceremony, the proceedings began. The clerk read the indictment[2] and the rejoinder, after which the plaintiff was called on to make his speech, and was followed by the defendant. The law directed that every man should conduct his own case, but it became customary when a man was not a good speaker himself, or when the case was very important, for the court to allow others (συνήγοροι) to come to his aid,[3] as in this case Anytus and Lyco came to the aid of Meletus. When the speeches were ended the herald called on the dicasts to vote, which was done by each casting a ballot (ψῆφος) into one or the other of two vessels, according as he wished to convict or acquit. If the vote was to convict, and if there was no regular penalty provided, the plaintiff in a speech proposed the penalty (τίμησις)

---

[1] On the oath of the jurors, see article by Fränkel in *Hermes*, XIII., p. 452.

[2] *Apol.* 19 B.

[3] *Der Attische Process*, p. 920.

which he desired, after which the defendant made a counter proposal (ἀντιτίμησις). The vote on the penalty was then taken.[1] If the plaintiff did not secure a fifth part of the votes, he was fined a thousand drachmae.[2] If the accused was found guilty and condemned to imprisonment or death, he was taken charge of by the officers called the Eleven (οἱ ἕνδεκα).[3]

29. Speech of his Accusers. — The principal speech for the accusers, it would seem, was made by Meletus, since Socrates refers to him chiefly in his reply. But Anytus and Lyco also came forward (*Apol.* 36 A. ἀνέβη Ἄνυτος καὶ Λύκων) and spoke. Of these two, however, only Anytus is actually cited by Socrates.[4]

In regard to the first count in their indictment, that Socrates did not acknowledge the gods which the city acknowledged, his accusers seem to have urged simply the claim he made to be directed by (θεῖόν τι καὶ δαιμόνιον) the divine influence, which they perverted to mean a new divinity.[5]

In regard to the second count, that he corrupted the youth, his accusers urged : that he taught his associates to despise the established laws, especially election by lot ; that Critias and Alcibiades, who had associated with him, had turned out badly, Critias having been one of the most grasping and outrageous of the Thirty, and Alcibiades one of the most insolent and violent of the democratic party ; that he taught the young to disregard parents and guardians, and prefer his authority to theirs ; and that he quoted mischievous passages from Hesiod and Homer.[6]

THE APOLOGY OF SOCRATES

30. The Line of Argument. — After his accusers have finished speaking, Socrates mounts the bema and makes his defense. His line of thought will be given in detail, in the Notes, at the head of

[1] *Der Attische Process*, pp. 917–946.
[2] *Der Attische Process*, p. 951.
[3] *Der Attische Process*, p. 957.
[4] *Apol.* 29 C.
[5] Xen. *Mem.* I. 1.
[6] Xen. *Mem.* I. 2, 56.

each chapter. The first part of his speech, which is the defense proper, divides logically into five members, as follows:

1. Introduction (I.–II.).
   To conciliate his audience (I.).
   Plan of defense (II.): Of the two sets of accusers he will first defend himself against those of long standing, and afterward against his present accusers.
2. Defense against his old-time accusers (III.–X.).
3. Defense against his present accusers (XI.–XV.).
4. Socrates defends his past life in answering questions his opponents might ask in objection to it (XVI.–XXII.).
5. Peroration (XXIII.–XXIV.): He refuses to appeal to the pity of the jurors.

The judges then vote that Socrates was guilty, casting 281 ballots against him to 220 in his favor.

Meletus follows in a speech asking that the penalty, $\tau\iota\mu\eta\sigma\iota\varsigma$, be fixed at death.

Socrates in reply proposes the $\dot{\alpha}\nu\tau\iota\tau\iota\mu\eta\sigma\iota\varsigma$ (XXV.–XXVIII.). If they will not award him maintenance in the Prytaneum, let the penalty be a fine of thirty minae.

The jurors then decide on the penalty of death, by a majority, according to Diogenes Laertius, eighty larger than their former vote. While the officers are busy, Socrates talks first to those who voted against him, and then to those who voted in his favor (XXIX.–XXXIII.).

31. Dramatic Analysis. — The *Apology*, like the Dialogues, is constructed on dramatic as well as on logical lines. If we regard the *dialogi personae* as Aristophanes (representing the old-time accusers), Meletus, and Socrates, it conforms to Plato's usual method. The action of the dialogue is the discussion whether Socrates ought to be put to death, and the two indictments may be regarded as two antagonists which he summarily puts down. The piece falls naturally into a prologue, three episodes, and an epilogue, corresponding thus to a five act drama.

Act 1. Prologue (I.–II.) : Introduces the situation, characters, and beginning of the action.

Act 2. First Episode (III.–X.) : The δέσις or complication fairly begins.

Act 3. Second Episode (XI.–XV.) : The complication is developed. Note that the slighting treatment of Meletus here heightens the dramatic quality of the speech.

Act 4. Third Episode (XVI.–XXII.) : The λύσις, in which, opponents having been put aside, Socrates presents his life in the way which seems to him best.

Act 5. Epilogue (XXIII.–XXIV.) : The practical conclusion or τέλος. (My life is noble, for I will not do an ignoble thing to save it.)

The after speeches are to be regarded as dramatically reinforcing the epilogue of the main dramatic piece. His proposing of the penalty and his talk about the future display in still higher terms the nobility of his life and character.

32. The *Apology* substantially what Socrates said.[1] — The *Apology* is not, of course, a shorthand report of the very words used, but Plato was present as a most interested listener, and wrote it probably very soon afterward, while the matter was fresh in his mind. What Socrates said and the way he said it, under such conditions, must have been very unique and effective, so that Plato would have desired to report it as accurately as he could, especially as he was still under the immediate influence of his master, not having developed the comparative independence of a later period. His report would come at once into the hands of the other pupils and admirers of Socrates, who would resent any unnecessary deviation from what he had said. The individual traits of Socrates, as we otherwise know them, are here clearly seen, his homely direct method, his strain of irony, his

[1] For various views on this point see Grote's *Plato*, Chap. VII., and Zeller's *Plato and the Older Academy*, pp. 119 ff. on the one side, and Jowett's Introduction to his translation of the *Apology* and Riddell's *The Apology of Plato*, Introduction, 2, for another view.

dialectic skill, his moral courage, his civic devotion, his religious faith. Hence we may conclude that the *Apology* does give us, with substantial accuracy, a view of the person of Socrates, his method, and the process of his thought in his defense.

At the same time, we must remember, everything has passed through the artistic and idealizing mind and memory of the pupil, and Plato was himself a poet-philosopher of the very first rank. So it was unavoidable that this reported speech should take form and color somewhat from the medium through which it had passed. Not long before this, Thucydides in his history had given his masterly reports of the speeches of Pericles, and by viewing the *Apology* as a similar set speech, without any accompanying narrative, we shall best comprehend what it really is. But the greater intimacy and sympathy existing between Socrates and Plato makes certain here a far closer reproduction. A better parallel is the discourses of Jesus as reported for us by the beloved disciple.

33. Real Reasons for his Condemnation. — Why was Socrates found guilty and condemned to death? To us he appears as an interesting and noble character, perhaps the greatest glory of the city which saw fit to kill him. Aside from what is mentioned in the defense, namely, the distrust of him as being atheistic like the natural philosophers, and insincere like the sophists, and a corrupter of youth, and aside from the dislike which his cross-examination had caused, two other reasons may be mentioned.

His political views were not acceptable to the democracy. Socrates was a moderate oligarch. He did not believe in the election of officers of state by lot, nor in other features of a pure democracy. But in 399 B.C., only four years after the expulsion of the Thirty Tyrants, anything that savored of oligarchy was especially odious to the populace. Suspicion of this sort was probably present as a dark background, in the minds of the jurors. But as this is barely mentioned by Xenophon, in his review of what the accusers urged, and as it is not referred to in Plato's *Apology*, it cannot be regarded as having directly influenced the result very much.

The real, immediate reason why Socrates was treated so severely is the tone of fearless independence which he adopted all through his trial. To the jurors this must have seemed impertinence and insolence. At the outset he feels that the jurors are prejudiced, and he consistently abstains from giving them their ordinary official title. He refuses, for what probably seemed to the jurors simulated reasons, to give up the mode of life which they disliked in him, even if they would set him free. He refuses to appeal to the pity of the jurors at the end of the defense proper, although he knows that the refusal will displease some of them. He suggests as his penalty the right to dine with the honored guests of the city in the Prytaneum, which must have seemed to the jurors trifling impertinence.

This attitude of careless defiance fanned into a flame all the slumbering embers of old enmity and distrust. Xenophon expressly tells us that Socrates might have been acquitted "if in any moderate degree he would have conciliated the favor of the dicasts."

We are not to suppose that Socrates designed to irritate his judges. He simply speaks and acts just as sincerely and frankly as he would have done if his life had not been at stake. He does not flinch through fear of what his accusers may do. He regards this as a supreme moment in which to fulfil his mission, and impress his views of life and duty upon the city. It may be best for himself and for Athens that he be not acquitted. The whole matter of life and death he leaves entirely in the hands of God. Courage, self-sacrifice, and trust in the Divine guidance are the motives which appear conspicuously in all that he says and does.

THE CRITO

34. Its Subject. — This dialogue takes its name from Socrates' contemporary and fellow-demesman, who is the other interlocutor in it. He had abundant wealth and was a devoted friend. After Socrates was condemned, a month elapsed before he was put to death. The day before his trial the sacred ship was crowned, in token of the beginning of the embassy which every year was sent by Athens to the shrine of Apollo, at Delos. This embassy was in commemoration of the deliverance which Theseus was said to have wrought for the city by slaying the Cretan Minotaur and so saving his own life and that of his companions, the seven virgins and seven youths, sent every nine years as tribute to the monster. From the time when this ship was crowned until its return, the city was kept ceremonially clean, and it was unlawful to inflict the punishment of death upon condemned criminals.

During these thirty days in prison the friends of Socrates visited him frequently. Two of the conversations held in those days are preserved to us in the *Crito* and *Phaedo*. In the *Crito* the subject discussed is : *Is it ever right for a man who has been wronged to retaliate?* in its practical application to the case of Socrates, who has been unjustly condemned by the laws and is now urged by his friend to escape from prison. Crito has made every arrangement to get him away, but Socrates refuses on the ground that so to do would violate his obligations as a citizen.

35. The Line of Argument :

1. Introduction (I.–II.): Socrates must die on the third day.
2. Crito urges him to escape from prison (III.–V.).
3. Socrates justifies his refusal (VI.–X.).
4. The laws enforce the argument of Socrates (XI.–XVI.).
5. Conclusion (XVII.): He cannot disregard the arguments of the laws.

36. Dramatic Analysis. — The *Crito* is an example of a dialogue in which the conversation is given directly, and not merely reported as it is in the main part of the *Phaedo*. So the characters are introduced and the situation is developed by implication, as is the case in the tragedies of Aeschylus and Sophocles. The

dramatic skill exhibited in this introduction is not inferior to that of even those great masters. The action of the dialogue is the discussion whether Socrates may justly escape from prison. This dialogue also corresponds to a five-act drama.

Act 1. Prologue (I.–II.) : Introduces the situation, characters and beginning of the action.

Act 2. First Episode (III.–V.) : The δέσις or complication begins.

Act 3. Second Episode (VI.–X.) : The complication heightened.

Act 4. Third Episode (XI.–XVI.) : The λύσις, in which the crisis of the argument is past and the conclusion is unavoidable.

Act 5. Epilogue (XVII.) : The practical conclusion (The laws must be obeyed).

THE PHAEDO

37. Characters and Setting. — Phaedo, a native of Elis of noble birth, brought to Athens as a captive in war, probably only two or three years before the death of Socrates, after being liberated, had become his devoted follower. Not long after his master's death, possibly on his way to Elis just after that time, at Phlius, south of Sicyon in the valley of the Asopus, he narrates to Echecrates and other sympathetic Phliasians the last sayings and doings of Socrates. This narration takes us back to Athens, to the prison where, on the last day of his life, the disciples and friends of Socrates are assembled. Phaedo explains to the Phliasians how it was that the execution of Socrates was deferred so long a time after his sentence, until the return of the sacred ship from Delos, and tells who the friends were who were present. Prominent among these were the two Thebans, Simmias and Cebes, referred to in the *Crito*, who bear, after Socrates, the chief part in the discussion which follows. Another was Crito, who is represented here as in the *Crito* as being interested in everything pertaining to the personal comfort of Socrates. As he had tried there to induce Socrates to save his life by escaping from prison, here Crito is represented as receiving in private his master's last instructions in regard to his family, and finally closed his eyes in death.   Plato was not in the little company.   He was ill, perhaps from grief, as Plutarch says.

When the friends of Socrates enter the prison, Xanthippe and the three children are sent home in the care of one of Crito's servants, but return, toward evening, for a final farewell.   We find in her here no trace of the shrewish temper with which she is generally credited, though she is evidently ungoverned and violent in her emotions.

38. Analysis. — In the first three chapters (which is all of the prologue contained in this book), we have given to us the characters and the situation.   Because the situation is narrated and not given directly as in the *Crito*, a better opportunity is afforded to describe in detail just what happened and how Socrates conducted himself.

The main body of the Dialogue (omitted in this book) is an argument, conducted by Socrates, to show that the wise and virtuous man will meet death with cheerfulness, because the soul is immortal.

The last four chapters, which form the epilogue, are a practical illustration by Socrates of the truth of his theme.   He meets death calmly and cheerfully, unshaken even by the sobs and tears of his friends.

ΑΠΟΛΟΓΙΑ ΣΩΚΡΑΤΟΥΣ

[ἠθικός]

I. Ὅ τι μὲν ὑμεῖς, ὦ ἄνδρες Ἀθηναῖοι, πεπόν- A
θατε ὑπὸ τῶν ἐμῶν κατηγόρων, οὐκ οἶδα· ἐγὼ δ᾽
οὖν καὶ αὐτὸς ὑπ᾽ αὐτῶν ὀλίγου ἐμαυτοῦ ἐπελαθό-
μην· οὕτω πιθανῶς ἔλεγον. καίτοι ἀληθές γε, ὡς
5 ἔπος εἰπεῖν, οὐδὲν εἰρήκασιν. μάλιστα δὲ αὐτῶν
ἓν ἐθαύμασα τῶν πολλῶν ὧν ἐψεύσαντο, τοῦτο, ἐν
ᾧ ἔλεγον ὡς χρὴ ὑμᾶς εὐλαβεῖσθαι, μὴ ὑπ᾽ ἐμοῦ
ἐξαπατηθῆτε ὡς δεινοῦ ὄντος λέγειν. τὸ γὰρ μὴ B
αἰσχυνθῆναι ὅτι αὐτίκα ὑπ᾽ ἐμοῦ ἐξελεγχθήσονται
10 ἔργῳ, ἐπειδὰν μηδ᾽ ὁπωστιοῦν φαίνωμαι δεινὸς λέγειν, τοῦτό μοι ἔδοξεν αὐτῶν ἀναισχυντότατον εἶναι,
εἰ μὴ ἄρα δεινὸν καλοῦσιν οὗτοι λέγειν τὸν τἀληθῆ
λέγοντα· εἰ μὲν γὰρ τοῦτο λέγουσιν, ὁμολογοίην
ἂν ἔγωγε οὐ κατὰ τούτους εἶναι ῥήτωρ. οὗτοι μὲν
15 οὖν, ὥσπερ ἐγὼ λέγω, ἤ τι ἢ οὐδὲν ἀληθὲς εἰρήκα-
σιν· ὑμεῖς δ᾽ ἐμοῦ ἀκούσεσθε πᾶσαν τὴν ἀλήθειαν.
οὐ μέντοι μὰ Δία, ὦ ἄνδρες Ἀθηναῖοι, κεκαλλιεπημένους γε λόγους, ὥσπερ οἱ τούτων, ῥήμασί τε
καὶ ὀνόμασιν οὐδὲ κεκοσμημένους, ἀλλὰ ἀκού- C
20 σεσθε εἰκῇ λεγόμενα τοῖς ἐπιτυχοῦσιν ὀνόμασιν·
πιστεύω γὰρ δίκαια εἶναι ἃ λέγω, καὶ μηδεὶς ὑμῶν

41

προσδοκησάτω ἄλλως· οὐδὲ γὰρ ἂν δήπου πρέποι, 17
ὦ ἄνδρες, τῇδε τῇ ἡλικίᾳ ὥσπερ μειρακίῳ πλάττοντι λόγους εἰς ὑμᾶς εἰσιέναι. καὶ μέντοι καὶ
25 πάνυ, ὦ ἄνδρες Ἀθηναῖοι, τοῦτο ὑμῶν δέομαι καὶ
παρίεμαι· ἐὰν διὰ τῶν αὐτῶν λόγων ἀκούητέ μου
ἀπολογουμένου δι' ὧνπερ εἴωθα λέγειν καὶ ἐν
ἀγορᾷ ἐπὶ τῶν τραπεζῶν, ἵνα ὑμῶν πολλοὶ ἀκη-
κόασι, καὶ ἄλλοθι, μήτε θαυμάζειν μήτε θορυ- D
30 βεῖν τούτου ἕνεκα. ἔχει γὰρ οὑτωσί. νῦν ἐγὼ
πρῶτον ἐπὶ δικαστήριον ἀναβέβηκα, ἔτη γεγονὼς
ἑβδομήκοντα· ἀτεχνῶς οὖν ξένως ἔχω τῆς ἐνθάδε
λέξεως. ὥσπερ οὖν ἄν, εἰ τῷ ὄντι ξένος ἐτύγχανον
ὤν, ξυνεγιγνώσκετε δήπου ἄν μοι εἰ ἐν ἐκείνῃ τῇ
35 φωνῇ τε καὶ τῷ τρόπῳ ἔλεγον ἐν οἷσπερ ἐτεθράμ- 18
μην, καὶ δὴ καὶ νῦν τοῦτο ὑμῶν δέομαι δίκαιον, ὥς
γέ μοι δοκῶ, τὸν μὲν τρόπον τῆς λέξεως ἐᾶν· ἴσως
μὲν γὰρ χείρων, ἴσως δὲ βελτίων ἂν εἴη· αὐτὸ δὲ
τοῦτο σκοπεῖν καὶ τούτῳ τὸν νοῦν προσέχειν, εἰ
40 δίκαια λέγω ἢ μή· δικαστοῦ μὲν γὰρ αὕτη ἀρετή,
ῥήτορος δὲ τἀληθῆ λέγειν.

II. Πρῶτον μὲν οὖν δίκαιός εἰμι ἀπολογήσασθαι, ὦ ἄνδρες Ἀθηναῖοι, πρὸς τὰ πρῶτά μου
ψευδῆ κατηγορημένα καὶ τοὺς πρώτους κατηγόρους,
ἔπειτα δὲ πρὸς τὰ ὕστερα καὶ τοὺς ὑστέρους. ἐμοῦ B
5 γὰρ πολλοὶ κατήγοροι γεγόνασι πρὸς ὑμᾶς καὶ
πάλαι πολλὰ ἤδη ἔτη καὶ οὐδὲν ἀληθὲς λέγοντες,
οὓς ἐγὼ μᾶλλον φοβοῦμαι ἢ τοὺς ἀμφὶ Ἄνυτον,
καίπερ ὄντας καὶ τούτους δεινούς· ἀλλ' ἐκεῖνοι

δεινότεροι, ὦ ἄνδρες, οἳ ὑμῶν τοὺς πολλοὺς ἐκ 18
10 παίδων παραλαμβάνοντες ἔπειθόν τε καὶ κατηγόρουν ἐμοῦ οὐδὲν ἀληθές, ὡς "ἔστι τις Σωκράτης,
σοφὸς ἀνήρ, τά τε μετέωρα φροντιστὴς καὶ τὰ ὑπὸ
γῆς ἅπαντα ἀνεζητηκὼς καὶ τὸν ἥττω λόγον κρείττω
ποιῶν." οὗτοι, ὦ ἄνδρες Ἀθηναῖοι, οἱ ταύτην τὴν C
15 φήμην κατασκεδάσαντες, οἱ δεινοί εἰσίν μου κατή-
γοροι· οἱ γὰρ ἀκούοντες ἡγοῦνται τοὺς ταῦτα
ζητοῦντας οὐδὲ θεοὺς νομίζειν. ἔπειτά εἰσιν οὗτοι
οἱ κατήγοροι πολλοὶ καὶ πολὺν χρόνον ἤδη κατη-
γορηκότες, ἔτι δὲ καὶ ἐν ταύτῃ τῇ ἡλικίᾳ λέγοντες
20 πρὸς ὑμᾶς, ἐν ᾗ ἂν μάλιστα ἐπιστεύσατε παῖδες
ὄντες, ἔνιοι δ᾿ ὑμῶν καὶ μειράκια, ἀτεχνῶς ἐρήμην
κατηγοροῦντες ἀπολογουμένου οὐδενός. ὃ δὲ πάντων ἀλογώτατον, ὅτι οὐδὲ τὰ ὀνόματα οἷόν τε αὐτῶν
εἰδέναι καὶ εἰπεῖν, πλὴν εἴ τις κωμῳδιοποιὸς τυγ- D
25 χάνει ὤν. ὅσοι δὲ φθόνῳ καὶ διαβολῇ χρώμενοι
ὑμᾶς ἀνέπειθον, οἱ δὲ καὶ αὐτοὶ πεπεισμένοι ἄλλους
πείθοντες, οὗτοι πάντες ἀπορώτατοί εἰσιν· οὐδὲ
γὰρ ἀναβιβάσασθαι οἷόν τ᾿ ἐστὶν αὐτῶν ἐνταυθοῖ
οὐδ᾿ ἐλέγξαι οὐδένα, ἀλλ᾿ ἀνάγκη ἀτεχνῶς ὥσπερ
30 σκιαμαχεῖν ἀπολογούμενόν τε καὶ ἐλέγχειν μηδενὸς
ἀποκρινομένου. ἀξιώσατε οὖν καὶ ὑμεῖς, ὥσπερ
ἐγὼ λέγω, διττούς μου τοὺς κατηγόρους γεγονέναι,
ἑτέρους μὲν τοὺς ἄρτι κατηγορήσαντας, ἑτέρους
δὲ τοὺς πάλαι οὓς ἐγὼ λέγω, καὶ οἰήθητε δεῖν E
35 πρὸς ἐκείνους πρῶτόν με ἀπολογήσασθαι· καὶ
γὰρ ὑμεῖς ἐκείνων πρότερον ἠκούσατε κατηγορούν-

τῶν καὶ πολὺ μᾶλλον ἢ τῶνδε τῶν ὕστερον. εἶεν· 18
ἀπολογητέον δή, ὦ ἄνδρες Ἀθηναῖοι, καὶ ἐπιχει- 19
ρητέον ὑμῶν ἐξελέσθαι τὴν διαβολήν, ἣν ὑμεῖς ἐν
40 πολλῷ χρόνῳ ἔσχετε, ταύτην ἐν οὕτως ὀλίγῳ χρόνῳ.
βουλοίμην μὲν οὖν ἂν τοῦτο οὕτως γενέσθαι, εἴ τι
ἄμεινον καὶ ὑμῖν καὶ ἐμοί, καὶ πλέον τί με ποιῆσαι
ἀπολογούμενον· οἶμαι δὲ αὐτὸ χαλεπὸν εἶναι, καὶ
οὐ πάνυ με λανθάνει οἷόν ἐστιν. ὅμως τοῦτο μὲν
45 ἴτω ὅπῃ τῷ θεῷ φίλον, τῷ δὲ νόμῳ πειστέον καὶ
ἀπολογητέον.

III. Ἀναλάβωμεν οὖν ἐξ ἀρχῆς, τίς ἡ κατη-
γορία ἐστὶν ἐξ ἧς ἡ ἐμὴ διαβολὴ γέγονεν, ᾗ δὴ
καὶ πιστεύων Μέλητός με ἐγράψατο τὴν γραφὴν B
ταύτην. εἶεν· τί δὴ λέγοντες διέβαλλον οἱ διαβάλ-
5 λοντες; ὥσπερ οὖν κατηγόρων τὴν ἀντωμοσίαν
δεῖ ἀναγνῶναι αὐτῶν· "Σωκράτης ἀδικεῖ καὶ περιεργάζεται ζητῶν τά τε ὑπὸ γῆς καὶ οὐράνια καὶ
τὸν ἥττω λόγον κρείττω ποιῶν καὶ ἄλλους τὰ αὐτὰ
ταῦτα διδάσκων." τοιαύτη τίς ἐστι· ταῦτα γὰρ C
10 ἑωρᾶτε καὶ αὐτοὶ ἐν τῇ Ἀριστοφάνους κωμῳδίᾳ,
Σωκράτη τινὰ ἐκεῖ περιφερόμενον, φάσκοντά τε
ἀεροβατεῖν καὶ ἄλλην πολλὴν φλυαρίαν φλυα-
ροῦντα, ὧν ἐγὼ οὐδὲν οὔτε μέγα οὔτε μικρὸν πέρι
ἐπαΐω. καὶ οὐχ ὡς ἀτιμάζων λέγω τὴν τοιαύτην
15 ἐπιστήμην, εἴ τις περὶ τῶν τοιούτων σοφός ἐστιν·
μή πως ἐγὼ ὑπὸ Μελήτου τοσαύτας δίκας φύγοιμι·
ἀλλὰ γὰρ ἐμοὶ τούτων, ὦ ἄνδρες Ἀθηναῖοι, οὐδὲν
μέτεστιν. μάρτυρας δὲ αὐτοὺς ὑμῶν τοὺς πολλοὺς D

παρέχομαι, καὶ ἀξιῶ ὑμᾶς ἀλλήλους διδάσκειν τε 19
20 καὶ φράζειν, ὅσοι ἐμοῦ πώποτε ἀκηκόατε διαλεγο-
μένου· πολλοὶ δὲ ὑμῶν οἱ τοιοῦτοί εἰσιν· φράζετε
οὖν ἀλλήλοις, εἰ πώποτε ἢ μικρὸν ἢ μέγα ἤκουσέ
τις ὑμῶν ἐμοῦ περὶ τῶν τοιούτων διαλεγομένου·
καὶ ἐκ τούτων γνώσεσθε ὅτι τοιαῦτ' ἐστὶ καὶ τἄλλα
25 περὶ ἐμοῦ ἃ οἱ πολλοὶ λέγουσιν.

IV. Ἀλλὰ γὰρ οὔτε τούτων οὐδέν ἐστιν, οὐδέ
γ' εἴ τινος ἀκηκόατε ὡς ἐγὼ παιδεύειν ἐπιχειρῶ
ἀνθρώπους καὶ χρήματα πράττομαι, οὐδὲ τοῦτο E
ἀληθές. ἐπεὶ καὶ τοῦτό γέ μοι δοκεῖ καλὸν εἶναι,
5 εἴ τις οἷός τ' εἴη παιδεύειν ἀνθρώπους ὥσπερ
Γοργίας τε ὁ Λεοντῖνος καὶ Πρόδικος ὁ Κεῖος καὶ
Ἱππίας ὁ Ἠλεῖος. τούτων γὰρ ἕκαστος, ὦ ἄνδρες,
οἷός τ' ἐστὶν ἰὼν εἰς ἑκάστην τῶν πόλεων τοὺς νέους,
οἷς ἔξεστι τῶν ἑαυτῶν πολιτῶν προῖκα ξυνεῖναι ᾧ
10 ἂν βούλωνται, τούτους πείθουσι τὰς ἐκείνων ξυνου-
σίας ἀπολιπόντας σφίσιν ξυνεῖναι χρήματα δι- 20
δόντας καὶ χάριν προσειδέναι. ἐπεὶ καὶ ἄλλος
ἀνήρ ἐστι Πάριος ἐνθάδε σοφὸς ὃν ἐγὼ ᾐσθόμην
ἐπιδημοῦντα· ἔτυχον γὰρ προσελθὼν ἀνδρὶ ὃς
15 τετέλεκε χρήματα σοφισταῖς πλείω ἢ ξύμπαντες
οἱ ἄλλοι, Καλλίᾳ τῷ Ἱππονίκου· τοῦτον οὖν ἀνη-
ρόμην—ἐστὸν γὰρ αὐτῷ δύο υἱέε—"ὦ Καλλία,"
ἦν δ' ἐγώ, "εἰ μέν σου τὼ υἱέε πώλω ἢ μόσχω
ἐγενέσθην, εἴχομεν ἂν αὐτοῖν ἐπιστάτην λαβεῖν
20 καὶ μισθώσασθαι, ὃς ἔμελλεν αὐτὼ καλώ τε καὶ
ἀγαθὼ ποιήσειν τὴν προσήκουσαν ἀρετήν· ἦν B

δ' ἂν οὗτος ἦ τῶν ἱππικῶν τις ἢ τῶν γεωργικῶν · 20
νῦν δ' ἐπειδὴ ἀνθρώπω ἐστόν, τίνα αὐτοῖν ἐν νῷ
ἔχεις ἐπιστάτην λαβεῖν; τίς τῆς τοιαύτης ἀρε-
25 τῆς, τῆς ἀνθρωπίνης τε καὶ πολιτικῆς, ἐπιστήμων
ἐστίν; οἶμαι γάρ σε ἐσκέφθαι διὰ τὴν τῶν υἱέων
κτῆσιν. ἔστιν τις," ἔφην ἐγώ, "ἢ οὔ;" "πάνυ γε,"
ἦ δ' ὅς. "τίς," ἦν δ' ἐγώ, "καὶ ποδαπός, καὶ πόσου
διδάσκει;" "Εὔηνος," ἔφη, "ὦ Σώκρατες, Πάριος,
30 πέντε μνῶν." καὶ ἐγὼ τὸν Εὔηνον ἐμακάρισα, εἰ
ὡς ἀληθῶς ἔχοι ταύτην τὴν τέχνην καὶ οὕτως C
ἐμμελῶς διδάσκει. ἐγὼ οὖν καὶ αὐτὸς ἐκαλλυ-
νόμην τε καὶ ἡβρυνόμην ἄν, εἰ ἠπιστάμην ταῦτα ·
ἀλλ' οὐ γὰρ ἐπίσταμαι, ὦ ἄνδρες Ἀθηναῖοι.

V. Ὑπολάβοι ἂν οὖν τις ὑμῶν ἴσως · "ἀλλ', ὦ
Σώκρατες, τὸ σὸν τί ἐστι πρᾶγμα; πόθεν αἱ δια-
βολαί σοι αὗται γεγόνασιν; οὐ γὰρ δήπου σοῦ γε
οὐδὲν τῶν ἄλλων περιττότερον πραγματευομένου
5 ἔπειτα τοσαύτη φήμη τε καὶ λόγος γέγονεν, εἰ μή
τι ἔπραττες ἀλλοῖον ἢ οἱ πολλοί · λέγε οὖν ἡμῖν
τί ἐστιν, ἵνα μὴ ἡμεῖς περὶ σοῦ αὐτοσχεδιάζωμεν." D
ταυτί μοι δοκεῖ δίκαια λέγειν ὁ λέγων, κἀγὼ ὑμῖν
πειράσομαι ἀποδεῖξαι τί ποτ' ἔστιν τοῦτο ὃ ἐμοὶ
10 πεποίηκεν τό τε ὄνομα καὶ τὴν διαβολήν. ἀκούετε
δή. καὶ ἴσως μὲν δόξω τισὶν ὑμῶν παίζειν, εὖ
μέντοι ἴστε, πᾶσαν ὑμῖν τὴν ἀλήθειαν ἐρῶ. ἐγὼ
γάρ, ὦ ἄνδρες Ἀθηναῖοι, δι' οὐδὲν ἀλλ' ἢ διὰ
σοφίαν τινὰ τοῦτο τὸ ὄνομα ἔσχηκα. ποίαν δὴ
15 σοφίαν ταύτην; ἥπερ ἐστὶν ἴσως ἀνθρωπίνη

σοφία. τῷ ὄντι γὰρ κινδυνεύω ταύτην εἶναι 20
σοφός· οὗτοι δὲ τάχ' ἂν οὓς ἄρτι ἔλεγον, μείζω
τινὰ ἢ κατ' ἄνθρωπον σοφίαν σοφοὶ εἶεν, ἢ οὐκ Ε
ἔχω τί λέγω· οὐ γὰρ δὴ ἔγωγε αὐτὴν ἐπίσταμαι,
20 ἀλλ' ὅστις φησὶ ψεύδεταί τε καὶ ἐπὶ διαβολῇ τῇ
ἐμῇ λέγει. καί μοι, ὦ ἄνδρες Ἀθηναῖοι, μὴ θορυβήσητε, μηδὲ ἂν δόξω τι ὑμῖν μέγα λέγειν· οὐ
γὰρ ἐμὸν ἐρῶ τὸν λόγον ὃν ἂν λέγω, ἀλλ' εἰς
ἀξιόχρεων ὑμῖν τὸν λέγοντα ἀνοίσω. τῆς γὰρ
25 ἐμῆς, εἰ δή τίς ἐστιν σοφία καὶ οἵα, μάρτυρα
ὑμῖν παρέξομαι τὸν θεὸν τὸν ἐν Δελφοῖς. Χαιρε-
φῶντα γὰρ ἴστε που. οὗτος ἐμός τε ἑταῖρος ἦν 21
ἐκ νέου καὶ ὑμῶν τῷ πλήθει ἑταῖρός τε καὶ ξυν-
έφυγε τὴν φυγὴν ταύτην καὶ μεθ' ὑμῶν κατῆλθε.
30 καὶ ἴστε δὴ οἷος ἦν Χαιρεφῶν, ὡς σφοδρὸς ἐφ'
ὅ τι ὁρμήσειεν. καὶ δή ποτε καὶ εἰς Δελφοὺς ἐλθὼν
ἐτόλμησε τοῦτο μαντεύσασθαι· καί, ὅπερ λέγω,
μὴ θορυβεῖτε, ὦ ἄνδρες· ἤρετο γὰρ δὴ εἴ τις
ἐμοῦ εἴη σοφώτερος. ἀνεῖλεν οὖν ἡ Πυθία μηδένα
35 σοφώτερον εἶναι. καὶ τούτων πέρι ὁ ἀδελφὸς ὑμῖν
αὐτοῦ οὑτοσὶ μαρτυρήσει, ἐπειδὴ ἐκεῖνος τετελεύτηκεν.

VI. Σκέψασθε δὲ ὧν ἕνεκα ταῦτα λέγω· μέλλω Β
γὰρ ὑμᾶς διδάξειν ὅθεν μοι ἡ διαβολὴ γέγονε.
ταῦτα γὰρ ἐγὼ ἀκούσας ἐνεθυμούμην οὑτωσί· "τί
ποτε λέγει ὁ θεός, καὶ τί ποτε αἰνίττεται; ἐγὼ γὰρ
5 δὴ οὔτε μέγα οὔτε σμικρὸν ξύνοιδα ἐμαυτῷ σοφὸς
ὤν· τί οὖν ποτε λέγει φάσκων ἐμὲ σοφώτατον

εἶναι; οὐ γὰρ δήπου ψεύδεταί γε· οὐ γὰρ θέμις 21
αὐτῷ.   καὶ πολὺν μὲν χρόνον ἠπόρουν τί ποτε
λέγει. ἔπειτα μόγις πάνυ ἐπὶ ζήτησιν αὐτοῦ τοι-
10 αύτην τινὰ ἐτραπόμην. ἦλθον ἐπί τινα τῶν δοκούντων σοφῶν εἶναι, ὡς ἐνταῦθα, εἴπερ που, ἐλέγ- C
ξων τὸ μαντεῖον καὶ ἀποφανῶν τῷ χρησμῷ ὅτι
" οὑτοσὶ ἐμοῦ σοφώτερός ἐστι, σὺ δ' ἐμὲ ἔφησθα."
διασκοπῶν οὖν τοῦτον — ὀνόματι γὰρ οὐδὲν δέομαι
15 λέγειν, ἦν δέ τις τῶν πολιτικῶν πρὸς ὃν ἐγὼ σκοπῶν
τοιοῦτόν τι ἔπαθον, ὦ ἄνδρες Ἀθηναῖοι, — καὶ διαλεγόμενος αὐτῷ, ἔδοξέ μοι οὗτος ὁ ἀνὴρ δοκεῖν
μὲν εἶναι σοφὸς ἄλλοις τε πολλοῖς ἀνθρώποις καὶ
μάλιστα ἑαυτῷ, εἶναι δ' οὔ· κἄπειτα ἐπειρώμην
20 αὐτῷ δεικνύναι ὅτι οἴοιτο μὲν εἶναι σοφός, εἴη δ'
οὔ. ἐντεῦθεν οὖν τούτῳ τε ἀπηχθόμην καὶ πολλοῖς D
τῶν παρόντων, πρὸς ἐμαυτὸν δ' οὖν ἀπιὼν ἐλογιζόμην ὅτι "τούτου μὲν τοῦ ἀνθρώπου ἐγὼ σοφώτερός εἰμι· κινδυνεύει μὲν γὰρ ἡμῶν οὐδέτερος οὐδὲν
25 καλὸν κἀγαθὸν εἰδέναι, ἀλλ' οὗτος μὲν οἴεταί τι
εἰδέναι οὐκ εἰδώς, ἐγὼ δέ, ὥσπερ οὖν οὐκ οἶδα,
οὐδὲ οἴομαι· ἔοικα γοῦν τούτου γε σμικρῷ τινι
αὐτῷ τούτῳ σοφώτερος εἶναι, ὅτι ἃ μὴ οἶδα οὐδὲ
οἴομαι εἰδέναι." ἐντεῦθεν ἐπ' ἄλλον ᾖα τῶν ἐκείνου
30 δοκούντων σοφωτέρων εἶναι, καί μοι ταὐτὰ ταῦτα Ε
ἔδοξε· καὶ ἐνταῦθα κἀκείνῳ καὶ ἄλλοις πολλοῖς
ἀπηχθόμην.

VII. Μετὰ ταῦτ' οὖν ἤδη ἐφεξῆς ᾖα, αἰσθανόμενος μὲν καὶ λυπούμενος καὶ δεδιὼς ὅτι ἀπηχθανόμην,

ὅμως δὲ ἀναγκαῖον ἐδόκει εἶναι τὸ τοῦ θεοῦ περὶ 21
πλείστου ποιεῖσθαι· ἰτέον οὖν σκοποῦντι τὸν χρη-
5 σμόν, τί λέγει, ἐπὶ ἅπαντας τούς τι δοκοῦντας
εἰδέναι.   καὶ νὴ τὸν κύνα, ὦ ἄνδρες Ἀθηναῖοι 22
— δεῖ γὰρ πρὸς ὑμᾶς τἀληθῆ λέγειν — ἦ μὴν ἐγὼ
ἔπαθόν τι τοιοῦτον· οἱ μὲν μάλιστα εὐδοκιμοῦντες
ἔδοξάν μοι ὀλίγου δεῖν τοῦ πλείστου ἐνδεεῖς εἶναι
10 ζητοῦντι κατὰ τὸν θεόν, ἄλλοι δὲ δοκοῦντες φαυλό-
τεροι ἐπιεικέστεροι εἶναι ἄνδρες πρὸς τὸ φρονίμως
ἔχειν. δεῖ δὴ ὑμῖν τὴν ἐμὴν πλάνην ἐπιδεῖξαι
ὥσπερ πόνους τινὰς πονοῦντος, ἵνα μοι καὶ ἀνέλεγκτος ἡ μαντεία γένοιτο. μετὰ γὰρ τοὺς πολιτι-
15 κοὺς ᾖα ἐπὶ τοὺς ποιητὰς τούς τε τῶν τραγῳδιῶν
καὶ τοὺς τῶν διθυράμβων καὶ τοὺς ἄλλους, ὡς B
ἐνταῦθα ἐπ᾽ αὐτοφώρῳ καταληψόμενος ἐμαυτὸν
ἀμαθέστερον ἐκείνων ὄντα. ἀναλαμβάνων οὖν
αὐτῶν τὰ ποιήματα ἅ μοι ἐδόκει μάλιστα πεπραγ-
20 ματεῦσθαι αὐτοῖς, διηρώτων ἂν αὐτοὺς τί λέγοιεν,
ἵν᾽ ἅμα τι καὶ μανθάνοιμι παρ᾽ αὐτῶν. αἰσχύνομαι
οὖν ὑμῖν εἰπεῖν, ὦ ἄνδρες, τἀληθῆ· ὅμως δὲ ῥητέον.
ὡς ἔπος γὰρ εἰπεῖν ὀλίγου αὐτῶν ἅπαντες οἱ παρόντες ἂν βέλτιον ἔλεγον περὶ ὧν αὐτοὶ ἐπεποιήκε-
25 σαν. ἔγνων οὖν καὶ περὶ τῶν ποιητῶν ἐν ὀλίγῳ
τοῦτο, ὅτι οὐ σοφίᾳ ποιοῖεν ἃ ποιοῖεν, ἀλλὰ C
φύσει τινὶ καὶ ἐνθουσιάζοντες, ὥσπερ οἱ θεομάν-
τεις καὶ οἱ χρησμῳδοί· καὶ γὰρ οὗτοι λέγουσι
μὲν πολλὰ καὶ καλά, ἴσασιν δὲ οὐδὲν ὧν λέγουσι.
30 τοιοῦτόν τί μοι ἐφάνησαν πάθος καὶ οἱ ποιηταὶ

πεπονθότες· καὶ ἅμα ἠσθόμην αὐτῶν διὰ τὴν 22
ποίησιν οἰομένων καὶ τἆλλα σοφωτάτων εἶναι
ἀνθρώπων, ἃ οὐκ ἦσαν. ἀπῇα οὖν καὶ ἐντεῦθεν
τῷ αὐτῷ οἰόμενος περιγεγονέναι ᾧπερ καὶ τῶν
35 πολιτικῶν.

VIII. Τελευτῶν οὖν ἐπὶ τοὺς χειροτέχνας ᾖα·
ἐμαυτῷ γὰρ ξυνῄδη οὐδὲν ἐπισταμένῳ, ὡς ἔπος D
εἰπεῖν, τούτους δέ γ᾽ ᾔδη ὅτι εὑρήσοιμι πολλὰ καὶ
καλὰ ἐπισταμένους. καὶ τούτου μὲν οὐκ ἐψεύσθην,
5 ἀλλ᾽ ἠπίσταντο ἃ ἐγὼ οὐκ ἠπιστάμην καί μου
ταύτῃ σοφώτεροι ἦσαν. ἀλλ᾽, ὦ ἄνδρες Ἀθηναῖοι,
ταὐτόν μοι ἔδοξαν ἔχειν ἁμάρτημα ὅπερ καὶ οἱ
ποιηταί, καὶ οἱ ἀγαθοὶ δημιουργοί· διὰ τὸ τὴν
τέχνην καλῶς ἐξεργάζεσθαι ἕκαστος ἠξίου καὶ
10 τἆλλα τὰ μέγιστα σοφώτατος εἶναι, καὶ αὐτῶν
αὕτη ἡ πλημμέλεια ἐκείνην τὴν σοφίαν ἀπέκρυπτεν·
ὥστ᾽ ἐμὲ ἐμαυτὸν ἀνερωτᾶν ὑπὲρ τοῦ χρησμοῦ, E
πότερα δεξαίμην ἂν οὕτω ὥσπερ ἔχω ἔχειν, μήτε
τι σοφὸς ὢν τὴν ἐκείνων σοφίαν μήτε ἀμαθὴς τὴν
15 ἀμαθίαν, ἢ ἀμφότερα ἃ ἐκεῖνοι ἔχουσιν ἔχειν.
ἀπεκρινάμην οὖν ἐμαυτῷ καὶ τῷ χρησμῷ ὅτι μοι
λυσιτελοῖ ὥσπερ ἔχω ἔχειν.

IX. Ἐκ ταυτησὶ δὴ τῆς ἐξετάσεως, ὦ ἄνδρες
Ἀθηναῖοι, πολλαὶ μὲν ἀπέχθειαί μοι γεγόνασι 23
καὶ οἶαι χαλεπώταται καὶ βαρύταται, ὥστε πολλὰς
διαβολὰς ἀπ᾽ αὐτῶν γεγονέναι, ὄνομα δὲ τοῦτο λέ-
5 γεσθαι, σοφὸς εἶναι. οἴονται γάρ με ἑκάστοτε οἱ
παρόντες ταῦτα αὐτὸν εἶναι σοφόν, ἃ ἂν ἄλλον

ἐξελέγξω· τὸ δὲ κινδυνεύει, ὦ ἄνδρες, τῷ ὄντι ὁ 23
θεὸς σοφὸς εἶναι, καὶ ἐν τῷ χρησμῷ τούτῳ τοῦτο
λέγειν, ὅτι ἡ ἀνθρωπίνη σοφία ὀλίγου τινὸς ἀξία
10 ἐστὶν καὶ οὐδενός· καὶ φαίνεται τοῦτ' οὐ λέγειν τὸν
Σωκράτη, προσκεχρῆσθαι δὲ τῷ ἐμῷ ὀνόματι, ἐμὲ
παράδειγμα ποιούμενος, ὥσπερ ἂν εἰ εἴποι ὅτι Β
"οὗτος ὑμῶν, ὦ ἄνθρωποι, σοφώτατός ἐστιν, ὅστις
ὥσπερ Σωκράτης ἔγνωκεν ὅτι οὐδενὸς ἄξιός ἐστι
15 τῇ ἀληθείᾳ πρὸς σοφίαν." ταῦτ' οὖν ἐγὼ μὲν ἔτι
καὶ νῦν περιιὼν ζητῶ καὶ ἐρευνῶ κατὰ τὸν θεόν, καὶ
τῶν ἀστῶν καὶ ξένων ἄν τινα οἴωμαι σοφὸν εἶναι·
καὶ ἐπειδάν μοι μὴ δοκῇ, τῷ θεῷ βοηθῶν ἐνδείκνυ-
μαι ὅτι οὐκ ἔστι σοφός. καὶ ὑπὸ ταύτης τῆς ἀσχο-
20 λίας οὔτε τι τῶν τῆς πόλεως πρᾶξαί μοι σχολὴ
γέγονεν ἄξιον λόγου οὔτε τῶν οἰκείων, ἀλλ' ἐν
πενίᾳ μυρίᾳ εἰμὶ διὰ τὴν τοῦ θεοῦ λατρείαν. C

X. Πρὸς δὲ τούτοις οἱ νέοι μοι ἐπακολουθοῦντες,
οἷς μάλιστα σχολή ἐστιν, οἱ τῶν πλουσιωτάτων,
αὐτόματοι χαίρουσιν ἀκούοντες ἐξεταζομένων τῶν
ἀνθρώπων, καὶ αὐτοὶ πολλάκις ἐμὲ μιμοῦνται, εἶτα
5 ἐπιχειροῦσιν ἄλλους ἐξετάζειν· κἄπειτα, οἶμαι,
εὑρίσκουσι πολλὴν ἀφθονίαν οἰομένων μὲν εἰδέναι
τι ἀνθρώπων, εἰδότων δὲ ὀλίγα ἢ οὐδέν. ἐντεῦθεν
οὖν οἱ ὑπ' αὐτῶν ἐξεταζόμενοι ἐμοὶ ὀργίζονται, ἀλλ'
οὐχ αὑτοῖς, καὶ λέγουσιν ὡς "Σωκράτης τίς ἐστι μια-
10 ρώτατος καὶ διαφθείρει τοὺς νέους·" καὶ ἐπειδάν τις D
αὐτοὺς ἐρωτᾷ ὅ τι ποιῶν καὶ ὅ τι διδάσκων, ἔχουσι
μὲν οὐδὲν εἰπεῖν, ἀλλ' ἀγνοοῦσιν, ἵνα δὲ μὴ δοκῶσιν

ἀπορεῖν, τὰ κατὰ πάντων τῶν φιλοσοφούντων πρό- 23
χειρα ταῦτα λέγουσιν, ὅτι τὰ μετέωρα καὶ τὰ ὑπὸ
15 γῆς καὶ θεοὺς μὴ νομίζειν καὶ τὸν ἥττω λόγον
κρείττω ποιεῖν. τὰ γὰρ ἀληθῆ, οἶμαι, οὐκ ἂν
ἐθέλοιεν λέγειν, ὅτι κατάδηλοι γίγνονται προσποιούμενοι μὲν εἰδέναι, εἰδότες δὲ οὐδέν. ἅτε
οὖν, οἶμαι, φιλότιμοι ὄντες καὶ σφοδροὶ καὶ Ε
20 πολλοί, καὶ ξυντεταγμένως καὶ πιθανῶς λέγοντες
περὶ ἐμοῦ, ἐμπεπλήκασιν ὑμῶν τὰ ὦτα καὶ πάλαι
καὶ σφοδρῶς διαβάλλοντες. ἐκ τούτων καὶ Μέλητός μοι ἐπέθετο καὶ Ἄνυτος καὶ Λύκων, Μέλητος
μὲν ὑπὲρ τῶν ποιητῶν ἀχθόμενος, Ἄνυτος δὲ ὑπὲρ
25 τῶν δημιουργῶν καὶ τῶν πολιτικῶν, Λύκων δὲ 24
ὑπὲρ τῶν ῥητόρων· ὥστε, ὅπερ ἀρχόμενος ἐγὼ
ἔλεγον, θαυμάζοιμ᾽ ἂν εἰ οἷός τ᾽ εἴην ἐγὼ ὑμῶν
ταύτην τὴν διαβολὴν ἐξελέσθαι ἐν οὕτως ὀλίγῳ
χρόνῳ οὕτω πολλὴν γεγονυῖαν. ταῦτ᾽ ἔστιν ὑμῖν,
30 ὦ ἄνδρες Ἀθηναῖοι, τἀληθῆ, καὶ ὑμᾶς οὔτε μέγα
οὔτε μικρὸν ἀποκρυψάμενος ἐγὼ λέγω οὐδ᾽ ὑπο-
στειλάμενος. καίτοι οἶδα σχεδὸν ὅτι τοῖς αὐτοῖς
ἀπεχθάνομαι· ὃ καὶ τεκμήριον ὅτι ἀληθῆ λέγω
καὶ ὅτι αὕτη ἐστὶν ἡ διαβολὴ ἡ ἐμὴ καὶ τὰ αἴτια
35 ταῦτά ἐστιν. καὶ ἐάν τε νῦν ἐάν τε αὖθις ζητήσητε Β
ταῦτα, οὕτως εὑρήσετε.

XI. Περὶ μὲν οὖν ὧν οἱ πρῶτοί μου κατήγοροι
κατηγόρουν αὕτη ἐστὶν ἱκανὴ ἀπολογία πρὸς ὑμᾶς.
πρὸς δὲ Μέλητον τὸν ἀγαθόν τε καὶ φιλόπολιν, ὥς
φησι, καὶ τοὺς ὑστέρους μετὰ ταῦτα πειράσομαι

5 ἀπολογεῖσθαι. αὖθις γὰρ δή, ὥσπερ ἑτέρων τού- 24
των ὄντων κατηγόρων, λάβωμεν αὖ τὴν τούτων
ἀντωμοσίαν. ἔχει δέ πως ὧδε· Σωκράτη φησὶν
ἀδικεῖν τούς τε νέους διαφθείροντα καὶ θεοὺς οὓς
ἡ πόλις νομίζει οὐ νομίζοντα, ἕτερα δὲ δαιμόνια C
10 καινά. τὸ μὲν δὴ ἔγκλημα τοιοῦτόν ἐστιν· τούτου δὲ τοῦ ἐγκλήματος ἓν ἕκαστον ἐξετάσωμεν.
φησὶ γὰρ δὴ τοὺς νέους ἀδικεῖν με διαφθείροντα.
ἐγὼ δέ γε, ὦ ἄνδρες Ἀθηναῖοι, ἀδικεῖν φημι Μέλητον, ὅτι σπουδῇ χαριεντίζεται, ῥᾳδίως εἰς ἀγῶνα
15 καθιστὰς ἀνθρώπους, περὶ πραγμάτων προσποιού-
μενος σπουδάζειν καὶ κήδεσθαι ὧν οὐδὲν τούτῳ
πώποτε ἐμέλησεν. ὡς δὲ τοῦτο οὕτως ἔχει, πειράσομαι καὶ ὑμῖν ἐπιδεῖξαι.

XII. Καί μοι δεῦρο, ὦ Μέλητε, εἰπέ· ἄλλο τι
ἢ περὶ πολλοῦ ποιεῖ ὅπως ὡς βέλτιστοι οἱ νεώ- D
τεροι ἔσονται; "ἔγωγε." ἴθι δή νυν εἰπὲ τούτοις
τίς αὐτοὺς βελτίους ποιεῖ. δῆλον γὰρ ὅτι οἶσθα,
5 μέλον γέ σοι. τὸν μὲν γὰρ διαφθείροντα ἐξευρών,
ὡς φῄς, ἐμὲ εἰσάγεις τουτοισὶ καὶ κατηγορεῖς· τὸν
δὲ δὴ βελτίους ποιοῦντα ἴθι εἰπὲ καὶ μήνυσον αὐτοῖς τίς ἐστιν. ὁρᾷς, ὦ Μέλητε, ὅτι σιγᾷς καὶ
οὐκ ἔχεις εἰπεῖν; καίτοι οὐκ αἰσχρόν σοι δοκεῖ
10 εἶναι καὶ ἱκανὸν τεκμήριον οὗ δὴ ἐγὼ λέγω, ὅτι
σοι οὐδὲν μεμέληκεν; ἀλλ' εἰπέ, ὦ 'γαθέ, τίς
αὐτοὺς ἀμείνους ποιεῖ. "οἱ νόμοι." ἀλλ' οὐ
τοῦτο ἐρωτῶ, ὦ βέλτιστε, ἀλλὰ τίς ἄνθρωπος, E
ὅστις πρῶτον καὶ αὐτὸ τοῦτο οἶδε, τοὺς νόμους.

15 " οὗτοι, ὦ Σώκρατες, οἱ δικασταί." πῶς λέγεις, ὦ 24
Μέλητε ; οἴδε τοὺς νέους παιδεύειν οἷοί τέ εἰσι
καὶ βελτίους ποιοῦσιν ; "μάλιστα." πότερον
ἅπαντες, ἢ οἱ μὲν αὐτῶν, οἱ δ' οὔ ; "ἅπαντες."
εὖ γε νὴ τὴν Ἥραν λέγεις, καὶ πολλὴν ἀφθονίαν
20 τῶν ὠφελούντων. τί δὲ δή ; οἴδε οἱ ἀκροαταὶ
βελτίους ποιοῦσιν ἢ οὔ ; "καὶ οὗτοι." τί δὲ 25
οἱ βουλευταί ; "καὶ οἱ βουλευταί." ἀλλ' ἄρα,
ὦ Μέλητε, μὴ οἱ ἐν τῇ ἐκκλησίᾳ, οἱ ἐκκλησιασταί,
διαφθείρουσι τοὺς νεωτέρους ; ἢ κἀκεῖνοι βελτίους
25 ποιοῦσιν ἅπαντες ; "κἀκεῖνοι." πάντες ἄρα, ὡς
ἔοικεν, Ἀθηναῖοι καλοὺς κἀγαθοὺς ποιοῦσι πλὴν
ἐμοῦ, ἐγὼ δὲ μόνος διαφθείρω. οὕτω λέγεις ;
"πάνυ σφόδρα ταῦτα λέγω." πολλήν γ' ἐμοῦ
κατέγνωκας δυστυχίαν. καί μοι ἀπόκριναι · ἦ
30 καὶ περὶ ἵππους οὕτω σοι δοκεῖ ἔχειν ; οἱ μὲν
βελτίους ποιοῦντες αὐτοὺς πάντες ἄνθρωποι εἶναι, Β
εἷς δέ τις ὁ διαφθείρων ; ἢ τοὐναντίον τούτου πᾶν
εἷς μέν τις ὁ βελτίους οἷός τ' ὢν ποιεῖν ἢ πάνυ
ὀλίγοι, οἱ ἱππικοί · οἱ δὲ πολλοὶ ἐάν περ ξυνῶσι
35 καὶ χρῶνται ἵπποις, διαφθείρουσιν ; οὐχ οὕτως
ἔχει, ὦ Μέλητε, καὶ περὶ ἵππων καὶ τῶν ἄλλων
ἁπάντων ζῴων ; πάντως δήπου, ἐάν τε σὺ καὶ
Ἄνυτος οὐ φῆτε ἐάν τε φῆτε · πολλὴ γὰρ ἄν τις
εὐδαιμονία εἴη περὶ τοὺς νέους, εἰ εἷς μὲν μόνος
40 αὐτοὺς διαφθείρει, οἱ δ' ἄλλοι ὠφελοῦσιν. ἀλλὰ
γάρ, ὦ Μέλητε, ἱκανῶς ἐπιδείκνυσαι ὅτι οὐδεπώ- C
ποτε ἐφρόντισας τῶν νέων, καὶ σαφῶς ἀποφαίνεις

τὴν σαυτοῦ ἀμέλειαν, ὅτι οὐδέν σοι μεμέληκεν περὶ 25
ὧν ἐμὲ εἰσάγεις.

XIII. Ἔτι δὲ ἡμῖν εἰπέ, ὦ πρὸς Διός, Μέλητε,
πότερόν ἐστιν οἰκεῖν ἄμεινον ἐν πολίταις χρηστοῖς
ἢ πονηροῖς; ὦ τάν, ἀπόκριναι· οὐδὲν γάρ τοι
χαλεπὸν ἐρωτῶ. οὐχ οἱ μὲν πονηροὶ κακόν τι
5 ἐργάζονται τοὺς ἀεὶ ἐγγυτάτω ἑαυτῶν ὄντας, οἱ δ᾽
ἀγαθοὶ ἀγαθόν τι; "πάνυ γε." ἔστιν οὖν ὅστις
βούλεται ὑπὸ τῶν ξυνόντων βλάπτεσθαι μᾶλλον D
ἢ ὠφελεῖσθαι; ἀπόκριναι, ὦ ἀγαθέ· καὶ γὰρ ὁ
νόμος κελεύει ἀποκρίνεσθαι. ἔσθ᾽ ὅστις βούλεται
10 βλάπτεσθαι; "οὐ δῆτα." φέρε δή, πότερον ἐμὲ
εἰσάγεις δεῦρο ὡς διαφθείροντα τοὺς νεωτέρους καὶ
πονηροτέρους ποιοῦντα ἑκόντα ἢ ἄκοντα; "ἑκόντα
ἔγωγε." τί δῆτα, ὦ Μέλητε; τοσοῦτον σὺ ἐμοῦ
σοφώτερος εἶ τηλικούτου ὄντος τηλικόσδε ὤν, ὥστε
15 σὺ μὲν ἔγνωκας ὅτι οἱ μὲν κακοὶ κακόν τι ἐργάζονται ἀεὶ τοὺς μάλιστα πλησίον ἑαυτῶν, οἱ δὲ E
ἀγαθοὶ ἀγαθόν· ἐγὼ δὲ δὴ εἰς τοσοῦτον ἀμαθίας
ἥκω ὥστε καὶ τοῦτ᾽ ἀγνοῶ, ὅτι, ἐάν τινα μοχθηρὸν
ποιήσω τῶν ξυνόντων, κινδυνεύσω κακόν τι λαβεῖν
20 ἀπ᾽ αὐτοῦ, ὥστε τοῦτο τὸ τοσοῦτον κακὸν ἑκὼν
ποιῶ, ὡς φῂς σύ; ταῦτα ἐγώ σοι οὐ πείθομαι, ὦ
Μέλητε, οἶμαι δὲ οὐδὲ ἄλλον ἀνθρώπων οὐδένα·
ἀλλ᾽ ἢ οὐ διαφθείρω, ἢ εἰ διαφθείρω, ἄκων, ὥστε 26
σύ γε κατ᾽ ἀμφότερα ψεύδει. εἰ δὲ ἄκων διαφθείρω,
25 τῶν τοιούτων καὶ ἀκουσίων ἁμαρτημάτων οὐ δεῦρο
νόμος εἰσάγειν ἐστίν, ἀλλὰ ἰδίᾳ λαβόντα διδάσκειν

καὶ νουθετεῖν· δῆλον γὰρ ὅτι, ἐὰν μάθω, παύσομαι 26
ὅ γε ἄκων ποιῶ. σὺ δὲ ξυγγενέσθαι μέν μοι καὶ
διδάξαι ἔφυγες καὶ οὐκ ἠθέλησας, δεῦρο δὲ εἰσ-
30 άγεις οἷ νόμος ἐστὶν εἰσάγειν τοὺς κολάσεως δεομέ-
νους, ἀλλ᾽ οὐ μαθήσεως.

XIV. Ἀλλὰ γάρ, ὦ ἄνδρες Ἀθηναῖοι, τοῦτο
μὲν δῆλον ἤδη ἐστὶν ὃ ἐγὼ ἔλεγον, ὅτι Μελήτῳ Β
τούτων οὔτε μέγα οὔτε μικρὸν πώποτε ἐμέλησεν.
ὅμως δὲ δὴ λέγε ἡμῖν, πῶς με φὴς διαφθείρειν,
5 ὦ Μέλητε, τοὺς νεωτέρους; ἢ δῆλον δὴ ὅτι κατὰ
τὴν γραφὴν ἣν ἐγράψω, θεοὺς διδάσκοντα μὴ
νομίζειν οὓς ἡ πόλις νομίζει, ἕτερα δὲ δαιμόνια
καινά; οὐ ταῦτα λέγεις ὅτι διδάσκων διαφθείρω;
"πάνυ μὲν οὖν σφόδρα ταῦτα λέγω." πρὸς αὐτῶν
10 τοίνυν, ὦ Μέλητε, τούτων τῶν θεῶν ὧν νῦν ὁ λόγος
ἐστίν, εἰπὲ ἔτι σαφέστερον καὶ ἐμοὶ καὶ τοῖς Γ
ἀνδράσιν τούτοις. ἐγὼ γὰρ οὐ δύναμαι μαθεῖν
πότερον λέγεις διδάσκειν με νομίζειν εἶναί τινας
θεούς, καὶ αὐτὸς ἄρα νομίζω εἶναι θεούς, καὶ οὐκ
15 εἰμὶ τὸ παράπαν ἄθεος οὐδὲ ταύτῃ ἀδικῶ, οὐ μέντοι
οὕσπερ γε ἡ πόλις ἀλλὰ ἑτέρους, καὶ τοῦτ᾽ ἔστιν
ὅ μοι ἐγκαλεῖς, ὅτι ἑτέρους· ἢ παντάπασί με φὴς
οὔτε αὐτὸν νομίζειν θεοὺς τούς τε ἄλλους ταῦτα
διδάσκειν. "ταῦτα λέγω, ὡς τὸ παράπαν οὐ
20 νομίζεις θεούς." ὦ θαυμάσιε Μέλητε, ἵνα τί
ταῦτα λέγεις; οὐδὲ ἥλιον οὐδὲ σελήνην ἄρα Δ
νομίζω θεοὺς εἶναι, ὥσπερ οἱ ἄλλοι ἄνθρωποι;
"μὰ Δί᾽, ὦ ἄνδρες δικασταί, ἐπεὶ τὸν μὲν ἥλιον

λίθον φησὶν εἶναι, τὴν δὲ σελήνην γῆν." ᾿Αναξα- 26
25 γόρου οἴει κατηγορεῖν, ὦ φίλε Μέλητε, καὶ οὕτω
καταφρονεῖς τῶνδε καὶ οἴει αὐτοὺς ἀπείρους γραμ-
μάτων εἶναι, ὥστε οὐκ εἰδέναι ὅτι τὰ ᾿Αναξαγόρου
βιβλία τοῦ Κλαζομενίου γέμει τούτων τῶν λόγων ;
καὶ δὴ καὶ οἱ νέοι ταῦτα παρ᾽ ἐμοῦ μανθάνουσιν ἃ
30 ἔξεστιν ἐνίοτε, εἰ πάνυ πολλοῦ, δραχμῆς ἐκ τῆς Ε
ὀρχήστρας πριαμένοις Σωκράτους καταγελᾶν, ἐὰν
προσποιῆται ἑαυτοῦ εἶναι, ἄλλως τε καὶ οὕτως
ἄτοπα ὄντα. ἀλλ᾽, ὦ πρὸς Διός, οὑτωσί σοι δοκῶ
οὐδένα νομίζειν θεὸν εἶναι ; "οὐ μέντοι μὰ Δία
35 οὐδ᾽ ὁπωστιοῦν." ἄπιστός γ᾽ εἶ, ὦ Μέλητε, καὶ
ταῦτα μέντοι, ὡς ἐμοὶ δοκεῖς, σαυτῷ, ἐμοὶ γὰρ
δοκεῖ οὑτοσί, ὦ ἄνδρες ᾿Αθηναῖοι, πάνυ εἶναι
ὑβριστὴς καὶ ἀκόλαστος, καὶ ἀτεχνῶς τὴν γραφὴν
ταύτην ὕβρει τινὶ καὶ ἀκολασίᾳ καὶ νεότητι γρά-
40 ψασθαι. ἔοικεν γὰρ ὥσπερ αἴνιγμα ξυντιθέντι 27
διαπειρωμένῳ· "ἆρα γνώσεται Σωκράτης ὁ σοφὸς
δὴ ἐμοῦ χαριεντιζομένου καὶ ἐναντί᾽ ἐμαυτῷ λέγοντος, ἢ ἐξαπατήσω αὐτὸν καὶ τοὺς ἄλλους τοὺς
ἀκούοντας ;" οὗτος γὰρ ἐμοὶ φαίνεται τὰ ἐναντία
45 λέγειν αὐτὸς ἑαυτῷ ἐν τῇ γραφῇ, ὥσπερ ἂν εἰ εἴποι·
"ἀδικεῖ Σωκράτης θεοὺς οὐ νομίζων, ἀλλὰ θεοὺς
νομίζων." καίτοι τοῦτό ἐστι παίζοντος.

XV. Ξυνεπισκέψασθε δή, ὦ ἄνδρες, ᾗ μοι
φαίνεται ταῦτα λέγειν· σὺ δὲ ἡμῖν ἀπόκριναι, ὦ
Μέλητε· ὑμεῖς δέ, ὅπερ κατ᾽ ἀρχὰς ὑμᾶς παρη- Β
τησάμην, μέμνησθέ μοι μὴ θορυβεῖν, ἐὰν ἐν τῷ

5 εἰωθότι τρόπῳ τοὺς λόγους ποιῶμαι. ἔστιν ὅστις 27
ἀνθρώπων, ὦ Μέλητε, ἀνθρώπεια μὲν νομίζει πράγ-
ματ᾽ εἶναι, ἀνθρώπους δὲ οὐ νομίζει; ἀποκρινέ-
σθω, ὦ ἄνδρες, καὶ μὴ ἄλλα καὶ ἄλλα θορυβείτω·
ἔσθ᾽ ὅστις ἵππους μὲν οὐ νομίζει, ἱππικὰ δὲ πράγ-
10 ματα; ἢ αὐλητὰς μὲν οὐ νομίζει εἶναι, αὐλητικὰ
δὲ πράγματα; οὐκ ἔστιν, ὦ ἄριστε ἀνδρῶν· εἰ
μὴ σὺ βούλει ἀποκρίνασθαι, ἐγὼ σοὶ λέγω καὶ τοῖς
ἄλλοις τουτοισί. ἀλλὰ τὸ ἐπὶ τούτῳ γε ἀπόκριναι·
ἔσθ᾽ ὅστις δαιμόνια μὲν νομίζει πράγματ᾽ εἶναι, C
15 δαίμονας δὲ οὐ νομίζει; "οὐκ ἔστιν." ὡς ὤνησας, ὅτι μόγις ἀπεκρίνω ὑπὸ τουτωνὶ ἀναγκαζόμε-
νος. οὐκοῦν δαιμόνια μὲν φῄς με καὶ νομίζειν καὶ
διδάσκειν, εἴ τ᾽ οὖν καινὰ εἴ τε παλαιά· ἀλλ᾽ οὖν
δαιμόνιά γε νομίζω κατὰ τὸν σὸν λόγον, καὶ ταῦτα
20 καὶ διωμόσω ἐν τῇ ἀντιγραφῇ. εἰ δὲ δαιμόνια
νομίζω, καὶ δαίμονας δήπου πολλὴ ἀνάγκη νομίζειν
μέ ἐστιν· οὐχ οὕτως ἔχει; ἔχει δή· τίθημι γάρ
σε ὁμολογοῦντα, ἐπειδὴ οὐκ ἀποκρίνει. τοὺς δὲ
δαίμονας οὐχὶ ἤτοι θεούς γε ἡγούμεθα ἢ θεῶν D
25 παῖδας; φῂς ἢ οὔ; "πάνυ γε." οὐκοῦν εἴ περ
δαίμονας ἡγοῦμαι, ὡς σὺ φῄς, εἰ μὲν θεοί τινές
εἰσιν οἱ δαίμονες, τοῦτ᾽ ἂν εἴη ὃ ἐγώ φημί σε αἰνίττεσθαι καὶ χαριεντίζεσθαι, θεοὺς οὐχ ἡγούμενον
φάναι ἐμὲ θεοὺς αὖ ἡγεῖσθαι πάλιν, ἐπειδήπερ γε
30 δαίμονας ἡγοῦμαι· εἰ δ᾽ αὖ οἱ δαίμονες θεῶν παῖδές
εἰσιν νόθοι τινὲς ἢ ἐκ νυμφῶν ἢ ἔκ τινων ἄλλων,
ὧν δὴ καὶ λέγονται, τίς ἂν ἀνθρώπων θεῶν μὲν

παῖδας ἡγοῖτο εἶναι, θεοὺς δὲ μή; ὁμοίως γὰρ ἂν 27
ἄτοπον εἴη ὥσπερ ἂν εἴ τις ἵππων μὲν παῖδας Ε
35 ἡγοῖτο [ἢ] καὶ ὄνων, τοὺς ἡμιόνους, ἵππους δὲ καὶ
ὄνους μὴ ἡγοῖτο εἶναι. ἀλλ᾽, ὦ Μέλητε, οὐκ ἔστιν
ὅπως σὺ ταῦτα οὐχὶ ἀποπειρώμενος ἡμῶν ἐγράψω
τὴν γραφὴν ταύτην ἢ ἀπορῶν ὅ τι ἐγκαλοῖς ἐμοὶ
ἀληθὲς ἀδίκημα· ὅπως δὲ σύ τινα πείθοις ἂν καὶ
40 σμικρὸν νοῦν ἔχοντα ἀνθρώπων, ὡς οὐ τοῦ αὐτοῦ
ἐστιν καὶ δαιμόνια καὶ θεῖα ἡγεῖσθαι, καὶ αὖ τοῦ
αὐτοῦ μήτε δαίμονας μήτε θεοὺς μήτε ἥρωας, 28
οὐδεμία μηχανή ἐστιν.

XVI. Ἀλλὰ γάρ, ὦ ἄνδρες Ἀθηναῖοι, ὡς μὲν
ἐγὼ οὐκ ἀδικῶ κατὰ τὴν Μελήτου γραφήν, οὐ
πολλῆς μοι δοκεῖ εἶναι ἀπολογίας, ἀλλὰ ἱκανὰ καὶ
ταῦτα· ὃ δὲ καὶ ἐν τοῖς ἔμπροσθεν ἔλεγον, ὅτι
5 πολλή μοι ἀπέχθεια γέγονεν καὶ πρὸς πολλούς, εὖ
ἴστε ὅτι ἀληθές ἐστιν. καὶ τοῦτ᾽ ἔστιν ὃ ἐμὲ
αἱρήσει, ἐάν περ αἱρῇ, οὐ Μέλητος οὐδὲ Ἄνυτος,
ἀλλ᾽ ἡ τῶν πολλῶν διαβολή τε καὶ φθόνος. ἃ δὴ
πολλοὺς καὶ ἄλλους καὶ ἀγαθοὺς ἄνδρας ᾕρηκεν,
10 οἶμαι δὲ καὶ αἱρήσειν· οὐδὲν δὲ δεινὸν μὴ ἐν Β
ἐμοὶ στῇ. ἴσως δ᾽ ἂν οὖν εἴποι τις· "εἶτ᾽ οὐκ
αἰσχύνει, ὦ Σώκρατες, τοιοῦτον ἐπιτήδευμα ἐπιτη-
δεύσας, ἐξ οὗ κινδυνεύεις νυνὶ ἀποθανεῖν;" ἐγὼ δὲ
τούτῳ ἂν δίκαιον λόγον ἀντείποιμι, ὅτι "οὐ καλῶς
15 λέγεις, ὦ ἄνθρωπε, εἰ οἴει δεῖν κίνδυνον ὑπολογίζεσθαι τοῦ ζῆν ἢ τεθνάναι ἄνδρα ὅτου τι καὶ
σμικρὸν ὄφελός ἐστιν, ἀλλ᾽ οὐκ ἐκεῖνο μόνον σκο-

πεῖν, ὅταν πράττῃ, πότερα δίκαια ἢ ἄδικα πράττει, 28
καὶ ἀνδρὸς ἀγαθοῦ ἔργα ἢ κακοῦ.   φαῦλοι γὰρ ἂν
20 τῷ γε σῷ λόγῳ εἶεν τῶν ἡμιθέων ὅσοι ἐν Τροίᾳ C
τετελευτήκασιν οἵ τε ἄλλοι καὶ ὁ τῆς Θέτιδος υἱός,
ὃς τοσοῦτον τοῦ κινδύνου κατεφρόνησεν παρὰ τὸ
αἰσχρόν τι ὑπομεῖναι, ὥστε ἐπειδὴ εἶπεν ἡ μήτηρ
αὐτῷ προθυμουμένῳ Ἕκτορα ἀποκτεῖναι, θεὸς οὖσα,
25 οὑτωσί πως, ὡς ἐγὼ οἶμαι· 'ὦ παῖ, εἰ τιμωρήσεις
Πατρόκλῳ τῷ ἑταίρῳ τὸν φόνον καὶ Ἕκτορα ἀποκτε-
νεῖς, αὐτὸς ἀποθανεῖ· αὐτίκα γάρ τοι,' φησί, 'μεθ᾽
Ἕκτορα πότμος ἑτοῖμος·' ὁ δὲ ταῦτα ἀκούσας τοῦ
μὲν θανάτου καὶ τοῦ κινδύνου ὠλιγώρησε, πολὺ
30 δὲ μᾶλλον δείσας τὸ ζῆν κακὸς ὢν καὶ τοῖς φίλοις D
μὴ τιμωρεῖν, 'αὐτίκα,' φησί, 'τεθναίην δίκην ἐπιθεὶς
τῷ ἀδικοῦντι, ἵνα μὴ ἐνθάδε μένω καταγέλαστος
παρὰ νηυσὶ κορωνίσιν ἄχθος ἀρούρης.'   μὴ αὐτὸν
οἴει φροντίσαι θανάτου καὶ κινδύνου;"   οὕτω γὰρ
35 ἔχει, ὦ ἄνδρες Ἀθηναῖοι, τῇ ἀληθείᾳ· οὗ ἄν τις
ἑαυτὸν τάξῃ ἡγησάμενος βέλτιστον εἶναι ἢ ὑπ᾽
ἄρχοντος ταχθῇ, ἐνταῦθα δεῖ, ὡς ἐμοὶ δοκεῖ, μέ-
νοντα κινδυνεύειν, μηδὲν ὑπολογιζόμενον μήτε
θάνατον μήτε ἄλλο μηδὲν πρὸ τοῦ αἰσχροῦ.

XVII. Ἐγὼ οὖν δεινὰ ἂν εἴην εἰργασμένος, ὦ
ἄνδρες Ἀθηναῖοι, εἰ, ὅτε μέν με οἱ ἄρχοντες ἔτατ- E
τον οὓς ὑμεῖς εἵλεσθε ἄρχειν μου, καὶ ἐν Ποτιδαίᾳ
καὶ ἐν Ἀμφιπόλει καὶ ἐπὶ Δηλίῳ, τότε μὲν οὗ ἐκεῖνοι
5 ἔταττον ἔμενον ὥσπερ καὶ ἄλλος τις καὶ ἐκινδύνευον
ἀποθανεῖν, τοῦ δὲ θεοῦ τάττοντος, ὡς ἐγὼ ᾠήθην

τε καὶ ὑπέλαβον, φιλοσοφοῦντά με δεῖν ζῆν καὶ 28
ἐξετάζοντα ἐμαυτὸν καὶ τοὺς ἄλλους, ἐνταῦθα δὲ
φοβηθεὶς ἢ θάνατον ἢ ἄλλο ὁτιοῦν πρᾶγμα λί- 29
10 ποιμι τὴν τάξιν. δεινόν τἂν εἴη, καὶ ὡς ἀληθῶς
τότ᾽ ἄν με δικαίως εἰσάγοι τις εἰς δικαστήριον, ὅτι
οὐ νομίζω θεοὺς εἶναι ἀπειθῶν τῇ μαντείᾳ καὶ δεδιὼς
θάνατον καὶ οἰόμενος σοφὸς εἶναι οὐκ ὤν. τὸ γὰρ
τοι θάνατον δεδιέναι, ὦ ἄνδρες, οὐδὲν ἄλλο ἐστὶν
15 ἢ δοκεῖν σοφὸν εἶναι μὴ ὄντα· δοκεῖν γὰρ εἰδέναι
ἐστὶν ἃ οὐκ οἶδεν. οἶδε μὲν γὰρ οὐδεὶς τὸν θάνατον οὐδ᾽ εἰ τυγχάνει τῷ ἀνθρώπῳ πάντων μέγιστον
ὂν τῶν ἀγαθῶν, δεδίασι δ᾽ ὡς εὖ εἰδότες ὅτι μέγιστον τῶν κακῶν ἐστι. καὶ τοῦτο πῶς οὐκ ἀμαθία B
20 ἐστὶν αὕτη ἡ ἐπονείδιστος, ἡ τοῦ οἴεσθαι εἰδέναι ἃ
οὐκ οἶδεν; ἐγὼ δ᾽, ὦ ἄνδρες, τούτῳ καὶ ἐνταῦθα
ἴσως διαφέρω τῶν πολλῶν ἀνθρώπων, καὶ εἰ δή τῳ
σοφώτερός του φαίην εἶναι, τούτῳ ἄν, ὅτι οὐκ εἰδὼς
ἱκανῶς περὶ τῶν ἐν Ἅιδου οὕτω καὶ οἴομαι οὐκ
25 εἰδέναι· τὸ δὲ ἀδικεῖν καὶ ἀπειθεῖν τῷ βελτίονι,
καὶ θεῷ καὶ ἀνθρώπῳ, ὅτι κακὸν καὶ αἰσχρόν ἐστιν
οἶδα. πρὸ οὖν τῶν κακῶν ὧν οἶδα ὅτι κακά ἐστιν,
ἃ μὴ οἶδα εἰ ἀγαθὰ ὄντα τυγχάνει οὐδέποτε φοβή-
σομαι οὐδὲ φεύξομαι· ὥστε οὐδ᾽ εἴ με νῦν ὑμεῖς
30 ἀφίετε Ἀνύτῳ ἀπιστήσαντες, ὃς ἔφη ἢ τὴν ἀρχὴν C
οὐ δεῖν ἐμὲ δεῦρο εἰσελθεῖν ἤ, ἐπειδὴ εἰσῆλθον, οὐχ
οἷόν τ᾽ εἶναι τὸ μὴ ἀποκτεῖναί με, λέγων πρὸς ὑμᾶς
ὡς, εἰ διαφευξοίμην, "ἤδη ἂν ὑμῶν οἱ υἱεῖς ἐπιτηδεύοντες ἃ Σωκράτης διδάσκει πάντες παντάπασι

35 διαφθαρήσονται," — εἴ μοι πρὸς ταῦτα εἴποιτε· 29
"ὦ Σώκρατες, νῦν μὲν Ἀνύτῳ οὐ πεισόμεθα, ἀλλ'
ἀφίεμέν σε, ἐπὶ τούτῳ μέντοι, ἐφ' ᾧ τε μηκέτι ἐν
ταύτῃ τῇ ζητήσει διατρίβειν μηδὲ φιλοσοφεῖν·
ἐὰν δὲ ἁλῷς ἔτι τοῦτο πράττων, ἀποθανεῖ·" εἰ
40 οὖν με, ὅπερ εἶπον, ἐπὶ τούτοις ἀφίοιτε, εἴποιμ' ἂν D
ὑμῖν ὅτι "ἐγὼ ὑμᾶς, ἄνδρες Ἀθηναῖοι, ἀσπάζομαι
μὲν καὶ φιλῶ, πείσομαι δὲ μᾶλλον τῷ θεῷ ἢ ὑμῖν,
καὶ ἕωσπερ ἂν ἐμπνέω καὶ οἷός τε ὦ, οὐ μὴ παύσωμαι φιλοσοφῶν καὶ ὑμῖν παρακελευόμενός τε
45 καὶ ἐνδεικνύμενος ὅτῳ ἂν ἀεὶ ἐντυγχάνω ὑμῶν,
λέγων οἷάπερ εἴωθα, ὅτι 'ὦ ἄριστε ἀνδρῶν, Ἀθηναῖος ὤν, πόλεως τῆς μεγίστης καὶ εὐδοκιμωτάτης
εἰς σοφίαν καὶ ἰσχύν, χρημάτων μὲν οὐκ αἰσχύνει
ἐπιμελούμενος ὅπως σοι ἔσται ὡς πλεῖστα καὶ
50 δόξης καὶ τιμῆς, φρονήσεως δὲ καὶ ἀληθείας καὶ E
τῆς ψυχῆς ὅπως ὡς βελτίστη ἔσται οὐκ ἐπιμελεῖ
οὐδὲ φροντίζεις;' καὶ ἐάν τις ὑμῶν ἀμφισβητῇ καὶ
φῇ ἐπιμελεῖσθαι, οὐκ εὐθὺς ἀφήσω αὐτὸν οὐδ' ἄπειμι, ἀλλ' ἐρήσομαι αὐτὸν καὶ ἐξετάσω καὶ ἐλέγξω,
55 καὶ ἐάν μοι μὴ δοκῇ κεκτῆσθαι ἀρετήν, φάναι
δέ, ὀνειδιῶ ὅτι τὰ πλείστου ἄξια περὶ ἐλαχίστου 30
ποιεῖται, τὰ δὲ φαυλότερα περὶ πλείονος. ταῦτα
καὶ νεωτέρῳ καὶ πρεσβυτέρῳ, ὅτῳ ἂν ἐντυγχάνω,
ποιήσω, καὶ ξένῳ καὶ ἀστῷ, μᾶλλον δὲ τοῖς ἀστοῖς,
60 ὅσῳ μου ἐγγυτέρω ἐστὲ γένει. ταῦτα γὰρ κελεύει
ὁ θεός, εὖ ἴστε, καὶ ἐγὼ οἴομαι οὐδέν πω ὑμῖν
μεῖζον ἀγαθὸν γενέσθαι ἐν τῇ πόλει ἢ τὴν ἐμὴν

τῷ θεῷ ὑπηρεσίαν. οὐδὲν γὰρ ἄλλο πράττων ἐγὼ 30
περιέρχομαι ἢ πείθων ὑμῶν καὶ νεωτέρους καὶ
65 πρεσβυτέρους μήτε σωμάτων ἐπιμελεῖσθαι μήτε
χρημάτων πρότερον μηδὲ οὕτω σφόδρα ὡς τῆς B
ψυχῆς ὅπως ὡς ἀρίστη ἔσται, λέγων ὅτι οὐκ ἐκ
χρημάτων ἀρετὴ γίγνεται, ἀλλ᾽ ἐξ ἀρετῆς χρήματα
καὶ τὰ ἄλλα ἀγαθὰ τοῖς ἀνθρώποις ἅπαντα καὶ
70 ἰδίᾳ καὶ δημοσίᾳ. εἰ μὲν οὖν ταῦτα λέγων διαφθείρω τοὺς νέους, ταῦτ᾽ ἂν εἴη βλαβερά· εἰ δέ τίς
μέ φησιν ἄλλα λέγειν ἢ ταῦτα, οὐδὲν λέγει. πρὸς
ταῦτα," φαίην ἄν, "ὦ Ἀθηναῖοι, ἢ πείθεσθε Ἀνύτῳ
ἢ μή, καὶ ἢ ἀφίετε ἢ μὴ ἀφίετε, ὡς ἐμοῦ οὐκ ἂν
75 ποιήσοντος ἄλλα, οὐδ᾽ εἰ μέλλω πολλάκις τεθνάναι." C

XVIII. Μὴ θορυβεῖτε, ἄνδρες Ἀθηναῖοι, ἀλλ᾽
ἐμμείνατέ μοι οἷς ἐδεήθην ὑμῶν, μὴ θορυβεῖν ἐφ᾽
οἷς ἂν λέγω, ἀλλ᾽ ἀκούειν· καὶ γάρ, ὡς ἐγὼ οἶμαι,
ὀνήσεσθε ἀκούοντες. μέλλω γὰρ οὖν ἄττα ὑμῖν
5 ἐρεῖν καὶ ἄλλα ἐφ᾽ οἷς ἴσως βοήσεσθε· ἀλλὰ
μηδαμῶς ποιεῖτε τοῦτο. εὖ γὰρ ἴστε, ἐὰν ἐμὲ
ἀποκτείνητε τοιοῦτον ὄντα οἷον ἐγὼ λέγω, οὐκ ἐμὲ
μείζω βλάψετε ἢ ὑμᾶς αὐτούς· ἐμὲ μὲν γὰρ οὐδὲν
ἂν βλάψειεν οὔτε Μέλητος οὔτε Ἄνυτος· οὐδὲ γὰρ
10 ἂν δύναιτο· οὐ γὰρ οἴομαι θεμιτὸν εἶναι ἀμείνονι D
ἀνδρὶ ὑπὸ χείρονος βλάπτεσθαι. ἀποκτείνειε μεντἂν ἴσως ἢ ἐξελάσειεν ἢ ἀτιμώσειεν· ἀλλὰ ταῦτα
οὗτος μὲν ἴσως οἴεται καὶ ἄλλος τίς που μεγάλα
κακά, ἐγὼ δ᾽ οὐκ οἴομαι, ἀλλὰ πολὺ μᾶλλον ποιεῖν
15 ἃ οὗτος νυνὶ ποιεῖ, ἄνδρα ἀδίκως ἐπιχειρεῖν ἀπο-

κτεινύναι. νῦν οὖν, ὦ ἄνδρες Ἀθηναῖοι, πολλοῦ 3ᵃ
δέω ἐγὼ ὑπὲρ ἐμαυτοῦ ἀπολογεῖσθαι, ὥς τις ἂν
οἴοιτο, ἀλλὰ ὑπὲρ ὑμῶν, μή τι ἐξαμάρτητε περὶ τὴν
τοῦ θεοῦ δόσιν ὑμῖν ἐμοῦ καταψηφισάμενοι. ἐὰν
20 γὰρ ἐμὲ ἀποκτείνητε, οὐ ῥᾳδίως ἄλλον τοιοῦτον Ε
εὑρήσετε, ἀτεχνῶς, εἰ καὶ γελοιότερον εἰπεῖν προσκείμενον τῇ πόλει ὑπὸ τοῦ θεοῦ, ὥσπερ ἵππῳ
μεγάλῳ μὲν καὶ γενναίῳ, ὑπὸ μεγέθους δὲ νωθε-
στέρῳ καὶ δεομένῳ ἐγείρεσθαι ὑπὸ μύωπός τινος·
25 οἷον δή μοι δοκεῖ ὁ θεὸς ἐμὲ τῇ πόλει προστεθει-
κέναι τοιοῦτόν τινα ὃς ὑμᾶς ἐγείρων καὶ πείθων
καὶ ὀνειδίζων ἕνα ἕκαστον οὐδὲν παύομαι τὴν 31
ἡμέραν ὅλην πανταχοῦ προσκαθίζων. τοιοῦτος
οὖν ἄλλος οὐ ῥᾳδίως ὑμῖν γενήσεται, ὦ ἄνδρες,
30 ἀλλ' ἐὰν ἐμοὶ πείθησθε, φείσεσθέ μου· ὑμεῖς δ'
ἴσως τάχ' ἂν ἀχθόμενοι, ὥσπερ οἱ νυστάζοντες
ἐγειρόμενοι, κρούσαντες ἄν με, πειθόμενοι Ἀνύτῳ,
ῥᾳδίως ἂν ἀποκτείναιτε, εἶτα τὸν λοιπὸν βίον καθεύ-
δοντες διατελοῖτε ἄν, εἰ μή τινα ἄλλον ὁ θεὸς ὑμῖν
35 ἐπιπέμψειεν κηδόμενος ὑμῶν. ὅτι δ' ἐγὼ τυγχάνω
ὢν τοιοῦτος οἷος ὑπὸ τοῦ θεοῦ τῇ πόλει δεδόσθαι,
ἐνθένδε ἂν κατανοήσαιτε· οὐ γὰρ ἀνθρωπίνῳ ἔοικε Β
τὸ ἐμὲ τῶν μὲν ἐμαυτοῦ ἁπάντων ἠμεληκέναι καὶ
ἀνέχεσθαι τῶν οἰκείων ἀμελουμένων τοσαῦτα ἤδη
40 ἔτη, τὸ δὲ ὑμέτερον πράττειν ἀεί, ἰδίᾳ ἑκάστῳ
προσιόντα ὥσπερ πατέρα ἢ ἀδελφὸν πρεσβύτερον,
πείθοντα ἐπιμελεῖσθαι ἀρετῆς. καὶ εἰ μέν τι ἀπὸ
τούτων ἀπέλαυον καὶ μισθὸν λαμβάνων ταῦτα

παρεκελευόμην, εἶχον ἄν τινα λόγον· νῦν δὲ ὁρᾶτε 31
45 δὴ καὶ αὐτοὶ ὅτι οἱ κατήγοροι, τἆλλα πάντα ἀναι-
σχύντως οὕτω κατηγοροῦντες, τοῦτό γε οὐχ οἷοί τε
ἐγένοντο ἀπαναισχυντῆσαι, παρασχόμενοι μάρ- C
τυρα ὡς ἐγώ ποτέ τινα ἢ ἐπραξάμην μισθὸν ἢ
ᾔτησα. ἱκανὸν γάρ, οἶμαι, ἐγὼ παρέχομαι τὸν
50 μάρτυρα ὡς ἀληθῆ λέγω, τὴν πενίαν.

XIX. Ἴσως ἂν οὖν δόξειεν ἄτοπον εἶναι ὅτι
δὴ ἐγὼ ἰδίᾳ μὲν ταῦτα ξυμβουλεύω περιιὼν καὶ
πολυπραγμονῶ, δημοσίᾳ δὲ οὐ τολμῶ ἀναβαίνων
εἰς τὸ πλῆθος τὸ ὑμέτερον ξυμβουλεύειν τῇ πόλει.
5 τούτου δὲ αἴτιόν ἐστιν ὃ ὑμεῖς ἐμοῦ πολλάκις ἀκηκόατε πολλαχοῦ λέγοντος, ὅτι μοι θεῖόν τι καὶ D
δαιμόνιον γίγνεται [φωνή], ὃ δὴ καὶ ἐν τῇ γραφῇ
ἐπικωμῳδῶν Μέλητος ἐγράψατο· ἐμοὶ δὲ τοῦτ᾽
ἔστιν ἐκ παιδὸς ἀρξάμενον φωνή τις γιγνομένη,
10 ἣ ὅταν γένηται ἀεὶ ἀποτρέπει με τοῦτο ὃ ἂν μέλλω
πράττειν, προτρέπει δὲ οὔποτε· τοῦτ᾽ ἔστιν ὅ μοι
ἐναντιοῦται τὰ πολιτικὰ πράττειν. καὶ παγκάλως
γέ μοι δοκεῖ ἐναντιοῦσθαι· εὖ γὰρ ἴστε, ὦ ἄνδρες
Ἀθηναῖοι, εἰ ἐγὼ πάλαι ἐπεχείρησα πράττειν τὰ
15 πολιτικὰ πράγματα, πάλαι ἂν ἀπολώλη καὶ οὔτ᾽
ἂν ὑμᾶς ὠφελήκη οὐδὲν οὔτ᾽ ἂν ἐμαυτόν. καί E
μοι μὴ ἄχθεσθε λέγοντι τἀληθῆ· οὐ γὰρ ἔστιν
ὅστις ἀνθρώπων σωθήσεται οὔτε ὑμῖν οὔτε ἄλλῳ
πλήθει οὐδενὶ γνησίως ἐναντιούμενος καὶ διακω-
20 λύων πολλὰ ἄδικα καὶ παράνομα ἐν τῇ πόλει γίγνεσθαι, ἀλλ᾽ ἀναγκαῖόν ἐστι τὸν τῷ ὄντι μαχούμενον 32

ὑπὲρ τοῦ δικαίου, καὶ εἰ μέλλει ὀλίγον χρόνον 32
σωθήσεσθαι, ἰδιωτεύειν ἀλλὰ μὴ δημοσιεύειν.

XX. Μεγάλα δ᾽ ἔγωγε ὑμῖν τεκμήρια παρέξομαι τούτων, οὐ λόγους, ἀλλ᾽ ὃ ὑμεῖς τιμᾶτε, ἔργα.
ἀκούσατε δή μου τὰ ἐμοὶ ξυμβεβηκότα, ἵνα εἰδῆτε
ὅτι οὐδ᾽ ἂν ἑνὶ ὑπεικάθοιμι παρὰ τὸ δίκαιον δείσας
5 θάνατον, μὴ ὑπείκων δὲ ἅμα κἂν ἀπολοίμην. ἐρῶ
δὲ ὑμῖν φορτικὰ μὲν καὶ δικανικά, ἀληθῆ δέ. ἐγὼ
γάρ, ὦ Ἀθηναῖοι, ἄλλην μὲν ἀρχὴν οὐδεμίαν πώ- B
ποτε ἦρξα ἐν τῇ πόλει, ἐβούλευσα δέ· καὶ ἔτυχεν
ἡμῶν ἡ φυλὴ [Ἀντιοχὶς] πρυτανεύουσα, ὅτε ὑμεῖς
10 τοὺς δέκα στρατηγοὺς τοὺς οὐκ ἀνελομένους τοὺς
ἐκ τῆς ναυμαχίας ἐβούλεσθε ἀθρόους κρίνειν, παρανόμως, ὡς ἐν τῷ ὑστέρῳ χρόνῳ πᾶσιν ὑμῖν ἔδοξε.
τότ᾽ ἐγὼ μόνος τῶν πρυτάνεων ἠναντιώθην μηδὲν
ποιεῖν παρὰ τοὺς νόμους καὶ ἐναντία ἐψηφισάμην·
15 καὶ ἑτοίμων ὄντων ἐνδεικνύναι με καὶ ἀπάγειν τῶν
ῥητόρων, καὶ ὑμῶν κελευόντων καὶ βοώντων, μετὰ
τοῦ νόμου καὶ τοῦ δικαίου ᾤμην μᾶλλόν με δεῖν C
διακινδυνεύειν ἢ μεθ᾽ ὑμῶν γενέσθαι μὴ δίκαια
βουλευομένων, φοβηθέντα δεσμὸν ἢ θάνατον. καὶ
20 ταῦτα μὲν ἦν ἔτι δημοκρατουμένης τῆς πόλεως·
ἐπειδὴ δὲ ὀλιγαρχία ἐγένετο, οἱ τριάκοντα αὖ με-
ταπεμψάμενοί με πέμπτον αὐτὸν εἰς τὴν θόλον
προσέταξαν ἀγαγεῖν ἐκ Σαλαμῖνος Λέοντα τὸν Σα-
λαμίνιον, ἵνα ἀποθάνοι· οἷα δὴ καὶ ἄλλοις ἐκεῖνοι
25 πολλοῖς πολλὰ προσέταττον, βουλόμενοι ὡς πλεί-
στους ἀναπλῆσαι αἰτιῶν· τότε μέντοι ἐγὼ οὐ

λόγῳ ἀλλ' ἔργῳ αὖ ἐνεδειξάμην ὅτι ἐμοὶ θανάτου 32
μὲν μέλει, εἰ μὴ ἀγροικότερον ἦν εἰπεῖν, οὐδ' ὁτι- D
οῦν, τοῦ δὲ μηδὲν ἄδικον μηδ' ἀνόσιον ἐργάζεσθαι,
30 τούτου δὲ τὸ πᾶν μέλει. ἐμὲ γὰρ ἐκείνη ἡ ἀρχὴ
οὐκ ἐξέπληξεν οὕτως ἰσχυρὰ οὖσα, ὥστε ἄδικόν τι
ἐργάσασθαι, ἀλλ' ἐπειδὴ ἐκ τῆς θόλου ἐξήλθομεν,
οἱ μὲν τέτταρες ᾤχοντο εἰς Σαλαμῖνα καὶ ἤγαγον
Λέοντα, ἐγὼ δὲ ᾠχόμην ἀπιὼν οἴκαδε. καὶ ἴσως ἂν
35 διὰ ταῦτα ἀπέθανον, εἰ μὴ ἡ ἀρχὴ διὰ ταχέων κα-
τελύθη· καὶ τούτων ὑμῖν ἔσονται πολλοὶ μάρτυρες. E

XXI. Ἆρ' οὖν ἂν με οἴεσθε τοσάδε ἔτη διαγενέσθαι, εἰ ἔπραττον τὰ δημόσια, καὶ πράττων
ἀξίως ἀνδρὸς ἀγαθοῦ ἐβοήθουν τοῖς δικαίοις καί,
ὥσπερ χρή, τοῦτο περὶ πλείστου ἐποιούμην; πολ-
5 λοῦ γε δεῖ, ὦ ἄνδρες Ἀθηναῖοι. οὐδὲ γὰρ ἂν
ἄλλος ἀνθρώπων οὐδείς. ἀλλ' ἐγὼ διὰ παντὸς 33
τοῦ βίου δημοσίᾳ τε, εἴ πού τι ἔπραξα, τοιοῦτος
φανοῦμαι, καὶ ἰδίᾳ ὁ αὐτὸς οὗτος, οὐδενὶ πώποτε
ξυγχωρήσας οὐδὲν παρὰ τὸ δίκαιον οὔτε ἄλλῳ
10 οὔτε τούτων οὐδενὶ οὓς οἱ διαβάλλοντες ἐμέ φασιν ἐμοὺς μαθητὰς εἶναι. ἐγὼ δὲ διδάσκαλος μὲν
οὐδενὸς πώποτ' ἐγενόμην· εἰ δέ τίς μου λέγοντος
καὶ τὰ ἐμαυτοῦ πράττοντος ἐπιθυμοῖ ἀκούειν, εἴ τε
νεώτερος εἴ τε πρεσβύτερος, οὐδενὶ πώποτε ἐφθό-
15 νησα, οὐδὲ χρήματα μὲν λαμβάνων διαλέγομαι, B
μὴ λαμβάνων δὲ οὔ, ἀλλ' ὁμοίως καὶ πλουσίῳ καὶ
πένητι παρέχω ἐμαυτὸν ἐρωτᾶν, καὶ ἐάν τις βούληται ἀποκρινόμενος ἀκούειν ὧν ἂν λέγω. καὶ τού-

τῶν ἐγὼ εἴ τέ τις χρηστὸς γίγνεται εἴ τε μή, οὐκ ἂν 33
20 δικαίως τὴν αἰτίαν ὑπέχοιμι, ὧν μήτε ὑπεσχόμην
μηδενὶ μηδὲν πώποτε μάθημα μήτε ἐδίδαξα· εἰ
δέ τίς φησι παρ' ἐμοῦ πώποτέ τι μαθεῖν ἢ ἀκοῦ-
σαι ἰδίᾳ ὅ τι μὴ καὶ οἱ ἄλλοι πάντες, εὖ ἴστε ὅτι
οὐκ ἀληθῆ λέγει.

XXII. Ἀλλὰ διὰ τί δή ποτε μετ' ἐμοῦ χαί-
ρουσί τινες πολὺν χρόνον διατρίβοντες; ἀκηκό- C
ατε, ὦ ἄνδρες Ἀθηναῖοι· πᾶσαν ὑμῖν τὴν ἀλήθειαν
ἐγὼ εἶπον, ὅτι ἀκούοντες χαίρουσιν ἐξεταζομένοις
5 τοῖς οἰομένοις μὲν εἶναι σοφοῖς, οὖσι δ' οὔ· ἔστι
γὰρ οὐκ ἀηδές. ἐμοὶ δὲ τοῦτο, ὡς ἐγώ φημι, προσ-
τέτακται ὑπὸ τοῦ θεοῦ πράττειν, καὶ ἐκ μαντείων
καὶ ἐξ ἐνυπνίων καὶ παντὶ τρόπῳ ᾧπέρ τίς ποτε
καὶ ἄλλη θεία μοῖρα ἀνθρώπῳ καὶ ὁτιοῦν προσ-
10 έταξε πράττειν. ταῦτα, ὦ Ἀθηναῖοι, καὶ ἀληθῆ
ἐστιν καὶ εὐέλεγκτα. εἰ γὰρ δὴ ἔγωγε τῶν νέων
τοὺς μὲν διαφθείρω, τοὺς δὲ διέφθαρκα, χρῆν D
δήπου, εἴ τε τινὲς αὐτῶν πρεσβύτεροι γενόμενοι
ἔγνωσαν ὅτι νέοις οὖσιν αὐτοῖς ἐγὼ κακὸν πώποτέ
15 τι ξυνεβούλευσα, νυνὶ αὐτοὺς ἀναβαίνοντας ἐμοῦ
κατηγορεῖν καὶ τιμωρεῖσθαι· εἰ δὲ μὴ αὐτοὶ ἤθελον, τῶν οἰκείων τινὰς τῶν ἐκείνων, πατέρας καὶ
ἀδελφοὺς καὶ ἄλλους τοὺς προσήκοντας, εἴ περ ὑπ'
ἐμοῦ τι κακὸν ἐπεπόνθεσαν αὐτῶν οἱ οἰκεῖοι, νῦν
20 μεμνῆσθαι καὶ τιμωρεῖσθαι. πάντως δὲ πάρει-
σιν αὐτῶν πολλοὶ ἐνταυθοῖ οὓς ἐγὼ ὁρῶ, πρῶτον
μὲν Κρίτων οὑτοσί, ἐμὸς ἡλικιώτης καὶ δημότης, E

Κριτοβούλου τοῦδε πατήρ, ἔπειτα Λυσανίας ὁ Σφήτ- 33
τιος, Αἰσχίνου τοῦδε πατήρ, ἔτι Ἀντιφῶν ὁ Κηφι-
25 σιεὺς οὑτοσί, Ἐπιγένους πατήρ, ἄλλοι τοίνυν οὗτοι
ὧν οἱ ἀδελφοὶ ἐν ταύτῃ τῇ διατριβῇ γεγόνασιν,
Νικόστρατος ὁ Θεοζοτίδου, ἀδελφὸς Θεοδότου —
καὶ ὁ μὲν Θεόδοτος τετελεύτηκεν, ὥστε οὐκ ἂν
ἐκεῖνός γε αὐτοῦ καταδεηθείη, — καὶ Πάραλος
30 ὅδε ὁ Δημοδόκου οὗ ἦν Θεάγης ἀδελφός· ὅδε δὲ
Ἀδείμαντος ὁ Ἀρίστωνος, οὗ ἀδελφὸς οὑτοσὶ Πλά- 34
των, καὶ Αἰαντόδωρος οὗ Ἀπολλόδωρος ὅδε ἀδελφός. καὶ ἄλλους πολλοὺς ἐγὼ ἔχω ὑμῖν εἰπεῖν, ὧν
τινα ἐχρῆν μάλιστα μὲν ἐν τῷ ἑαυτοῦ λόγῳ παρα-
35 σχέσθαι Μέλητον μάρτυρα· εἰ δὲ τότε ἐπελάθετο,
νῦν παρασχέσθω, ἐγὼ παραχωρῶ, καὶ λεγέτω, εἴ
τι ἔχει τοιοῦτον. ἀλλὰ τούτου πᾶν τοὐναντίον εὑρήσετε, ὦ ἄνδρες, πάντας ἐμοὶ βοηθεῖν ἑτοίμους
τῷ διαφθείροντι, τῷ κακὰ ἐργαζομένῳ τοὺς οἰκείους
40 αὐτῶν, ὥς φασι Μέλητος καὶ Ἄνυτος. αὐτοὶ μὲν Β
γὰρ οἱ διεφθαρμένοι τάχ' ἂν λόγον ἔχοιεν βοηθοῦν-
τες· οἱ δὲ ἀδιάφθαρτοι, πρεσβύτεροι ἤδη ἄνδρες,
οἱ τούτων προσήκοντες, τίνα ἄλλον ἔχουσι λόγον
βοηθοῦντες ἐμοὶ ἀλλ' ἢ τὸν ὀρθόν τε καὶ δίκαιον,
45 ὅτι ξυνίσασι Μελήτῳ μὲν ψευδομένῳ, ἐμοὶ δὲ ἀλη-
θεύοντι ;

XXIII. Εἶεν δή, ὦ ἄνδρες· ἃ μὲν ἐγὼ ἔχοιμ' ἂν
ἀπολογεῖσθαι, σχεδόν ἐστι ταῦτα καὶ ἄλλα ἴσως
τοιαῦτα. τάχα δ' ἄν τις ὑμῶν ἀγανακτήσειεν ἀνα- C
μνησθεὶς ἑαυτοῦ, εἰ ὁ μὲν καὶ ἐλάττω τουτουῒ τοῦ

5 ἀγῶνος ἀγῶνα ἀγωνιζόμενος ἐδεήθη τε καὶ ἱκέτευσε 34
τοὺς δικαστὰς μετὰ πολλῶν δακρύων, παιδία τε
αὐτοῦ ἀναβιβασάμενος, ἵνα ὅτι μάλιστα ἐλεηθείη,
καὶ ἄλλους τῶν οἰκείων καὶ φίλων πολλούς, ἐγὼ δὲ
οὐδὲν ἄρα τούτων ποιήσω, καὶ ταῦτα κινδυνεύων,
10 ὡς ἂν δόξαιμι, τὸν ἔσχατον κίνδυνον. τάχ᾽ οὖν
τις ταῦτα ἐννοήσας αὐθαδέστερον ἂν πρός με σχοίη,
καὶ ὀργισθεὶς αὐτοῖς τούτοις θεῖτο ἂν μετ᾽ ὀργῆς
τὴν ψῆφον. εἰ δή τις ὑμῶν οὕτως ἔχει, — οὐκ D
ἀξιῶ μὲν γὰρ ἔγωγε, εἰ δ᾽ οὖν, — ἐπιεικῆ ἄν μοι
15 δοκῶ πρὸς τοῦτον λέγειν λέγων ὅτι "ἐμοί, ὦ ἄριστε,
εἰσὶν μέν πού τινες καὶ οἰκεῖοι· καὶ γὰρ τοῦτο
αὐτὸ τὸ τοῦ Ὁμήρου, οὐδ᾽ ἐγὼ ἀπὸ δρυὸς οὐδ᾽ ἀπὸ
πέτρης πέφυκα, ἀλλ᾽ ἐξ ἀνθρώπων," ὥστε καὶ οἰκεῖοί
μοί εἰσι καὶ υἱεῖς, ὦ ἄνδρες Ἀθηναῖοι, τρεῖς, εἷς
20 μὲν μειράκιον ἤδη, δύο δὲ παιδία· ἀλλ᾽ ὅμως οὐδένα αὐτῶν δεῦρο ἀναβιβασάμενος δεήσομαι ὑμῶν
ἀποψηφίσασθαι. τί δὴ οὖν οὐδὲν τούτων ποιήσω;
οὐκ αὐθαδιζόμενος, ὦ Ἀθηναῖοι, οὐδ᾽ ὑμᾶς ἀτιμά- E
ζων, ἀλλ᾽ εἰ μὲν θαρραλέως ἐγὼ ἔχω πρὸς θάνατον
25 ἢ μή, ἄλλος λόγος, πρὸς δ᾽ οὖν δόξαν καὶ ἐμοὶ καὶ
ὑμῖν καὶ ὅλῃ τῇ πόλει οὔ μοι δοκεῖ καλὸν εἶναι ἐμὲ
τούτων οὐδὲν ποιεῖν καὶ τηλικόνδε ὄντα καὶ τοῦτο
τοὔνομα ἔχοντα, εἴ τ᾽ οὖν ἀληθὲς εἴ τ᾽ οὖν ψεῦδος·
ἀλλ᾽ οὖν δεδογμένον γέ ἐστι τὸ Σωκράτη διαφέρειν
30 τινὶ τῶν πολλῶν ἀνθρώπων. εἰ οὖν ὑμῶν οἱ δοκοῦν- 35
τες διαφέρειν εἴ τε σοφίᾳ εἴ τε ἀνδρείᾳ εἴ τε ἄλλῃ
ᾑτινιοῦν ἀρετῇ τοιοῦτοι ἔσονται, αἰσχρὸν ἂν εἴη·

οἵουσπερ ἐγὼ πολλάκις ἑώρακά τινας, ὅταν κρί- 35
νωνται, δοκοῦντας μέν τι εἶναι, θαυμάσια δὲ ἐρ-
35 γαζομένους, ὡς δεινόν τι οἰομένους πείσεσθαι εἰ
ἀποθανοῦνται, ὥσπερ ἀθανάτων ἐσομένων ἂν ὑμεῖς
αὐτοὺς μὴ ἀποκτείνητε· οἳ ἐμοὶ δοκοῦσιν αἰσχύ-
νην τῇ πόλει περιάπτειν, ὥστ᾽ ἄν τινα καὶ τῶν
ξένων ὑπολαβεῖν ὅτι οἱ διαφέροντες Ἀθηναίων εἰς
40 ἀρετήν, οὓς αὐτοὶ ἑαυτῶν ἔν τε ταῖς ἀρχαῖς καὶ B
ταῖς ἄλλαις τιμαῖς προκρίνουσιν, οὗτοι γυναικῶν
οὐδὲν διαφέρουσι. ταῦτα γάρ, ὦ ἄνδρες Ἀθηναῖοι,
οὔτε ὑμᾶς χρὴ ποιεῖν τοὺς δοκοῦντας καὶ ὁτιοῦν
εἶναι, οὔτ᾽, ἂν ἡμεῖς ποιῶμεν, ὑμᾶς ἐπιτρέπειν,
45 ἀλλὰ τοῦτο αὐτὸ ἐνδείκνυσθαι, ὅτι πολὺ μᾶλλον
καταψηφιεῖσθε τοῦ τὰ ἐλεεινὰ ταῦτα δράματα εἰσ-
άγοντος καὶ καταγέλαστον τὴν πόλιν ποιοῦντος ἢ
τοῦ ἡσυχίαν ἄγοντος.

XXIV. Χωρὶς δὲ τῆς δόξης, ὦ ἄνδρες, οὐδὲ
δίκαιόν μοι δοκεῖ εἶναι δεῖσθαι τοῦ δικαστοῦ οὐδὲ C
δεόμενον ἀποφεύγειν, ἀλλὰ διδάσκειν καὶ πείθειν.
οὐ γὰρ ἐπὶ τούτῳ κάθηται ὁ δικαστής, ἐπὶ τῷ κατα-
5 χαρίζεσθαι τὰ δίκαια, ἀλλ᾽ ἐπὶ τῷ κρίνειν ταῦτα·
καὶ ὀμώμοκεν οὐ χαριεῖσθαι οἷς ἂν δοκῇ αὐτῷ,
ἀλλὰ δικάσειν κατὰ τοὺς νόμους. οὔκουν χρὴ οὔτε
ἡμᾶς ἐθίζειν ὑμᾶς ἐπιορκεῖν οὔθ᾽ ὑμᾶς ἐθίζεσθαι·
οὐδέτεροι γὰρ ἂν ἡμῶν εὐσεβοῖεν. μὴ οὖν ἀξιοῦτέ
10 με, ὦ ἄνδρες Ἀθηναῖοι, τοιαῦτα δεῖν πρὸς ὑμᾶς
πράττειν, ἃ μήτε ἡγοῦμαι καλὰ εἶναι μήτε δίκαια
μήτε ὅσια, ἄλλως τε μέντοι νὴ Δία πάντως καὶ D

ἀσεβείας φεύγοντα ὑπὸ Μελήτου τουτουΐ.   σαφῶς 35
γὰρ ἄν, εἰ πείθοιμι ὑμᾶς καὶ τῷ δεῖσθαι βιαζοί-
15 μην ὀμωμοκότας, θεοὺς ἂν διδάσκοιμι μὴ ἡγεῖσθαι
ὑμᾶς εἶναι, καὶ ἀτεχνῶς ἀπολογούμενος κατηγο-
ροίην ἂν ἐμαυτοῦ ὡς θεοὺς οὐ νομίζω.   ἀλλὰ πολλοῦ δεῖ οὕτως ἔχειν· νομίζω τε γάρ, ὦ ἄνδρες
Ἀθηναῖοι, ὡς οὐδεὶς τῶν ἐμῶν κατηγόρων, καὶ ὑμῖν
20 ἐπιτρέπω καὶ τῷ θεῷ κρῖναι περὶ ἐμοῦ ὅπῃ μέλλει
ἐμοί τε ἄριστα εἶναι καὶ ὑμῖν.

———

XXV. Τὸ μὲν μὴ ἀγανακτεῖν, ὦ ἄνδρες Ἀθη- E
ναῖοι, ἐπὶ τούτῳ τῷ γεγονότι, ὅτι μου κατεψηφί- 36
σασθε, ἄλλα τέ μοι πολλὰ ξυμβάλλεται, καὶ οὐκ
ἀνέλπιστόν μοι γέγονεν τὸ γεγονὸς τοῦτο, ἀλλὰ
5 πολὺ μᾶλλον θαυμάζω ἑκατέρων τῶν ψήφων τὸν
γεγονότα ἀριθμόν.   οὐ γὰρ ᾠόμην ἔγωγε οὕτω
παρ' ὀλίγον ἔσεσθαι, ἀλλὰ παρὰ πολύ· νῦν δέ,
ὡς ἔοικεν, εἰ τριάκοντα μόναι μετέπεσον τῶν ψήφων, ἀπεπεφεύγη ἄν.   Μέλητον μὲν οὖν, ὡς ἐμοὶ
10 δοκῶ, καὶ νῦν ἀποπέφευγα, καὶ οὐ μόνον ἀποπέφευγα, ἀλλὰ παντὶ δῆλον τοῦτό γε, ὅτι, εἰ μὴ
ἀνέβη Ἄνυτος καὶ Λύκων κατηγορήσοντες ἐμοῦ,
κἂν ὦφλε χιλίας δραχμάς, οὐ μεταλαβὼν τὸ B
πέμπτον μέρος τῶν ψήφων.

XXVI. Τιμᾶται δ' οὖν μοι ὁ ἀνὴρ θανάτου.
εἶεν· ἐγὼ δὲ δὴ τίνος ὑμῖν ἀντιτιμήσομαι, ὦ ἄνδρες Ἀθηναῖοι; ἢ δῆλον ὅτι τῆς ἀξίας; τί οὖν;
τί ἄξιός εἰμι παθεῖν ἢ ἀποτεῖσαι, ὅ τι μαθὼν ἐν τῷ

5 βίῳ οὐχ ἡσυχίαν ἦγον, ἀλλ᾽ ἀμελήσας ὧνπερ οἱ 36
πολλοί, χρηματισμοῦ τε καὶ οἰκονομίας καὶ στρα-
τηγιῶν καὶ δημηγοριῶν καὶ τῶν ἄλλων ἀρχῶν καὶ
ξυνωμοσιῶν καὶ στάσεων τῶν ἐν τῇ πόλει γιγνο-
μένων, ἡγησάμενος ἐμαυτὸν τῷ ὄντι ἐπιεικέστερον
10 εἶναι ἢ ὥστε εἰς ταῦτ᾽ ἰόντα σῴζεσθαι, ἐνταῦθα C
μὲν οὐκ ᾖα οἷ ἐλθὼν μήτε ὑμῖν μήτε ἐμαυτῷ ἔμελλον μηδὲν ὄφελος εἶναι, ἐπὶ δὲ τὸ ἰδίᾳ ἕκαστον ἰὼν
εὐεργετεῖν τὴν μεγίστην εὐεργεσίαν, ὡς ἐγώ φημι,
ἐνταῦθα ᾖα, ἐπιχειρῶν ἕκαστον ὑμῶν πείθειν μὴ
15 πρότερον μήτε τῶν ἑαυτοῦ μηδενὸς ἐπιμελεῖσθαι,
πρὶν ἑαυτοῦ ἐπιμεληθείη, ὅπως ὡς βέλτιστος καὶ
φρονιμώτατος ἔσοιτο, μήτε τῶν τῆς πόλεως, πρὶν
αὐτῆς τῆς πόλεως, τῶν τε ἄλλων οὕτω κατὰ τὸν
αὐτὸν τρόπον ἐπιμελεῖσθαι· τί οὖν εἰμι ἄξιος πα-
20 θεῖν τοιοῦτος ὤν; ἀγαθόν τι, ὦ ἄνδρες Ἀθηναῖοι, D
εἰ δεῖ γε κατὰ τὴν ἀξίαν τῇ ἀληθείᾳ τιμᾶσθαι· καὶ
ταῦτά γε ἀγαθὸν τοιοῦτον ὅ τι ἂν πρέποι ἐμοί. τί
οὖν πρέπει ἀνδρὶ πένητι εὐεργέτῃ, δεομένῳ ἄγειν
σχολὴν ἐπὶ τῇ ὑμετέρᾳ παρακελεύσει; οὐκ ἔσθ᾽ ὅ
25 τι μᾶλλον, ὦ ἄνδρες Ἀθηναῖοι, πρέπει οὕτως ὡς
τὸν τοιοῦτον ἄνδρα ἐν πρυτανείῳ σιτεῖσθαι, πολύ
γε μᾶλλον ἢ εἴ τις ὑμῶν ἵππῳ ἢ ξυνωρίδι ἢ ζεύγει
νενίκηκεν Ὀλυμπίασιν. ὁ μὲν γὰρ ὑμᾶς ποιεῖ εὐ-
δαίμονας δοκεῖν εἶναι, ἐγὼ δὲ εἶναι· καὶ ὁ μὲν Ε
30 τροφῆς οὐδὲν δεῖται, ἐγὼ δὲ δέομαι. εἰ οὖν δεῖ με
κατὰ τὸ δίκαιον τῆς ἀξίας τιμᾶσθαι, τούτου τιμῶ- 37
μαι, ἐν πρυτανείῳ σιτήσεως.

XXVII. Ἴσως οὖν ὑμῖν καὶ ταυτὶ λέγων παρα- 37
πλησίως δοκῶ λέγειν ὥσπερ περὶ τοῦ οἴκτου καὶ
τῆς ἀντιβολήσεως, ἀπαυθαδιζόμενος· τὸ δὲ οὐκ
ἔστιν, ὦ Ἀθηναῖοι, τοιοῦτον, ἀλλὰ τοιόνδε μᾶλλον.
5 πέπεισμαι ἐγὼ ἑκὼν εἶναι μηδένα ἀδικεῖν ἀνθρώπων, ἀλλὰ ὑμᾶς τοῦτο οὐ πείθω· ὀλίγον γὰρ χρόνον ἀλλήλοις διειλέγμεθα· ἐπεί, ὡς ἐγᾦμαι, εἰ ἦν
ὑμῖν νόμος, ὥσπερ καὶ ἄλλοις ἀνθρώποις, περὶ
θανάτου μὴ μίαν ἡμέραν μόνον κρίνειν, ἀλλὰ B
10 πολλάς, ἐπείσθητε ἄν· νῦν δ᾽ οὐ ῥᾴδιον ἐν χρόνῳ
ὀλίγῳ μεγάλας διαβολὰς ἀπολύεσθαι. πεπεισμένος
δὴ ἐγὼ μηδένα ἀδικεῖν πολλοῦ δέω ἐμαυτόν γε
ἀδικήσειν καὶ κατ᾽ ἐμαυτοῦ ἐρεῖν αὐτός, ὡς ἄξιός
εἰμί του κακοῦ καὶ τιμήσεσθαι τοιούτου τινὸς
15 ἐμαυτῷ. τί δείσας; ἦ μὴ πάθω τοῦτο, οὗ Μέλητός μοι τιμᾶται, ὅ φημι οὐκ εἰδέναι οὔτ᾽ εἰ ἀγαθὸν
οὔτ᾽ εἰ κακόν ἐστιν; ἀντὶ τούτου δὴ ἕλωμαι ὧν εὖ
οἶδ᾽ ὅτι κακῶν ὄντων; τοῦ τιμησάμενος; πότερον
δεσμοῦ; καὶ τί με δεῖ ζῆν ἐν δεσμωτηρίῳ, δου- C
20 λεύοντα τῇ ἀεὶ καθισταμένῃ ἀρχῇ, τοῖς ἕνδεκα;
ἀλλὰ χρημάτων, καὶ δεδέσθαι ἕως ἂν ἐκτείσω;
ἀλλὰ ταὐτόν μοί ἐστιν ὅπερ νῦν δὴ ἔλεγον· οὐ
γὰρ ἔστι μοι χρήματα ὁπόθεν ἐκτείσω. ἀλλὰ δὴ
φυγῆς τιμήσωμαι; ἴσως γὰρ ἄν μοι τούτου τιμή-
25 σαιτε. πολλὴ μεντἂν με φιλοψυχία ἔχοι, εἰ οὕτως
ἀλόγιστός εἰμι ὥστε μὴ δύνασθαι λογίζεσθαι ὅτι
ὑμεῖς μὲν ὄντες πολῖταί μου οὐχ οἷοί τε ἐγένεσθε
ἐνεγκεῖν τὰς ἐμὰς διατριβὰς καὶ τοὺς λόγους, D

ἀλλ᾽ ὑμῖν βαρύτεραι γεγόνασιν καὶ ἐπιφθονώτε- 37
30 ραι, ὥστε ζητεῖτε αὐτῶν νυνὶ ἀπαλλαγῆναι. ἄλλοι
δὲ ἄρα αὐτὰς οἴσουσι ῥᾳδίως; πολλοῦ γε δεῖ, ὦ
Ἀθηναῖοι. καλὸς οὖν ἄν μοι ὁ βίος εἴη ἐξελθόντι
τηλικῷδε ἀνθρώπῳ ἄλλην ἐξ ἄλλης πόλεως ἀμειβομένῳ καὶ ἐξελαυνομένῳ ζῆν. εὖ γὰρ οἶδ᾽ ὅτι,
35 ὅποι ἂν ἔλθω, λέγοντος ἐμοῦ ἀκροάσονται οἱ νέοι
ὥσπερ ἐνθάδε· κἂν μὲν τούτους ἀπελαύνω, οὗτοι
ἐμὲ αὐτοὶ ἐξελῶσι, πείθοντες τοὺς πρεσβυτέρους·
ἐὰν δὲ μὴ ἀπελαύνω, οἱ τούτων πατέρες τε καὶ Ε
οἰκεῖοι δι᾽ αὐτοὺς τούτους.

XXVIII. Ἴσως οὖν ἄν τις εἴποι· "σιγῶν δὲ καὶ
ἡσυχίαν ἄγων, ὦ Σώκρατες, οὐχ οἷός τ᾽ ἔσει ἡμῖν
ἐξελθὼν ζῆν;" τουτὶ δή ἐστι πάντων χαλεπώτατον
πεῖσαί τινας ὑμῶν. ἐάν τε γὰρ λέγω ὅτι τῷ θεῷ
5 ἀπειθεῖν τοῦτ᾽ ἔστιν καὶ διὰ τοῦτο ἀδύνατον ἡσυχίαν ἄγειν, οὐ πείσεσθέ μοι ὡς εἰρωνευομένῳ·
ἐάν τ᾽ αὖ λέγω ὅτι καὶ τυγχάνει μέγιστον ἀγαθὸν 38
ὂν ἀνθρώπῳ τοῦτο, ἑκάστης ἡμέρας περὶ ἀρετῆς
τοὺς λόγους ποιεῖσθαι καὶ τῶν ἄλλων περὶ ὧν
10 ὑμεῖς ἐμοῦ ἀκούετε διαλεγομένου καὶ ἐμαυτὸν καὶ
ἄλλους ἐξετάζοντος, ὁ δὲ ἀνεξέταστος βίος οὐ βιω-
τὸς ἀνθρώπῳ, ταῦτα δ᾽ ἔτι ἧττον πείσεσθέ μοι λέγοντι. τὰ δὲ ἔχει μὲν οὕτως, ὡς ἐγώ φημι, ὦ
ἄνδρες, πείθειν δὲ οὐ ῥᾴδια. καὶ ἐγὼ ἅμα οὐκ
15 εἴθισμαι ἐμαυτὸν ἀξιοῦν κακοῦ οὐδενός. εἰ μὲν
γὰρ ἦν μοι χρήματα, ἐτιμησάμην ἂν χρημάτων Β
ὅσα ἔμελλον ἐκτείσειν· οὐδὲν γὰρ ἂν ἐβλάβην· νῦν

δέ—οὐ γὰρ ἔστιν, εἰ μὴ ἄρα ὅσον ἂν ἐγὼ δυναίμην 38
ἐκτεῖσαι, τοσούτου βούλεσθέ μοι τιμῆσαι. ἴσως
20 δ' ἂν δυναίμην ἐκτεῖσαι ὑμῖν μνᾶν ἀργυρίου · τοσούτου οὖν τιμῶμαι. Πλάτων δὲ ὅδε, ὦ ἄνδρες
Ἀθηναῖοι, καὶ Κρίτων καὶ Κριτόβουλος καὶ Ἀπολλόδωρος κελεύουσί με τριάκοντα μνῶν τιμήσασθαι,
αὐτοὶ δ' ἐγγυᾶσθαι · τιμῶμαι οὖν τοσούτου, ἐγγυη-
25 ταὶ δὲ ὑμῖν ἔσονται τοῦ ἀργυρίου οὗτοι ἀξιόχρεῳ. C

XXIX. Οὐ πολλοῦ γ' ἕνεκα χρόνου, ὦ ἄνδρες
Ἀθηναῖοι, ὄνομα ἕξετε καὶ αἰτίαν ὑπὸ τῶν βουλο-
μένων τὴν πόλιν λοιδορεῖν, ὡς Σωκράτη ἀπεκτόνατε,
ἄνδρα σοφόν · φήσουσι γὰρ δή με σοφὸν εἶναι, εἰ
5 καὶ μή εἰμι, οἱ βουλόμενοι ὑμῖν ὀνειδίζειν. εἰ οὖν
περιεμείνατε ὀλίγον χρόνον, ἀπὸ τοῦ αὐτομάτου ἂν
ὑμῖν τοῦτο ἐγένετο · ὁρᾶτε γὰρ δὴ τὴν ἡλικίαν, ὅτι
πόρρω ἤδη ἐστὶ τοῦ βίου, θανάτου δὲ ἐγγύς. λέγω
δὲ τοῦτο οὐ πρὸς πάντας ὑμᾶς, ἀλλὰ πρὸς τοὺς
10 ἐμοῦ καταψηφισαμένους θάνατον. λέγω δὲ καὶ D
τόδε πρὸς τοὺς αὐτοὺς τούτους. ἴσως με οἴεσθε,
ὦ ἄνδρες, ἀπορίᾳ λόγων ἑαλωκέναι τοιούτων οἷς
ἂν ὑμᾶς ἔπεισα, εἰ ᾤμην δεῖν ἅπαντα ποιεῖν καὶ
λέγειν, ὥστε ἀποφυγεῖν τὴν δίκην. πολλοῦ γε δεῖ.
15 ἀλλ' ἀπορίᾳ μὲν ἑάλωκα, οὐ μέντοι λόγων, ἀλλὰ
τόλμης καὶ ἀναισχυντίας καὶ τοῦ ἐθέλειν λέγειν
πρὸς ὑμᾶς τοιαῦτα οἷ' ἂν ὑμῖν ἥδιστα ἦν ἀκούειν,
θρηνοῦντός τέ μου καὶ ὀδυρομένου καὶ ἄλλα ποιοῦντος καὶ λέγοντος πολλὰ καὶ ἀνάξια ἐμοῦ, ὡς E

20 ἐγώ φημι· οἷα δὴ καὶ εἴθισθε ὑμεῖς τῶν ἄλλων 38
ἀκούειν. ἀλλ᾽ οὔτε τότε ᾠήθην δεῖν ἕνεκα τοῦ
κινδύνου πρᾶξαι οὐδὲν ἀνελεύθερον, οὔτε νῦν μοι
μεταμέλει οὕτως ἀπολογησαμένῳ, ἀλλὰ πολὺ μᾶλλον αἱροῦμαι ὧδε ἀπολογησάμενος τεθνάναι ἢ
25 ἐκείνως ζῆν. οὔτε γὰρ ἐν δίκῃ οὔτ᾽ ἐν πολέμῳ
οὔτ᾽ ἐμὲ οὔτ᾽ ἄλλον οὐδένα δεῖ τοῦτο μηχανᾶ- 39
σθαι, ὅπως ἀποφεύξεται πᾶν ποιῶν θάνατον. καὶ
γὰρ ἐν ταῖς μάχαις πολλάκις δῆλον γίγνεται ὅτι
τό γε ἀποθανεῖν ἄν τις ἐκφύγοι καὶ ὅπλα ἀφεὶς
30 καὶ ἐφ᾽ ἱκετείαν τραπόμενος τῶν διωκόντων· καὶ
ἄλλαι μηχαναὶ πολλαί εἰσιν ἐν ἑκάστοις τοῖς κιν-
δύνοις, ὥστε διαφεύγειν θάνατον, ἐάν τις τολμᾷ
πᾶν ποιεῖν καὶ λέγειν. ἀλλὰ μὴ οὐ τοῦτ᾽ ᾖ χαλεπόν, ὦ ἄνδρες, θάνατον ἐκφυγεῖν, ἀλλὰ πολὺ χαλε-
35 πώτερον πονηρίαν· θᾶττον γὰρ θανάτου θεῖ. καὶ
νῦν ἐγὼ μὲν ἅτε βραδὺς ὢν καὶ πρεσβύτης ὑπὸ τοῦ B
βραδυτέρου ἑάλων, οἱ δ᾽ ἐμοὶ κατήγοροι ἅτε δεινοὶ
καὶ ὀξεῖς ὄντες ὑπὸ τοῦ θάττονος, τῆς κακίας. καὶ
νῦν ἐγὼ μὲν ἄπειμι ὑφ᾽ ὑμῶν θανάτου δίκην ὄφλων,
40 οὗτοι δ᾽ ὑπὸ τῆς ἀληθείας ὠφληκότες μοχθηρίαν
καὶ ἀδικίαν. καὶ ἔγωγε τῷ τιμήματι ἐμμένω καὶ
οὗτοι. ταῦτα μέν που ἴσως οὕτως καὶ ἔδει σχεῖν,
καὶ οἶμαι αὐτὰ μετρίως ἔχειν.

XXX. Τὸ δὲ δὴ μετὰ τοῦτο ἐπιθυμῶ ὑμῖν
χρησμῳδῆσαι, ὦ καταψηφισάμενοί μου· καὶ γὰρ C
εἰμι ἤδη ἐνταῦθα ἐν ᾧ μάλιστα ἄνθρωποι χρησμῳδοῦσιν, ὅταν μέλλωσιν ἀποθανεῖσθαι. φημὶ γάρ,

5 ὦ ἄνδρες, οἳ ἐμὲ ἀπεκτόνατε, τιμωρίαν ὑμῖν ἥξειν 39
εὐθὺς μετὰ τὸν ἐμὸν θάνατον πολὺ χαλεπωτέραν
νὴ Δία ἢ οἵαν ἐμὲ ἀπεκτόνατε· νῦν γὰρ τοῦτο
εἴργασθε οἰόμενοι ἀπαλλάξεσθαι τοῦ διδόναι ἔλεγ-
χον τοῦ βίου, τὸ δὲ ὑμῖν πολὺ ἐναντίον ἀποβή-
10 σεται, ὡς ἐγώ φημι.   πλείους ἔσονται ὑμᾶς οἱ
ἐλέγχοντες, οὓς νῦν ἐγὼ κατεῖχον, ὑμεῖς δὲ οὐκ D
ᾐσθάνεσθε· καὶ χαλεπώτεροι ἔσονται ὅσῳ νεώτε-
ροί εἰσιν, καὶ ὑμεῖς μᾶλλον ἀγανακτήσετε. εἰ γὰρ
οἴεσθε ἀποκτείνοντες ἀνθρώπους ἐπισχήσειν τοῦ
15 ὀνειδίζειν τινὰ ὑμῖν ὅτι οὐκ ὀρθῶς ζῆτε, οὐκ ὀρθῶς
διανοεῖσθε· οὐ γὰρ ἔσθ' αὕτη ἡ ἀπαλλαγὴ οὔτε
πάνυ δυνατὴ οὔτε καλή, ἀλλ' ἐκείνη καὶ καλλίστη
καὶ ῥᾴστη, μὴ τοὺς ἄλλους κολούειν, ἀλλ' ἑαυτὸν
παρασκευάζειν ὅπως ἔσται ὡς βέλτιστος. ταῦτα
20 μὲν οὖν ὑμῖν τοῖς καταψηφισαμένοις μαντευσά-
μενος ἀπαλλάττομαι.
                                                          E
  XXXI. Τοῖς δὲ ἀποψηφισαμένοις ἡδέως ἂν
διαλεχθείην ὑπὲρ τοῦ γεγονότος τουτουὶ πράγμα-
τος, ἐν ᾧ οἱ ἄρχοντες ἀσχολίαν ἄγουσι καὶ οὔπω
ἔρχομαι οἷ ἐλθόντα με δεῖ τεθνάναι. ἀλλά μοι, ὦ
5 ἄνδρες, παραμείνατε τοσοῦτον χρόνον· οὐδὲν γὰρ
κωλύει διαμυθολογῆσαι πρὸς ἀλλήλους ἕως ἔξεστιν. ὑμῖν γὰρ ὡς φίλοις οὖσιν ἐπιδεῖξαι ἐθέλω 40
τὸ νυνί μοι ξυμβεβηκὸς τί ποτε νοεῖ. ἐμοὶ γάρ, ὦ
ἄνδρες δικασταί — ὑμᾶς γὰρ δικαστὰς καλῶν ὀρ-
10 θῶς ἂν καλοίην — θαυμάσιόν τι γέγονεν. ἡ γὰρ
εἰωθυῖά μοι μαντικὴ ἡ τοῦ δαιμονίου ἐν μὲν τῷ

πρόσθεν χρόνῳ παντὶ πάνυ πυκνὴ ἀεὶ ἦν καὶ πάνυ 40
ἐπὶ σμικροῖς ἐναντιουμένη, εἴ τι μέλλοιμι μὴ ὀρθῶς
πράξειν· νυνὶ δὲ ξυμβέβηκέ μοι, ἅπερ ὁρᾶτε καὶ
15 αὐτοί, ταυτὶ ἅ γε δὴ οἰηθείη ἄν τις καὶ νομίζεται
ἔσχατα κακῶν εἶναι. ἐμοὶ δὲ οὔτε ἐξιόντι ἕωθεν
οἴκοθεν ἠναντιώθη τὸ τοῦ θεοῦ σημεῖον, οὔτε ἡνίκα B
ἀνέβαινον ἐνταυθοῖ ἐπὶ τὸ δικαστήριον, οὔτε ἐν τῷ
λόγῳ οὐδαμοῦ μέλλοντί τι ἐρεῖν· καίτοι ἐν ἄλλοις
20 λόγοις πολλαχοῦ δή με ἐπέσχε λέγοντα μεταξύ·
νῦν δὲ οὐδαμοῦ περὶ ταύτην τὴν πρᾶξιν οὔτ᾽ ἐν ἔργῳ
οὐδενὶ οὔτ᾽ ἐν λόγῳ ἠναντίωταί μοι. τί οὖν αἴτιον
εἶναι ὑπολαμβάνω; ἐγὼ ὑμῖν ἐρῶ· κινδυνεύει γάρ
μοι τὸ ξυμβεβηκὸς τοῦτο ἀγαθὸν γεγονέναι, καὶ
25 οὐκ ἔσθ᾽ ὅπως ἡμεῖς ὀρθῶς ὑπολαμβάνομεν ὅσοι
οἰόμεθα κακὸν εἶναι τὸ τεθνάναι. μέγα μοι τεκ- C
μήριον τούτου γέγονεν· οὐ γὰρ ἔσθ᾽ ὅπως οὐκ
ἠναντιώθη ἄν μοι τὸ εἰωθὸς σημεῖον, εἰ μή τι
ἔμελλον ἐγὼ ἀγαθὸν πράξειν.

XXXII. Ἐννοήσωμεν δὲ καὶ τῇδε ὡς πολλὴ
ἐλπίς ἐστιν ἀγαθὸν αὐτὸ εἶναι. δυοῖν γὰρ θάτερόν
ἐστιν τὸ τεθνάναι· ἢ γὰρ οἷον μηδὲν εἶναι μηδὲ
αἴσθησιν μηδεμίαν μηδενὸς ἔχειν τὸν τεθνεῶτα, ἢ
5 κατὰ τὰ λεγόμενα μεταβολή τις τυγχάνει οὖσα καὶ
μετοίκησις τῇ ψυχῇ τοῦ τόπου τοῦ ἐνθένδε εἰς
ἄλλον τόπον. καὶ εἴ τε μηδεμία αἴσθησίς ἐστιν,
ἀλλ᾽ οἷον ὕπνος, ἐπειδάν τις καθεύδων μηδ᾽ ὄναρ D
μηδὲν ὁρᾷ, θαυμάσιον κέρδος ἂν εἴη ὁ θάνατος.
10 ἐγὼ γὰρ ἂν οἶμαι, εἴ τινα ἐκλεξάμενον δέοι ταύτην

τὴν νύκτα ἐν ᾗ οὕτω κατέδαρθεν ὥστε μηδὲ ὄναρ 40
ἰδεῖν, καὶ τὰς ἄλλας νύκτας τε καὶ ἡμέρας τὰς τοῦ
βίου τοῦ ἑαυτοῦ ἀντιπαραθέντα ταύτῃ τῇ νυκτὶ δέοι
σκεψάμενον εἰπεῖν, πόσας ἄμεινον καὶ ἥδιον ἡμέ-
15 ρας καὶ νύκτας ταύτης τῆς νυκτὸς βεβίωκεν ἐν τῷ
ἑαυτοῦ βίῳ, οἶμαι ἂν μὴ ὅτι ἰδιώτην τινά, ἀλλὰ
τὸν μέγαν βασιλέα εὐαριθμήτους ἂν εὑρεῖν αὐτὸν E
ταύτας πρὸς τὰς ἄλλας ἡμέρας καὶ νύκτας. εἰ οὖν
τοιοῦτον ὁ θάνατός ἐστιν, κέρδος ἔγωγε λέγω· καὶ
20 γὰρ οὐδὲν πλείων ὁ πᾶς χρόνος φαίνεται οὕτω δὴ
εἶναι ἢ μία νύξ. εἰ δ᾽ αὖ οἷον ἀποδημῆσαί ἐστιν
ὁ θάνατος ἐνθένδε εἰς ἄλλον τόπον, καὶ ἀληθῆ
ἐστιν τὰ λεγόμενα, ὡς ἄρα ἐκεῖ εἰσιν ἅπαντες οἱ
τεθνεῶτες, τί μεῖζον ἀγαθὸν τούτου εἴη ἄν, ὦ ἄν-
25 δρες δικασταί; εἰ γάρ τις ἀφικόμενος εἰς Ἅιδου,
ἀπαλλαγεὶς τούτων τῶν φασκόντων δικαστῶν 41
εἶναι, εὑρήσει τοὺς ἀληθῶς δικαστάς, οἵπερ καὶ
λέγονται ἐκεῖ δικάζειν, Μίνως τε καὶ Ῥαδάμανθυς
καὶ Αἰακὸς καὶ Τριπτόλεμος καὶ ἄλλοι ὅσοι τῶν
30 ἡμιθέων δίκαιοι ἐγένοντο ἐν τῷ ἑαυτῶν βίῳ, ἆρα
φαύλη ἂν εἴη ἡ ἀποδημία; ἢ αὖ Ὀρφεῖ ξυγγενέσθαι καὶ Μουσαίῳ καὶ Ἡσιόδῳ καὶ Ὁμήρῳ ἐπὶ
πόσῳ ἄν τις δέξαιτ᾽ ἂν ὑμῶν; ἐγὼ μὲν γὰρ πολλάκις θέλω τεθνάναι, εἰ ταῦτ᾽ ἔστιν ἀληθῆ· ἐπεὶ
35 ἔμοιγε καὶ αὐτῷ θαυμαστὴ ἂν εἴη ἡ διατριβὴ αὐ-
τόθι, ὁπότε ἐντύχοιμι Παλαμήδει καὶ Αἴαντι τῷ B
Τελαμῶνος καὶ εἴ τις ἄλλος τῶν παλαιῶν διὰ κρίσιν ἄδικον τέθνηκεν, ἀντιπαραβάλλοντι τὰ ἐμαυτοῦ

πάθη πρὸς τὰ ἐκείνων, ὡς ἐγὼ οἶμαι, οὐκ ἂν ἀηδὲς 41
40 εἴη. καὶ δὴ τὸ μέγιστον, τοὺς ἐκεῖ ἐξετάζοντα καὶ
ἐρευνῶντα ὥσπερ τοὺς ἐνταῦθα διάγειν, τίς αὐτῶν
σοφός ἐστιν καὶ τίς οἴεται μέν, ἔστιν δ' οὔ. ἐπὶ
πόσῳ δ' ἄν τις, ὦ ἄνδρες δικασταί, δέξαιτο ἐξετάσαι τὸν ἐπὶ Τροίαν ἀγαγόντα τὴν πολλὴν στρατιὰν
45 ἢ Ὀδυσσέα ἢ Σίσυφον, ἢ ἄλλους μυρίους ἄν τις C
εἴποι καὶ ἄνδρας καὶ γυναῖκας; οἷς ἐκεῖ διαλέγε-
σθαι καὶ ξυνεῖναι καὶ ἐξετάζειν ἀμήχανον ἂν εἴη
εὐδαιμονίας. πάντως οὐ δήπου τούτου γε ἕνεκα οἱ
ἐκεῖ ἀποκτείνουσι· τά τε γὰρ ἄλλα εὐδαιμονέστε-
50 ροί εἰσιν οἱ ἐκεῖ τῶν ἐνθάδε, καὶ ἤδη τὸν λοιπὸν
χρόνον ἀθάνατοί εἰσιν, εἴ περ γε τὰ λεγόμενα ἀληθῆ
ἐστιν.

XXXIII. Ἀλλὰ καὶ ὑμᾶς χρή, ὦ ἄνδρες δικασταί, εὐέλπιδας εἶναι πρὸς τὸν θάνατον, καὶ ἕν
τι τοῦτο διανοεῖσθαι ἀληθές, ὅτι οὐκ ἔστιν ἀνδρὶ
ἀγαθῷ κακὸν οὐδὲν οὔτε ζῶντι οὔτε τελευτήσαντι, D
5 οὐδὲ ἀμελεῖται ὑπὸ θεῶν τὰ τούτου πράγματα·
οὐδὲ τὰ ἐμὰ νῦν ἀπὸ τοῦ αὐτομάτου γέγονεν, ἀλλά
μοι δῆλόν ἐστι τοῦτο, ὅτι ἤδη τεθνάναι καὶ ἀπηλ-
λάχθαι πραγμάτων βέλτιον ἦν μοι. διὰ τοῦτο καὶ
ἐμὲ οὐδαμοῦ ἀπέτρεψεν τὸ σημεῖον, καὶ ἔγωγε τοῖς
10 καταψηφισαμένοις μου καὶ τοῖς κατηγόροις οὐ πάνυ
χαλεπαίνω. καίτοι οὐ ταύτῃ τῇ διανοίᾳ κατεψη-
φίζοντό μου καὶ κατηγόρουν, ἀλλ' οἰόμενοι βλάπ-
τειν· τοῦτο αὐτοῖς ἄξιον μέμφεσθαι. τοσόνδε E
μέντοι αὐτῶν δέομαι· τοὺς υἱεῖς μου, ἐπειδὰν

15 ἡβήσωσι, τιμωρήσασθε, ὦ ἄνδρες, ταὐτὰ ταῦτα 41
λυποῦντες ἅπερ ἐγὼ ὑμᾶς ἐλύπουν, ἐὰν ὑμῖν δοκῶσιν ἢ χρημάτων ἢ ἄλλου του πρότερον ἐπιμελεῖσθαι ἢ ἀρετῆς, καὶ ἐὰν δοκῶσί τι εἶναι μηδὲν
ὄντες, ὀνειδίζετε αὐτοῖς, ὥσπερ ἐγὼ ὑμῖν, ὅτι οὐκ
20 ἐπιμελοῦνται ὧν δεῖ, καὶ οἴονταί τι εἶναι ὄντες οὐδενὸς ἄξιοι. καὶ ἐὰν ταῦτα ποιῆτε, δίκαια πεπονθὼς 42
ἐγὼ ἔσομαι ὑφ᾽ ὑμῶν αὐτός τε καὶ οἱ υἱεῖς. ἀλλὰ
γὰρ ἤδη ὥρα ἀπιέναι, ἐμοὶ μὲν ἀποθανουμένῳ,
ὑμῖν δὲ βιωσομένοις· ὁπότεροι δὲ ἡμῶν ἔρχονται
25 ἐπὶ ἄμεινον πρᾶγμα, ἄδηλον παντὶ πλὴν ἢ τῷ θεῷ.

ΚΡΙΤΩΝ

[ἢ περὶ πρακτέου, ἠθικός]

TA TOY ΔΙΑΛΟΓΟΥ ΠΡΟΣΩΠΑ
ΣΩΚΡΑΤΗΣ, ΚΡΙΤΩΝ

St. I.
p. 43

I. ΣΩ. Τί τηνικάδε ἀφῖξαι, ὦ Κρίτων; ἢ οὐ A
πρῷ ἔτι ἐστίν;

ΚΡ. Πάνυ μὲν οὖν.

ΣΩ. Πηνίκα μάλιστα;

5 ΚΡ. Ὄρθρος βαθύς.

ΣΩ. Θαυμάζω ὅπως ἠθέλησέ σοι ὁ τοῦ δεσμωτηρίου φύλαξ ὑπακοῦσαι.

ΚΡ. Ξυνήθης ἤδη μοί ἐστιν, ὦ Σώκρατες, διὰ
τὸ πολλάκις δεῦρο φοιτᾶν, καί τι καὶ εὐεργέτηται
10 ὑπ' ἐμοῦ.

ΣΩ. Ἄρτι δὲ ἥκεις ἢ πάλαι;

ΚΡ. Ἐπιεικῶς πάλαι.

ΣΩ. Εἶτα πῶς οὐκ εὐθὺς ἐπήγειράς με, ἀλλὰ B
σιγῇ παρακάθησαι;

15 ΚΡ. Οὐ μὰ τὸν Δία, ὦ Σώκρατες, οὐδ' ἂν αὐτὸς
ἤθελον ἐν τοσαύτῃ τε ἀγρυπνίᾳ καὶ λύπῃ εἶναι.
ἀλλὰ καὶ σοῦ πάλαι θαυμάζω αἰσθανόμενος ὡς
ἡδέως καθεύδεις· καὶ ἐπιτηδές σε οὐκ ἤγειρον, ἵνα
ὡς ἥδιστα διάγῃς. καὶ πολλάκις μὲν δή σε καὶ

83

20 πρότερον ἐν παντὶ τῷ βίῳ εὐδαιμόνισα τοῦ τρόπου, 43
πολὺ δὲ μάλιστα ἐν τῇ νυνὶ παρεστώσῃ ξυμφορᾷ,
ὡς ῥᾳδίως αὐτὴν καὶ πράως φέρεις.

ΣΩ. Καὶ γὰρ ἄν, ὦ Κρίτων, πλημμελὲς εἴη ἀγανακτεῖν τηλικοῦτον ὄντα, εἰ δεῖ ἤδη τελευτᾶν.   C

25 ΚΡ. Καὶ ἄλλοι, ὦ Σώκρατες, τηλικοῦτοι ἐν τοι-
αύταις ξυμφοραῖς ἁλίσκονται, ἀλλ᾽ οὐδὲν αὐτοὺς
ἐπιλύεται ἡ ἡλικία τὸ μὴ οὐχὶ ἀγανακτεῖν τῇ
παρούσῃ τύχῃ.

ΣΩ. Ἔστι ταῦτα. ἀλλὰ τί δὴ οὕτω πρῲ ἀφῖξαι;

30 ΚΡ. Ἀγγελίαν, ὦ Σώκρατες, φέρων χαλεπήν, οὐ
σοί, ὡς ἐμοὶ φαίνεται, ἀλλ᾽ ἐμοὶ καὶ τοῖς σοῖς ἐπι-
τηδείοις πᾶσιν καὶ χαλεπὴν καὶ βαρεῖαν, ἣν ἐγώ,
ὡς ἐμοὶ δοκῶ, ἐν τοῖς βαρύτατ᾽ ἂν ἐνέγκαιμι.

ΣΩ. Τίνα ταύτην; ἢ τὸ πλοῖον ἀφῖκται ἐκ Δή-
35 λου, οὗ δεῖ ἀφικομένου τεθνάναι με;   D

ΚΡ. Οὔτοι δὴ ἀφῖκται, ἀλλὰ δοκεῖ μέν μοι ἥξειν
τήμερον ἐξ ὧν ἀπαγγέλλουσιν ἥκοντές τινες ἀπὸ
Σουνίου καὶ καταλιπόντες ἐκεῖ αὐτό. δῆλον οὖν ἐκ
τούτων [τῶν ἀγγέλων] ὅτι ἥξει τήμερον, καὶ ἀνάγ-
40 κη δὴ εἰς αὔριον ἔσται, ὦ Σώκρατες, τὸν βίον σε
τελευτᾶν.

II. ΣΩ. Ἀλλ᾽, ὦ Κρίτων, τύχῃ ἀγαθῇ. εἰ ταύτῃ
τοῖς θεοῖς φίλον, ταύτῃ ἔστω. οὐ μέντοι οἶμαι ἥξειν
αὐτὸ τήμερον.
    44

ΚΡ. Πόθεν τοῦτο τεκμαίρει;

5 ΣΩ. Ἐγώ σοι ἐρῶ. τῇ γὰρ που ὑστεραίᾳ δεῖ
με ἀποθνήσκειν ἢ ᾗ ἂν ἔλθῃ τὸ πλοῖον.

ΚΡ. Φασί γέ τοι δὴ οἱ τούτων κύριοι.   44

ΣΩ. Οὐ τοίνυν τῆς ἐπιούσης ἡμέρας οἶμαι αὐτὸ
ἥξειν, ἀλλὰ τῆς ἑτέρας. τεκμαίρομαι δὲ ἔκ τινος
10 ἐνυπνίου ὃ ἑώρακα ὀλίγον πρότερον ταύτης τῆς
νυκτός· καὶ κινδυνεύεις ἐν καιρῷ τινι οὐκ ἐγεῖ-
ραί με.

ΚΡ. Ἦν δὲ δὴ τί τὸ ἐνύπνιον;

ΣΩ. Ἐδόκει τίς μοι γυνὴ προσελθοῦσα καλὴ
15 καὶ εὐειδής, λευκὰ ἱμάτια ἔχουσα, καλέσαι με
καὶ εἰπεῖν· "ὦ Σώκρατες,   B

ἤματί κεν τριτάτῳ Φθίην ἐρίβωλον ἵκοιο."

ΚΡ. Ἄτοπον τὸ ἐνύπνιον, ὦ Σώκρατες.

ΣΩ. Ἐναργὲς μὲν οὖν, ὥς γέ μοι δοκεῖ, ὦ Κρίτων.

III. ΚΡ. Λίαν γε, ὡς ἔοικεν. ἀλλ᾽, ὦ δαιμόνιε
Σώκρατες, ἔτι καὶ νῦν ἐμοὶ πείθου καὶ σώθητι· ὡς
ἐμοί, ἐὰν σὺ ἀποθάνῃς, οὐ μία ξυμφορά ἐστιν,
ἀλλὰ χωρὶς μὲν τοῦ ἐστερῆσθαι τοιούτου ἐπιτη-
5 δείου οἷον ἐγὼ οὐδένα μή ποτε εὑρήσω, ἔτι δὲ καὶ
πολλοῖς δόξω οἳ ἐμὲ καὶ σὲ μὴ σαφῶς ἴσασιν, ὡς
οἷός τ᾽ ὢν σε σῴζειν, εἰ ἤθελον ἀναλίσκειν χρή-   C
ματα, ἀμελῆσαι. καίτοι τίς ἂν αἰσχίων εἴη ταύτης
δόξα ἢ δοκεῖν χρήματα περὶ πλείονος ποιεῖσθαι ἢ
10 φίλους; οὐ γὰρ πείσονται οἱ πολλοὶ ὡς σὺ αὐτὸς οὐκ
ἠθέλησας ἀπιέναι ἐνθένδε ἡμῶν προθυμουμένων.

ΣΩ. Ἀλλὰ τί ἡμῖν, ὦ μακάριε Κρίτων, οὕτω τῆς
τῶν πολλῶν δόξης μέλει; οἱ γὰρ ἐπιεικέστατοι, ὧν
μᾶλλον ἄξιον φροντίζειν, ἡγήσονται αὐτὰ οὕτω πε-
15 πρᾶχθαι ὥσπερ ἂν πραχθῇ.

ΚΡ. Ἀλλ᾽ ὁρᾷς δὴ ὅτι ἀνάγκη, ὦ Σώκρατες, 44
καὶ τῆς τῶν πολλῶν δόξης μέλειν. αὐτὰ δὲ δῆλα D
τὰ παρόντα νυνί, ὅτι οἷοί τ᾽ εἰσὶν οἱ πολλοὶ οὐ τὰ
σμικρότατα τῶν κακῶν ἐξεργάζεσθαι, ἀλλὰ τὰ μέ-
20 γιστα σχεδόν, ἐάν τις ἐν αὐτοῖς διαβεβλημένος ᾖ.

ΣΩ. Εἰ γὰρ ὤφελον, ὦ Κρίτων, οἷοί τ᾽ εἶναι οἱ
πολλοὶ τὰ μέγιστα κακὰ ἐργάζεσθαι, ἵνα οἷοί τ᾽
ἦσαν καὶ τὰ μέγιστα ἀγαθά, καὶ καλῶς ἂν εἶχεν·
νῦν δὲ οὐδέτερα οἷοί τε· οὔτε γὰρ φρόνιμον οὔτε
25 ἄφρονα δυνατοὶ ποιῆσαι, ποιοῦσι δὲ τοῦτο ὅ τι ἂν
τύχωσι.

IV. ΚΡ. Ταῦτα μὲν δὴ οὕτως ἐχέτω· τάδε δέ, E
ὦ Σώκρατες, εἰπέ μοι. ἆρά γε μὴ ἐμοῦ προμηθεῖ
καὶ τῶν ἄλλων ἐπιτηδείων, μή, ἐὰν σὺ ἐνθένδε
ἐξέλθῃς, οἱ συκοφάνται ἡμῖν πράγματα παρέχω-
5 σιν ὡς σὲ ἐνθένδε ἐκκλέψασιν, καὶ ἀναγκασθῶμεν
ἢ καὶ πᾶσαν τὴν οὐσίαν ἀποβαλεῖν ἢ συχνὰ
χρήματα, ἢ καὶ ἄλλο τι πρὸς τούτοις παθεῖν ;
εἰ γάρ τι τοιοῦτον φοβεῖ, ἔασον αὐτὸ χαίρειν· 45
ἡμεῖς γάρ που δίκαιοί ἐσμεν σώσαντές σε κινδυ-
10 νεύειν τοῦτον τὸν κίνδυνον καί, ἐὰν δέῃ, ἔτι τούτου
μείζω. ἀλλ᾽ ἐμοὶ πείθου καὶ μὴ ἄλλως ποίει.

ΣΩ. Καὶ ταῦτα προμηθοῦμαι, ὦ Κρίτων, καὶ
ἄλλα πολλά.

ΚΡ. Μήτε τοίνυν ταῦτα φοβοῦ· καὶ γὰρ οὐδὲ
15 πολὺ τἀργύριόν ἐστιν ὃ θέλουσι λαβόντες τινὲς
σῶσαί σε καὶ ἐξαγαγεῖν ἐνθένδε. ἔπειτα οὐχ
ὁρᾷς τούτους τοὺς συκοφάντας ὡς εὐτελεῖς, καὶ

οὐδὲν ἂν δέοι ἐπ᾽ αὐτοὺς πολλοῦ ἀργυρίου; σοὶ 45
δὲ ὑπάρχει μὲν τὰ ἐμὰ χρήματα, ὡς ἐγὼ οἶμαι, Β
20 ἱκανά· ἔπειτα καὶ εἴ τι ἐμοῦ κηδόμενος οὐκ οἴει
δεῖν ἀναλίσκειν τἀμά, ξένοι οὗτοι ἐνθάδε ἕτοιμοι
ἀναλίσκειν· εἷς δὲ καὶ κεκόμικεν ἐπ᾽ αὐτὸ τοῦτο
ἀργύριον ἱκανόν, Σιμμίας ὁ Θηβαῖος· ἕτοιμος δὲ
καὶ Κέβης καὶ ἄλλοι πολλοὶ πάνυ. ὥστε, ὅπερ
25 λέγω, μήτε ταῦτα φοβούμενος ἀποκάμῃς σαυτὸν
σῶσαι, μήτε, ὃ ἔλεγες ἐν τῷ δικαστηρίῳ, δυσχερές
σοι γενέσθω, ὅτι οὐκ ἂν ἔχοις ἐξελθὼν ὅ τι χρῷο
σαυτῷ· πολλαχοῦ μὲν γὰρ καὶ ἄλλοσε ὅποι ἂν
ἀφίκῃ ἀγαπήσουσί σε· ἐὰν δὲ βούλῃ εἰς Θεττα- C
30 λίαν ἰέναι, εἰσὶν ἐμοὶ ἐκεῖ ξένοι, οἵ σε περὶ πολλοῦ
ποιήσονται καὶ ἀσφάλειάν σοι παρέξονται ὥστε
σε μηδένα λυπεῖν τῶν κατὰ Θετταλίαν.

V. Ἔτι δέ, ὦ Σώκρατες, οὐδὲ δίκαιόν μοι δοκεῖς ἐπιχειρεῖν πρᾶγμα, σαυτὸν προδοῦναι, ἐξὸν
σωθῆναι· καὶ τοιαῦτα σπεύδεις περὶ σαυτὸν γενέσθαι, ἅπερ ἂν καὶ οἱ ἐχθροί σου σπεύσαιέν τε καὶ
5 ἔσπευσάν σε διαφθεῖραι βουλόμενοι. πρὸς δὲ τούτοις καὶ τοὺς υἱεῖς τοὺς σαυτοῦ ἔμοιγε δοκεῖς προδιδόναι, οὕς σοι ἐξὸν καὶ ἐκθρέψαι καὶ ἐκπαιδεῦσαι D
οἰχήσει καταλιπών, καὶ τὸ σὸν μέρος, ὅ τι ἂν τύχωσι,
τοῦτο πράξουσιν· τεύξονται δέ, ὡς τὸ εἰκός, τοιού-
10 των οἷάπερ εἴωθεν γίγνεσθαι ἐν ταῖς ὀρφανίαις περὶ
τοὺς ὀρφανούς. ἢ γὰρ οὐ χρὴ ποιεῖσθαι παῖδας ἢ
ξυνδιαταλαιπωρεῖν καὶ τρέφοντα καὶ παιδεύοντα·
σὺ δέ μοι δοκεῖς τὰ ῥᾳθυμότατα αἱρεῖσθαι· χρὴ

δέ, ἅπερ ἂν ἀνὴρ ἀγαθὸς καὶ ἀνδρεῖος ἕλοιτο, ταῦτα 45
15 αἱρεῖσθαι, φάσκοντά γε δὴ ἀρετῆς διὰ παντὸς τοῦ
βίου ἐπιμελεῖσθαι· ὡς ἔγωγε καὶ ὑπὲρ σοῦ καὶ
ὑπὲρ ἡμῶν τῶν σῶν ἐπιτηδείων αἰσχύνομαι, μὴ Ε
δόξῃ ἅπαν τὸ πρᾶγμα τὸ περὶ σὲ ἀνανδρίᾳ τινὶ τῇ
ἡμετέρᾳ πεπρᾶχθαι, καὶ ἡ εἴσοδος τῆς δίκης εἰς τὸ
20 δικαστήριον ὡς εἰσῆλθεν ἐξὸν μὴ εἰσελθεῖν, καὶ
αὐτὸς ὁ ἀγὼν τῆς δίκης ὡς ἐγένετο, καὶ τὸ τελευταῖον δὴ τουτὶ ὥσπερ κατάγελως τῆς πράξεως,
κακίᾳ τινὶ καὶ ἀνανδρίᾳ τῇ ἡμετέρᾳ διαπεφευγέ- 46
ναι ἡμᾶς δοκεῖν, οἵτινές σε οὐχὶ ἐσώσαμεν οὐδὲ
25 σὺ σαυτόν, οἷόν τε ὂν καὶ δυνατόν, εἴ τι καὶ μικρὸν
ἡμῶν ὄφελος ἦν. ταῦτα οὖν, ὦ Σώκρατες, ὅρα μὴ
ἅμα τῷ κακῷ καὶ αἰσχρὰ ᾖ σοί τε καὶ ἡμῖν. ἀλλὰ
βουλεύου, μᾶλλον δὲ οὐδὲ βουλεύεσθαι ἔτι ὥρα,
ἀλλὰ βεβουλεῦσθαι. μία δὲ βουλή· τῆς γὰρ
30 ἐπιούσης νυκτὸς πάντα ταῦτα δεῖ πεπρᾶχθαι. εἰ
δέ τι περιμενοῦμεν, ἀδύνατον καὶ οὐκέτι οἷόν τε.
ἀλλὰ παντὶ τρόπῳ ὦ Σώκρατες, πείθου μοι καὶ
μηδαμῶς ἄλλως ποίει.

VI. ΣΩ. Ὦ φίλε Κρίτων, ἡ προθυμία σου Β
πολλοῦ ἀξία, εἰ μετά τινος ὀρθότητος εἴη· εἰ δὲ
μή, ὅσῳ μείζων, τοσούτῳ χαλεπωτέρα. σκοπεῖ-
σθαι οὖν χρὴ ἡμᾶς εἴ τε ταῦτα πρακτέον εἴ τε μή·
5 ὡς ἐγὼ οὐ μόνον νῦν ἀλλὰ καὶ ἀεὶ τοιοῦτος οἷος
τῶν ἐμῶν μηδενὶ ἄλλῳ πείθεσθαι ἢ τῷ λόγῳ ὃς ἂν
μοι λογιζομένῳ βέλτιστος φαίνηται. τοὺς δὲ λόγους οὓς ἐν τῷ ἔμπροσθεν ἔλεγον οὐ δύναμαι νῦν

ἐκβαλεῖν, ἐπειδή μοι ἥδε ἡ τύχη γέγονεν, ἀλλὰ 46
10 σχεδόν τι ὅμοιοι φαίνονταί μοι, καὶ τοὺς αὐτοὺς
πρεσβεύω καὶ τιμῶ οὕσπερ καὶ πρότερον· ὧν C
ἐὰν μὴ βελτίω ἔχωμεν λέγειν ἐν τῷ παρόντι, εὖ
ἴσθι ὅτι οὐ μή σοι ξυγχωρήσω, οὐδ᾽ ἂν πλείω τῶν
νῦν παρόντων ἡ τῶν πολλῶν δύναμις ὥσπερ παῖδας
15 ἡμᾶς μορμολύττηται, δεσμοὺς καὶ θανάτους ἐπι-
πέμπουσα καὶ χρημάτων ἀφαιρέσεις. πῶς οὖν ἂν
μετριώτατα σκοποίμεθα αὐτά; εἰ πρῶτον μὲν τοῦτον τὸν λόγον ἀναλάβοιμεν ὃν σὺ λέγεις περὶ τῶν
δοξῶν, πότερον καλῶς ἐλέγετο ἑκάστοτε ἢ οὔ, ὅτι
20 ταῖς μὲν δεῖ τῶν δοξῶν προσέχειν τὸν νοῦν, ταῖς D
δὲ οὔ· ἢ πρὶν μὲν ἐμὲ δεῖν ἀποθνήσκειν καλῶς
ἐλέγετο, νῦν δὲ κατάδηλος ἄρα ἐγένετο ὅτι ἄλλως
ἕνεκα λόγου ἐλέγετο, ἦν δὲ παιδιὰ καὶ φλυαρία ὡς
ἀληθῶς; ἐπιθυμῶ δ᾽ ἔγωγ᾽ ἐπισκέψασθαι, ὦ Κρί-
25 των, κοινῇ μετὰ σοῦ, εἴ τί μοι ἀλλοιότερος φανεῖται,
ἐπειδὴ ὧδε ἔχω, ἢ ὁ αὐτός, καὶ ἐάσομεν χαίρειν ἢ
πεισόμεθα αὐτῷ. ἐλέγετο δέ πως, ὡς ἐγῷμαι, ἑκάστοτε ὧδε ὑπὸ τῶν οἰομένων τὶ λέγειν, ὥσπερ νῦν
δὴ ἐγὼ ἔλεγον, ὅτι τῶν δοξῶν ἃς οἱ ἄνθρωποι
30 δοξάζουσιν, δέοι τὰς μὲν περὶ πολλοῦ ποιεῖσθαι, E
τὰς δὲ μή. τοῦτο πρὸς θεῶν, ὦ Κρίτων, οὐ δοκεῖ
καλῶς σοι λέγεσθαι; σὺ γάρ, ὅσα γε τἀνθρώπεια,
ἐκτὸς εἶ τοῦ μέλλειν ἀποθνήσκειν αὔριον, καὶ οὐκ 47
ἄν σε παρακρούοι ἡ παροῦσα ξυμφορά· σκόπει
35 δή· οὐχ ἱκανῶς δοκεῖ σοι λέγεσθαι, ὅτι οὐ πάσας
χρὴ τὰς δόξας τῶν ἀνθρώπων τιμᾶν, ἀλλὰ τὰς μέν,

τὰς δ᾽ οὔ;   οὐδὲ πάντων, ἀλλὰ τῶν μέν, τῶν δ᾽ οὔ; 47
τί φῇς;   ταῦτα οὐχὶ καλῶς λέγεται;

ΚΡ. Καλῶς.

40   ΣΩ. Οὐκοῦν τὰς μὲν χρηστὰς τιμᾶν, τὰς δὲ πο-
νηρὰς μή;

ΚΡ. Ναί.

ΣΩ. Χρησταὶ δὲ οὐχ αἱ τῶν φρονίμων, πονηραὶ
δὲ αἱ τῶν ἀφρόνων;

45   ΚΡ. Πῶς δ᾽ οὔ;

VII.   ΣΩ. Φέρε δή, πῶς αὖ τὰ τοιαῦτα ἐλέγετο;
γυμναζόμενος ἀνὴρ καὶ τοῦτο πράττων |πότερον| B
παντὸς ἀνδρὸς ἐπαίνῳ καὶ ψόγῳ καὶ δόξῃ τὸν νοῦν
προσέχει, ἢ ἑνὸς μόνου ἐκείνου, ὃς ἂν τυγχάνῃ
5 ἰατρὸς ἢ παιδοτρίβης ὤν;

ΚΡ. Ἑνὸς μόνου.

ΣΩ. Οὐκοῦν φοβεῖσθαι χρὴ τοὺς ψόγους καὶ
ἀσπάζεσθαι τοὺς ἐπαίνους τοὺς τοῦ ἑνὸς ἐκείνου,
ἀλλὰ μὴ τοὺς τῶν πολλῶν.

10   ΚΡ. Δῆλα δή.

ΣΩ. Ταύτῃ ἄρα αὐτῷ πρακτέον καὶ γυμναστέον
καὶ ἐδεστέον γε καὶ ποτέον, ᾗ ἂν τῷ ἑνὶ δοκῇ τῷ
ἐπιστάτῃ καὶ ἐπαΐοντι, μᾶλλον ἢ ᾗ ξύμπασι τοῖς
ἄλλοις.

15   ΚΡ. Ἔστι ταῦτα.

ΣΩ. Εἶεν. ἀπειθήσας δὲ τῷ ἑνὶ καὶ ἀτιμάσας C
αὐτοῦ τὴν δόξαν καὶ τοὺς ἐπαίνους, τιμήσας δὲ
τοὺς τῶν πολλῶν λόγους καὶ μηδὲν ἐπαϊόντων, ἆρα
οὐδὲν κακὸν πείσεται;

20 ΚΡ. Πῶς γὰρ οὔ;   47

ΣΩ. Τί δ᾽ ἔστι τὸ κακὸν τοῦτο; καὶ ποῖ τείνει,
καὶ εἰς τί τῶν τοῦ ἀπειθοῦντος;

ΚΡ. Δῆλον ὅτι εἰς τὸ σῶμα· τοῦτο γὰρ διόλλυσι.

25 ΣΩ. Καλῶς λέγεις. οὐκοῦν καὶ τἆλλα, ὦ Κρίτων, οὕτως, ἵνα μὴ πάντα διίωμεν, καὶ δὴ καὶ περὶ
τῶν δικαίων καὶ ἀδίκων καὶ αἰσχρῶν καὶ καλῶν
καὶ ἀγαθῶν καὶ κακῶν περὶ ὧν νῦν ἡ βουλὴ ἡμῖν
ἐστιν, πότερον τῇ τῶν πολλῶν δόξῃ δεῖ ἡμᾶς D
30 ἔπεσθαι καὶ φοβεῖσθαι αὐτὴν ἢ τῇ τοῦ ἑνός, εἴ τίς
ἐστιν ἐπαΐων, ὃν δεῖ καὶ αἰσχύνεσθαι καὶ φοβεῖσθαι μᾶλλον ἢ ξύμπαντας τοὺς ἄλλους; ᾧ εἰ μὴ
ἀκολουθήσομεν, διαφθεροῦμεν ἐκεῖνο καὶ λωβησό-
μεθα ὃ τῷ μὲν δικαίῳ βέλτιον ἐγίγνετο, τῷ δὲ
35 ἀδίκῳ ἀπώλλυτο. ἢ οὐδέν ἐστι τοῦτο;

ΚΡ. Οἶμαι ἔγωγε, ὦ Σώκρατες.

VIII. ΣΩ. Φέρε δή, ἐὰν τὸ ὑπὸ τοῦ ὑγιεινοῦ
μὲν βέλτιον γιγνόμενον, ὑπὸ τοῦ νοσώδους δὲ δια-
φθειρόμενον διολέσωμεν, πειθόμενοι μὴ τῇ τῶν
ἐπαϊόντων δόξῃ, ἆρα βιωτὸν ἡμῖν ἐστιν διεφθαρ- E
5 μένου αὐτοῦ; ἔστι δέ που τοῦτο σῶμα· ἢ οὐχί;

ΚΡ. Ναί.

ΣΩ. Ἆρ᾽ οὖν βιωτὸν ἡμῖν ἐστιν μετὰ μοχθηροῦ
καὶ διεφθαρμένου σώματος;

ΚΡ. Οὐδαμῶς.

10 ΣΩ. Ἀλλὰ μετ᾽ ἐκείνου ἆρ᾽ ἡμῖν βιωτὸν διεφθαρμένου ᾧ τὸ ἄδικον μὲν λωβᾶται, τὸ δὲ δίκαιον ὀνί-

νησιν; ἢ φαυλότερον ἡγούμεθα εἶναι τοῦ σώματος 47
ἐκεῖνο, ὅ τι ποτ᾽ ἐστὶ τῶν ἡμετέρων, περὶ ὃ ἥ τε 48
ἀδικία καὶ ἡ δικαιοσύνη ἐστίν;

15   ΚΡ. Οὐδαμῶς.

      ΣΩ. Ἀλλὰ τιμιώτερον;

      ΚΡ. Πολύ γε.

      ΣΩ. Οὐκ ἄρα, ὦ βέλτιστε, πάνυ ἡμῖν οὕτω φρον-
τιστέον τί ἐροῦσιν οἱ πολλοὶ ἡμᾶς, ἀλλ᾽ ὅ τι ὁ
20 ἐπαΐων περὶ τῶν δικαίων καὶ ἀδίκων, ὁ εἷς καὶ αὐτὴ
ἡ ἀλήθεια. ὥστε πρῶτον μὲν ταύτῃ οὐκ ὀρθῶς
εἰσηγεῖ, εἰσηγούμενος τῆς τῶν πολλῶν δόξης δεῖν
ἡμᾶς φροντίζειν περὶ τῶν δικαίων καὶ καλῶν καὶ
ἀγαθῶν καὶ τῶν ἐναντίων. "ἀλλὰ μὲν δή," φαίη γ᾽ ἄν
25 τις, "οἷοί τέ εἰσιν ἡμᾶς οἱ πολλοὶ ἀποκτεινύναι."   Β

      ΚΡ. Δῆλα δὴ καὶ ταῦτα· φαίη γὰρ ἄν, ὦ Σώκρατες.

      ΣΩ. Ἀληθῆ λέγεις. ἀλλ᾽, ὦ θαυμάσιε, οὗτός τε
ὁ λόγος ὃν διεληλύθαμεν, ἔμοιγε δοκεῖ ὅμοιος εἶναι
[τῷ] καὶ πρότερον· καὶ τόνδε αὖ σκόπει, εἰ ἔτι
30 μένει ἡμῖν ἢ οὔ, ὅτι οὐ τὸ ζῆν περὶ πλείστου ποιητέον, ἀλλὰ τὸ εὖ ζῆν.

      ΚΡ. Ἀλλὰ μένει.

      ΣΩ. Τὸ δὲ εὖ καὶ καλῶς καὶ δικαίως ὅτι ταὐτόν
ἐστιν, μένει ἢ οὐ μένει;

35   ΚΡ. Μένει.

      IX. ΣΩ. Οὐκοῦν ἐκ τῶν ὁμολογουμένων τοῦτο
σκεπτέον, πότερον δίκαιον ἐμὲ ἐνθένδε πειρᾶσθαι
ἐξιέναι μὴ ἀφιέντων Ἀθηναίων ἢ οὐ δίκαιον· καὶ Ϲ
ἐὰν μὲν φαίνηται δίκαιον, πειρώμεθα, εἰ δὲ μή,

5 ἐῶμεν. ἃς δὲ σὺ λέγεις τὰς σκέψεις περί τε ἀνα- 48
λώσεως χρημάτων καὶ δόξης καὶ παίδων τροφῆς,
μὴ ὡς ἀληθῶς ταῦτα, ὦ Κρίτων, σκέμματα ᾖ τῶν
ῥᾳδίως ἀποκτεινύντων καὶ ἀναβιωσκομένων γ᾽ ἄν,
εἰ οἷοί τ᾽ ἦσαν, οὐδενὶ ξὺν νῷ, τούτων τῶν πολλῶν.
10 ἡμῖν δ᾽, ἐπειδὴ ὁ λόγος οὕτως αἱρεῖ, μὴ οὐδὲν ἄλλο
σκεπτέον ᾖ ἢ ὅπερ νῦν δὴ ἐλέγομεν, πότερον δίκαια
πράξομεν καὶ χρήματα τελοῦντες τούτοις τοῖς ἐμὲ
ἐνθένδε ἐξάξουσι καὶ χάριτας, καὶ αὐτοὶ ἐξάγοντές D
τε καὶ ἐξαγόμενοι, ἢ τῇ ἀληθείᾳ ἀδικήσομεν πάντα
15 ταῦτα ποιοῦντες· κἂν φαινώμεθα ἄδικα αὐτὰ ἐργα-
ζόμενοι, μὴ οὐ δέῃ ὑπολογίζεσθαι οὔτ᾽ εἰ ἀποθνήσκειν δεῖ παραμένοντας καὶ ἡσυχίαν ἄγοντας, οὔτε
ἄλλο ὁτιοῦν πάσχειν πρὸ τοῦ ἀδικεῖν.

ΚΡ. Καλῶς μέν μοι δοκεῖς λέγειν, ὦ Σώκρατες.
20 ὅρα δὲ τί δρῶμεν.

ΣΩ. Σκοπῶμεν, ὦ ἀγαθέ, κοινῇ, καὶ εἴ πῃ ἔχεις
ἀντιλέγειν ἐμοῦ λέγοντος, ἀντίλεγε, καί σοι πείσο-
μαι· εἰ δὲ μή, παῦσαι ἤδη, ὦ μακάριε, πολλάκις E
μοι λέγων τὸν αὐτὸν λόγον, ὡς χρὴ ἐνθένδε ἀκόν-
25 των Ἀθηναίων ἐμὲ ἀπιέναι· ὡς ἐγὼ περὶ πολλοῦ
ποιοῦμαι πείσας σε ταῦτα πράττειν, ἀλλὰ μὴ ἄκοντος. ὅρα δὲ δὴ τῆς σκέψεως τὴν ἀρχήν, ἐάν σοι
ἱκανῶς λέγηται, καὶ πειρῶ ἀποκρίνεσθαι τὸ ἐρω- 49
τώμενον, ᾗ ἂν μάλιστα οἴῃ.

30 ΚΡ. Ἀλλὰ πειράσομαι.

Χ. ΣΩ. Οὐδενὶ τρόπῳ φαμὲν ἑκόντας ἀδικητέον
εἶναι, ἢ τινὶ μὲν ἀδικητέον τρόπῳ, τινὶ δὲ οὔ; ἢ

οὐδαμῶς τό γε ἀδικεῖν οὔτε ἀγαθὸν οὔτε καλόν, ὡς 49
πολλάκις ἡμῖν καὶ ἐν τῷ ἔμπροσθεν χρόνῳ ὡμολο-
5 γήθη; [ὅπερ καὶ ἄρτι ἐλέγετο·] ἢ πᾶσαι ἡμῖν
ἐκεῖναι αἱ πρόσθεν ὁμολογίαι ἐν ταῖσδε ταῖς ὀλί-
γαις ἡμέραις ἐκκεχυμέναι εἰσίν, καὶ πάλαι, ὦ Κρίτων, ἄρα τηλικοίδε γέροντες ἄνδρες πρὸς ἀλλήλους
σπουδῇ διαλεγόμενοι ἐλάθομεν ἡμᾶς αὐτοὺς παί- B
10 δων οὐδὲν διαφέροντες; ἢ παντὸς μᾶλλον οὕτως
ἔχει ὥσπερ τότε ἐλέγετο ἡμῖν, εἴ τε φασὶν οἱ πολλοὶ
εἴ τε μή, καὶ εἴ τε δεῖ ἡμᾶς ἔτι τῶνδε χαλεπώτερα
πάσχειν εἴ τε καὶ πρᾳότερα, ὅμως τό γε ἀδικεῖν τῷ
ἀδικοῦντι καὶ κακὸν καὶ αἰσχρὸν τυγχάνει ὃν παντὶ
15 τρόπῳ; φαμὲν ἢ οὔ;

ΚΡ. Φαμέν.

ΣΩ. Οὐδαμῶς ἄρα δεῖ ἀδικεῖν.

ΚΡ. Οὐ δῆτα.

ΣΩ. Οὐδὲ ἀδικούμενον ἄρα ἀνταδικεῖν, ὡς οἱ
20 πολλοὶ οἴονται, ἐπειδή γε οὐδαμῶς δεῖ ἀδικεῖν. C

ΚΡ. Οὐ φαίνεται.

ΣΩ. Τί δὲ δή; κακουργεῖν δεῖ, ὦ Κρίτων, ἢ οὔ;

ΚΡ. Οὐ δεῖ δήπου, ὦ Σώκρατες.

ΣΩ. Τί δέ; ἀντικακουργεῖν κακῶς πάσχοντα, ὡς
25 οἱ πολλοί φασιν, δίκαιον ἢ οὐ δίκαιον;

ΚΡ. Οὐδαμῶς.

ΣΩ. Τὸ γάρ που κακῶς ποιεῖν ἀνθρώπους τοῦ
ἀδικεῖν οὐδὲν διαφέρει.

ΚΡ. ᾿Αληθῆ λέγεις.

30 ΣΩ. Οὔτε ἄρα ἀνταδικεῖν δεῖ οὔτε κακῶς ποιεῖν

οὐδένα ἀνθρώπων, οὐδ᾿ ἂν ὁτιοῦν πάσχῃ ὑπ᾿ αὐτῶν. 49
καὶ ὅρα, ὦ Κρίτων, ταῦτα καθομολογῶν, ὅπως μὴ
παρὰ δόξαν ὁμολογῇς. οἶδα γὰρ ὅτι ὀλίγοις D
τισὶ ταῦτα καὶ δοκεῖ καὶ δόξει. οἷς οὖν οὕτω δέ-
35 δοκται καὶ οἷς μή, τούτοις οὐκ ἔστι κοινὴ βουλή,
ἀλλὰ ἀνάγκη τούτους ἀλλήλων καταφρονεῖν, ὁρῶν-
τας τὰ ἀλλήλων βουλεύματα. σκόπει δὴ οὖν καὶ
σὺ εὖ μάλα, πότερον κοινωνεῖς καὶ ξυνδοκεῖ σοι
καὶ ἀρχώμεθα ἐντεῦθεν βουλευόμενοι, ὡς οὐδέποτε
40 ὀρθῶς ἔχοντος οὔτε τοῦ ἀδικεῖν οὔτε τοῦ ἀνταδικεῖν
οὔτε κακῶς πάσχοντα ἀμύνεσθαι ἀντιδρῶντα κα-
κῶς· ἢ ἀφίστασαι καὶ οὐ κοινωνεῖς τῆς ἀρχῆς;
ἐμοὶ μὲν γὰρ καὶ πάλαι οὕτω καὶ νῦν ἔτι δοκεῖ, E
σοὶ δὲ εἴ πῃ ἄλλῃ δέδοκται, λέγε καὶ δίδασκε. εἰ
45 δ᾿ ἐμμένεις τοῖς πρόσθε, τὸ μετὰ τοῦτο ἄκουε.

ΚΡ. Ἀλλ᾿ ἐμμένω τε καὶ ξυνδοκεῖ μοι· ἀλλὰ
λέγε.

ΣΩ. Λέγω δὴ αὖ τὸ μετὰ τοῦτο, μᾶλλον δ᾿
ἐρωτῶ· πότερον ἃ ἄν τις ὁμολογήσῃ τῳ δίκαια
50 ὄντα ποιητέον ἢ ἐξαπατητέον;

ΚΡ. Ποιητέον.

ΧΙ. ΣΩ. Ἐκ τούτων δὴ ἄθρει. ἀπιόντες ἐνθένδε ἡμεῖς μὴ πείσαντες τὴν πόλιν πότερον 50
κακῶς τινας ποιοῦμεν, καὶ ταῦτα οὓς ἥκιστα δεῖ,
ἢ οὔ; καὶ ἐμμένομεν οἷς ὡμολογήσαμεν δικαίοις
5 οὖσιν ἢ οὔ;

ΚΡ. Οὐκ ἔχω, ὦ Σώκρατες, ἀποκρίνασθαι πρὸς
ὃ ἐρωτᾷς· οὐ γὰρ ἐννοῶ.

ΣΩ. Ἀλλ' ὧδε σκόπει. εἰ μέλλουσιν ἡμῖν ἐν- 50
θένδε εἴ τε ἀποδιδράσκειν, εἴ θ' ὅπως δεῖ ὀνομάσαι
10 τοῦτο, ἐλθόντες οἱ νόμοι καὶ τὸ κοινὸν τῆς πόλεως
ἐπιστάντες ἔροιντο· "εἰπέ μοι, ὦ Σώκρατες, τί ἐν
νῷ ἔχεις ποιεῖν; ἄλλο τι ἢ τούτῳ τῷ ἔργῳ ᾧ
ἐπιχειρεῖς διανοεῖ τούς τε νόμους ἡμᾶς ἀπολέσαι B
καὶ ξύμπασαν τὴν πόλιν τὸ σὸν μέρος; ἢ δοκεῖ
15 σοι οἷόν τε ἔτι ἐκείνην τὴν πόλιν εἶναι καὶ μὴ
ἀνατετράφθαι, ἐν ᾗ αἱ γενόμεναι δίκαι μηδὲν ἰσχύ-
ουσιν, ἀλλὰ ὑπὸ ἰδιωτῶν ἄκυροί τε γίγνονται καὶ
διαφθείρονται;" τί ἐροῦμεν, ὦ Κρίτων, πρὸς ταῦτα
καὶ ἄλλα τοιαῦτα; πολλὰ γὰρ ἄν τις ἔχοι, ἄλλως
20 τε καὶ ῥήτωρ, εἰπεῖν ὑπὲρ τούτου τοῦ νόμου ἀπολλυμένου, ὃς τὰς δίκας τὰς δικασθείσας προστάττει
κυρίας εἶναι. ἢ ἐροῦμεν πρὸς αὐτοὺς ὅτι "ἠδίκει γὰρ
ἡμᾶς ἡ πόλις καὶ οὐκ ὀρθῶς τὴν δίκην ἔκρινεν"; C
ταῦτα ἢ τί ἐροῦμεν;

25 ΚΡ. Ταῦτα νὴ Δία, ὦ Σώκρατες.

XII. ΣΩ. Τί οὖν ἂν εἴπωσιν οἱ νόμοι· "ὦ
Σώκρατες, ἦ καὶ ταῦτα ὡμολόγητο ἡμῖν τε καὶ
σοί, ἢ ἐμμένειν ταῖς δίκαις αἷς ἂν ἡ πόλις δικάζῃ;"
εἰ οὖν αὐτῶν θαυμάζοιμεν λεγόντων, ἴσως ἂν εἴποιεν
5 ὅτι "ὦ Σώκρατες, μὴ θαύμαζε· τὰ λεγόμενα, ἀλλ'
ἀποκρίνου, ἐπειδὴ καὶ εἴωθας χρῆσθαι τῷ ἐρωτᾶν
τε καὶ ἀποκρίνεσθαι. φέρε γάρ, τί ἐγκαλῶν ἡμῖν D
καὶ τῇ πόλει ἐπιχειρεῖς ἡμᾶς ἀπολλύναι; οὐ πρῶτον μέν σε ἐγεννήσαμεν ἡμεῖς καὶ δι' ἡμῶν ἐλάμ-
10 βανεν τὴν μητέρα σου ὁ πατὴρ καὶ ἐφύτευσέν σε;

φράσον οὖν, τούτοις ἡμῶν, τοῖς νόμοις τοῖς περὶ 50
τοὺς γάμους, μέμφει τι, ὡς οὐ καλῶς ἔχουσιν;"
"οὐ μέμφομαι," φαίην ἄν. " ἀλλὰ τοῖς περὶ τὴν
τοῦ γενομένου τροφήν τε καὶ παιδείαν ἐν ᾗ καὶ
15 σὺ ἐπαιδεύθης; ἢ οὐ καλῶς προσέταττον ἡμῶν
οἱ ἐπὶ τούτοις τεταγμένοι νόμοι, παραγγέλλοντες
τῷ πατρὶ τῷ σῷ σε ἐν μουσικῇ καὶ γυμναστικῇ
παιδεύειν;" "καλῶς," φαίην ἄν. " εἶεν. ἐπειδὴ Ε
δὲ ἐγένου τε καὶ ἐξετράφης καὶ ἐπαιδεύθης, ἔχοις
20 ἂν εἰπεῖν πρῶτον μὲν ὡς οὐχὶ ἡμέτερος ἦσθα καὶ
ἔκγονος καὶ δοῦλος, αὐτός τε καὶ οἱ σοὶ πρόγονοι;
καὶ εἰ τοῦθ' οὕτως ἔχει, ἆρ' ἐξ ἴσου οἴει εἶναι σοὶ
τὸ δίκαιον καὶ ἡμῖν, καὶ ἅττ' ἂν ἡμεῖς σε ἐπιχειρῶμεν ποιεῖν, καὶ σοὶ ταῦτα ἀντιποιεῖν οἴει δίκαιον
25 εἶναι; ἢ πρὸς μὲν ἄρα σοι τὸν πατέρα οὐκ ἐξ
ἴσου ἦν τὸ δίκαιον καὶ πρὸς τὸν δεσπότην, εἴ σοι
ὦν ἐτύγχανεν, ὥστε, ἅπερ πάσχοις, ταῦτα καὶ ἀντιποιεῖν, οὔτε κακῶς ἀκούοντα ἀντιλέγειν οὔτε τυπτό- 51
μενον ἀντιτύπτειν οὔτε ἄλλα τοιαῦτα πολλά · πρὸς
30 δὲ τὴν πατρίδα ἄρα καὶ τοὺς νόμους ἐξέσται σοι,
ὥστε, ἐάν σε ἐπιχειρῶμεν ἡμεῖς ἀπολλύναι δίκαιον
ἡγούμενοι εἶναι, καὶ σὺ δὲ ἡμᾶς τοὺς νόμους καὶ
τὴν πατρίδα, καθ' ὅσον δύνασαι, ἐπιχειρήσεις
ἀνταπολλύναι, καὶ φήσεις ταῦτα ποιῶν δίκαια
35 πράττειν, ὁ τῇ ἀληθείᾳ τῆς ἀρετῆς ἐπιμελόμενος;
ἢ οὕτως εἶ σοφὸς ὥστε λέληθέν σε ὅτι μητρός
τε καὶ πατρὸς καὶ τῶν ἄλλων προγόνων ἁπάντων
τιμιώτερόν ἐστιν ἡ πατρὶς καὶ σεμνότερον καὶ

ἁγιώτερον καὶ ἐν μείζονι μοίρᾳ καὶ παρὰ θεοῖς 51
40 καὶ παρ' ἀνθρώποις τοῖς νοῦν ἔχουσι, καὶ σέβε- B
σθαι δεῖ καὶ μᾶλλον ὑπείκειν καὶ θωπεύειν πατρίδα
χαλεπαίνουσαν ἢ πατέρα, καὶ ἢ πείθειν ἢ ποιεῖν ἃ
ἂν κελεύῃ, καὶ πάσχειν, ἐάν τι προστάττῃ παθεῖν,
ἡσυχίαν ἄγοντα, ἐάν τε τύπτεσθαι ἐάν τε δεῖσθαι,
45 ἐάν τε εἰς πόλεμον ἄγῃ τρωθησόμενον ἢ ἀποθανού-
μενον, ποιητέον ταῦτα, καὶ τὸ δίκαιον οὕτως ἔχει,
καὶ οὐχὶ ὑπεικτέον οὐδὲ ἀναχωρητέον οὐδὲ λειπτέον
τὴν τάξιν, ἀλλὰ καὶ ἐν πολέμῳ καὶ ἐν δικαστηρίῳ
καὶ πανταχοῦ ποιητέον ἃ ἂν κελεύῃ ἡ πόλις καὶ C
50 ἡ πατρίς, ἢ πείθειν αὐτὴν ᾗ τὸ δίκαιον πέφυκε,
βιάζεσθαι δὲ οὐχ ὅσιον οὔτε μητέρα οὔτε πατέρα,
πολὺ δὲ τούτων ἔτι ἧττον τὴν πατρίδα;" τί φήσο-
μεν πρὸς ταῦτα, ὦ Κρίτων; ἀληθῆ λέγειν τοὺς
νόμους ἢ οὔ;

55			ΚΡ. Ἔμοιγε δοκεῖ.

			XIII. ΣΩ. "Σκόπει τοίνυν, ὦ Σώκρατες," φαῖεν
ἂν ἴσως οἱ νόμοι, "εἰ ἡμεῖς ταῦτα ἀληθῆ λέγομεν,
ὅτι οὐ δίκαια ἡμᾶς ἐπιχειρεῖς δρᾶν ἃ νῦν ἐπιχειρεῖς. ἡμεῖς γάρ σε γεννήσαντες, ἐκθρέψαντες,
5 παιδεύσαντες, μεταδόντες ἁπάντων ὧν οἷοί τ' ἦμεν
καλῶν σοὶ καὶ τοῖς ἄλλοις πᾶσιν πολίταις, ὅμως D
προαγορεύομεν τῷ ἐξουσίαν πεποιηκέναι Ἀθηναίων
τῷ βουλομένῳ, ἐπειδὰν δοκιμασθῇ καὶ ἴδῃ τὰ ἐν
τῇ πόλει πράγματα καὶ ἡμᾶς τοὺς νόμους, ᾧ ἂν
10 μὴ ἀρέσκωμεν ἡμεῖς, ἐξεῖναι λαβόντα τὰ αὑτοῦ
ἀπιέναι ὅποι ἂν βούληται. καὶ οὐδεὶς ἡμῶν τῶν

νόμων ἐμποδών ἐστιν οὐδ᾽ ἀπαγορεύει, ἐάν τέ τις 51
βούληται ὑμῶν εἰς ἀποικίαν ἰέναι, εἰ μὴ ἀρέσκοιμεν ἡμεῖς τε καὶ ἡ πόλις, ἐάν τε μετοικεῖν ἄλλοσέ
15 ποι ἐλθών, ἰέναι ἐκεῖσε ὅποι ἂν βούληται, ἔχοντα
τὰ αὑτοῦ. ὃς δ᾽ ἂν ὑμῶν παραμείνῃ, ὁρῶν ὃν E
τρόπον ἡμεῖς τάς τε δίκας δικάζομεν καὶ τἆλλα
τὴν πόλιν διοικοῦμεν, ἤδη φαμὲν τοῦτον ὡμολογη-
κέναι ἔργῳ ἡμῖν ἃ ἂν ἡμεῖς κελεύωμεν ποιήσειν
20 ταῦτα, καὶ τὸν μὴ πειθόμενον τριχῇ φαμεν ἀδικεῖν,
ὅτι τε γεννηταῖς οὖσιν ἡμῖν οὐ πείθεται, καὶ ὅτι
τροφεῦσι, καὶ ὅτι ὁμολογήσας ἡμῖν πείθεσθαι οὔτε
πείθεται οὔτε πείθει ἡμᾶς, εἰ μὴ καλῶς τι ποιοῦμεν,
προτιθέντων ἡμῶν καὶ οὐκ ἀγρίως ἐπιταττόντων 52
25 ποιεῖν ἃ ἂν κελεύωμεν, ἀλλὰ ἐφιέντων δυοῖν θάτερα,
ἢ πείθειν ἡμᾶς ἢ ποιεῖν, τούτων οὐδέτερα ποιεῖ.

XIV. "Ταύταις δή φαμεν καὶ σέ, ὦ Σώκρατες,
ταῖς αἰτίαις ἐνέξεσθαι, εἴ περ ποιήσεις ἃ ἐπινοεῖς,
καὶ οὐχ ἥκιστα Ἀθηναίων σέ, ἀλλ᾽ ἐν τοῖς μάλιστα." εἰ οὖν ἐγὼ εἴποιμι· "διὰ τί δή;" ἴσως ἄν
5 μου δικαίως καθάπτοιντο λέγοντες ὅτι ἐν τοῖς
μάλιστα Ἀθηναίων ἐγὼ αὐτοῖς ὡμολογηκὼς τυγχάνω ταύτην τὴν ὁμολογίαν. φαῖεν γὰρ ἂν ὅτι
"ὦ Σώκρατες, μεγάλα ἡμῖν τούτων τεκμήριά ἐστιν, B
ὅτι σοι καὶ ἡμεῖς ἠρέσκομεν καὶ ἡ πόλις· οὐ γὰρ
10 ἄν ποτε τῶν ἄλλων Ἀθηναίων ἁπάντων διαφερόντως
ἐν αὐτῇ ἐπεδήμεις, εἰ μή σοι διαφερόντως ἤρεσκεν,
καὶ οὔτ᾽ ἐπὶ θεωρίαν πώποτ᾽ ἐκ τῆς πόλεως ἐξῆλθες
[, ὅ τι μὴ ἅπαξ εἰς Ἰσθμόν,] οὔτε ἄλλοσε οὐδαμόσε,

εἰ μή ποι στρατευσόμενος, οὔτε ἄλλην ἀποδημίαν 52
15 ἐποιήσω πώποτε, ὥσπερ οἱ ἄλλοι ἄνθρωποι, οὐδ᾽
ἐπιθυμία σε ἄλλης πόλεως οὐδὲ ἄλλων νόμων ἔλα-
βεν εἰδέναι, ἀλλὰ ἡμεῖς σοι ἱκανοὶ ἦμεν καὶ ἡ
ἡμετέρα πόλις· οὕτω σφόδρα ἡμᾶς ᾑροῦ, καὶ C
ὡμολόγεις καθ᾽ ἡμᾶς πολιτεύσεσθαι, τά τε ἄλλα
20 καὶ παῖδας ἐν αὐτῇ ἐποιήσω, ὡς ἀρεσκούσης σοι
τῆς πόλεως. ἔτι τοίνυν ἐν αὐτῇ τῇ δίκῃ ἐξῆν σοι
φυγῆς τιμήσασθαι, εἰ ἐβούλου, καὶ ὅπερ νῦν ἀκού-
σης τῆς πόλεως ἐπιχειρεῖς, τότε ἑκούσης ποιῆσαι.
σὺ δὲ τότε μὲν ἐκαλλωπίζου ὡς οὐκ ἀγανακτῶν, εἰ
25 δέοι τεθνάναι σε, ἀλλὰ ᾑροῦ, ὡς ἔφησθα, πρὸ τῆς
φυγῆς θάνατον· νῦν δὲ οὔτ᾽ ἐκείνους τοὺς λόγους
αἰσχύνει, οὔτε ἡμῶν τῶν νόμων ἐντρέπει, ἐπιχειρῶν
διαφθεῖραι, πράττεις τε ἅπερ ἂν δοῦλος φαυλό- D
τατος πράξειεν, ἀποδιδράσκειν ἐπιχειρῶν παρὰ τὰς
30 ξυνθήκας τε καὶ τὰς ὁμολογίας καθ᾽ ἃς ἡμῖν ξυν-
έθου πολιτεύεσθαι. πρῶτον μὲν οὖν ἡμῖν τοῦτ᾽ αὐτὸ
ἀπόκριναι, εἰ ἀληθῆ λέγομεν φάσκοντές σε ὡμολο-
γηκέναι πολιτεύεσθαι καθ᾽ ἡμᾶς ἔργῳ, ἀλλ᾽ οὐ
λόγῳ, ἢ οὐκ ἀληθῆ." τί φῶμεν πρὸς ταῦτα, ὦ
35 Κρίτων; ἄλλο τι ἢ ὁμολογῶμεν;

ΚΡ. Ἀνάγκη, ὦ Σώκρατες.

ΣΩ. "Ἄλλο τι οὖν," ἂν φαῖεν, "ἢ ξυνθήκας τὰς
πρὸς ἡμᾶς αὐτοὺς καὶ ὁμολογίας παραβαίνεις, οὐχ
ὑπὸ ἀνάγκης ὁμολογήσας οὐδὲ ἀπατηθεὶς οὐδὲ ἐν E
40 ὀλίγῳ χρόνῳ ἀναγκασθεὶς βουλεύσασθαι, ἀλλ᾽ ἐν
ἔτεσιν ἑβδομήκοντα, ἐν οἷς ἐξῆν σοι ἀπιέναι, εἰ μὴ

ἠρέσκομεν ἡμεῖς μηδὲ δίκαιαι ἐφαίνοντό σοι αἱ 52
ὁμολογίαι εἶναι. σὺ δὲ οὔτε Λακεδαίμονα προ-
ῃροῦ οὔτε Κρήτην, ἃς δὴ ἑκάστοτε φῂς εὐνομεῖσθαι,
45 οὔτε ἄλλην οὐδεμίαν τῶν Ἑλληνίδων πόλεων οὐδὲ
τῶν βαρβαρικῶν, ἀλλὰ ἐλάττω ἐξ αὐτῆς ἀπεδή- 53
μησας ἢ οἱ χωλοί τε καὶ τυφλοὶ καὶ οἱ ἄλλοι ἀνά-
πηροι· οὕτω σοι διαφερόντως τῶν ἄλλων Ἀθηναίων
ἤρεσκεν ἡ πόλις τε καὶ ἡμεῖς οἱ νόμοι δῆλον ὅτι·
50 τίνι γὰρ ἂν πόλις ἀρέσκοι ἄνευ νόμων; νῦν δὲ δὴ
οὐκ ἐμμένεις τοῖς ὡμολογημένοις; ἐὰν ἡμῖν γε
πείθῃ, ὦ Σώκρατες· καὶ οὐ καταγέλαστός γε ἔσει
ἐκ τῆς πόλεως ἐξελθών.

XV. "Σκόπει γὰρ δή, ταῦτα παραβὰς καὶ ἐξαμαρτάνων τι τούτων τί ἀγαθὸν ἐργάσει σαυτὸν ἢ
τοὺς ἐπιτηδείους τοὺς σαυτοῦ. ὅτι μὲν γὰρ κιν- B
δυνεύσουσί γέ σου οἱ ἐπιτήδειοι καὶ αὐτοὶ φεύγειν
5 καὶ στερηθῆναι τῆς πόλεως ἢ τὴν οὐσίαν ἀπολέσαι,
σχεδόν τι δῆλον· αὐτὸς δὲ πρῶτον μὲν ἐὰν εἰς τῶν
ἐγγύτατά τινα πόλεων ἔλθῃς, ἢ Θήβαζε ἢ Μέγα-
ράδε — εὐνομοῦνται γὰρ ἀμφότεραι, — πολέμιος
ἥξεις, ὦ Σώκρατες, τῇ τούτων πολιτείᾳ, καὶ ὅσοι-
10 περ κήδονται τῶν αὑτῶν πόλεων, ὑποβλέψονταί σε
διαφθορέα ἡγούμενοι τῶν νόμων, καὶ βεβαιώσεις
τοῖς δικασταῖς τὴν δόξαν, ὥστε δοκεῖν ὀρθῶς τὴν
δίκην δικάσαι· ὅστις γὰρ νόμων διαφθορεύς C
ἐστιν, σφόδρα που δόξειεν ἂν νέων γε καὶ ἀνοήτων
15 ἀνθρώπων διαφθορεὺς εἶναι. πότερον οὖν φεύξει
τάς τε εὐνομουμένας πόλεις καὶ τῶν ἀνδρῶν τοὺς

κοσμιωτάτους ; καὶ τοῦτο ποιοῦντι ἆρα ἄξιόν σοι 53
ζῆν ἔσται ; ἢ πλησιάσεις τούτοις καὶ ἀναισχυν-
τήσεις διαλεγόμενος — τίνας λόγους, ὦ Σώκρατες ;
20 ἢ οὕσπερ ἐνθάδε, ὡς ἡ ἀρετὴ καὶ ἡ δικαιοσύνη
πλείστου ἄξιον τοῖς ἀνθρώποις καὶ τὰ νόμιμα καὶ
οἱ νόμοι ; καὶ οὐκ οἴει ἄσχημον ἂν φανεῖσθαι τὸ
τοῦ Σωκράτους πρᾶγμα ; οἴεσθαί γε χρή. ἀλλ᾿ D
ἐκ μὲν τούτων τῶν τόπων ἀπαρεῖς, ἥξεις δὲ εἰς
25 Θετταλίαν παρὰ τοὺς ξένους τοὺς Κρίτωνος · ἐκεῖ
γὰρ δὴ πλείστη ἀταξία καὶ ἀκολασία, καὶ ἴσως ἂν
ἡδέως σου ἀκούοιεν ὡς γελοίως ἐκ τοῦ δεσμωτηρίου
ἀπεδίδρασκες σκευήν τέ τινα περιθέμενος, ἢ διφθέραν λαβὼν ἢ ἄλλα οἷα δὴ εἰώθασιν ἐνσκευάζεσθαι
30 οἱ ἀποδιδράσκοντες, καὶ τὸ σχῆμα τὸ σαυτοῦ μετ-
αλλάξας · ὅτι δὲ γέρων ἀνὴρ σμικροῦ χρόνου τῷ
βίῳ λοιποῦ ὄντος, ὡς τὸ εἰκός, ἐτόλμησας οὕτως E
αἰσχρῶς ἐπιθυμεῖν ζῆν, νόμους τοὺς μεγίστους
παραβάς, οὐδεὶς ὃς ἐρεῖ ; ἴσως, ἂν μή τινα
35 λυπῇς · εἰ δὲ μή, ἀκούσει, ὦ Σώκρατες, πολλὰ καὶ
ἀνάξια σαυτοῦ. ὑπερχόμενος δὴ βιώσει πάντας
ἀνθρώπους καὶ δουλεύων — τί ποιῶν ; ἢ εὐωχούμε-
νος ἐν Θετταλίᾳ, ὥσπερ ἐπὶ δεῖπνον ἀποδεδημηκὼς
εἰς Θετταλίαν ; λόγοι δὲ ἐκεῖνοι οἱ περὶ δικαιο-
40 σύνης τε καὶ τῆς ἄλλης ἀρετῆς ποῦ ἡμῖν ἔσονται ; 54
ἀλλὰ δὴ τῶν παίδων ἕνεκα βούλει ζῆν, ἵνα αὐτοὺς
ἐκθρέψῃς καὶ παιδεύσῃς ; τί δέ ; εἰς Θετταλίαν
αὐτοὺς ἀγαγὼν θρέψεις τε καὶ παιδεύσεις, ξένους
ποιήσας, ἵνα καὶ τοῦτο ἀπολαύσωσιν ; ἢ τοῦτο

45 μὲν οὔ, αὐτοῦ δὲ τρεφόμενοι σοῦ ζῶντος βέλτιον 54
θρέψονται καὶ παιδεύσονται, μὴ ξυνόντος σοῦ αὐτοῖς; οἱ γὰρ ἐπιτήδειοι οἱ σοὶ ἐπιμελήσονται
αὐτῶν. πότερον ἐὰν εἰς Θετταλίαν ἀποδημήσῃς,
ἐπιμελήσονται, ἐὰν δὲ εἰς Ἅιδου ἀποδημήσῃς,
50 οὐχὶ ἐπιμελήσονται; εἴ πέρ γέ τι ὄφελος αὐτῶν
ἐστιν τῶν σοι φασκόντων ἐπιτηδείων εἶναι, οἴεσθαί B
γε χρή.

XVI. "Ἀλλ', ὦ Σώκρατες, πειθόμενος ἡμῖν τοῖς
σοῖς τροφεῦσι μήτε παῖδας περὶ πλείονος ποιοῦ
μήτε τὸ ζῆν μήτε ἄλλο μηδὲν πρὸ τοῦ δικαίου, ἵνα
εἰς Ἅιδου ἐλθὼν ἔχῃς πάντα ταῦτα ἀπολογήσασθαι
5 τοῖς ἐκεῖ ἄρχουσιν· οὔτε γὰρ ἐνθάδε σοι φαίνεται
ταῦτα πράττοντι ἄμεινον εἶναι οὐδὲ δικαιότερον
οὐδὲ ὁσιώτερον, οὐδὲ ἄλλῳ τῶν σῶν οὐδενί, οὔτε
ἐκεῖσε ἀφικομένῳ ἄμεινον ἔσται. ἀλλὰ νῦν μὲν
ἠδικημένος ἄπει, ἐὰν ἀπίῃς, οὐχ ὑφ' ἡμῶν τῶν
10 νόμων ἀλλὰ ὑπ' ἀνθρώπων· ἐὰν δὲ ἐξέλθῃς οὕτως C
αἰσχρῶς ἀνταδικήσας τε καὶ ἀντικακουργήσας,
τὰς σαυτοῦ ὁμολογίας τε καὶ ξυνθήκας τὰς πρὸς
ἡμᾶς παραβὰς καὶ κακὰ ἐργασάμενος τούτους οὓς
ἥκιστα ἔδει, σαυτόν τε καὶ φίλους καὶ πατρίδα καὶ
15 ἡμᾶς, ἡμεῖς τέ σοι χαλεπανοῦμεν ζῶντι, καὶ ἐκεῖ οἱ
ἡμέτεροι ἀδελφοὶ οἱ ἐν Ἅιδου νόμοι οὐκ εὐμενῶς
σε ὑποδέξονται, εἰδότες ὅτι καὶ ἡμᾶς ἐπεχείρησας
ἀπολέσαι τὸ σὸν μέρος. ἀλλὰ μή σε πείσῃ Κρίτων ποιεῖν ἃ λέγει μᾶλλον ἢ ἡμεῖς."
D
XVII. Ταῦτα, ὦ φίλε ἑταῖρε Κρίτων, εὖ ἴσθι

ὅτι ἐγὼ δοκῶ ἀκούειν, ὥσπερ οἱ κορυβαντιῶντες 54
τῶν αὐλῶν δοκοῦσιν ἀκούειν, καὶ ἐν ἐμοὶ αὕτη ἡ
ἠχὴ τούτων τῶν λόγων βομβεῖ καὶ ποιεῖ μὴ δύνα-
5 σθαι τῶν ἄλλων ἀκούειν· ἀλλὰ ἴσθι, ὅσα γε τὰ
νῦν ἐμοὶ δοκοῦντα, ἐὰν λέγῃς παρὰ ταῦτα, μάτην
ἐρεῖς. ὅμως μέντοι εἴ τι οἴει πλέον ποιήσειν, λέγε.

ΚΡ. Ἀλλ᾽, ὦ Σώκρατες, οὐκ ἔχω λέγειν.

ΣΩ. Ἔα τοίνυν, ὦ Κρίτων, καὶ πράττωμεν ταύτῃ, Ε
10 ἐπειδὴ ταύτῃ ὁ θεὸς ὑφηγεῖται.

ΦΑΙΔΩΝ

[ἢ περὶ ψυχῆς, ἠθικός]

TA TOΥ ΔΙΑΛΟΓΟΥ ΠΡΟΣΩΠΑ
ΕΧΕΚΡΑΤΗΣ, ΦΑΙΔΩΝ, ΑΠΟΛΛΟΔΩΡΟΣ,
ΣΩΚΡΑΤΗΣ, ΚΕΒΗΣ, ΣΙΜΜΙΑΣ, ΚΡΙΤΩΝ,
Ο ΤΩΝ ΕΝΔΕΚΑ ΥΠΗΡΕΤΗΣ

St. I.
p. 57

I. ΕΧΕΚΡΑΤΗΣ. Αὐτός, ὦ Φαίδων, παρεγένου A
Σωκράτει ἐκείνῃ τῇ ἡμέρᾳ ᾗ τὸ φάρμακον ἔπιεν
ἐν τῷ δεσμωτηρίῳ, ἢ ἄλλου του ἤκουσας;
ΦΑΙΔΩΝ. Αὐτός, ὦ Ἐχέκρατες.

5   ΕΧ. Τί οὖν δή ἐστιν ἄττα εἶπεν ὁ ἀνὴρ πρὸ τοῦ
θανάτου; καὶ πῶς ἐτελεύτα; ἡδέως γὰρ ἂν ἐγὼ
ἀκούσαιμι. καὶ γὰρ οὔτε τῶν πολιτῶν Φλειασίων
οὐδεὶς πάνυ τι ἐπιχωριάζει τὰ νῦν Ἀθήναζε, οὔτε
τις ξένος ἀφῖκται χρόνου συχνοῦ ἐκεῖθεν, ὅστις ἂν
10 ἡμῖν σαφές τι ἀγγεῖλαι οἷός τ᾽ ἦν περὶ τούτων, B
πλήν γε δὴ ὅτι φάρμακον πιὼν ἀποθάνοι· τῶν δὲ
ἄλλων οὐδὲν εἶχεν φράζειν.

ΦΑΙΔ. Οὐδὲ τὰ περὶ τῆς δίκης ἄρα ἐπύθεσθε 58
ὃν τρόπον ἐγένετο;

15 ΕΧ. Ναί, ταῦτα μὲν ἡμῖν ἤγγειλέ τις, καὶ ἐθαυ-
μάζομέν γε ὅτι πάλαι γενομένης αὐτῆς πολλῷ
ὕστερον φαίνεται ἀποθανών. τί οὖν ἦν τοῦτο, ὦ
Φαίδων;

105

ΦΑΙΔ. Τύχη τις αὐτῷ, ὦ Ἐχέκρατες, συνέβη · 58
20 ἔτυχεν γὰρ τῇ προτεραίᾳ τῆς δίκης ἡ πρύμνα
ἐστεμμένη τοῦ πλοίου ὃ εἰς Δῆλον Ἀθηναῖοι
πέμπουσιν.

ΕΧ. Τοῦτο δὲ δὴ τί ἐστιν;

ΦΑΙΔ. Τοῦτ᾽ ἔστι τὸ πλοῖον, ὥς φασιν Ἀθηναῖοι,
25 ἐν ᾧ Θησεύς ποτε εἰς Κρήτην τοὺς δὶς ἑπτὰ ἐκείνους ᾤχετο ἄγων καὶ ἔσωσέ τε καὶ αὐτὸς ἐσώθη. Β
τῷ οὖν Ἀπόλλωνι εὔξαντο, ὡς λέγεται, τότε, εἰ
σωθεῖεν, ἑκάστου ἔτους θεωρίαν ἀπάξειν εἰς Δῆλον ·
ἣν δὴ ἀεὶ καὶ νῦν ἔτι ἐξ ἐκείνου κατ᾽ ἐνιαυτὸν τῷ
30 θεῷ πέμπουσιν. ἐπειδὰν οὖν ἄρξωνται τῆς θεωρίας, νόμος ἐστὶν αὐτοῖς ἐν τῷ χρόνῳ τούτῳ καθα-
ρεύειν τὴν πόλιν καὶ δημοσίᾳ μηδένα ἀποκτεινύναι,
πρὶν ἂν εἰς Δῆλόν τε ἀφίκηται τὸ πλοῖον καὶ πάλιν
δεῦρο · τοῦτο δ᾽ ἐνίοτε ἐν πολλῷ χρόνῳ γίγνεται,
35 ὅταν τύχωσιν ἄνεμοι ἀπολαβόντες αὐτούς. ἀρχὴ
δ᾽ ἐστὶ τῆς θεωρίας, ἐπειδὰν ὁ ἱερεὺς τοῦ Ἀπόλ- C
λωνος στέψῃ τὴν πρύμναν τοῦ πλοίου · τοῦτο δ᾽
ἔτυχεν, ὥσπερ λέγω, τῇ προτεραίᾳ τῆς δίκης γε-
γονός. διὰ ταῦτα καὶ πολὺς χρόνος ἐγένετο τῷ
40 Σωκράτει ἐν τῷ δεσμωτηρίῳ ὁ μεταξὺ τῆς δίκης
τε καὶ θανάτου.

II. ΕΧ. Τί δὲ δὴ τὰ περὶ αὐτὸν τὸν θάνατον,
ὦ Φαίδων ; τί ἦν τὰ λεχθέντα καὶ πραχθέντα, καὶ
τίνες οἱ παραγενόμενοι τῶν ἐπιτηδείων τῷ ἀνδρί ;
ἢ οὐκ εἴων οἱ ἄρχοντες παρεῖναι, ἀλλ᾽ ἔρημος ἐτε-
5 λεύτα φίλων ;

ΦΑΙΔ. Οὐδαμῶς, ἀλλὰ παρῆσάν τινες καὶ πολ- 58
λοί γε.   D

ΕΧ. Ταῦτα δὴ πάντα προθυμήθητι ὡς σαφέσ-
τατα ἡμῖν ἀπαγγεῖλαι, εἰ μή τίς σοι ἀσχολία
10 τυγχάνει οὖσα.

ΦΑΙΔ. Ἀλλὰ σχολάζω γε καὶ πειράσομαι ὑμῖν
διηγήσασθαι· καὶ γὰρ τὸ μεμνῆσθαι Σωκράτους
καὶ αὐτὸν λέγοντα καὶ ἄλλου ἀκούοντα ἔμοιγε ἀεὶ
πάντων ἥδιστον.

15 ΕΧ. Ἀλλὰ μήν, ὦ Φαίδων, καὶ τοὺς ἀκουσομέ-
νους γε τοιούτους ἑτέρους ἔχεις· ἀλλὰ πειρῶ ὡς ἂν
δύνῃ ἀκριβέστατα διεξελθεῖν πάντα.

ΦΑΙΔ. Καὶ μὴν ἔγωγε θαυμάσια ἔπαθον παρα- Ε
γενόμενος. οὔτε γὰρ ὡς θανάτῳ παρόντα με ἀν-
20 δρὸς ἐπιτηδείου ἔλεος εἰσῄει· εὐδαίμων γάρ μοι
ἀνὴρ ἐφαίνετο, ὦ Ἐχέκρατες, καὶ τοῦ τρόπου καὶ
τῶν λόγων, ὡς ἀδεῶς καὶ γενναίως ἐτελεύτα, ὥστε
μοι ἐκεῖνον παρίστασθαι μηδ᾽ εἰς Ἅιδου ἰόντα ἄνευ
θείας μοίρας ἰέναι, ἀλλὰ καὶ ἐκεῖσε ἀφικόμενον εὖ
25 πράξειν, εἴ πέρ τις πώποτε καὶ ἄλλος. διὰ δὴ 59
ταῦτα οὐδὲν πάνυ μοι ἐλεεινὸν εἰσῄει, ὡς εἰκὸς ἂν
δόξειεν εἶναι παρόντι πένθει· οὔτε αὖ ἡδονὴ ὡς ἐν
φιλοσοφίᾳ ἡμῶν ὄντων, ὥσπερ εἰώθειμεν· καὶ γὰρ
οἱ λόγοι τοιοῦτοί τινες ἦσαν· ἀλλ᾽ ἀτεχνῶς ἄτοπόν
30 τί μοι πάθος παρῆν καί τις ἀήθης κρᾶσις ἀπό τε
τῆς ἡδονῆς συγκεκραμένη ὁμοῦ καὶ ἀπὸ τῆς λύπης, τοῦ κεράννυ-
ἐνθυμουμένῳ ὅτι αὐτίκα ἐκεῖνος ἔμελλε τελευτᾶν,
καὶ πάντες οἱ παρόντες σχεδόν τι οὕτω διεκείμεθα,

ότὲ μὲν γελῶντες, ἐνίοτε δὲ δακρύοντες, εἷς δὲ ἡμῶν 59
35 καὶ διαφερόντως, Ἀπολλόδωρος · οἶσθα γάρ που
τὸν ἄνδρα καὶ τὸν τρόπον αὐτοῦ.   B

ΕΧ. Πῶς γὰρ οὔ;

ΦΑΙΔ. Ἐκεῖνός τε τοίνυν παντάπασιν οὕτως εἶχεν,
καὶ αὐτὸς ἔγωγε ἐτεταράγμην καὶ οἱ ἄλλοι.

40   ΕΧ. Ἔτυχον δέ, ὦ Φαίδων, τίνες παραγενόμενοι;

ΦΑΙΔ. Οὗτός τε δὴ ὁ Ἀπολλόδωρος τῶν ἐπιχωρίων παρῆν καὶ ὁ Κριτόβουλος καὶ ὁ πατὴρ αὐτοῦ
[Κρίτων], καὶ ἔτι Ἑρμογένης καὶ Ἐπιγένης καὶ
Αἰσχίνης καὶ Ἀντισθένης · ἦν δὲ καὶ Κτήσιππος
45 ὁ Παιανιεὺς καὶ Μενέξενος καὶ ἄλλοι τινὲς τῶν
ἐπιχωρίων · Πλάτων δέ, οἶμαι, ἠσθένει.

ΕΧ. Ξένοι δέ τινες παρῆσαν;   C

ΦΑΙΔ. Ναί, Σιμμίας τέ γε ὁ Θηβαῖος καὶ Κέβης
καὶ Φαιδωνίδης καὶ Μεγαρόθεν Εὐκλείδης τε καὶ
50 Τερψίων.

ΕΧ. Τί δέ; Ἀρίστιππος καὶ Κλεόμβροτος παρ-
εγένοντο;

ΦΑΙΔ. Οὐ δῆτα · ἐν Αἰγίνῃ γὰρ ἐλέγοντο εἶναι.

ΕΧ. Ἄλλος δέ τις παρῆν;

55   ΦΑΙΔ. Σχεδόν τι οἶμαι τούτους παραγενέσθαι.

ΕΧ. Τί οὖν δή; τίνες, φής, ἦσαν οἱ λόγοι;

III. ΦΑΙΔ. Ἐγώ σοι ἐξ ἀρχῆς πάντα πειράσομαι διηγήσασθαι. ἀεὶ γὰρ δὴ καὶ τὰς πρόσθεν
ἡμέρας εἰώθειμεν φοιτᾶν καὶ ἐγὼ καὶ οἱ ἄλλοι D
παρὰ τὸν Σωκράτη, συλλεγόμενοι ἔωθεν εἰς τὸ
5 δικαστήριον ἐν ᾧ καὶ ἡ δίκη ἐγένετο · πλησίον

γὰρ ἦν τοῦ δεσμωτηρίου. περιεμένομεν οὖν ἑκά- 59
στοτε ἕως ἀνοιχθείη τὸ δεσμωτήριον, διατρίβοντες
μετ᾽ ἀλλήλων· ἀνεῴγετο γὰρ οὐ πρῴ· ἐπειδὴ δὲ
ἀνοιχθείη, εἰσῆμεν παρὰ τὸν Σωκράτη καὶ τὰ
10 πολλὰ διημερεύομεν μετ᾽ αὐτοῦ. καὶ δὴ καὶ τότε
πρωιαίτερον συνελέγημεν. τῇ γὰρ προτεραίᾳ
ἡμέρᾳ ἐπειδὴ ἐξήλθομεν ἐκ τοῦ δεσμωτηρίου
ἑσπέρας, ἐπυθόμεθα ὅτι τὸ πλοῖον ἐκ Δήλου ἀφιγ-   E
μένον εἴη. παρηγγείλαμεν οὖν ἀλλήλοις ἥκειν
15 ὡς πρωιαίτατα εἰς τὸ εἰωθός. καὶ ἥκομεν καὶ
ἡμῖν ἐξελθὼν ὁ θυρωρός, ὅσπερ εἰώθει ὑπακούειν,
εἶπεν περιμένειν καὶ μὴ πρότερον παριέναι ἕως
ἂν αὐτὸς κελεύσῃ. "λύουσι γάρ," ἔφη, "οἱ ἕνδεκα
Σωκράτη καὶ παραγγέλλουσιν ὅπως ἂν τῇδε τῇ
20 ἡμέρᾳ τελευτήσῃ." οὐ πολὺν δ᾽ οὖν χρόνον ἐπι-
σχὼν ἧκεν καὶ ἐκέλευεν ἡμᾶς εἰσιέναι. εἰσιόντες
οὖν κατελαμβάνομεν τὸν μὲν Σωκράτη ἄρτι λελυ-   60
μένον, τὴν δὲ Ξανθίππην — γιγνώσκεις γάρ —
ἔχουσάν τε τὸ παιδίον αὐτοῦ καὶ παρακαθημένην.
25 ὡς οὖν εἶδεν ἡμᾶς ἡ Ξανθίππη, ἀνευφήμησέ τε καὶ
τοιαῦτ᾽ ἄττα εἶπεν οἷα δὴ εἰώθασιν αἱ γυναῖκες,
ὅτι "ὦ Σώκρατες, ὕστατον δή σε προσεροῦσι νῦν
οἱ ἐπιτήδειοι καὶ σὺ τούτους." καὶ ὁ Σωκράτης
βλέψας εἰς τὸν Κρίτωνα· "ὦ Κρίτων," ἔφη, "ἀπα-
30 γέτω τις αὐτὴν οἴκαδε." καὶ ἐκείνην μὲν ἀπῆγόν
τινες τῶν τοῦ Κρίτωνος βοῶσάν τε καὶ κοπτομέ-   B
νην· ὁ δὲ Σωκράτης ἀνακαθιζόμενος εἰς τὴν κλίνην
συνέκαμψέ τε τὸ σκέλος καὶ ἐξέτριψε τῇ χειρί, καὶ

τρίβων ἅμα· "ὡς ἄτοπον," ἔφη, "ὦ ἄνδρες, ἔοικέ τι 60
35 εἶναι τοῦτο ὃ καλοῦσιν οἱ ἄνθρωποι ἡδύ· ὡς θαυ-
μασίως πέφυκε πρὸς τὸ δοκοῦν ἐναντίον εἶναι, τὸ
λυπηρόν, τὸ ἅμα μὲν αὐτὼ μὴ ἐθέλειν παραγίγνε-
σθαι τῷ ἀνθρώπῳ, ἐὰν δέ τις διώκῃ τὸ ἕτερον καὶ
λαμβάνῃ, σχεδόν τι ἀναγκάζεσθαι λαμβάνειν καὶ τὸ
40 ἕτερον, ὥσπερ ἐκ μιᾶς κορυφῆς συνημμένω δύ' ὄντε.
καί μοι δοκεῖ," ἔφη, "εἰ ἐνενόησεν αὐτὰ Αἴσωπος, C
μῦθον ἂν συνθεῖναι ὡς ὁ θεὸς βουλόμενος αὐτὰ
διαλλάξαι πολεμοῦντα, ἐπειδὴ οὐκ ἐδύνατο, συνῆψεν
εἰς ταὐτὸν αὐτοῖς τὰς κορυφάς, καὶ διὰ ταῦτα ᾧ ἂν
45 τὸ ἕτερον παραγένηται ἐπακολουθεῖ ὕστερον καὶ τὸ
ἕτερον. ὥσπερ οὖν καὶ αὐτῷ μοι ἔοικεν· ἐπειδὴ ὑπὸ
τοῦ δεσμοῦ ἦν ἐν τῷ σκέλει [πρότερον] τὸ ἀλγεινόν,
ἥκειν δὴ φαίνεται ἐπακολουθοῦν τὸ ἡδύ."

LXIV. Ταῦτα δὴ εἰπόντος αὐτοῦ ὁ Κρίτων 115
"εἶεν," ἔφη, "ὦ Σώκρατες· τί δὲ τούτοις ἢ ἐμοὶ B
ἐπιστέλλεις ἢ περὶ τῶν παίδων ἢ περὶ ἄλλου του,
ὅ τι ἄν σοι ποιοῦντες ἡμεῖς ἐν χάριτι μάλιστα
5 ποιοῖμεν;" "ἅπερ ἀεὶ λέγω," ἔφη, "ὦ Κρίτων,
οὐδὲν καινότερον· ὅτι ὑμῶν αὐτῶν ἐπιμελούμενοι
ὑμεῖς καὶ ἐμοὶ καὶ τοῖς ἐμοῖς καὶ ὑμῖν αὐτοῖς ἐν
χάριτι ποιήσετε ἅττ' ἂν ποιῆτε, κἂν μὴ νῦν ὁμολο-
γήσητε· ἐὰν δὲ ὑμῶν μὲν αὐτῶν ἀμελῆτε καὶ μὴ
10 θέλητε ὥσπερ κατ' ἴχνη κατὰ τὰ νῦν τε εἰρημένα
καὶ τὰ ἐν τῷ ἔμπροσθεν χρόνῳ ζῆν, οὐδὲ ἐὰν πολλὰ
ὁμολογήσητε ἐν τῷ παρόντι καὶ σφόδρα, οὐδὲν C

πλέον ποιήσετε." "ταῦτα μὲν τοίνυν προθυμηθη- 115
σόμεθα," ἔφη, "οὕτω ποιεῖν· θάπτωμεν δέ σε τίνα
15 τρόπον;" "ὅπως ἄν," ἔφη, "βούλησθε, ἐάν πέρ γε
λάβητέ με καὶ μὴ ἐκφύγω ὑμᾶς." γελάσας δὲ ἅμα
ἡσυχῇ καὶ πρὸς ἡμᾶς ἀποβλέψας εἶπεν· "οὐ πείθω,
ὦ ἄνδρες, Κρίτωνα ὡς ἐγώ εἰμι οὗτος Σωκράτης,
ὁ νυνὶ διαλεγόμενος καὶ διατάττων ἕκαστον τῶν
20 λεγομένων, ἀλλ' οἴεταί με ἐκεῖνον εἶναι ὃν ὄψεται
ὀλίγον ὕστερον νεκρόν, καὶ ἐρωτᾷ δὴ πῶς με D
θάπτῃ. ὅτι δὲ ἐγὼ πάλαι πολὺν λόγον πεποίημαι
ὡς, ἐπειδὰν πίω τὸ φάρμακον, οὐκέτι ὑμῖν παρα-
μενῶ, ἀλλ' οἰχήσομαι ἀπιὼν εἰς μακάρων δή τινας
25 εὐδαιμονίας, ταῦτά μοι δοκῶ αὐτῷ ἄλλως λέγειν,
παραμυθούμενος ἅμα μὲν ὑμᾶς, ἅμα δ' ἐμαυτόν.
ἐγγυήσασθε οὖν με πρὸς Κρίτωνα," ἔφη, "τὴν
ἐναντίαν ἐγγύην ἢ ἣν οὗτος πρὸς τοὺς δικαστὰς
ἠγγυᾶτο. οὗτος μὲν γὰρ ἦ μὴν παραμενεῖν· ὑμεῖς
30 δὲ ἦ μὴν μὴ παραμενεῖν ἐγγυήσασθε ἐπειδὰν ἀπο-
θάνω, ἀλλὰ οἰχήσεσθαι ἀπιόντα, ἵνα Κρίτων ῥᾷον E
φέρῃ, καὶ μὴ ὁρῶν μου τὸ σῶμα ἢ καιόμενον ἢ
κατορυττόμενον ἀγανακτῇ ὑπὲρ ἐμοῦ ὡς δεινὰ πά-
σχοντος, μηδὲ λέγῃ ἐν τῇ ταφῇ ὡς ἢ προτίθεται
35 Σωκράτη ἢ ἐκφέρει ἢ κατορύττει. εὖ γὰρ ἴσθι,"
ἦ δ' ὅς, "ὦ ἄριστε Κρίτων, τὸ μὴ καλῶς λέγειν οὐ
μόνον εἰς αὐτὸ τοῦτο πλημμελές, ἀλλὰ καὶ κακόν
τι ἐμποιεῖ ταῖς ψυχαῖς. ἀλλὰ θαρρεῖν τε χρὴ καὶ
φάναι τοὐμὸν σῶμα θάπτειν, καὶ θάπτειν οὕτως ὅπως 116
40 ἄν σοι φίλον ᾖ καὶ μάλιστα ἡγῇ νόμιμον εἶναι."

LXV. Ταῦτ᾽ εἰπὼν ἐκεῖνος μὲν ἀνίστατο εἰς 116
οἴκημά τι ὡς λουσόμενος, καὶ ὁ Κρίτων εἵπετο
αὐτῷ, ἡμᾶς δ᾽ ἐκέλευε περιμένειν. περιεμένομεν
οὖν πρὸς ἡμᾶς αὐτοὺς διαλεγόμενοι περὶ τῶν εἰρη-
5 μένων καὶ ἀνασκοποῦντες, τοτὲ δ᾽ αὖ περὶ τῆς ξυμ-
φορᾶς διεξιόντες ὅση ἡμῖν γεγονυῖα εἴη, ἀτεχνῶς
ἡγούμενοι ὥσπερ πατρὸς στερηθέντες διάξειν ὀρ-
φανοὶ τὸν ἔπειτα βίον. ἐπειδὴ δὲ ἐλούσατο καὶ B
ἠνέχθη παρ᾽ αὐτὸν τὰ παιδία — δύο γὰρ αὐτῷ
10 υἱεῖς σμικροὶ ἦσαν, εἷς δὲ μέγας — καὶ αἱ οἰκεῖαι
γυναῖκες ἀφίκοντο, ἐκείναις ἐναντίον τοῦ Κρίτωνος
διαλεχθείς τε καὶ ἐπιστείλας ἅττα ἐβούλετο, τὰς
μὲν γυναῖκας καὶ τὰ παιδία ἀπιέναι ἐκέλευσεν,
αὐτὸς δὲ ἧκε παρ᾽ ἡμᾶς. καὶ ἦν ἤδη ἐγγὺς ἡλίου
15 δυσμῶν· χρόνον γὰρ πολὺν διέτριψεν ἔνδον. ἐλθὼν
δ᾽ ἐκαθέζετο λελουμένος, καὶ οὐ πολλὰ μετὰ ταῦτα
διελέχθη, καὶ ἧκεν ὁ τῶν ἕνδεκα ὑπηρέτης καὶ στὰς
παρ᾽ αὐτόν· "ὦ Σώκρατες," ἔφη, "οὐ καταγνώσομαι C
σοῦ ὅπερ ἄλλων καταγιγνώσκω, ὅτι μοι χαλεπαί-
20 νουσι καὶ καταρῶνται ἐπειδὰν αὐτοῖς παραγγέλλω
πίνειν τὸ φάρμακον ἀναγκαζόντων τῶν ἀρχόντων.
σὲ δὲ ἐγὼ καὶ ἄλλως ἔγνωκα ἐν τούτῳ τῷ χρόνῳ
γενναιότατον καὶ πρᾳότατον καὶ ἄριστον ἄνδρα
ὄντα τῶν πώποτε δεῦρο ἀφικομένων, καὶ δὴ καὶ νῦν
25 εὖ οἶδ᾽ ὅτι οὐκ ἐμοὶ χαλεπαίνεις, γιγνώσκεις γὰρ
τοὺς αἰτίους, ἀλλὰ ἐκείνοις. νῦν, οἶσθα γὰρ ἃ
ἦλθον ἀγγέλλων, χαῖρέ τε καὶ πειρῶ ὡς ῥᾷστα
φέρειν τὰ ἀναγκαῖα." καὶ ἅμα δακρύσας μετα- D

στρεφόμενος ἀπῄει.   καὶ ὁ Σωκράτης ἀναβλέψας 116
30 πρὸς αὐτόν· "καὶ σύ," ἔφη, "χαῖρε, καὶ ἡμεῖς ταῦτα
ποιήσομεν."   καὶ ἅμα πρὸς ἡμᾶς· "ὡς ἀστεῖος,"
ἔφη, "ὁ ἄνθρωπος· καὶ παρὰ πάντα μοι τὸν χρόνον προσῄει καὶ διελέγετο ἐνίοτε καὶ ἦν ἀνδρῶν
λῷστος, καὶ νῦν ὡς γενναίως με ἀποδακρύει.   ἀλλ᾽
35 ἄγε δή, ὦ Κρίτων, πειθώμεθα αὐτῷ, καὶ ἐνεγκάτω
τις τὸ φάρμακον, εἰ τέτριπται· εἰ δὲ μή, τριψάτω
ὁ ἄνθρωπος."   καὶ ὁ Κρίτων· "ἀλλ᾽ οἶμαι," ἔφη,
"ἔγωγε, ὦ Σώκρατες, ἔτι ἥλιον εἶναι ἐπὶ τοῖς ὄρεσιν Ε
καὶ οὔπω δεδυκέναι.   καὶ ἅμα ἐγὼ οἶδα καὶ ἄλλους
40 πάνυ ὀψὲ πίνοντας, ἐπειδὰν παραγγελθῇ αὐτοῖς,
δειπνήσαντάς τε καὶ πιόντας εὖ μάλα, καὶ ξυγγε-
νομένους γ᾽ ἐνίους ὧν ἂν τύχωσιν ἐπιθυμοῦντες.
ἀλλὰ μηδὲν ἐπείγου· ἔτι γὰρ ἐγχωρεῖ."   καὶ ὁ
Σωκράτης· "εἰκότως γε," ἔφη, "ὦ Κρίτων, ἐκεῖνοί
45 τε ταῦτα ποιοῦσιν οὓς σὺ λέγεις, οἴονται γὰρ κερδαίνειν ταῦτα ποιήσαντες, καὶ ἔγωγε ταῦτα εἰκότως
οὐ ποιήσω· οὐδὲν γὰρ οἶμαι κερδαίνειν ὀλίγον 117
ὕστερον πιὼν ἄλλο γε ἢ γέλωτα ὀφλήσειν παρ᾽
ἐμαυτῷ, γλιχόμενος τοῦ ζῆν καὶ φειδόμενος οὐδε-
50 νὸς ἔτι ἐνόντος.   ἀλλ᾽ ἴθι," ἔφη, "πιθοῦ καὶ μὴ
ἄλλως ποίει."

LXVI. Καὶ ὁ Κρίτων ἀκούσας ἔνευσε τῷ παιδὶ
πλησίον ἑστῶτι.   καὶ ὁ παῖς ἐξελθὼν καὶ συχνὸν
χρόνον διατρίψας ἧκεν ἄγων τὸν μέλλοντα διδόναι
τὸ φάρμακον, ἐν κύλικι φέροντα τετριμμένον· ἰδὼν
5 δὲ ὁ Σωκράτης τὸν ἄνθρωπον· "εἶεν," ἔφη, "ὦ βέλ-

τιστε, σὺ γὰρ τούτων ἐπιστήμων, τί χρὴ ποιεῖν;" 117
"οὐδὲν ἄλλο," ἔφη, "ἢ πιόντα περιιέναι ἕως ἄν σου
βάρος ἐν τοῖς σκέλεσι γένηται, ἔπειτα κατακεῖ- B
σθαι· καὶ οὕτως αὐτὸ ποιήσει." καὶ ἅμα ὤρεξε
10 τὴν κύλικα τῷ Σωκράτει· καὶ ὃς λαβὼν καὶ μάλα
ἵλεως, ὦ Ἐχέκρατες, οὐδὲν τρέσας οὐδὲ διαφθείρας
οὔτε τοῦ χρώματος οὔτε τοῦ προσώπου, ἀλλ᾽, ὥσπερ
εἰώθει, ταυρηδὸν ὑποβλέψας πρὸς τὸν ἄνθρωπον·
"τί λέγεις," ἔφη, "περὶ τοῦδε τοῦ πώματος πρὸς τὸ
15 ἀποσπεῖσαί τινι; ἔξεστιν ἢ οὔ;" "τοσοῦτον," ἔφη,
"ὦ Σώκρατες, τρίβομεν ὅσον οἰόμεθα μέτριον εἶναι
πιεῖν." "μανθάνω," ἦ δ᾽ ὅς· "ἀλλ᾽ εὔχεσθαί γέ που
τοῖς θεοῖς ἔξεστί τε καὶ χρὴ τὴν μετοίκησιν τὴν C
ἐνθένδε ἐκεῖσε εὐτυχῆ γενέσθαι· ἃ δὴ καὶ ἐγὼ εὔ-
20 χομαί τε καὶ γένοιτο ταύτῃ." καὶ ἅμ᾽ εἰπὼν ταῦτα
ἐπισχόμενος καὶ μάλα εὐχερῶς καὶ εὐκόλως ἐξέ-
πιεν. καὶ ἡμῶν οἱ πολλοὶ τέως μὲν ἐπιεικῶς οἷοί
τε ἦσαν κατέχειν τὸ μὴ δακρύειν, ὡς δὲ εἴδομεν
πίνοντά τε καὶ πεπωκότα, οὐκέτι, ἀλλ᾽ ἐμοῦ γε βίᾳ
25 καὶ αὐτοῦ ἀστακτὶ ἐχώρει τὰ δάκρυα, ὥστε ἐγκα-
λυψάμενος ἀπέκλαιον ἐμαυτόν· οὐ γὰρ δὴ ἐκεῖνόν
γε, ἀλλὰ τὴν ἐμαυτοῦ τύχην, οἵου ἀνδρὸς ἑταίρου D
ἐστερημένος εἴην. ὁ δὲ Κρίτων ἔτι πρότερος ἐμοῦ,
ἐπειδὴ οὐχ οἷός τ᾽ ἦν κατέχειν τὰ δάκρυα, ἐξανέ-
30 στη. Ἀπολλόδωρος δὲ καὶ ἐν τῷ ἔμπροσθεν χρόνῳ
οὐδὲν ἐπαύετο δακρύων, καὶ δὴ καὶ τότε ἀναβρυ-
χησάμενος κλαίων καὶ ἀγανακτῶν οὐδένα ὅντινα
οὐ κατέκλασε τῶν παρόντων πλήν γε αὐτοῦ Σωκρά-

τους. ἐκεῖνος δέ· "οἷα," ἔφη, "ποιεῖτε, ὦ θαυμά-117
35 σιοι. ἐγὼ μέντοι οὐχ ἥκιστα τούτου ἕνεκα τὰς
γυναῖκας ἀπέπεμψα, ἵνα μὴ τοιαῦτα πλημμελοῖεν·
καὶ γὰρ ἀκήκοα ὅτι ἐν εὐφημίᾳ χρὴ τελευτᾶν. Ε
ἀλλ᾽ ἡσυχίαν τε ἄγετε καὶ καρτερεῖτε." καὶ ἡμεῖς
ἀκούσαντες ᾐσχύνθημέν τε καὶ ἐπέσχομεν τοῦ δα-
40 κρύειν. ὁ δὲ περιελθών, ἐπειδή οἱ βαρύνεσθαι
ἔφη τὰ σκέλη, κατεκλίθη ὕπτιος· οὕτω γὰρ ἐκέλευεν ὁ ἄνθρωπος· καὶ ἅμα ἐφαπτόμενος αὐτοῦ
οὗτος ὁ δοὺς τὸ φάρμακον, διαλιπὼν χρόνον ἐπε-
σκόπει τοὺς πόδας καὶ τὰ σκέλη, κἄπειτα σφόδρα
45 πιέσας αὐτοῦ τὸν πόδα ἤρετο εἰ αἰσθάνοιτο· ὁ δ᾽
οὐκ ἔφη· καὶ μετὰ τοῦτο αὖθις τὰς κνήμας· καὶ 118
ἐπανιὼν οὕτως ἡμῖν ἐπεδείκνυτο ὅτι ψύχοιτό τε
καὶ πηγνῦτο. καὶ αὐτὸς ἥπτετο καὶ εἶπεν ὅτι,
ἐπειδὰν πρὸς τῇ καρδίᾳ γένηται αὐτῷ, τότε οἰχή-
50 σεται. ἤδη οὖν σχεδόν τι αὐτοῦ ἦν τὰ περὶ τὸ
ἦτρον ψυχόμενα, καὶ ἐκκαλυψάμενος — ἐνεκεκάλυπτο γάρ — εἶπεν ὃ δὴ τελευταῖον ἐφθέγξατο·
"ὦ Κρίτων," ἔφη, "τῷ Ἀσκληπιῷ ὀφείλομεν ἀλε-
κτρυόνα· ἀλλὰ ἀπόδοτε καὶ μὴ ἀμελήσητε."
55 "ἀλλὰ ταῦτα," ἔφη, "ἔσται," ὁ Κρίτων· "ἀλλ᾽ ὅρα,
εἴ τι ἄλλο λέγεις." ταῦτα ἐρομένου αὐτοῦ οὐδὲν
ἔτι ἀπεκρίνατο, ἀλλ᾽ ὀλίγον χρόνον διαλιπὼν ἐκινήθη τε καὶ ὁ ἄνθρωπος ἐξεκάλυψεν αὐτόν, καὶ ὃς
τὰ ὄμματα ἔστησεν· ἰδὼν δὲ ὁ Κρίτων συνέλαβε
60 τὸ στόμα καὶ τοὺς ὀφθαλμούς.

LXVII. Ἥδε ἡ τελευτή, ὦ Ἐχέκρατες, τοῦ

ἑταίρου ἡμῖν ἐγένετο, ἀνδρός, ὡς ἡμεῖς φαῖμεν 118
ἄν, τῶν τότε ὧν ἐπειράθημεν ἀρίστου καὶ ἄλλως
φρονιμωτάτου καὶ δικαιοτάτου.

ABBREVIATIONS

H. — Hadley's Greek Grammar, revised by Allen.

G. — Goodwin's Greek Grammar.

GMT. — Goodwin's Greek Moods and Tenses.

B. — Babbitt's Greek Grammar.

Go. — Goodell's School Grammar of Attic Greek.

M. AND S. — Meier und Schömann, *Der Attische Process*
    (neu bearbeitet von H. Lipsius, Berlin, 1883 ff.).

INT. — Introduction.

APP. — Appendix.

NOTES ON THE APOLOGY

St. I. p. 17. These initials and numbers found in the margin of modern editions of Plato refer to the corresponding volume and page of the edition of Henricus Stephanus (Henri Estienne, the distinguished French scholar and printer), which appeared in 1578 and has been adopted as the standard for reference. Each page is divided into five parts by the letters (a) b c d e down the margin. (Appendix II., 1, a.)

Title, ΑΠΟΛΟΓΙΑ ΣΩΚΡΑΤΟΥΣ. For details as to the prosecutors, the charge, the court, and the trial, see Introduction, 26–29. As to how exact a report this is of what Socrates actually said, see Introduction, 32. [ἠθι-κός] : Thrasyllus (70 A.D.), who arranged the Dialogues of Plato into tetralogies (Int. 3), also made a philosophical distribution of them into classes, according to their subject or method and spirit. (See Diogenes Laertius, III. 56; Grote's *Plato*, chap. IV.) The *Apology* he put under the head ἠθικοί, or *ethical*.

The other Dialogues of Plato have a list of the *dialogi personae*, ΤΑ ΤΟΥ ΔΙΑΛΟΓΟΥ ΠΡΟΣΩΠΑ, prefixed. The *Apology*, being a monologue, has none, but it is constructed on the same dramatic plan as the other Dialogues, the two sets of accusers taking the place of two interlocutors or antagonists, whom the protagonist Socrates overthrows. The whole introduction of the speech forms the dramatic prologue (Int. 31).

I.–II. INTRODUCTION (PROLOGUE)

I. (To conciliate his audience.) *My accusers have spoken mostly falsehoods, but in an elaborate manner. I will speak only the truth. Permit me to do it in my ordinary, simple, conversational way.*

1. ὅ τι . . . πεπόνθατε, *how you have been affected.* — ὅ τι : cognate acc. of neuter adjective. H. 716, b; G. 1054; B. 334; Go. 536, b. — The contrast suggested by ὅ τι μέν is not strictly carried out. Socrates goes on, in ἐγὼ δ' οὖν, to set over against each other the subjects more prominently than the objects of πεπόνθατε. For the form ὅ τι, see App. III. — ὦ ἄνδρες Ἀθηναῖοι : In this form it is that Socrates addresses the dicasts, and never by their official title, ὦ ἄνδρες δικασταί, until in XXXI. 8, where he is speaking only to

117

those who voted in his favor. Meletus, the only time he addresses them (XIV. 23), calls them ἄνδρες δικασταί. Socrates, from the outset believing that the majority of the court was prejudiced against him, regards them as not fair judges and purposely abstains from giving them the title he does not think they deserve. **2. ὑπὸ . . . κατηγόρων**: although πεπόνθατε is active in form, it is passive in signification, and so is followed by ὑπό with the genitive. H. 820; G. 1241; B. 513; Go. 499, a. — **δ' οὖν**, *at any rate*. What is certain is set over against that which is uncertain. **3. καὶ αὐτός**, *even myself*, of whom it was least to have been expected. — **ὀλίγου** = ὀλίγου δεῖ, has the force of an adverb. H. 743; G. 1116, b; B. 642, note 1; Go. 569. — **ἐμαυτοῦ ἐπελαθόμην**, *forgot who I was*. **4. γέ** intensifies ἀληθές, and so contrasts it with πιθανῶς. In translation, here as often, this force of γέ may be indicated by emphasizing the preceding word. — **ὡς ἔπος εἰπεῖν**: the denial is possibly too sweeping, and is qualified in this way. For the infinitive, see H. 956; G. 1534; B. 642, 1; Go. 569. **5. αὐτῶν** (subjective gen. after ἔν) = 'they said,' and is explained by τῶν . . . ἐψεύσαντο. A similar construction is αὐτῶν in l. 11. **6. ὧν**: relative attracted into the case of its antecedent, for ἅ which would be cognate acc. — **τοῦτο** is resumptive of ἔν. **7. χρή** is strictly a noun. Plato may have intended that either ἐστί or the opt. εἴη should be supplied with it. H. 932, 2; G. 1487; B. 267; Go. 390. (App. III.) **8. ὡς** marks the reason as offered by his accusers, not by himself. H. 978; G. 1574; B. 656, 3; Go. 593, c. **11. τοῦτο**: resumptive of τὸ . . . μὴ αἰσχυνθῆναι. **12. εἰ μὴ ἄρα**, Lat. *nisi*

forte, ironical. His opponents, of course, would make no such statement. **13. εἰ μὲν γάρ**, *for truly if*. μέν is here evidently a weak form of μήν, and no correlative clause with δέ is to be supplied. Note that the condition and conclusion in this sentence are of different forms. H. 901, b; G. 1421, 1; B. 612, 2; Go. 646. **14. οὐ κατὰ τούτους**, *not after their fashion*, as explained in l. 17. **16. ὑμεῖς δ' ἐμοῦ**: we should have expected ἐμοῦ δέ, as the speakers really are contrasted. **17. κεκαλλιεπημένους . . . ῥήμασί τε καὶ ὀνόμασιν**, *arguments expressed in beautiful words and phrases*. This refers to the choice and arrangement of words, while **κεκοσμημένους** (l. 19) means *adorned with tropes* or rhetorical figures. Their discourse was as elaborate as it was untrue. **21. γὰρ δίκαια**: γάρ introduces the reason why he is not anxious about the precise words he may use or the form his speech may take. He knows that he has right on his side. **22. προσδοκησάτω**: for the imperat., see H. 874, b; G. 1347; B. 584, note; Go. 485. **23. τῇδε τῇ ἡλικίᾳ**, *for a man of my age*. The abstract for the concrete. — **μειρακίῳ**, according to our idiom, instead of being in the dative, would be in the nominative, the subject of ἂν πλάττοι to be supplied from the participle. — **πλάττοντι** (*fabricating*) agrees in case with ἡλικίῳ, but in gender with the person suggested. The reference here (as far as εἰσιέναι) is not to elaboration, but to falsification, to which idea δίκαια in l. 21 brings back his thoughts. " A μειράκιον, to hide a fault, uses falsehood and not rhetoric " (Riddell). **24. καὶ μέντοι**, *and yet*, though he is neither elaborate nor false, for another reason he has to beg that allowance be made for him. — **καὶ πάνυ**, *very earnestly*. **27. ἐν ἀγορᾷ ... καὶ ἄλλοθι**: the Apology is in the conversational key throughout, and often so in form, as was Socrates' ordinary discourse (Int. 21). **28. ἵνα**, *where*. In this sense ἵνα is rare in good Attic prose. **32. ἑβδομήκοντα**: see App. III. and Int. 5, note 1. — **33. λέξεως**: the gen. depends on ξένως. H. 756; G. 1147; B. 362, 3; Go. 518, b. — **ἄν**: this particle is repeated, as often when the sentence is long. H. 864; G. 1312; B. 439, note 2. **35. φωνῇ**, *dialect*. Athens compelled her subject states to bring many of their causes for trial to her courts, so that strange dialects were not infrequently heard by Athenian jurors (M. and S. p. 753, and note 19). **36. καὶ δὴ καί**: after ὥσπερ we should have looked for οὕτω καί. By καὶ δὴ καί especial attention is called to a particular case under a general statement. **38. χείρων, βελτίων**: there are advantages and disadvantages in Socrates' conversational style of speaking when compared with that of his accusers, but style is here a quite subordinate matter. — **ἂν εἴη**, *may prove to be*. For this use of the potential opt., see H. 872; G. 1331; B. 563; Go. 479. — **αὐτὸ δὲ τοῦτο**, *but this alone*. The intensive αὐτό with δέ emphasizes τοῦτο in contrast with τὸν μὲν τρόπον (l. 37). **40. αὕτη** (for τοῦτο), referring to the sentence αὐτὸ ... μή, is attracted into the gender of ἀρετή.

II. (Plan of defense.) *My accusers are of two kinds, those of long standing who are the more formidable, and my present accusers. Let me first defend myself against the first.*

- **1.** For **δίκαιος** used personally with the infin., see H. 944, a; G. 1527; B.

634. — **ἀπολογήσασθαι**: notice the force of the middle form. The active voice of this verb is not in use. **2. πρός** is used to express action toward an object, with or without a hostile sense. Compare πρὸς ὑμᾶς, l. 5. **5. καὶ πάλαι**: καί is intensive. The *Clouds* of Aristophanes had appeared in 423 B.C., twenty-four years before (Int. 22). **6. πολλὰ ἤδη ἔτη** makes prominent the continuance of that which began (πάλαι) *long ago*. — **καί**: in accordance with the Greek idiom, but superfluous in English. See XVI. 9, πολλοὺς ... καὶ ἀγαθοὺς ἄνδρας, 'many good men.' **7. τοὺς ἀμφὶ Ἄνυτον**, *Anytus and his party*. H. 791, 3; G. 1202, 3; B. 400, 2. Anytus is mentioned because he was the most influential of the accusers (Int. 26). **9. ὑμῶν τοὺς πολλούς**, *most of you*. For οἱ πολλοί in this sense, see H. 665; G. 967. Notice position of the personal pronoun. H. 673, b; G. 977, 1; B. 457, 1; Go. 554. **10. παραλαμβάνοντες**, *taking in charge*. The word often means to take in order to educate, as pupils. **11. ἐμοῦ οὐδὲν ἀληθές**: for various readings of the text, see App. III. — **τὶς Σωκράτης**, *a certain Socrates*. τὶς by its indefiniteness is depreciatory and contemptuous. **12. σοφὸς ἀνήρ**: this expression might refer to either natural philosopher or sophist, and so the prejudice popularly felt toward both those classes is unjustly directed toward Socrates (Int. 26). — The items of the charge which follows are derived from the *Clouds*, μετέωρα φροντιστής from ψυχῶν σοφῶν ... φροντιστήριον, l. 94, and τὰ ὑπὸ γῆς ἅπαντα ἀναζητηκώς from ζητοῦσιν οὗτοι τὰ κατὰ γῆς, l. 188. These two imply that Socrates was a natural philosopher (Int. 13). — **τὸν**

120   NOTES ON THE APOLOGY

ἥττω λόγον κρείττω ποιῶν (l. 13) is
suggested by the *Clouds*, 112 ff., and
later in that comedy Δίκαιος Λόγος and
Ἄδικος Λόγος are introduced.   This
last item implies that Socrates was a
sophist (Int. 14 and 15). — μετέωρα
φροντιστής: the acc. depends on the
verbal idea which is contained in the
noun. H. 713; G. 1050; B. 330; Go.
531. On φροντιστής, see App. III.
15. οἱ δεινοί : the article with the
predicate makes it equivalent to a
relative clause, *who are formidable*.
17. οὐδέ, 'do *not* believe in the gods
either.' Atheism was charged against
Socrates and his followers, in the
Clouds. **20.** ἐν ᾗ ἂν ... ἐπιστεύσατε,
*in which you would have been most
likely to believe them*. This is not the
hypothetical, but the potential, indicative. GMT. 244. This must be carefully distinguished from the use of ἄν
with imp. or aor. to denote customary
action. H. 835; G. 1296; B. 565;
Go. 461, b. Notice that in this expression Socrates avoids saying that any
of his audience actually had believed
his accusers. See note on III. 4.
21. ἐρήμην (δίκην) κατηγοροῦντες,
prosecuting a suit that went altogether
by default. A suit was said to be ἐρήμη
when the defendant did not appear.
Socrates of course could not be present
to defend himself, when all throughout
Athens and during so many years these
things were being said about him.
22. ὁ δὲ πάντων ἀλογώτατον : supply
τοῦτό ἐστιν. H. 611; G. 891, 1; B.
308; Go. 493, b. **24.** πλὴν εἰ, *except
in case*. πλήν represents the apodosis.
GMT. 477. — κωμῳδιοποιός : here
Aristophanes chiefly is alluded to,
although other comic poets, as Eupolis
and Ameipsias, had ridiculed Socrates.

25. With the comic poets who are
known, ὅσοι δέ contrasts the unknown
assailants, who again in what follows
are divided into the malicious and the
innocent. **26.** οἱ δὲ καί, *others also*,
just as if there had been οἱ μέν after
ὅσοι δέ. (οἱ μὲν) ... χρώμενοι and οἱ
δὲ ... πείθοντες together make up ὅσοι
δέ. **27.** ἀπορώτατοι, *most difficult to
deal with*. When Socrates was slan-
dered he was not present to defend
himself, and now when he is to defend
himself he cannot get his accusers before him. **30.** σκιαμαχεῖν is figurative
in meaning but is so defined by ἀπολο-
γούμενον that it is readily coördinated
by τὲ καί with ἐλέγχειν. **37.** εἶεν, *well
then*. This interjection is used when
the speaker implies that what has been
said, being quite evident, is of course
accepted by his hearers, and he will
pass on to something else. **39.** διαβολή here means *prejudice* excited by
false accusations. **40.** ἔσχετε, *you
acquired*. The aor. is inceptive. **41.** εἴ
τι ἄμεινον : the fact that it is his own
life which is at stake does not prevent
Socrates from being entirely judicial.
It may not be best for the city or for
himself that he should be acquitted.
This expression gives us the key to
Socrates' whole attitude in this defense.
He is "ready to be offered," if needs
be (Int. 33). **42.** πλέον τί με ποιῆσαι,
that I should accomplish something.
πλέον='more than if I did not.' **45.** τῷ
θεῷ, *God*, not 'the god' (Int. 10).
Along with perfect fearlessness of man
or death Socrates joins entire trust in
God.

The dramatic prologue ends here, —
the actors (Socrates and his two sets
of accusers), the scene and the attend-

ant circumstances (the court room and the trial), and the subject of contention (Is Socrates guilty of the charge?), all having been introduced. The eight chapters which follow correspond to the first episode or second act.

III.–X. Defense against his Old-Time Accusers

III. *My old-time accusers charge me with being a physicist and teaching men such things. I am not a physicist, — I do not know about and never talked about such things.*

4. οἱ διαβάλλοντες : the exciters of this prejudice Socrates represents as being certain individuals who, with time and perseverance, had done their work. He thus adroitly avoids both imputing this charge to the judges, which would have further offended them, and designating the whole people as guilty of misrepresenting him. These prejudices and accusations are made more tangible by throwing them into the form of a technical indictment, supposed to be preferred by certain men and read before the court. **5. ὥσπερ** qualifies not only κατηγόρων but also ἀντωμοσίαν and ἀναγνῶναι : ' to read, as it were, their indictment, so to speak, just as though they were plaintiffs.' Really there is no technical indictment, nor any formal reading by the official court reader (Int. 28), just as the accusers are only imagined as present in court. — ἀντωμοσίαν is here the sworn charge or *indictment* of the prosecuting party. **6.** In this fictitious indictment Socrates gathers together and formulates the prejudices of many years. It practically repeats II. 11–14. περί in περιεργάζεται indi-

cates excessive zeal. He takes more pains than enough = *is a busybody*. **9. τοιαύτη τίς**, *somewhat such.* It is not possible to give the exact words of such imaginary accusers. **10. ἑωρᾶτε :** the imperfect denotes the time when they had seen the *Clouds* acted. In that comedy Aristophanes had given expression to these widespread accusations. **11. Σωκράτη τινά :** the indefinite indicates that the character in the comedy bore no resemblance to the real Socrates. — περιφερόμενον : in the *Clouds* Socrates was represented as a foolish speculator in celestial phenomena, suspended aloft in a basket, saying in l. 225, ἀεροβατῶ καὶ περιφρονῶ τὸν ἥλιον. **13.** Note the unusual separation of πέρι from the case it governs. This is the only preposition which, in prose, stands after its case and suffers anastrophe. H. 110; G. 116, 1 ; B. 68. **14. οὐκ ὡς ἀτιμάζων :** according to Xenophon (*Mem.* I. 1, 11) Socrates did disparage the study of physics. Plato represents him as disparaging no truth, but as doubting whether it had been attained in the domain of physics. **16. μή . . . δίκας φύγοιμι,** *may I never be prosecuted by Meletus on such charges.* See App. III. δίκην φεύγειν is equivalent to the pass. διώκεσθαι, and so is followed by ὑπό with gen. of the agent. See note on I. 2. **17. ἀλλὰ γάρ,** *but really.* There is an ellipsis here. The full expression would be, ' *but* I need say no more, *for.*' **18. αὐτούς,** *yourselves,* is in apposition with ὑμῶν τοὺς πολλούς, and is in the acc. instead of the gen. because τοὺς πολλούς is the more emphatic. For another reading of the text here, see App. III. **21. οἱ τοιοῦτοι** is the subject, as is indicated by the

article, *those of you who are such.*
πολλοί is made emphatic by the position which it occupies.

IV. *I am not a teacher of men for money. To be a teacher is a very fine thing, for various reasons; but I do not profess to have this skill.*

1. ἀλλὰ γάρ resumes the ἀλλὰ γάρ of l. 17 in the preceding chapter. — **ἐστίν** has for its predicate ἀληθές in l. 4. By being kept in suspense till the close of the sentence, ἀληθές is emphasized. — **οὐδέ,** *nor yet.* It differs from οὔτε, which we might have expected, in that an adversative idea is introduced. οὐδέ, l. 3, repeats the οὐδέ of l. 1, and the resumptive clause may be rendered : *that is not true either.* One of the main points in which Socrates differed from the sophists was just this, that he did not take money for teaching his pupils (Int. 14 and 22). **4. ἐπεί,** ' (and yet I should be glad to), since,' or omitting the clause to be supplied, *although.* — **καὶ τοῦτό . . . καλὸν εἶναι,** *this too* (as well as the study of physics, III. 14) *seems to me to be a fine thing.* **5. εἰ . . . εἴη** : the optative indicates considerable doubt whether any one really can. **6. Γοργίας τε ὁ Δεοντῖνος** : for Gorgias and the sophists in general, see Int. 14. Protagoras was no longer living (d. 411). **7. γάρ** introduces the first reason for καλόν, l. 4. **8. οἷός τ᾽ ἐστίν** would naturally be followed by πείθειν (governing τοὺς νέους), which appears, in anacoluthon, as πείθουσι. By this change of construction the indicative makes more prominent that which is remarkable. The subject of πείθουσι is ἕκαστος used as a collective. H. 609, a; G. 900; B. 500; Go. 498, a. If οἷός τ᾽ ἐστίν is omitted,

the irregularity disappears. See App. III. **9. τῶν ἑαυτῶν πολιτῶν** : the genitive depends upon the ᾧ which follows. **12. πρός** in προσειδέναι has the force of *besides.* To gain gratitude, as well as money, caps the climax. — **ἐπεὶ καί** : *since* there is another sophist *also,* as well as the ones just mentioned. In the following reported conversation with Callias, a second reason is introduced why it is a fine thing (καλόν, l. 4) to teach young men. It is : if it is good to train young colts and steers, much more must it be to fit young men for life and work. **16. Καλλίᾳ** : Callias was a very wealthy Athenian who was exceedingly hospitable to sophists, as is represented humorously in the first chapters of the *Protagoras.* **20. ὃς ἔμελλεν,** *whose duty it would be.* For the omission of ἄν in this conclusion, see H. 897, b; G. 1402, 3; B. 567, 1; Go. 460, a. For the fut. infin. in ποιήσειν, see H. 855, a; G. 1277; B. 549, 1; Go. 570, b. **21. ἀρετήν** : cognate acc. after the adjectives. H. 717; G. 1053; B. 332; Go. 536, d. **25. τῆς ἀνθρωπίνης τε καὶ πολιτικῆς** : the appropriate excellence of young men is to be good *men* and good *citizens.* **26. τῶν υἱέων** : objective gen. after κτῆσιν. **28. ἦ δ᾽ ὅς** : for the use of the relative form as a demonstrative, see H. 655, a; G. 1023, 2; B. 443, 3; Go. 560. **29. Εὔηνος** : a sophist and teacher of secondary rank, judging from his fee. Protagoras charged 100 minae. **31. ἔχοι . . . διδάσκει** : in the indirect discourse, after a past tense either we may have the optative or the mode of the direct discourse may be retained. See note on I. 7. Here, as very often in Herodotus and sometimes in Xenophon, we have both usages in the same sentence. (App. III.) The apodosis is implied in ἐμακάρισα = *told him he was happy.* GMT. 696. 32. ἐμμελῶς (from ἐμμελής, 'in harmony'), *reasonably*, combining the two ideas of appropriately and cheaply. This is spoken ironically. 34. ἀλλ' (οὐ καλλύνομαι καὶ ἀβρύνομαι) οὐ γὰρ ἐπίσταμαι, *but really I do not understand them.* Compare III. 17.

V. *The prejudice against me is the result of the Delphic oracle's reply to Chaerephon, that no one was wiser than I.*

2. τὸ σὸν τί ἐστι πρᾶγμα; *what have you been doing?* 4. περιττότερον πραγματευομένου: the participle is not conditional, or the negative would not have been οὐδέν. H. 1025; G. 1612; B. 431, 1; Go. 486. It denotes cause, *since you were not busying yourself more than others.* It has been charged that Socrates was a busybody (III. 6, περιεργάζεται), but he has denied ιt. 5. ἔπειτα, *in that case.* 6. ἀλλοῖον: if he was not a busybody, he must have been in some way eccentric. 7. αὐτοσχεδιάζωμεν, *act unadvisedly;* properly said of those who say or do anything suddenly, on the impulse of the moment, and here refers to hasty decision on the part of the judges. 10. ὄνομα refers to σοφός. See II. 12. 14. σοφίαν τινά, *a sort of wisdom.* The indefinite is depreciatory. H. 702; G. 1016; B. 491, note 1. The wisdom which he possesses is very humble compared with that claimed by the physicists and sophists. — ἔσχηκα, (*have acquired* and so) *have.* — ποίαν . . . ταύτην: H. 1012, a; G. 1602; B. 575, note 1. Fully expressed, this would be ποία σοφία

ἐστὶν αὕτη δι' ἣν τοῦτο . . . ἔσχηκα. 15. ἥπερ . . . σοφία, "My wisdom is precisely (-περ) that only wisdom, as I believe (ἴσως), which is possible to man" (Riddell). 16. κινδυνεύω: since the running a risk implies a chance of success, this verb is used to express what may probably or possibly happen to be; *I may be.* — ταύτην: cog. acc. after σοφός. 19. λέγω is in the subjunctive mode. H. 866, 3; G. 1358; B. 577; Go. 471. 20. τῇ ἐμῇ: in place of an objective gen. 21. μὴ θορυβήσητε: the aor. (instead of pres. as in I. 29 and V. 33, etc.) denotes that he fears that, at the moment when he shall make the remarkable statement he is leading up to, they will raise a disturbance. 22. τὶ . . . μέγα λέγειν, *something great*, in the sense of big or *boastful.* 23. ἐμόν, *as mine own.* This is in the predicate, as is ἀξιόχρεων in l. 24. — ἀλλ' . . . ἀνοίσω *but I will refer to a speaker who is, you will admit (ὑμῖν), responsible.* For the ethical dative, see H. 770; G. 1171; B. 381; Go. 523, a. 24. τῆς γὰρ ἐμῆς: Socrates modestly refrains from adding σοφίας, which is contained in the following depreciatory conditional clause. 26. τὸν θεὸν τὸν ἐν Δελφοῖς: for the relation which the oracle bore to the development of Socrates' missionary career, see Int. 22. He must have been already a well-known personage, or Chaerephon would hardly have consulted the oracle about him. 28. ὑμῶν τῷ πλήθει ἑταῖρος: ἑταῖρος in a political sense, an *adherent* or partisan. See App. III. Chaerephon was a partisan of the πλῆθος in the sense of δῆμος or δημοκρατία. This fact is mentioned to dispose the court to listen more indulgently to the

story which is to follow. The recol-
lection of the rapacity and cruelty of
the Thirty Tyrants (June, 404–Feb.,
403) was still vivid. **29. φυγήν** refers
to the expulsion from Athens of all
opposed to the oligarchical government, and **κατῆλθε** to the return of the
democracy under Thrasybulus at the
end of the eight months' reign of
the Thirty. **30. οἷος ἦν Χαιρεφῶν:**
Chaerephon's energetic and enthusiastic disposition is caricatured by
Aristophanes, *Clouds*, l. 104. In the
Charmides he is termed μανικός. His
devotion to Socrates is indicated by
the words ἐμός τε ἑταῖρος (l. 27) and
by the act here described. **31. καὶ
δή ποτε καί,** *once in particular*.
Chaerephon has been called σφοδρός.
καὶ δὴ καί introduces a special instance of this quality. **32. ὅπερ λέγω,**
as I say. ὅπερ refers to μὴ θορυβήσητε,
l. 21. **33. δή,** *really*, again calls attention to the extraordinary nature of
the question. **34. ἀνεῖλεν οὖν ἡ Πυθία:** the words of the Pythian priestess,
according to Diogenes Laertius (II. 37),
were ἀνδρῶν ἁπάντων Σωκράτης σοφώτατος. The scholiast on Aristoph.
Clouds, l. 144, gives them, σοφὸς Σο-
φοκλῆς, σοφώτερος δ' Εὐριπίδης, ἀνδρῶν
δὲ πάντων Σωκράτης σοφώτατος. **35. ὁ
ἀδελφός:** Chaerecrates. Socrates calls
on this brother as a witness who would
know the facts at first hand.

VI. *I found this true in regard to
men in public life.*

4. τί ποτε αἰνίττεται, *what, pray,
does he intimate in his dark saying?*
Note the vividness which ποτέ gives
to these questions. Socrates modestly
feels that the plain meaning of the
oracle is apparently false, but it must
have some meaning,—what is it?

5. σοφὸς ὤν: by a different construction in VIII. 2, the participle is put in
the dative. GMT. 908. **7. ψεύδεταί γε:**
the force of γέ may be given by emphasizing the preceding word. Whatever explanation may be suggested, he
does not *lie*. That is ruled out by the
very nature of the god, οὐ γὰρ θέμις
αὐτῷ. **9. μόγις πάνυ,** *after long cogi-
tation.* — **τοιαύτην τινά:** predicate,
somewhat as follows. **12. τὸ μαντεῖον,
τῷ χρησμῷ,** *the oracle, the response.*
— ὅτι introduces direct discourse and
is equivalent to quotation marks. H.
928, b; G. 1477; Go. 623. So also in
l. 23. **14. διασκοπῶν . . . καὶ διαλεγόμενος** are in the nom. instead of
the dat., as is not infrequent with
ἔδοξέ μοι, in anacoluthon. διά in διασκοπῶν signifies *carefully* considering.
διαλεγόμενος resumes the thought after
the parenthetic clause, and indicates
that conversation was the test he applied. (App. III.) **15. τῶν πολιτικῶν,**
of the men in public life. 'States-
men' is too good a word here, as
'politicians' is too bad a one. — **πρὸς
ὅν . . . τι ἔπαθον,** *with reference to
whom I had an experience somewhat
like this.* **17. ἔδοξέ μοι** (inceptive aor.),
I came to the conclusion. **22. πρὸς
ἐμαυτὸν . . . ἐλογιζόμην:** like our *I
thought to myself*. **25. καλὸν κἀγαθόν:**
these words are almost always joined
together, as if they expressed one
idea. The masc. of this phrase denotes the perfect man, who is as he
should be. *Which we ought* gives
nearly the sense. On Socrates' pro-
fession of ignorance, see Int. 17.
26. ὥσπερ οὖν, *as really, you see.*
27. σμικρῷ τινι αὐτῷ τούτῳ, *by just
this little point* ('something,' τινί).
Dat. of degree of difference.

VII. *Also in the case of the poets I found the oracle true.*

1. ἐφεξῆς, *to one after another.* From this time we may date Socrates' more continuous devotion to teaching his fellow-men, in doing which he incurred the hostility of so many (Int. 26). **2. ὅτι** is declarative after αἰσθανόμενος, and subordinate to this are λυπούμενος and δεδιώς, circumstantial participles of manner, *perceiving with grief and apprehension.* **3. ἐδόκει** would naturally be a participle (ἡγούμενος), contrasted by δέ with αἰσθανόμενος μέν. The finite verb makes more prominent Socrates' determination.—**τὸ τοῦ θεοῦ,** *the service of the god.* **4. ἰτέον** (εἶναι) depends on ἐδόκει. It resumes ἦα of l. 1, the verbal giving the idea of necessity which ἀναγκαῖον in the intermediate clause has brought in.—**σκοποῦντι** agrees with ἐμοί, the dative of the agent, not expressed.—**τὸν χρησμόν** is, proleptically, outside of the relative clause to which it belongs. **6. νὴ τὸν κύνα,** as also in *Gorgias,* 482 B, μὰ τὸν κύνα τὸν Αἰγυπτίων θεόν, where the dog-headed Anubis is referred to. **9. ἐνδεεῖς** is the predicate after εἶναι, and is modified by τοῦ πλείστου, which in turn is qualified by ὀλίγου δεῖν. H. 956; G. 1534; B. 642, 1; Go. 569. **10. ζητοῦντι κατὰ τὸν θεόν:** his quest was *in accordance with the god's command,* because only by making it could he learn the real import of the response. **11. ἐπιεικέστεροι,** *more likely men.* **13. πόνους ... πονοῦντος:** the allusion is to the toils of Hercules. The participle agrees with the gen. implied in the possessive ἐμήν. H. 691; G. 1001; B. 477, note. (App. III.)—**καὶ ἀνέλεγκτος,** might *actually* (καί intensive) prove *irrefutable.* The result was exactly opposite

to his expectation and intent. (App. III.) **15. ποιητάς,** lit. 'makers.' The verbal idea (followed here by the objective gen.) is stronger in the Greek than in the corresponding English, *poets.* **20. διηρώτων ἄν:** the imperfect with ἄν denotes the repetition of the action. H. 835; G. 1296; GMT. 162; B. 568; Go. 461, a. So also ἄν ... ἔλεγον, l. 24. **21. ἅμα τι καί:** Socrates combined a quest for knowledge with his search as to the truth of the oracle (Int. 8). **23. αὐτῶν,** *than they themselves.* The genitive is after βέλτιον. **25. ἐν ὀλίγῳ** (χρόνῳ). **26. ποιοῖεν:** in the optative because the verb on which it depends is in the optative. H. 919, a; G. 1439; B. 316; Go. 642, d. **27. φύσει τινί,** *sort of naturally.* So in the *Ion,* 533 E, Socrates says that the excellent poets compose οὐκ ἐκ τέχνης ἀλλ' ἔνθεοι (*inspired*) ὄντες καὶ κατεχόμενοι (*possessed*). **29. πολλὰ καὶ καλά:** the καί is superfluous in our idiom. **32. σοφωτάτων:** the predicate is in the genitive because the participle on which εἶναι depends is in that case. H. 940, a; G. 931; B. 631; Go. 571, c. **33. ἀνθρώπων** is gen. of the whole.—**ἅ** is acc. of specification. **34. τῷ αὐτῷ ... ᾧπερ,** *in the very (-περ) same point in which.* (App. III.)

VIII. *In the case of the artisans likewise the oracle proved to be true.*

1. τελευτῶν: for a list of participles used adverbially, see H. 968, a; G. 1564; GMT. 834; B. 653, note 2; Go. 583, a. **4. τούτου:** for the gen. of separation with ψεύδομαι, see H. 748; G. 1117; B. 362, 1; Go. 509. **7. ὅπερ καὶ ... καὶ οἱ:** in English, one καί has to be omitted and the other translated by *also.* **10. τὰ μέγιστα** refers particularly to affairs of state. Many who had become rich through trade or business were aspiring to direct public affairs (Int. 16). **11. ἡ πλημμέλεια** means originally a mistake in music; here render *error*. **15. ἤ . . . ἔχειν,** *or to be both things which they are.*

IX. *Therefore great enmity has arisen against me as I have kept up this investigation ever since to my pecuniary ruin.*

4. λέγεσθαι is in the infin. under the influence of ὥστε, although with δέ (corresponding to μέν, l. 2) we should have expected ἐλεγόμην. The subject of the infin. is ἐμέ. If it had been expressed, we should have had σοφὸν εἶναι. H. 940; G. 927; B. 631; Go. 571. **5. σοφός** is in the nom. just as if we had had ἐλεγόμην instead of λέγεσθαι. — **εἶναι:** the infin. is frequently used in this way after ὀνομάζειν and similar expressions when the name indicates what the subject *is.* **7. τὸ δέ,** *but on the contrary.* Literally, 'this, on the other hand,' the sentence which follows being in apposition with τό. The correct view now to be stated is contrasted with another previously advanced. τό is used here as a demonstrative. **10. καὶ οὐδενός** corrects and heightens the force of ὀλίγου τινός, *or rather I should say, nothing.* — **τοῦτ' οὐ λέγειν τὸν Σωκράτη :** with this text (instead of τοῦτο λέγειν, see App. III.) Socrates offers this whole explanation as a conjecture. If he had intended to say, "the god evidently does not mean Socrates," we should need to have λέγων instead of λέγειν. H. 986; G. 1592; B. 661, note 3; Go. 588, c. The infin. προσκεχρῆσθαι confirms this view, for with the reading τοῦτο it should be a participle. τοῦτο = σοφὸν εἶναι. The two accusatives are after

λέγειν. H. 725, a; G. 1073; B. 340; Go. 536, c. **12. ὥσπερ ἂν εἰ :** with ἄν, ποιοῖτο must be supplied to complete the conclusion. **15. ταῦτα** is cognate acc. after ζητῶ and ἐρευνῶ, *I make these investigations and inquiries.* — **μέν** has in contrast with it δέ in X. l. 1. **17. ἀστῶν καὶ ξένων :** the genitives depend on τινά. **18. τῷ θεῷ βοηθῶν,** *bearing aid to the god* by proving the oracle true. **21. ἐν πενίᾳ μυρίᾳ,** *in extreme poverty.* In Xen. *Oeconomics* II. 3, Socrates says that perhaps he could sell his house and all his other property for five minae. **22. τοῦ θεοῦ** is objective gen., where we might have had the dative of the indirect object.

X. *Moreover the young men, my followers, have imitated me. The result is this great prejudice, which will be difficult to remove.*

3. αὐτόματοι is to be taken with ἐπακολουθοῦντες. Socrates disclaims responsibility not only for what these young men did, but for their following him at all. He had not sought them as pupils, as the sophists did. That they were the sons of rich men, by arousing class feeling, increased the odium they excited. **4. αὐτοί,** among *their own selves.* This signification of αὐτοί is indicated by the following εἶτα, implying a step in advance, and by the sharp contrast which ἄλλους offers in the next line. We should have expected καί before εἶτα. **9. αὐτοῖς :** the real trouble lay, not in the youth who questioned them, but in the men themselves, as is indicated in the context, lines 17, etc. (App. III.) **11. ποιῶν** and **διδάσκων** agree with the subject of διαφθείρει, to be supplied from the preceding line, and are circumstantial, denoting the means. **14. ταῦτα,** Lat. *ista*, is here expressive of contempt. —**ὅτι τὰ μετέωρα . . . ποιεῖν**: after ὅτι supply διδάσκων διαφθείρει τοὺς νέους, making τὰ μετέωρα, τὰ ὑπὸ γῆς, and the two infinitives νομίζειν and ποιεῖν depend on διδάσκων. Or, better, regard ὅτι as equivalent to quotation marks introducing direct discourse, and the accusatives and infinitives as in apposition with τὰ . . . πρόχειρα ταῦτα. In this latter way contempt is expressed still more forcibly. **17. κατάδηλοι . . . προσποιούμενοι . . . εἰδότες**: H. 981; G. 1589; B. 661; Go. 585, a. εἰδέναι may be taken absolutely = to have knowledge, or τί may be supplied from the following οὐδέν. **18. ἅτε ὄντες,** inasmuch as they are. H. 977; G. 1575; B. 656, 1; Go. 593, a. **20. ξυντεταγμένως,** concertedly. The metaphor is taken from soldiers arrayed in line of battle. (App. III.) **22. καὶ Μέλητός . . . ῥητόρων**: on the accusers, see Int. 26. The classes here mentioned correspond to those Socrates is described as having visited in chaps. VI., VII., and VIII., if we may regard the ῥήτορες here as the same with the πολιτικοί of chap. VI. καὶ τῶν πολιτικῶν, l. 25, is added because Anytus, the most influential of the three accusers, was both tanner and πολιτικός. (App. III.) **29. ταῦτ' . . . τἀληθῆ**: the article with the predicate indicates the truth promised in I. 16. ὑμῖν is ethical dative, I assure you. **32. τοῖς αὐτοῖς** refers to these very things he has just said so frankly. In this manner he has always spoken to them, and then as now they hated him for so doing. They have thus had an object lesson of the way in which this hatred had sprung up against him. (App. III.)

Here closes the first episode (or second act of the drama), one antagonist, the accusers of long ago, having been discomfited. In the second episode which follows, a second antagonist comes on to meet a like fate.

XI.–XV. Defense against his Present Accusers

In this part of his defense, note that Socrates does not think it worth while to reply directly and specifically to the charges, but he utterly destroys their force and rules Meletus out of court, as it were, by showing that he has no interest in the case. The dramatic value of thus slighting him is very evident (Int. 26 and 31). Later in his speech, in his own time and way, Socrates amply refutes the charges here urged against him.

XI. *My present accusers charge me with corrupting the youth and not believing in the gods the city believes in, but in δαιμόνια καινά. Meletus is the real evil-doer, for he brings this suit, although he cares nothing about the matters involved.*

2. πρὸς ὑμᾶς, πρὸς δὲ Μέλητον, *before you, but against Meletus.* See note on II. 2. **3. φιλόπολιν, ὥς φησι**: implying that few if any others would call him so. **5. αὖθις γὰρ δή . . . ἀντωμοσίαν,** *For again now just as though these accusers were a second set, let us in turn take up their indictment.* Really there is only one set of formal accusers, but since he has in imagination introduced his old-time accusers into court (III. 5, ὥσπερ οὖν), the one only actual set becomes *as it were* a second set. Notice also that the charges of the present accusers are the outgrowth of those earlier attacks and really identical, and so only *as it were* a second set. **7. πῶς ὧδε**: the indictment is not given here in the exact words. Diogenes Laertius says (II. 40) that Favorinus (who wrote a work on Socrates in the time of the emperor Hadrian) reports that the exact form of the indictment as preserved in the Metroon (or temple of Cybele at Athens, where the archives of the city were deposited) was as follows: ἀδικεῖ Σωκράτης οὓς μὲν ἡ πόλις νομίζει θεοὺς οὐ νομίζων ἕτερα δὲ καινὰ δαιμόνια εἰσηγούμενος · ἀδικεῖ δὲ καὶ τοὺς νέους διαφθείρων. τίμημα θάνατος. Notice that the order of the charges is reversed. **14. σπουδῇ χαριεντίζεται**: literally, 'jests in earnest,' *makes a jest of a very serious matter.* He jests because the charges he makes are so absurd and inconsistent as to be ridiculous, and yet it is a serious matter because it involves the reputation and life of an innocent man.— ῥᾳδίως, *lightly.* Lat. *temere.* — εἰς ἀγῶνα καθιστάς, *bringing to trial.* **16. ὧν** is gen. depending on ἐμέλησεν. — οὐδέν is an adverbial acc. **18. καὶ ὑμῖν**, *to you also* as well as I understand it myself.

XII. *Meletus shows his lack of interest in the matter by saying that all benefit the young except me, and that I alone corrupt them.*

1. δεῦρο has the same force as ἴθι, l. 3; GMT. 251. *Here now.* — εἰπέ: the accused could question his opponent and the law bade him respond. M. and S. p. 931. Socrates thus avails himself of his especial skill in cross questioning. — ἄλλο τι ἤ for ἄλλο τι ἔστιν ἤ = 'is anything else true than ?' = *do you not certainly ?* H. 1015, b; G. 1604; B. 573, note. A decidedly affirmative

reply is looked for. **2.** For ὅπως with future after an expression of effort, see H. 885; G. 1372; B. 593; Go. 638, a. **5. μέλον**: for acc. absolute, see H. 973; G. 1569; B. 658; Go. 591. — τὸν μέν is sharply contrasted with τὸν δέ, l. 6. — **6.** ἐμέ, which is really the object of εἰσάγεις, must be understood as also in predicate apposition with τὸν διαφθείροντα. — τουτοισί is instead of εἰς δικαστήριον or εἰς τοὺς δικαστάς. **10. οὗ . . . λέγω** refers to XI. 17. The rel. is attracted into the case of the omitted antecedent. **12.** In giving this impersonal answer (οἱ νόμοι), Meletus shows that he vaguely foresees the trap into which Socrates is leading him and tries to avoid it. Socrates sharply brings his nose back to the grindstone in ἀλλ' οὐ τοῦτο. **15. οἱ δικασταί**: Meletus, obliged unwillingly to give a pertinent answer, in this reply curries favor with the judges. He includes the whole six thousand, but in the οἴδε which follows (l. 16) Socrates limits it to the number, probably five hundred, actually present and serving in this case. Even then, logically, Meletus in what follows has to include the audience and the five hundred members of the βουλή, and then all the ecclesia, and finally everybody, in the number of those who benefit the young. This conversation is a good example of the way in which Socrates, by his method of questioning, would discomfit an adversary. **19. λέγεις** is modified first by the adverb εὖ and then by the object acc. ἀφθονίαν, by καί coördinated with the adverb. **22. ἀλλ' ἄρα**, *well now.* This ironically introduces the last suggestion, which caps the climax of absurdity in the position Meletus has taken. The ecclesiasts included all Athenians over twenty years of age. **23.** μή expects a negative answer. 'The ecclesiasts *don't*, do they?' **26.** καλοὺς κἀγαθούς, *what they ought to be.* See note VI. 25. **28.** πολλήν is emphatic, shown by its position, by the γέ which follows, and by its being placed in the predicate. **31.** εἶναι depends on δοκοῦσι (to be supplied from δοκεῖ, l. 30), of which οἱ μὲν . . . ποιοῦντες is the subject. ὁ διαφθείρων, l. 32, and ὁ . . . οἶός τ' ὤν, l. 33, are in like manner subjects of a δοκεῖ, after which εἷς δέ τις and εἷς μέν τις are predicate. In l. 35 διαφθείρουσιν is no longer under control of δοκεῖ. **38.** οὐ φῆτε, whether you admit it *or deny* it. GMT. 384. οὐ is so closely united with φῆτε as to form but one idea (Lat. *negare*), and so after the conditional particle the οὐ is retained. It really belongs not to φῆτε, but to a suppressed predicate; 'if you say that it is not so.' — πολλή . . . τις εὐδαιμονία, *a great piece of good fortune.* τὶς, although indefinite, by individualizing the case, makes it appear peculiar, and thus heightens the greatness of the good fortune. **40.** διαφθείρει, ὠφελοῦσιν: these indicatives (in place of optatives) ironically assume as true what Meletus has claimed. **43.** ἀμέλειαν . . . μεμέληκεν: the play on words is intended. Meletus, whose name suggests the idea of careful, is careless.

XIII. Meletus again shows his lack of interest in the matter by absurdly charging me with corrupting young men, although I know that if I do they will harm me, and so I must do it unwillingly. But in that case I need not punishment, but instruction.

1. ἔτι, *again*, introduces a second

KITCHEL'S PLATO — 9

proof of Meletus's lack of interest. — ὦ πρὸς Διός, Μέλητε: for various positions of exclamation and address, see XIV. 9 and 10, and the *Crito*, VI. 31. For the exclamation without the address, see XIV. 33; so Μέλητε here is to be taken by itself. (App. III.) **3.** ὦ τάν, *my friend.* **5.** ἀεὶ . . . ὄντας: with participles ἀεί often has the force of *for the time being.* **8.** ὁ νόμος. See note on XII. 1. **14.** τηλικούτου . . . τηλικόσδε: of such an age as they were respectively, hence, *so old . . . so young.* For the age of Meletus, see Int. 26. Notice the chiastic arrangement of the pronouns and the participles agreeing with them. The order is one, three, four, two, instead of the ordinary one. **17.** ἀμαθίας is partitive gen. after the neuter pronoun, denoting degree. H. 730, c; G. 1088; B. 355; Go. 507, c. **18.** ὥστε . . . ἀγνοῶ, *so that I don't know even this.* For the indic. after ὥστε, see H. 927; G. 1450; B. 595; Go. 639, a. **20.** ἀπ' αὐτοῦ. See App. III. **22.** οἶμαι δέ: we have to supply the infin. πείθεσθαι. **23.** ἄκων: understand διαφθείρω. (App. III.) *Unwillingly* because he knew better. Socrates held that knowledge and virtue were identical (Int. 17). If one knew right, he would wish to do right, and so if one knowingly did wrong, it must be involuntary. **25.** καί is redundant, as frequently with πολύς. Here, however, it is noticeable that no new idea is added in ἀκουσίων. (App. III.) — ἁμαρτημάτων is gen. after εἰσάγειν, a verb of judicial action. H. 745; G. 1121; B. 367; Go. 514. **27.** After παύσομαι supply ποιῶν. (App. III.) **29.** ἔφυγες καὶ οὐκ ἠθέλησας: we should reverse the order of the verbs.

XIV. *Not believing in the gods is the peculiarity of Anaxagoras and his school. Meletus is ridiculous in charging this on me. Moreover, he contradicts himself in the indictment.*

3. τούτων is gen. after ἐμέλησεν. **4.** ὅμως, *nevertheless*, implies that what has preceded is a sufficient reply to Meletus's charges, but for all that Socrates will go into some detail. **5.** ἤ: the disjunctive, in this use of it, introduces a direct question which follows a general question, suggesting the answer thereto. **8.** ταῦτα is to be taken with διδάσκων. **10.** ὧν is the objective gen. after λόγος, just as we have λέγειν τινά. No preposition, as περί, is needed in either case. **14.** αὐτὸς . . . νομίζω . . . ἀδικῶ: the direct discourse, instead of acc. and infin. after λέγεις, makes more clear and positive the truth in regard to Socrates' belief. In l. 16, however, we should revert to the indirect, supplying λέγεις νομίζειν, which governs οὔσπερ and ἑτέρους. **20.** ἵνα τί: supply γένηται. **21.** οὐδὲ . . . οὐδέ, *not even* (ne quidem) . . . *nor yet.* The sun and the moon have been worshiped not only by the Greeks (under the names of Apollo and Artemis), but by the common consent of almost all peoples from the earliest times. That Socrates did habitually pay reverence to the sun is shown in the *Symposium* 220 D, where he stands in a brown study all day and the following night until dawn, then προσευξάμενος τῷ ἡλίῳ (*after a prayer to the sun*) he went away. **23.** μά, used in strong protestations and oaths, is in itself neither affirmative nor negative, but is made so by prefixing ναί or οὐ. Here οὐ νομίζει must be supplied. — ὦ ἄν-

δρες δικασταί: this form of address, which Meletus here uses, Plato is careful not to put into the mouth of Socrates. See note on I. 1. **24.** Ἀναξαγόρου: Anaxagoras of Clazomenae (500–428) is reported (Diog. Laert. II.) as having taught that the sun was μύδρος διάπυρος (*a red-hot mass of metal*), and that the moon, like the earth, had οἰκήσεις καὶ λόφους καὶ φάραγγας (*dwellings, ridges, and ravines*). This view of the sun Xenophon (*Mem.* IV. 7, 7) makes Socrates particularly confute. (App. III.) **25.** οὕτω qualifies ἀπείρους as well as καταφρονεῖς. **27.** οὐκ εἰδέναι: οὐκ is used instead of μή because the infin. in the indirect, regularly with ὥστε, stands for the indic. ἴσασι of direct discourse. οὐκ represents their ignorance as an actual fact, and so emphasizes the impudence of Meletus's charge. H. 1023, b; G. 1450 and 1451; GMT. 594; B. 431, 2; Go. 564. **29.** καὶ δὴ καί, *and now in this case.* Here, as usually, these words produce a particular instance of a general statement just preceding. Meletus does despise his auditors (καταφρονεῖς τῶνδε), because he expects them to believe that the young men learned these things from Socrates. — ἅ . . . πριαμένοις: ἅ refers to the doctrines, not the books, because its antecedent ταῦτα can only mean that, and because books at this time probably could not have been bought for a drachma. In an account rendered by certain Athenian officers for building the Erechtheum (407 B.C.) — found in an inscription, *C.I.A.* I., no. 324, pp. 171, 175 — the following item occurs: χάρται ἐωνήθησαν δύο ἐς ἃ τὰ ἀντίγραφα ἐνεγράψαμεν ⊢ | | | |, *two sheets of papyrus were* *purchased, upon which we wrote down duplicates of our accounts, 2 drachmae 4 obols* (Riddell and Dyer). Each sheet of paper thus cost more than the sum here mentioned. On the other hand, the sheets of paper referred to in the inscription may have been of extra size or quality (Birt, *Das antike Buchwesen*, pp. 433 and 434, n. 4). Again, we have no knowledge that copies of the play were sold from the orchestra of the theater of Dionysus, nor from that part of the ἀγορά near which the statues of Harmodius and Aristogeiton stood, which was called ὀρχήστρα. The youth are to be regarded as purchasing these doctrines by paying the admission fee to the theater, where they heard in the plays the ideas of the philosophers either praised by Euripides, who had been especially influenced by Anaxagoras, or ridiculed by Aristophanes. **30.** ἐνίοτε: the plays were given only at stated times and did not all contain these views. — εἰ πάνυ πολλοῦ, *at the most.* Supply πρίαιντο. The ordinary price of admission into the theater was two obols (given as a gratuity to the poorer citizens since the time of Pericles). A drachma, or six obols, was the cost of a season ticket for the three days on which plays were given. **32.** ἄλλως τε καὶ οὕτως ἄτοπα ὄντα, *especially as they are so peculiar*, which would make the theft still more glaring. **33.** οὑτωσί, *even so*, if these views are not mine at all, *do you still claim* (σοὶ δοκῶ) *that your charge is true?* (App. III.) **35.** ἄπιστός γ᾽ εἶ . . . σαυτῷ, *no one can believe you, not even you yourself as it seems to me.* ἄπιστος signifies here, not to be believed, and σαυτῷ is dative of the agent after it;

the statement is, at first, general. Socrates, having shown that Meletus is ridiculously mistaken as to a matter of fact, goes on to prove that he knowingly contradicts himself in the indictment. **41.** διαπειρωμένῳ, *making trial.* — ξυντιθέντι, *by composing.* This participle denotes the means. The object of διαπειρωμένῳ would naturally be the gen. Σωκράτους, instead of which we have the question introduced by ἆρα. — ὁ σοφὸς δή, *the wise man, forsooth.* δή has an ironical force. **42.** ἐμοῦ χαριεντιζομένου: "The use of the gen. after verbs of knowing, seeing, and showing seems to be limited in Attic Greek to a noun joined with a participle" (Riddell). See VII. 31, ᾐσθόμην αὐτῶν οἰομένων. **47.** παίζοντος: H. 732, c; G. 1094, 1; B. 348, 1; Go. 508.

XV. *For if I believe in* δαιμόνια, *I must believe in* δαίμονες, *and so in* θεοί. **2.** ταῦτα λέγειν refers to ἀδικεῖ Σωκράτης ... νομίζων in XIV. 46. **3.** παρῃτησάμην refers to παρίεμαι of I. 26. **8.** μὴ ἄλλα καὶ ἄλλα θορυβείτω, *let him not keep making all sorts of disturbance.* Meletus foresees that Socrates is about to entrap him again, and so tries to avoid answering by making irrelevant outcries. At first Socrates has himself to make answer for him, till finally the court interposes and compels him (l. 16) to respond. ἄλλα is cognate acc. H. 716, b; G. 1054; B. 334; Go. 536, b. **13.** τὸ ἐπὶ τούτῳ γε ἀπόκριναι, *This next question at all events make answer to.* In the phrase τὸ ἐπὶ τούτῳ the preposition denotes succession, literally, 'the one after this.' γέ makes τούτῳ emphatic. The previous questions have been merely illustrative, but the one to come goes right to the point in question. **15.** ὡς ὤνησας, ὅτι, *How you have obliged me, in that.* **18.** Socrates is charged in the indictment with believing in δαιμόνια καινά, but whether they are new or old makes no difference, so far as the main question is concerned. — ἀλλ᾽ οὖν, *at any rate, then.* **21.** καὶ δαίμονας: the reasoning here is sound. δαιμόνια imply δαίμονες. This is quite different from the wrong inference of Meletus, who claims that when Socrates spoke of τὸ δαιμόνιον (meaning merely some divine agency) he meant some new δαίμων, different from any the city believed in. **23.** τοὺς δὲ δαίμονας: this definition is consistent with Greek usage from Homer to Plato. "The word δαίμων was used to denote either θεός or a spiritual being inferior to θεός. Its distinctive meaning as applied to either class is that it denotes such a being *in his dealings with men*" (Riddell). So in l. 26, δαίμονες are called θεοί τινες, *a sort of* gods. **27.** ἂν εἴη: this potential optative, where we should expect a positive indicative (after the two conditions with the indicative), insinuates a conclusion which is so clear that it can afford to be softened in stating it. — ὅ is cognate acc. after the following infinitives, *the riddle and jest which I say you are making.* **29.** φάναι, having the same subject with αἰνίττεσθαι, is in apposition with τοῦτο (l. 27), and explains it. **32.** ὦν for ἐξ ὦν. When the antecedent stands before the relative, a preposition belonging to both usually appears only with the first. H. 1007; G. 1025; B. 487, note. **33.** For μή in indirect discourse, see GMT. 685. **35.** The idea of hybrid or bastard

offspring introduced by νόθοι, l. 31, seems to require the retention of καί and τοὺς ἡμιόνους and the rejection of ἤ in completing the parallel. The present confused state of the text seems to be the result of an attempt to simplify the comparison by introducing ἤ and omitting καί and τοὺς ἡμιόνους. See App. III. **37.** ταῦτα is the object of ἐγράψω, and is further defined by τὴν γραφὴν ταύτην. — ἀποπειρώμενος looks back to διαπειρωμένῳ in XIV. 41. **38.** ἐγκαλοῖς represents a subjunctive of deliberation in direct discourse. H. 932, 2; G. 1490 and 1358; GMT. 677; B. 673; Go. 662. **40.** If οὐ in this line be retained, we have to suppose that in introducing the negative (μήτε) in the next line the speaker forgets how he began. In translating omit οὐ. (App. III.) **42.** ἥρωας is added as the more usual term to convey the idea of δαίμονες (which Socrates uses because Meletus had used δαιμόνια), and to show that his religious belief was quite as full as that of other Athenians. **43.** Notice the emphatic position of οὐδεμία μηχανή ἐστιν, about equivalent to *is absolutely impossible.*

Here, with the discomfiture of the second set of accusers, closes the second episode (or third act of the drama), which is also the end of the δέσις or complication (Int. 3) of this speech regarded as to its dramatic form. In the third episode (or fourth act) which follows begins the λύσις (unraveling or dénouement), in which Socrates pays no further attention to the indictment of his accusers, but under the form of answering certain objections to his life which might be suggested offers his own vindication of it.

XVI. – XXII.   SOCRATES ANSWERS
QUESTIONS HIS OPPONENTS MIGHT
ASK

XVI. *Am I not ashamed of a course
of life likely now to result in my being
put to death ?*

*No good man ought, through fear
of death, to think of doing anything
unjust.*

*Achilles would not play the coward
to save his life.*

1. ἀλλὰ γάρ as in IV. 1, XIV. 1,
etc.   2. οὐ πολλῆς . . . ἀπολογίας,
*does not seem to me to require a long
defense.*   The genitive is predicate of
characteristic.   H. 732, d; G. 1094;
B. 352, 1; Go. 508.   3. καὶ ταῦτα,
even this.   The intensive καί here
depreciates.   Socrates is aware that
he has not adequately considered the
indictment.   He has set it aside on
the ground of the insincerity and
inconsistency of Meletus.   6. ὃ ἐμὲ
αἱρήσει ἐάν περ αἱρῇ, *which will convict me if it does.*   αἱρεῖν in its technical
legal sense.   8. ἀλλ᾽ ἡ . . . φθόνος, in
apposition with τοῦτο, l. 6, repeats the
πολλὴ ἀπέχθεια of l. 5.   It is necessary,
rhetorically, to complete the antithesis
with οὐ Μέλητος οὐδὲ Ἄνυτος, and it is
that of which all the succeeding questions are the unfolding.   Hence its
prominence at the very end of the sentence.   9. πολλοὺς καὶ . . . καί: the
first καί is *also*, as often in comparisons.
The second is in accordance with the
Greek idiom with πολύς, but superfluous in English.   (App. III.)   10. οἶμαι
δὲ . . . οὐδὲν δέ: for the first δέ, in
the principal sentence after a relative
clause, as often in Homer, see H. 1046,
1, c; G. 1422.   The following καί = *too.*
The second δέ is used where our idiom

would have γάρ. — οὐδὲν δὲ . . . στῇ:
Socrates speaks, ironically, as though
he were afraid it would stop with him.
11. εἶτα in questions often expresses
surprise or indignation.   14. ὅτι here
introduces a direct quotation and is
equivalent to quotation marks.   See
note on VI. 12.   16. ὅτου τι καὶ σμικρὸν ὄφελός ἐστιν, *who is worth anything at all.*   Literally, ' of whom there
is even (καί) some little advantage.'
20. τῶν ἡμιθέων is equivalent to τῶν
ἡρώων.   Hesiod *Op.* 158, ἀνδρῶν ἡρώων
θεῖον γένος, οἳ καλέονται ἡμίθεοι.   21. ὁ
τῆς Θέτιδος υἱός: by identifying his
situation with that of Achilles, whom
all the Greeks regarded with enthusiastic admiration, Socrates appeals most
strongly to the kindly judgment of
his auditors.   See, also, *Crito* II. 17.
22. παρά, *in comparison with.*   H.
802, 3, c; G. 1213, 3, d; B. 411, 3, B.
24. θεὸς οὖσα, *goddess that she was,* and
so he knew that what she said would
certainly so happen.   25. οὑτωσί πως:
the words are quoted, not literally,
from *Il.* XVIII. 70 ff.   26. Πατρόκλῳ.
H. 764, 2, b; G. 1163; B. 376; Go.
520, a.   28. ὁ δέ is introduced because
so much has intervened since ὥστε,
l. 23 (which intended to introduce
something like ὠλιγώρησε), thus causing anacoluthon.   33. μὴ αὐτὸν οἴει,
you don't think that he.   μή calls for
a negative answer.   The position of
αὐτόν is emphatic.   39. πρὸ τοῦ αἰσχροῦ, *in preference to disgrace.*   Disgrace is the first thing to be taken into
account so as to avoid it.   By disgrace
Socrates means not ill repute among
men, but real dishonor, the opposite
of τὸ καλόν.

XVII. *No more will I desert my
post at which the god has stationed me.*

Besides, so to do would be to assert that death is an evil, which I do not know, while I know that to disobey the god is an evil. Even if you would let me go I would not alter my ways.

1. ἐγὼ οὖν: Socrates here makes an application to his own case of the principle just laid down and illustrated by the example of Achilles. — ἂν εἴην εἰργασμένος . . . εἰ . . . ἔμενον . . . λίποιμι: in this complex conditional sentence there are two conditions. In the first we have a past tense of the indicative referring to what had actually happened in Socrates' history. In the second we have the optative because it refers to a future action which is regarded as purely theoretical. The conclusion is in view of the combination of these conditions. *I then should have perpetrated a terrible crime if, though when the generals stationed me . . . I remained . . . yet when the god ordered that . . . I should desert my post.* GMT. 509. μέν (l. 2) contrasts οἱ ἄρχοντες with τοῦ δὲ θεοῦ (l. 6) and μέν (l. 4) contrasts τότε with ἐνταῦθα δέ (l. 8). **3.** *Potidaea*, on the isthmus of Pallene in Macedonia, rose against Athens in 432 B.C. Callias the Athenian general was slain; the city was besieged for two years and finally taken by the Athenians. This affair was one of the immediate occasions of the Peloponnesian war. In the battle at Potidaea Socrates saved the life of Alcibiades (Int. 9). *Amphipolis* was an Athenian colony on the river Strymon in Thrace. A battle took place there in 422 B.C. in which the Athenians were defeated and their general Cleon was killed. *Delium* was a sanctuary of Apollo in southeastern Boeotia. At a battle there in 424 B.C. the Athe-

nian general Hippocrates lost his life, and Socrates distinguished himself for coolness and intrepidity. **7.** δεῖν depends upon the idea of commanding in τάττοντος. The reference is of course to the command implied in the oracle of Apollo given to Chaerephon. **9.** λίποιμι τὴν τάξιν: λιποταξίου γραφή, an indictment for deserting one's post, the penalty for which was loss of rights of citizenship (ἀτιμία), would be at once suggested to an Athenian by these words. **10.** δεινόν τἂν εἴη repeats the δεινὰ ἂν εἴην εἰργασμένος of l. 1, regarding now as future what there, by the perfect tense, is regarded as past, not absolutely, but with reference to the future indicated in λίποιμι. **13.** καὶ οἰόμενος . . . οὐκ ὤν: Socrates here introduces the second reason why no good man would do wrong through fear of death. This would be to assume a knowledge which he has not, namely, that death is an evil. This quiet transition in one sentence from one part of the argument to the next is like XIV. 5-8. **16.** οἶδεν has the same indefinite subject with the preceding infinitives. — τὸν θάνατον, brought in before its proper place for emphasis, is the object of οἶδε instead of the subject of τυγχάνει. **17.** οὐδ' εἰ, *whether really*. **19.** τοῦτο is the subject of ἐστίν, after which ἀμαθία αὕτη is predicate. **20.** ἡ ἐπονείδιστος is equivalent to a relative clause, *which has been reproached*, in VI., VII., and VIII. **21.** τούτῳ and καὶ ἐνταῦθα, *here also*, as well as τούτῳ, repeated in l. 23, all make important this matter of death and his not presuming to know about it. (App. III.) **22.** Notice the two indefinites τῷ (dative of respect) and τοῦ. **23.** The suppression after τούτῳ ἂν of φαίην

εἶναι is a graceful evasion of self-asser-
tion. **25.** τῷ βελτίονι, *one's superior.*
27. πρό, *in preference to,* as in XVI.
39. **28.** τυγχάνει has the force of an
adverb, *perchance,* with ὄντα which is
to be translated as the verb. H. 984;
G. 1586; B. 660, note; Go. 585, a.
29. εἴ . . . ἀφίετε: this form of condition is merely logical and expresses no
opinion as to what will happen, but
when the condition reappears in its
final form, in l. 39 (εἰ . . . ἀφίοιτε),
after the intervening adverse considerations, the optative indicates that
the speaker has little expectation of
any such issue. **30.** ὃς ἔφη . . . ἀποκτεῖναί με: apparently a citation from
the preceding speech of Anytus. He
had said probably that Socrates might
have been ignored but now that he has
been brought into court, to acquit him
would be to sanction all he has done.
32. μή: after the negative expression,
μὴ οὐ is generally used. H. 1034; G.
1616; B. 434; Go. 572, a. **33.** εἰ
διαφευξοίμην: the future optative is
never used, except in indirect discourse
as the representative of the future indicative in direct. H. 855, a; G. 1287;
B. 548; Go. 483. The future indicative with εἰ in the direct would have
been the more vivid form used in
threats and warnings, as here. — ἄν
. . . διαφθαρήσονται: ἄν with the
future indicative is very rare in Attic
prose. H. 845; G. 1303; GMT. 197;
B. 563, a; Go. 666, a. To attempt to
take the ἄν with ἐπιτηδεύοντες is merely
an evasion. **37.** ἐπὶ τούτῳ, ἐφ' ᾧτε, *on
this condition however, provided that.*
This repetition emphasizes the condition. For the following infinitives, see
H. 999, a; G. 1460; GMT. 610; B.
645; Go. 567. **41.** For ὅτι, see on

XVI. 14. — ἄνδρες Ἀθηναῖοι: the ὦ
is omitted in the intensity of his feeling.
— ἀσπάζομαι means to salute respect-
fully, φιλῶ, to regard with affection.
Translate, *I respect and love you.*
42. πείσομαι: compare with the words
of Peter, *Acts* V. 29, πειθαρχεῖν δεῖ θεῷ
μᾶλλον ἢ ἀνθρώποις (Int. 9 and 10).
43. ἕωσπερ . . . οὐ μὴ παύσωμαι, *just
as long as . . . I certainly will not
cease.* Socrates makes his negation as
determined as possible. H. 1032; G.
1360; B. 569, 2; Go. 489, b. **47.** πόλεως is in apposition with the gen.
Ἀθηνῶν implied in Ἀθηναῖος. **54.** The
three verbs indicate the zeal of Socrates. **58.** νεωτέρῳ is dative of advantage and differs from the acc. (a
frequent construction after ποιῶ) in
denoting that it is for their benefit he
does as he does. **60.** ὅσῳ . . . ἐστὲ
γένει, *in proportion as you are nearer
of kin to me.* μοῦ is after the adverb
of place. γένει, dative of respect. The
correlative of ὅσῳ is to be supplied
with μᾶλλον. **63.** τῷ θεῷ: verbal
nouns are frequently followed by the
same case as the verbs from which they
are derived. We might have had here
the objective genitive. **66.** πρότερον
naturally calls for ἢ τῆς ψυχῆς, which
is readily supplied from ὡς τῆς ψυχῆς.
67. οὐκ ἐκ χρημάτων ἀρετή: at the
close of the Peloponnesian war the
opposite idea had become prevalent.
Low material standards prevailed (Int.
16). **71.** ταῦτα refers to ταῦτα λέγων,
l. 70. — ἄν εἴη: the optative with ἄν
implies that the condition is improbable. **72.** πρὸς ταῦτα, *in view of this.*
74. ἂν ποιήσοντος . . . εἰ μέλλω . . .
τεθνάναι: in this future conditional
sentence the condition has εἰ with the
periphrastic future because the condi-

tion here refers to something which in time is posterior to the time referred to in the conclusion. In the conclusion we should expect the strongest form of negation (as in l. 43), οὐ μὴ ποιήσω. But to denote that the reason here given is that of the hearers, not that of the speaker, ὡς with the genitive absolute is used. H. 978; G. 1574; B. 656, 3; Go. 593, c. The future participle ποιήσοντος with ἄν represents the future indicative with ἄν in direct discourse, of which only a few cases occur in Attic writers. GMT. 216. See l. 33 of this chapter and compare *Crito* XV. 22.

XVIII. *If you put me to death, you will injure the city more than you will me.*

1. μὴ θορυβεῖτε: enraged at the defiance of their power, many of the audience cry out against the speaker. **2. μὴ θορυβεῖν** is in apposition with the ἅ contained in οἷς (= τούτοις ἅ). **3. γάρ** introduces a reason for ἀκούειν, but γάρ, l. 4, the reason for μὴ θορυβεῖτε, l. 1. **10. θεμιτόν**, *possible in the nature of things.* **11. ἀνδρί**: in the dat. after θεμιτόν, where the acc. (subject of the infinitive) might have been used. — **ἀποκτείνειε μέντ᾽ ἄν ἴσως**, *to be sure he* (that is, ὁ χείρων of the preceding sentence) *might perhaps put him to death.* **12. ἀτιμόω** means to make ἄτιμος, that is to *deprive of civil rights.* **13. ἄλλος τίς που**, *many another man doubtless.* Literally, ' any other.' **14. ἀλλὰ πολὺ μᾶλλον** : understand οἴομαι μέγα κακόν. **15. ἀποκτεινύναι** explains ἅ . . . ποιεῖ. For the form see App. III. **21. γελοιότερον** : what is *very ridiculous* is the comparison of himself to a μύωψ, which idea, although it comes in later, is already suggested in his own mind by

the word he is about to use (προσκείμενον), for which he apologizes. — **πρόσκειμαι** serves as the passive of προστίθημι, used in l. 25, with the additional idea of urgent persistency, *applied to.* **24. ὑπὸ μύωπός τινος** may mean, *by a spur,* or *by a gadfly.* The first meaning is indicated by προσκείμενον, the last by προσκαθίζων (l. 28) and κρούσαντες (l. 32). **26. ἐγείρων** (suggested by ἐγείρεσθαι, l. 24), carrying on the comparison of the μύωψ, is explained by πείθων and ὀνειδίζων, which is what Socrates actually did. **28. προσκαθίζων**, *settling down on you,* as a fly persistently pesters a horse. **31. ἴσως τάχ᾽ ἄν**, *very likely.* — **ὥσπερ οἱ νυστάζοντες ἐγειρόμενοι**, *just like men waked from a nap* by a fly. **32. κρούσαντες**, *slapping me.* This the Athenians would do in *being persuaded by Anytus,* πειθόμενοι Ἀνύτῳ. For the repetition of ἄν in long sentences, see note on I. 33. **36.** With **οἷος** the infinitive is often used. H. 1000; G. 1526; B. 641; Go. 565. **37. οὐ γὰρ ἀνθρωπίνῳ ἔοικε** : having exhausted the idea that he is like a gadfly, Socrates takes up the other part of the conception, given in l. 22, that the god sent him. *For it is not like the way men act.* Such unselfish devotion to the welfare of others could have had only a divine source. **39. τῶν οἰκείων ἀμελουμένων** is the gen. absolute denoting concession. This is more unusual than to neglect one's public duties, referred to in the line preceding. **44. εἶχον ἄν τινα λόγον**, *I should have some reason,* and there would be no need of ascribing my course to divine intervention. (App. III.) **46. τοῦτό . . . ἀπαναισχυντῆσαι**, *to attain to this pitch of shamelessness.* τοῦτο is cognate acc. and is explained by παρα-σχόμενοι μάρτυρα. **49.** ἱκανόν is in predicate agreement with τὸν μάρτυρα.

Having considered the various phases of the question supposed to be raised by his adversaries in XVI. 11, viz., Are you not ashamed to have so conducted yourself as now to be in danger of being put to death? Socrates supposes a second question to be raised against him:

XIX. *Why do I work only in private, never taking part in public affairs?*

The divine voice prevents me.

Had I gone into public life with my idea of duty, I should quickly have been put to death as an inevitable result.

3. πολυπραγμονῶ, *am a busybody.* Socrates thus characterizes his cross-questioning of men in his endeavor to find out whether the oracle of the god was true. To his enemies his conduct appeared that of an inquisitive meddler. (App. III.) — οὐ . . . ἀναβαίνων εἰς τὸ πλῆθος: ἀνά in the compound participle refers to going up to the Pnyx, where the meetings of the people (τὸ πλῆθος) were held. Socrates felt that his mission of making men better could be fulfilled, not by the enactment of any law or the adoption of any particular measures, but only by dealing with them individually. **6.** μοὶ θεῖόν τι καὶ δαιμόνιον γίγνεται, *something godlike and divine comes to me.* φωνή, though appearing in all the manuscripts, is generally bracketed here because it anticipates unnecessarily the φωνή τις of l. 9. On the Socratic Δαιμόνιον, see Int. 10. **7.** ἐν τῇ γραφῇ, when Meletus spoke of the ἕτερα καινὰ δαιμόνια. The charge was a perversion of the truth, for Socrates never regarded or spoke of this voice

as a divinity, but merely as divine. This perversion Socrates here characterizes as a caricature by his use of the word ἐπικωμῳδῶν. **10.** τοῦτο is governed by πράττειν. **15.** πάλαι: the repetition of this word indicates that just as soon as he should have ventured into public activity, immediately he would have endangered his life. He might have begun fifty years before, since the rights and duties of Athenian citizenship began at the age of twenty years. — ἀπολώλη, ὠφελήκη : in the older Attic writers and in Plato the form of the pluperfect in η, instead of ειν, is used. H. 458, a; G. 777, 4; B. 222; Go. 288. **19.** πλήθει = δήμῳ, *populace.* — γνησίως, in a genuine or unfeigned way, *honestly.* **22.** καὶ εἰ, *even if,* signifies that the condition is highly improbable. εἰ καί, *although,* would express a condition which, although not disputed, is represented as of little moment. See XVIII. 21.

XX. *Shown by my experience in refusing to vote to try the ten generals together and in my refusing to go after Leon at the bidding of the Thirty.*

2. οὐ λόγους, ἀλλ᾽ . . . ἔργα: Socrates has facts which he proposes to state; he will not indulge in the idle declamation or the piteous appeals which the dicasts often hear from defendants. **4.** οὐδ᾽ ἂν ἑνί, *not even to any man,* is stronger than οὐδενὶ ἄν. **5.** μὴ ὑπείκων δέ, *although, if I should not yield.* μή shows that the participle is conditional. H. 1025; G. 1612; B. 431, 1; Go. 486. δέ here has a concessive force. (App. III.) **6.** φορτικὰ μὲν καὶ δικανικά, *vulgar and commonplace.* φορτικά from φόρτος (φέρω), a burden. δικανικά = such as are commonly heard in trials in court. **8.** ἐβούλευσα δέ, *but I was elected* (inceptive aor.) *senator*. The senate, or βουλή, consisting of 500 members (50 from each one of the 10 phylae), had for its principal business the preparation of resolutions (προβουλεύματα) to be laid before the ecclesia, or assembly of the people. The 50 members chosen from each tribe presided (πρυτανεύειν) in an order determined by lot, for one tenth of the year, 36 days at least, and while so acting were called πρυτάνεις. One of these 50 each day was chosen by lot ἐπιστάτης, or chief president, who presided at all meetings of the senate and ecclesia. **9.** [ʼΑντιοχίς]: see App. III. — ὅτε: after the victory off the Arginusae islands, 406 B.C. **10.** τοὺς δέκα στρατηγούς: of the ten in office at that time only eight were present at the battle, and of those two did not return to Athens, so only six were actually condemned and put to death. See Grote's *History of Greece*, chap. LXIV. — οὐκ ἀνελομένους: ἀναιρεῖσθαι is the word regularly used to signify the removal of the dead for burial, after a battle. The generals in this case maintained in their defense that the part of the fleet detailed for this purpose (while the main fleet went after the enemy) had been prevented from accomplishing their task by a storm. The great importance attached to a proper burial of the dead is here made very evident. **11.** ἐκ τῆς ναυμαχίας, instead of ἐν τῇ ναυμαχίᾳ, because the idea of removal from or after is also implied. Not only dead bodies are meant, but in this case also those clinging to the wrecks. — παρανόμως, *contrary to law*, because (1) they were not tried before a jury under oath, but in two excited meetings of the ecclesia,

and (2) they were tried ἄθροοι. **12.** ὡς ἐν τῷ ὑστέρῳ χρόνῳ . . . ἔδοξε: according to Xen. *Hellenica* I. 7, 12, καὶ οὐ πολλῷ χρόνῳ ὕστερον μετέμελε τοῖς ʼΑθηναίοις. The Athenians passed a decree that Callixenus, who proposed this illegal measure, and his accomplices, should be brought to trial; but they anticipated their sentence by voluntary exile. **13.** ἠναντιώθην μηδὲν ποιεῖν: this refers to Socrates' refusal as ἐπιστάτης on that day to put the question to vote in the ecclesia, which, it would seem, resulted in the adjournment of proceedings to the next day, when a more pliable ἐπιστάτης presided. The negative in μηδέν is redundant. H. 1029; G. 1615; B. 434; Go. 572. (App. III.) **14.** καὶ ἐναντία ἐψηφισάμην: when Socrates refused to put the question to vote in the ecclesia, they probably appealed to the whole body of prytanes, and in their deliberations Socrates voted against going on with the trial. (App. III.) **15.** ἐνδεικνύναι με καὶ ἀπάγειν, *to denounce and arrest me*. ἔνδειξις was laying information against one who discharged public functions for which he was not legally qualified. The immediate effect of it was to suspend the offender from office. ἀπαγωγή (ἀπάγειν) was a summary process by which a person caught in an unlawful act might be arrested by any citizen and led off to prison. See M. and S. pp. 270–294. — τῶν ῥητόρων: these orators held no office, but as they had access to the public ear, they exercised great influence, often, as here, for the bad. **18.** ἢ μεθʼ ὑμῶν γενέσθαι, *than to take sides with you*. **21.** οἱ τριάκοντα: after the disaster at Aegospotami and the capture of Athens by Lysander in

404 B.C., the Lacedaemonians set over it a hateful oligarchy of thirty, called the Thirty tyrants, or the Thirty. — αὖ, *in turn.* The Thirty now attempted to force Socrates to do through fear something which he regarded as wrong, just as the democracy had in the case of the generals. **22.** The θόλος, or Rotunda where the prytanes dined, was used by the Thirty as a banquet hall during their rule. **23.** Leon, born at Salamis but a citizen of Athens, had gone into voluntary exile to Salamis to avoid falling a victim to the Thirty, who coveted his wealth. For ἀποθνῄσκω as passive of ἀποκτείνω, see H. 820; G. 1241; B. 513; Go. 499, a. **26.** ἀναπλῆσαι, like Lat. *implere,* is used idiomatically of communicating pollution, here *to implicate in their crimes* (αἰτιῶν). **28.** εἰ μὴ ἀγροικότερον ἦν εἰπεῖν, *if it were not too boorish to say so.* This is apologetical for the extreme expression ὅτι ἐμοὶ θανάτου μὲν μέλει . . . οὐδ' ὁτιοῦν, which was very strong language for a defendant in peril of his life to use to his judges. **30.** τούτου δέ is resumptive of τοῦ δέ (l. 29) and makes very prominent Socrates' care to do nothing unjust. — τὸ πᾶν is adverbial. **31.** οὕτως ἰσχυρὰ οὖσα, *although it was so violent.* The later orators affirmed that more than 1500 victims were put to death without trial, by the Thirty. See Grote, chap. LXV. **34.** ᾠχόμην ἀπιών, *I went straightway.* The imp. of οἴχομαι equivalent to the pluperfect and reinforced by ἀπιών, indicates the prompt fearlessness of Socrates in this great peril. **35.** διὰ ταχέων: the rule of the Thirty lasted only eight months, June 404-Feb. 403, when they were expelled by Thrasybulus and the re-

turned exiles. **36.** ἔσονται: the fut. ind. seems to indicate that witnesses were here called to substantiate Socrates' statement. Compare XXII. 36 ff. It may mean simply that the court could have them if it sought for them.

XXI. *Why have some of my pupils turned out so badly? I never had any pupils for whom I assumed responsibility.*

1. ἆρ' οὖν: Socrates passes on to the third question of his opponents by a brief and forcible restatement of the point he has just made. — ἄν . . . διαγενέσθαι, εἰ ἔπραττον: the conclusion is in past time, but the conditions in present, indicating a course of action still pursued. H. 895; G. 1397; B. 606; Go. 646. **5.** οὐδέ, nor would any other man *either.* **7.** τοιοῦτος is explained by ξυγχωρήσας, l. 9. **9.** οὔτε ἄλλῳ οὔτε . . . οὐδενί: here again Socrates welds his argument together by gliding almost imperceptibly from one topic to another. See XIV. 5-8, XVII. 13, etc. **11.** ἐμοὺς μαθητάς: Alcibiades and Critias are probably referred to, whose vices were maliciously said to have arisen from the instruction of Socrates. — Socrates never became the διδάσκαλος of any one, in the technical and ordinary sense of the word, just as in l. 21 he says he never promised μάθημα to any one. He differed in important particulars from the professional teachers of the day. See Int. 14 and 21. **13.** τὰ ἐμαυτοῦ πράττοντος, *attending to my own business.* Socrates disclaims being a busybody, and asserts that conversation with men in obedience to the oracle is his proper business. **15.** οὐδέ denies the two clauses which follow, not singly but taken together, *nor, taking money do I con-verse but if I do not take it, not.* The sophists, on the contrary, taught when they were paid, and when they were not paid did not teach. **17.** ἐρωτᾶν, active where we should use the passive. H. 952, a; G. 1529; B. 641, note. — The conclusion to ἐάν τις βούληται . . . ἀκούειν is παρέχω ἐμαυτὸν ἀκούειν, to be supplied from the line preceding. **18.** τούτων is gen. of the whole after τίς, which alludes to Alcibiades and Critias. **19.** χρηστὸς γίγνεται, *turns out good.* **20.** τὴν αἰτίαν ὑπέχοιμι, incur the blame or *be responsible.*

XXII. *If my followers have been corrupted by me, why do not they them-selves or their relatives now accuse me?*

1. τί δή ποτε, *Why then, pray* (if I am not a regular teacher who pay me). **4.** εἶπον refers to what he said in X. 3. — ἀκούοντες and ἐξεταζομένοις are both supplemen-tary to χαίρουσιν, one agreeing with the subject, the other with the object. H. 980; G. 1578; B. 659; Go. 586, a. **6.** οὐκ ἀηδές : Litotes. A piquant way of saying ἥδιστον. **8.** ἐξ ἐνυπνίων : the importance which Socrates as-cribed to visions is illustrated in Crito II. (Int. 10 and 22). **9.** καὶ . . . καὶ ὁτιοῦν : in the Greek idiom καί is used in both clauses where we translate it only in one, *anything else what-soever.* — θεία μοῖρα, 'divine allot-ment' or, from the human side, *divine will.* **11.** εὐέλεγκτα, *easy to put to the proof* or *test.* **12.** χρῆν . . . κα-τηγορεῖν : for χρῆν with ἄν omitted in a conclusion of unfulfilled obliga-tion, see H. 897; G. 1400, 1 and 2; GMT. 415; B. 567; Go. 460. Here with the present infinitive χρῆν has the force of a present tense = *they*

ought (GMT. 417), and the whole conditional sentence is a present par-ticular one. H. 893; G. 1390; B. 602; Go. 647. The condition is a complex one, one part in present (or past) time (διαφθείρω and διέφθαρκα), the other in the past (ἔγνωσαν), and the con-clusion is in view of the combination of these conditions. Compare XVII. 1–10, where a past and a future con-dition are combined. **16.** εἰ δέ, instead of εἴ τε, introduces an adversative idea which is further emphasized by the in-tensive αὐτοί, *they themselves.* **17.** τῶν ἐκείνων : the genitive of the demon-strative here has the attributive posi-tion as if it were a reflexive. H. 673, b; G. 977, 1 ; B. 457, 2; Go. 554, a. Here it is in the second attributive position. G. 959, 2. **20.** μεμνῆσθαι καὶ τιμωρεῖσθαι : the infinitives de-pend on χρῆν, l. 12. See App. III. — πάντως δέ, *for surely.* δέ, here as often in Homer, is equivalent to γάρ. **22.** Κρίτων, *Crito* was a wealthy friend of Socrates, from whom the dialogue which follows the *Apology* was named. Critobulus, his son, famous for his beauty, was a frequent companion of Socrates. Crito and Socrates were of the same deme, Ἀλωπεκή, of the tribe Ἀντιοχίς. **23.** Lysanias, of the deme Σφηττός in the tribe Ἀκα-μαντίς, was the father of Aeschines (not the orator) called ὁ Σωκρατικός, who wrote Socratic dialogues and became a teacher for money of the Socratic doctrines. **24.** Antiphon (not the orator) was of the deme Κηφισιά of the tribe Ἐρεχθηίς. **25.** τοίνυν, *and then*, is transitional, only slightly infer-ential. — οὗτοι here refers to what follows, contrary to the ordinary state-ments of usage. **26.** ἐν ταύτῃ τῇ

διατριβῇ, *in this intercourse with me.*
Of Nicostratus and Theodotus we
know nothing further. The same
may be said of Paralus and Aeantodo-
rus, mentioned in the following lines.
Demodocus appears in the *Theages* and
Adimantus in the *Republic.* Apollodorus is mentioned frequently in Plato
and Xenophon. **29. καταδεηθείη,** *he
could not dissuade him,* literally, 'ask
of him against' (κατά) what is right or
his better judgment. **34. ἐχρῆν,** like
χρῆν, in l. 12, is a conclusion of unfulfilled obligation with ἄν omitted, here
in past time, as the infinitive is in a
past tense. **36. παραχωρῶ, καὶ λεγέτω :**
to complete the expression, ἐν τῷ ἐμῷ
ὕδατι should be added. The time
allowed to both plaintiff and defendant
was marked by the clepsydra or water
clock, made somewhat like a sand
glass with a narrow orifice through
which the water slowly trickled. **39. τῷ
διαφθείροντι** in apposition with ἐμοί
is ironical. **41. γάρ** introduces the
reason for πάντας βοηθεῖν ἑτοίμους, l. 38.
It is contained in the two clauses beginning αὐτοὶ μέν and οἱ δέ. *They
themselves who have been corrupted*
might be unwilling to confess that they
have been, while *those who are uncor-
rupted* can have no motive for aiding
me but the desire to see justice prevail. **44. ἀλλ᾽ ἤ,** *other than.* This
expression is used after ἄλλος and a
negative (here implied in the rhetorical question τίνα ἄλλον), and is probably a combination of two forms of
construction.

Here closes the main part of the
argument, and the peroration begins.
Dramatically, here is the end of the
fourth act, the epilogue which follows

serving as the fifth act of this dialectic
drama.

XXIII–XXIV. Peroration

XXIII. *I will not attempt to excite
the pity of you judges, for in so doing
I should act unworthily of a good
Athenian.*

2. ἀπολογεῖσθαι, *to offer in my
defense.* **3. ἄν ... ἀγανακτήσειεν ...
εἰ ... ἐδεήθη ... ποιήσω :** the conclusion is in view of the combination
of the two conditions, one in past,
the other in future time. Here, as in
XVII. 1–9, the μέν clause, in which is
the condition in past time, is entirely
subordinate : *some one of you may be
vexed, if* (while he in a less important
case entreated the court in various
ways, yet) *I shall do no one of these
things.* The second condition (ποιήσω) here is stated positively in the
indicative, to show Socrates' unwav-
ering determination. — **ἀναμνησθεὶς
ἑαυτοῦ,** *remembering his own conduct,*
implying that some of the dicasts had,
at one time or other, been defendants.
4. καὶ ἐλάττω, *of much less importance*
because not involving the life of the
defendant. **6. παιδία ... ἀναβιβασάμενος :** in regard to this custom of
defendants bringing their children or
even their wives into court, see M. and
S. p. 933. Compare Aristophanes'
Wasps, 566 ff. **9. ἄρα,** *then,* inferential, 'as is proved by my conduct.' —
καὶ ταῦτα : H. 612, a; G. 1573.
10. ὡς ἂν δόξαιμι, *as would be generally regarded;* literally 'as I should be
thought.' See Liddell and Scott, δοκέω,
II. 5. Socrates did not himself regard
death as the extremest danger. — **τάχ᾽
... ἄν** resumes the τάχα δ᾽ ἄν of l. 3.
14. γάρ gives the reason of the preced-

ing εἰ clause. 'I say "if," *for* I for my part (μέν) do not think it of you.' — εἰ δ' οὖν, *but if as I said any one feels so.* Supply ὑμῶν τις οὕτως ἔχει. Note the epanalepsis at the end of the parenthesis. — ἄν belongs with λέγειν, which represents an optative in the direct discourse. The condition is contained in λέγων. **15.** ἐμοί ... μέν πού τινες καὶ οἰκεῖοι, *I too doubtless have some relatives.* To μέν, ἀλλά in l. 20 is adversative. **16.** τοῦτο αὐτὸ τὸ τοῦ Ὁμήρου is in apposition with the following clause, *just as Homer says*, in *Odys.* XIX. 163, where Penelope asks Ulysses, whom she has not yet recognized, to relate from what race he has sprung. **19.** καὶ υἱεῖς, *yes, sons.* The fact that there are *three* and that two of them are *children* shows that Socrates could have made a very effective appeal had he been willing. The names of the three sons were Lamprocles, Sophroniscus, and Menexenus. That the oldest was still a youth when Socrates was seventy indicates that he did not marry till late in life (Int. 22). **24.** εἰ μὲν θαρραλέως: Socrates might have said positively (as the first reason why he will not appeal to the pity of the judges), "I am not afraid to face death," but such bluntness seemed to him not in good taste, so he only suggested it. Compare XX. 28. **25.** οὖν here and in l. 29, *at all events*, with reference to what precedes by way of confirmation. **26.** οὔ μοι δοκεῖ: here is a slight change in the structure of the sentence (anacoluthon). We should naturally have a participle, οἰόμενος perhaps, co-ordinate with αὐθαδιζόμενος, in l. 23. The intervening clause ἀλλ' ... ἄλλος λόγος occasions

the change. **27.** τοῦτο τοὔνομα is σοφός, which he says is at any rate applied to him, whether truly or falsely; literally, *whether it be true or a lie.* **29.** δεδογμένον γέ ἐστι, *it is generally regarded.* The force of γέ can best be given by specially accenting the preceding word. **30.** εἰ ... τοιοῦτοι ἔσονται is the protasis of a future cond. sentence instead of ἐάν with subjunctive, the indicative making the danger more imminent. This usage is customary in threats and warnings, as here. H. 899; G. 1405; Go. 648, b. **33.** οἵουσπερ, *of just which sort.* According to Plutarch, when Aspasia was tried on a charge of ἀσέβεια, Pericles besought the jurymen with tears and secured her acquittal. **35.** ὡς gives the idea as lying in the minds of the subject, so that οἰομένους is really superfluous. We might have had ὡς πεισομένους. **36.** ἀθανάτων ἐσομένων is the genitive absolute, although we should look for the acc. as in ἐργαζομένους. H. 970; G. 1568; B. 657, note 2. The separate construction here brings the subjects forward more prominently for scorn. **38.** καὶ τῶν ξένων, *even of strangers* who were regarded by the Athenians as inferior to themselves in the sense of propriety and decorum. **41.** οὗτοι: this repetition makes the subject very prominent. **42.** ταῦτα and ὑμᾶς are two accs. after ποιεῖν (H. 725, a; G. 1073; B. 340; Go. 536, c), of which the subject is τοὺς δοκοῦντας ... εἶναι. See App. III.

XXIV. *Also I should act unjustly and impiously.*

1. χωρὶς δὲ τῆς δόξης: the consideration with reference to reputation (πρὸς δόξαν) and τὸ καλόν, which began at XXIII. 25, here ends, and what is just and right is shown to be the chief question. **4. καταχαρίζεσθαι τὰ δίκαια,** *to give judgment by favor,* is added in explanation of τούτῳ, which would otherwise be vague. **5. ταῦτα** refers to τὰ δίκαια, *what justice is.* **6. ὁμώμοκεν:** the form of the oath as found in Demosthenes' speech against Timocrates is ψηφιοῦμαι κατὰ τοὺς νόμους καὶ τὰ ψηφίσματα τοῦ δήμου καὶ τῆς βουλῆς τῶν πεντακοσίων. — **οὐ** must be taken with the principal verb. The infin. would require μή. H. 1023, a; G. 1496; B. 431, note; Go. 564. **8. ἐθίζεσθαι,** "*allow yourselves to be habitutated,* an instance of the semi-middle sense" (Riddell). **12. ἄλλως τε . . . καί** is separated by μέντοι νὴ Δία, the phrase being apparently not yet so fixed a complex as to forbid such an introduction. — **πάντως** is brought in after the interruption and strengthens ἄλλως. The accumulated emphasis brings out the absurdity of his supposed action, under the circumstances. **13. ἀσεβείας φεύγοντα ὑπό,** *when a defendant on a charge of impiety brought by.* φεύγοντα is equivalent to the passive διωκόμενον and so is followed by ὑπό with gen. of the agent. See note on III. 16. ἀσεβείας is gen. of crime after the verb of judicial action. See note on XIII. 25. **20. καὶ τῷ θεῷ:** the peroration ends, like the prologue (II. 45), with an expression of confidence in God.

So far the order of trial has been, first, the speech of Meletus, supported by the other accusers, followed by this defense of Socrates. Then the dicasts decide that Socrates is guilty, by a vote of probably 281 to 220. Next in order, as this was an ἀγὼν τιμητός in which the penalty was not fixed by law, Meletus in a speech urges, as the τίμησις, the penalty of death named in the indictment (see note on XI. 7), to which Socrates replies, suggesting a counter penalty or ἀντιτίμησις (Int. 28).

XXV. EXORDIUM. *I wonder that the majority against me is so small.*

1. τὸ . . . ἀγανακτεῖν depends on ξυμβάλλεται, as if it were a word of prevention. We should expect here πρός or εἰς. The speaker did not, to begin with, have in mind the whole sentence. He puts first the subject he is to speak of, and then does not fully provide for its construction. *That I am not annoyed . . . many other things contribute.* The subject of the infin. is contained in μοι, l. 3. **2. ὅτι . . . κατεψηφίσασθε** explains ἐπὶ . . . γεγονότι and informs the reader, at the beginning of this second part, of the action which has just been taken. **6. οὕτω** is separated by the preposition from the adjective it modifies. **8. τριάκοντα** is the reading of the best manuscripts (App. III.). τρεῖς, which is in some manuscripts and was generally accepted formerly (see Grote and Curtius in their histories), was a variation doubtless introduced because so large a number as thirty seemed at variance with παρ' ὀλίγον. τριάκοντα better accords with the probable number (501) of the jury (Int. 28), if we accept the statement of Diogenes Laertius (II. 41) that 281 dicasts pronounced Socrates guilty. Then, to be exact, 31 votes *cast differently* (μετέπεσον) would reverse the verdict in the customary jury of 501; whereas, reading τρεῖς, three votes cast differently would give a minority of 275 and the improbable number 556 for the whole jury. **9.** Μέλητον . . . ἀποπέφευγα: the argument is: if Meletus, Anytus, and Lyco secured only 281 votes against him, Meletus alone would have secured only one third as many, not 100, the fifth part of the whole jury, which the prosecution must obtain or be liable to penalty. This penalty was affixed so as to prevent wanton litigation, in an age when suits at law were too readily resorted to. (App. III.) **12.** ἀνέβη: the singular because Anytus was much the more important of the two. Anytus and Lyco were back of Meletus, although apart from this word and the citation perhaps in XVII. 30 there is little to indicate it. **13.** ὦφλε χιλίας δραχμάς: the penalty included, besides the 1000 drachmae, deprivation of the right to bring an action of this sort in the future (M. and S. p. 951).

XXVI. *The penalty ought to be what I deserve, which I think is maintenance as a benefactor in the Prytaneum.*

1. τιμᾶται . . . μοι, *proposes as my penalty*. The middle is used of plaintiff or defendant, as parties immediately interested. The active is used of the judge or court. — θανάτου is gen. of value. H. 746, b; G. 1133; B. 367, note; Go. 514, a. **2.** τίνος ὑμῖν, *at what, pray*. The dat. is ethical. **3.** ἤ: the disjunctive, in this use of it, introduces a question which suggests the answer to a preceding question, as in XIV. 5. — τῆς ἀξίας: supply τιμῆς. **4.** παθεῖν ἤ ἀποτεῖσαι: the regular formula used in such cases, παθεῖν referring to corporal infliction, ἀποτεῖσαι to other penalty. — ὅ τι μαθών, *because I made up*

my mind, is the indirect form of τί μαθών. H. 968, c; G. 1566; GMT. 839 (b); B. 653, note 4. The literal translation is, 'because having learned what,' μαθών denoting the causal relation. **5.** With ὧνπερ οἱ πολλοί supply ἐπιμελοῦνται from ἀμελήσας. (App. III.) **7.** τῶν ἄλλων, *as well* or *besides*, since δημηγορία, *popular oratory*, was not an office. H. 705; G. 966, 2; B. 492, note 2. **8.** ξυνωμοσιῶν καὶ στάσεων, *political factions* (which were rife in Athens under the Thirty as during the Peloponnesian war) *and revolutions*. **9.** ἐπιεικέστερον, *too good* a man, in the acc. rather than nom. because the subject ἐμαυτόν is expressed. H. 940, b; G. 910; B. 630, note. **12.** ἐπί governs τὸ εὐεργετεῖν. — ἰών is repeated in ᾖα. This repetition in connection with ἰόντα and ᾖα of lines 10 and 11 emphasizes Socrates' restless activity; as he says in l. 5, οὐχ ἡσυχίαν ἦγον. (App. III.) **17.** ἔσοιτο: the fut. opt. is only used in indirect discourse, either actual or implied, as here. See note on XVII. 33. **19.** τί οὖν εἰμι ἄξιος repeats the question of l. 4, resuming the argument after the intervening lengthy characterization of himself. **21.** εἰ δεῖ γε, *if it is really necessary*. γέ, emphasizing δεῖ, feigns a reluctance to fix his penalty at what he does in what follows. **23.** πένητι εὐεργέτῃ, δεομένῳ: these words bring out the points which the award should be suited to. εὐεργέτης τοῦ δήμου was an honorary title conferred on those who had deserved well of the state. It was coveted even by kings. **25.** μᾶλλον would naturally be followed by ἤ, but οὕτως controls the form of what follows. The force of μᾶλλον may be freely given by 'so *exactly* suitable.' **26.** The Prytaneum must be distinguished from the θόλος (see XX. 22), where the prytanes of the senate dined. It was at the foot of the Acropolis, near the agora, and in it benefactors of the city, some on account of their own deserts as the victors in the Olympic and other games, others for what their ancestors (for instance, Harmodius and Aristogeiton) had done, were dined at the public expense. **27.** ἵππος is a single horse (κέλης), a chariot and two horses, and ζεῦγος one with four horses. **30.** οὐδὲν δεῖται, because only the very wealthy could afford to compete with horses in the great panhellenic festivals and, by being crowned as victors in them, so bring glory to their cities.

XXVII. *I will not fix my penalty at anything bad, least of all at exile.*

2. περὶ τοῦ οἴκτου refers to XXIII. **3.** ἀντιβόλησις is the same as ἱκετεία. **5.** ἑκὼν εἶναι differs from ἑκών in generally standing in a negative sentence. The infin. is in loose construction. H. 956; G. 1535; B. 642, 1; Go. 569. For μηδένα with the infinitive in ind. discourse, see note on XV. 33. So also in l. 12. **8.** ἄλλοις ἀνθρώποις: this was true of the Spartans. **13.** ἀδικήσειν and the fut. infinitives following represent the fut. indic. in direct discourse, πολλοῦ δέω being here equivalent to 'I think that I will not,' *I do not intend to.* H. 855, a; G. 1276; GMT. 113; B. 549; Go. 570, b. **15.** τί δείσας gives the reason of the infinitives which precede. **16.** ὁ φημι, viz. in XVII. **17.** ἔλωμαι ὧν ... ὄντων: from the fuller expression ἔλωμαί τι τούτων ἃ εὖ οἶδα ὅτι κακά ἐστιν, by the abbreviation of

τούτων ἅ to ὧν and changing κακά ἐστιν to κακῶν ὄντων in agreement with the relative, εὖ οἶδ' ὅτι being retained with a simply adverbial force in which ὅτι is superfluous. ἔλωμαι is the subjv. of deliberation. H. 866, 3; G. 1358; B. 577; Go. 471. So τιμήσωμαι in l. 24. **20.** τοῖς ἕνδεκα: the Eleven were the magistrates (one from each of the ten tribes, and a secretary) to whom persons condemned by public trial were handed over for punishment. See Int. 28 and App. III. **21.** ἀλλά, *well then,* implying that the preceding suggestion is not to be thought of, introduces another which is negatived by ἀλλά in the next line. **22.** νῦν δή, *just now.* **23.** ἐκτείσω is the subjunctive of deliberation in the dependent sentence. H. 866, 3; G. 1358; B. 672; Go. 661. **24.** τιμήσαιτε: the active here because its subject is the court. **30.** ἄλλοι ... οἴσουσι no longer depends on ὅτι as would be natural, but is made more forcible by being put ironically as a direct question. **31.** ἄρα, *do you suppose.* **32.** καλός, *a fine thing.* Ironical and by its position very emphatic. ζῆν is added to explain καλὸς ... βίος. **33.** ἄλλην ... ἀμειβομένῳ, *exchanging one city for another;* literally, *from* another, implying motion out of. The expression would suggest to the audience the wandering life led by the sophists.

XXVIII. *I could not in exile keep silent. The god forbids, nor do I wish it. But I am willing, since my friends advise it, to propose a fine of thirty minae.*

2. ἡμῖν, *pray;* the ethical dat. enlivens the question. **3.** τουτί is to be taken with πεῖσαι as cognate acc.

6. ὡς εἰρωνευομένῳ, *on the ground that I am jesting.* Socrates' irony, in which he was a master, consisted in pretending ignorance (or impotence, as here) in order to provoke or confound an antagonist (Int. 24). **7. ἐάν τε** introduces the second reason of χαλεπώτατον, l. 3. **11. ὁ δὲ ἀνεξέταστος βίος οὐ βιωτός** is still under the influence of ὅτι, l. 7. **12.** ταῦτα resumes and makes emphatic the reason just given. — δέ after ταῦτα contrasts it decidedly with the former reason advanced. — λέγοντι repeats the condition in ἐάν τ' αὖ λέγω, l. 7. **14.** ἅμα introduces as a new co-ordinate thought that which has been implied in l. 11 (where to live without cross-examining men is regarded as κακόν), and which from the outset Socrates has made the main principle in fixing his own penalty. **16.** γάρ introduces the reason of what is implied in the line preceding, namely, 'Anything that is not really bad I am willing to accept,' *for, if I had money, I would propose as my penalty as large a fine as I should be likely to pay.* **17.** ὅσα ἔμελλον ἐκτείσειν is an apodosis with ἄν omitted. See note on IV. 20. The protasis is contained in ἐτιμησάμην, which is itself the apodosis to εἰ ... ἦν ... χρήματα. — γάρ brings the payment of money in under the general principle he has fixed to govern him in this matter. To pay money would not be a real κακόν. **18.** εἰ μὴ ἄρα, *unless perchance.* The conclusion to this condition is to be supplied after νῦν δέ, *but now* I do not name any sum of money. The apparent contradiction in Socrates saying first that he has no money and then fixing his penalty at a money

payment is explained by the thought in his mind, that the little money he could pay would be too little to be accepted, as indeed a mina of silver, **μνᾶν ἀργυρίου** (about $18), was. His wealthy friends have to come to his aid. **24.** ἐγγυᾶσθαι depends upon the idea of saying in κελεύουσι.

Here the judges vote the penalty of death, and the formal trial is at an end. According to Diogenes Laertius (II. 5) the majority against Socrates was eighty votes greater than on the question of his guilt. Some delay on the part of the officers gives to him the opportunity to speak these last words to those judges who chose to remain and listen. Rarely would a man condemned to die have the equanimity, if he had the opportunity, so to speak.

XXIX. (To those who voted against him.) *You have brought disgrace on the city and yourselves, not on me.*

1. οὐ πολλοῦ ... χρόνου: the time between the present moment and the time of his natural death. **2.** ὑπό after ὄνομα ἕξετε, which is equivalent to a passive. **8.** πόρρω ... τοῦ βίου, *far on in life.* H. 757; G. 1149; B. 360; Go. 518, b. **14.** ὥστε ἀποφυγεῖν: the consequence is aimed at as a purpose. GMT. 587, 3. So also ὥστε διαφεύγειν in l. 32. **16.** τόλμης in a bad sense, *audacity.* **18.** θρηνοῦντός τέ μου, *had I wept.* Genitive absolute denoting condition. **26.** ἄλλον οὐδένα: Socrates possibly alludes to Anytus, who, Diodorus says, had become involved in an action for προδοσία, because when he had been sent with thirty triremes to save Pylos from the

Lacedaemonians he had failed to do so, but had escaped conviction by bribing the jury. **29.** γέ is depreciatory of τὸ ἀποθανεῖν in comparison with πονηρίαν, l. 35. **33.** μὴ οὐ . . . ᾖ χαλεπόν, *I suspect that this may not be a difficult thing.* For μὴ οὐ expressing a cautious negation or a suspicion that something may not be true, see H. 867; G. 1350; GMT. 265; B. 569, 1; Go. 474, a. **35.** θᾶττον γὰρ θανάτου θεῖ: notice the alliteration. **36.** ἅτε with the participle denotes the real reason as ὡς does an alleged one. **39.** ὑφ' ὑμῶν as if ὄφλων were passive, *at your hands.* They are characterized by being contrasted with ὑπὸ τῆς ἀληθείας in l. 40. — θανάτου δίκην ὄφλων, *incurring the penalty of death.* By the introduction of δίκην the judicial penalty is distinguished from the moral in the next line. ὀφλισκάνω may be followed by the cognate acc. of the penalty or by the genitive with or without δίκην. H. 745; G. 1122; B. 367; Go. 514. For the form ὄφλων, see App. III. **40.** ὠφληκότες: the perfect denotes that these have already incurred their penalty. **41.** καὶ οὗτοι, *and they as well.* **42.** ταῦτα μέν, *these things* connected with my trial are contrasted with τὸ δὲ, in XXX. 1. — που ἴσως, *I suppose perhaps.* This implies strongly that the necessity (ἔδει) lay in part at least in their own weakness and prejudice. — καὶ ἔδει σχεῖν, *really had to turn out* so. σχεῖν is the inceptive aorist. **43.** μετρίως, *all very well.* The result, both in his case and theirs, is the due measure and expression of their respective characters.

XXX. *You have not escaped the necessity of giving account of your lives.*

1. τό goes with μετὰ τοῦτο. The acc. is adverbial. δέ is adversative to μέν in XXIX. 42. **3.** ἐν ᾧ . . . χρησμῳδοῦσιν: "The opinion which connects prophetic enlightenment with the approach of death has maintained its hold in all ages. Patroclus foretells Hector's death, *Il.* XVI. 851, and Hector the death of Achilles, *Il.* XXII. 358, instances to which classical writers often appeal; thus Xen. *Apol.* 30, ἀνέθηκε μὲν καὶ Ὅμηρος ἔστιν οἷς τῶν ἐν καταλύσει τοῦ βίου προγιγνώσκειν τὰ μέλλοντα, βούλομαι δὲ καὶ ἐγὼ χρησμῳδῆσαί τι, Cic. *De Div.* I. 30, *Facilius evenit appropinquante morte ut animi futura augurentur; ex quo et illud est Calani, de quo ante dixi, et Homerici Hectoris qui moriens propinquam Achilli mortem denuntiat.* So Shakspeare, *Rich. II.* Act II. Sc. i. (Gaunt), 'Methinks I am a prophet new inspir'd; And thus expiring do foretell of him'" (Riddell). **5.** ἀπεκτόνατε: that is spoken of as already done which by their sentence the dicasts had made sure. **7.** With οἴαν understand τιμωρίαν, after which we should have expected τετιμώρησθε, making it a cognate acc. We have instead ἀπεκτόνατε, which more definite word makes evident the nature of the revenge they had taken. As it stands, the cognate acc. is after the analogy of μάχην with νικᾶν. Translate, *the punishment you have inflicted upon me in condemning me to death.* **10.** πλείους ἔσονται ὑμᾶς οἱ ἐλέγχοντες: the fact that this prophecy of Socrates was not fulfilled and yet is introduced here by Plato is adduced as evidence that he followed pretty closely the very expressions of Socrates. **16.** οὔτε πάνυ δυνατή, *neither at all practicable.* No-

tice the chiastic arrangement of the
predicate adjectives. **18.** κολούειν, *to
put down.* Literally, 'to cut short.'
21. ἀπαλλάττομαι, *I bid you farewell.*
Literally, 'I rid myself of.'

XXXI. (To those who voted for
him.)

*Death must be a good thing, for
the divine voice has not kept me back
from it.*

2. ὑπέρ, *in behalf of.* Socrates takes
the side of death and in what follows
makes a plea for it. **3.** οἱ ἄρχοντες
are the same as οἱ ἔνδεκα, *the officers.*
4. οἱ ἐλθόντα κτλ. is a euphemism
for prison. — ἀλλά is used not infrequently before the imperative or the
subjunctive of command to give greater
vivacity. See *Crito* IV. 11. **5.** οὐδὲν
γὰρ κωλύει: Socrates, in these words,
assures his friends that although just
condemned to death, a time when most
men are overcome with grief and agitation, his spirit is unperturbed, and he
is not only perfectly able to go on and
converse in a philosophic strain upon
the death which threatens him, but he
is especially desirous to comfort them
by so doing. Notice that γάρ occurs
five times in as many succeeding
clauses. **6.** ἕως ἔξεστιν, *while it is
allowed,* that is by the officers. **7.** ὡς
φίλοις οὖσιν, *in the assurance that
you are friends.* ὡς indicates that the
reason is one cherished in his own
mind. It is his own feeling about the
matter which is the chief thing. Generally ὡς with the participle denotes
that which is thought by some other
person than the speaker. H. 978; G.
1574; B. 656, 3; Go. 593, c. **9.** ὀρθῶς
ἂν καλοίην: here at last appears the
reason why Socrates has continually up
to this point addressed the jurors by the

expression which ignored their official
position. **12.** πάνυ (the second one)
modifies σμικροῖς and is in turn modified by the intensive καί. **13.** ὀρθῶς
refers, as we see from what follows,
not to the moral quality of what he
was at any time about to do, but to
the consequences to himself of intended
actions. (Int. 10.) **15.** ἅ is at once
the object of οἰηθείη and the subject
of νομίζεται. **16.** ἕωθεν: the session
of the court began early in the morning. M. and S. p. 946, 2. **20.** λέγοντα
μεταξύ, *in the midst of what I was
saying.* The adverb here really modifies the principal verb. H. 976, a;
G. 1572; GMT. 858; B. 655; Go.
592. **25.** ἡμεῖς: as if he shared in the
opinion, which he did not. **29.** ἀγαθὸν
(like εὖ) πράττειν, *to experience something good.*

XXXII. *In itself death is either like
a long sleep or it is the going to be
where are the just, the gifted, the unjustly condemned, and those who would
particularly repay investigation, with
whom to associate would be unspeakable
happiness.*

1. καὶ τῇδε, *in the following way
also,* that is, looking at the nature of
death itself. In the preceding chapter
death was surmised to be a good thing
from something external, namely, the
behavior of the divine voice in regard
to it. **2.** αὐτό, *in itself.* **3.** οἷον is
equivalent to τοιοῦτον ὥστε, and εἶναι
and ἔχειν τὸν τεθνεῶτα depend on it.
The subject of οἷον (supply ἐστί) is τὸ
τεθνάναι implied. **6.** τῇ ψυχῇ is dat.
of advantage, to be taken with τυγχάνει οὖσα. — τοῦ τόπου is gen. of separation after the verbal substantive
μετοίκησις. In ἐνθένδε the idea of
motion from is repeated redundantly.

7. εἴ τε has εἰ δ' αὖ, l. 21, introducing the second member of the alternative. **10.** ἄν belongs to εὑρεῖν, l. 17, where it is repeated, as well as in l. 16. Introduced thus early it shows that the whole sentence is to be hypothetical. — εἰ . . . δέοι: the condition is so long and interrupted that δέοι is repeated in l. 13. For the same reason the idea of ἐκλεξάμενον and ἀντιπαραθέντα is gathered up and repeated in σκεψάμενον, l. 14. **16.** οἶμαι here repeats οἶμαι of l. 10, this being necessary because so much has intervened that otherwise the dependence of the infin. εὑρεῖν would not be clear. This whole sentence illustrates the flexibility and grace of the conversational style. The thought is somewhat defective, because the pleasure of dreamless sleep is realized by a man only after he has waked, whereas, by this supposition, from death a man is not to wake, but is always to remain in unconsciousness. — μὴ ὅτι, *not to say.* H. 1035, a; G. 1504; B. 442, note. **17.** τὸν μέγα βασιλέα: the life of the king of Persia was regarded by the Greeks as one of great felicity. **18.** πρός, *in comparison with.* **23.** ἄρα, *then,* inferential from the admission that death is a migration from the earth to some other place. **26.** δικαστῶν is in the gen. because the participle is, upon which the infinitive depends. H. 940, a; G. 931; B. 631; Go. 571, c. **28.** Μίνως τε καὶ Ῥαδάμανθυς: the proper names agree with the relative οἵπερ. We should expect them in the acc. in apposition to δικαστάς. Minos, Rhadamanthys, and Aeacus, sons of Zeus, because of their regard for justice while living, were placed as judges in the infernal regions. Triptolemus,

son of Eleusis, is here reckoned by Plato (though not generally) as also one of the judges, partly because of his connection with the Eleusinian mysteries and also because he gave laws as well as taught agriculture to the Athenians. Notice the ascending interest in the personages mentioned in this passage, as well as in the sort of intercourse. He is to find the judges, associate with the poets (whose works Socrates was especially acquainted with and fond of). He is to compare experiences with those who, like himself, had died of unjust judgment, while, last and chiefest delight of all, he is to continue there as here his scrutinizing conversations with those who would best repay scrutiny. **32.** ἐπὶ πόσῳ ἄν τις δέξαιτ' ἂν ὑμῶν; *How much would any one of you give?* The condition is contained in ξυγγενέσθαι. **33.** γάρ introduces the reason why he thinks they would give a good deal, which is implied in the preceding question. **35.** ἔμοιγε καὶ αὐτῷ: the intensives indicate the especial fitness to the speaker of such a state of things. **36.** Παλαμήδει καὶ Αἴαντι: Palamedes, the son of Nauplius, was stoned to death by the Grecian army at Troy because it believed that he had betrayed it to Priam, in whose name Odysseus had caused a letter to be sent to Palamedes. This story is posthomeric. Ajax, by an unjust decision, did not receive the arms of Achilles which he contended for with Odysseus, and so took his own life. This account, founded on *Odyss.* XI. 543 ff., we find fully developed in a tragedy of Sophocles. **38.** ἀντιπαραβάλλοντι: the participle is supplementary. GMT. 901. **39.** οὐκ ἂν ἀηδὲς εἴη, at the close of the long sentence, repeats θαυμαστὴ ἂν εἴη at the beginning and has the same subject (ἡ διατριβή), causing anacoluthon but making the sentence periodic. (App. III.) **40. τὸ μέγιστον** is explained by the infinitive clause in apposition with it, which follows. **44. τὸν . . . ἀγαγόντα** is equivalent to a substantive, though it is a participle governing the acc. **45. ἢ ἄλλους μυρίους . . . εἴποι**, *or countless others one might mention.* This whole clause, taken together, is the fourth object of ἐξετάσαι. **47. ἀμήχανον . . . εὐδαιμονίας**, *an unspeakable* (lit. 'impracticable') *degree of happiness.* For the gen., see H. 730, c; G. 1088; B. 355; Go. 507, c. **48. πάντως οὐ δήπου τούτου γε ἕνεκα**, *Surely not, I suppose, for that.* The sarcasm is heightened to the utmost. **49. εὐδαιμονέστεροι**, *more fortunate* in that no one there would wish to put them to death for conversing, and they could not if they would, for ἀθάνατοί εἰσιν.

XXXIII. PERORATION. *You who have voted for me, be of good cheer therefore. You who have condemned me, treat my sons as I have treated you, and all will be right between us. It is now time for me to go away to death.*

3. The position of **τοῦτο** after ἔν τι is emphatic. Literally, 'one certain thing, namely this,' *this one thing in particular.* ἀληθές is pred. **8. πραγμάτων**, in a bad sense, *troubles.* — βέλτιον ἦν is a conclusion of unfulfilled obligation, with ἄν omitted. H. 897; G. 1400, 1; B. 567, 1; Go. 460. **13. τοῦτο** is cognate acc., as is ταὐτὰ in l. 15. **15. ἡβήσωσι**, *they shall have come of age.* The aor. is inceptive. **22. αὐτός τε καί** is epexegetical of ἐγώ. **25. πλὴν ἤ** is pleonastic, like ἄλλ' ἤ in V. 13. Socrates closes his peroration, as he did his prologue, with an expression of confidence in the divine guidance.

Here the Eleven lead Socrates away to prison.

NOTES ON THE CRITO

The circumstances under which this dialogue took place are explained in Int. 34.

Title, ΚΡΙΤΩΝ. This name of a person given by Plato himself to this Dialogue reminds us of the titles of the Greek tragedies, and was doubtless selected with reference to the dramatic form of the work. [ἢ περὶ **πρακτέου**, **ἠθικός**] : See on the sub-title to the *Apology*, p. 117.

For the reason why a list of the *dialogi personae* is prefixed, as to a play, see Int. 3 and 36.

The introduction is the dramatic prologue and is entirely dramatic in form, the conversation being given directly. In it the characters are introduced, and the situation is developed.

I.-II. INTRODUCTION. *Socrates must die on the third day.*

I. (Crito coming to the prison early in the morning, when Socrates awakes, says) *O Socrates, what a fortunate disposition you have, in that you can now sleep so sweetly. To-morrow probably you will be put to death.*

1. Κρίτων, *Crito* is mentioned twice in the *Apology;* as a contemporary and fellow-demesman of Socrates, in XXII. 22, as a wealthy friend, in XXVIII. 22. — **ἤ**: the disjunctive in the direct question following a general question suggests the answer thereto. So also in l. 34. **4. πηνίκα,** *what hour,* is more explicit than πότε. — **μάλιστα** is used as with numerals to indicate that only an approximation (though as near as possible to the exact truth) is intended. **5. βαθύς,** *early,* literally 'deep,' as if going back from sunrise far into the beginning of light. **7. ὑπα-κοῦσαι,** *to let you in,* literally, 'to hear to you' when you knocked; used of a janitor. The marvel was that Crito was admitted so early. **9. καί τι καὶ εὐερ-γέτηται ὑπ' ἐμοῦ,** *and, besides, he has received a trifle from me.* τί is cognate acc. of the neut. pronoun, retained in the passive. H. 725, c; G. 1239; B. 340, 1; Go. 536, c. **13. εἶτα** in questions often expresses wonder, as here. **16. ἐν τοσαύτῃ . . . λύπῃ,** *at once so sleepless and so distressed.* The position of τέ shows that τοσαύτῃ is to be taken both with ἀγρυπνίᾳ and λύπῃ. **17. ἀλλὰ καί,** *but further-more,* adding another reason why he did not wake Socrates. **18. ἐπίτηδες,** *purposely.* The purpose is indicated by the ἵνα which follows. **19. διάγῃς,** in the subj. instead of opt. though after

a past tense, the time when Crito conceived the purpose being indicated. H. 881, a; G. 1369; GMT. 318; B. 674; 659, a. **20. τοῦ τρόπου** is gen. of cause, which relation is expressed at the end of the sentence by the clause with ὡς, equivalent to ὅτι οὕτως. **23. πλημμελές,** *inconsistent,* from πλήν and μέλος, 'out of tune,' not in harmony with his advanced years. **27. μὴ οὐχί**: the double negative because ἐπιλύεται (used in the sense of preventing) has a negative force. H. 1034, a; G. 1616; GMT. 811; B. 435; Go. 572, a. Had the construction, τοῦ with the infinitive, been used, the negative would have been omitted. **29. ἀλλὰ τί δή,** *but why, pray?* returns to the question of line I. **33. ἐν τοῖς** (supply φέρουσιν) strengthens the superlative. **34. τίνα ταύτην**: the full expression would be τίς ἐστιν αὕτη ἡ ἀγγελία ἣν φέρεις; — **τὸ πλοῖον**: the sacred ship, in the absence of which the city was kept ceremonially clean, and no condemned criminal might be put to death. Int. 34 and *Phaedo* I. The words οὗ . . . με were not necessary for Crito, but are inserted for the reader. **36. μέν** has no δέ corresponding to it. The isolated μέν is often used to give force to assertions made by a person respecting himself in which opposition to other persons is implied. **38. Σουνίου**: "Sunium's marbled steep" (Byron's *Isles of Greece*) is the southern headland of Attica, on which are now the ruins of a temple of Athena. It is about twenty-five miles from Athens. — **ἐκ τούτων,** repeating the ἐξ ὧν of l. 37, must refer to things, and so **τῶν ἀγγέλων is** bracketed (App. III.).

II. *Judging from the dream I have just had, my execution will not take place till the day after to-morrow.*

1. τύχῃ ἀγαθῇ, *may fortune favor it*, a form often used by the Greeks to invoke a blessing upon a course of action, like Lat. *quod bene vertat.* H. 776; G. 1181. Socrates' hopeful spirit is contrasted by ἀλλά with the sorrowful tone in which Crito has spoken. **5.** γάρ introduces the first step in the reason why he does not think ἥξειν αὐτὸ τήμερον. The second is 'I am sure from my dream that I am not to die till day after to-morrow.' Therefore the ship will not come till to-morrow. **7.** γέ τοι δή is affirmative with some restrictions, '*At all events they say so* who have control of these matters' (referring to the Eleven). **8.** τοίνυν, *well then.*— ἐπιούσης ἡμέρας refers to the *oncoming day* in whose dawn they are. **9.** τῆς ἑτέρας is the other of two, so not 'to-day' but *to-morrow.* **11.** νυκτός is gen. of time. ὀλίγον πρότερον is inserted to indicate that the dream was after midnight, and so to be regarded as true. — καὶ κινδυνεύεις . . . με, *and probably* (implying that possibly the dream may have come before Crito reached the prison) *very opportunely you did not awake me.* **13.** δὴ τί, *what, pray?* **15.** λευκά : white garments are generally ascribed to supernatural appearances. See *Matt.* xxviii. 3, " His countenance was like lightning and his raiment white as snow." **17.** ἤματι . . . ἵκοιο: from *Iliad* IX. 363, only there the last word is ἱκοίμην. They are the words of Achilles, who in his anger at Agamemnon declares that he will return to his home in Thessaly, a two days' sail across the Aegean. Socrates re-

gards them as applying to his passage " from this place here to another." *Apol.* XXXII. 6. **19.** μὲν οὖν (Lat. *immo vero*) corrects by conceding still more, *say rather.*

Here ends the dramatic prologue. The next three chapters, in which the discussion begins, are the second act in this dialectic drama.

III.–V. CRITO URGES SOCRATES TO ESCAPE FROM PRISON

III. *If you refuse, the multitude will blame us as caring for money more than for you.*

1. γέ, *yes*, as often in replies. **2.** ἔτι καὶ νῦν, implying that he has often been importuned, but still there is opportunity. **3.** οὐ μία, *not one only*, but twofold, as he goes on to specify. **4.** τοῦ ἐστερῆσθαι: see App. III. **5.** οὐδένα μή with the fut. expresses emphatic negation. H. 1032; G. 1360; B. 569, 2; Go. 489, b. **6.** ὡς . . . ὤν, *although I was able, they would say*, to save you. ὡς (really repeating the δόξω of l. 6) implies that what is said in the concessive ὤν would be true only in the view of the many, and not really so. This suggests the contrariness to reality which we need in the conclusion of the condition εἰ ἤθελον. This conclusion ὤν is, being equivalent to ἦν with ἄν omitted. H. 897; G. 1400; GMT. 416 and 479; B. 567, 1; Go. 460. **8.** αἰσχίων . . . ταύτης . . . ἢ δοκεῖν: a gen. of a demonstrative after a comparative may be explained by a clause introduced by ἤ. Notice the redundancy. **17.** αὐτὰ . . . νυνί, ὅτι, *for the present situation itself is clear, that.* δέ, as often in Homer, is equivalent to γάρ. The intensive αὐτά implies that nothing more is needed than Socrates' own present situation to establish what Crito contends for. There is a slight anacoluthon in ὅτι . . . εἰσίν, the sentence continuing as if δηλοῖ (as some read) had preceded (App. III.). **19.** τὰ μέγιστα: Crito cannot view death as Socrates does. See *Apol.* XXXII. **21.** εἰ γὰρ ὤφελον expresses a wish which cannot be attained. H. 871, a; G. 1512; GMT. 734; B. 588, 2; Go. 470, b. It is really a condition contrary to reality. **22.** ἵνα . . . ἦσαν: the purpose is unattainable, depending upon a wish past attainment. H. 884; G. 1371; B. 590, note 4; Go. 642, c. **24.** οὔτε . . . φρόνιμον οὔτε ἄφρονα: the multitude cannot make one wise or foolish. They are unable to affect character. In Socrates' view life and death are of small account compared with the loss of integrity. **26.** With τύχωσι supply ποιοῦντες. The multitude are controlled by impulse, not principle.

IV. *Do not be anxious about the expense. It will cost little to procure escape. The informers can be bought off for a trifle. Other friends will assist if you dislike to use so much of my property. Nor be anxious what you can do, or where go.*

2. ἆρά γε μή, *Surely you are not* (are you). ἆρα μή calls for a negative answer, while γέ by its emphasis implies that even though he may deny it Crito really has this anxiety. **4.** παρέχωσιν: the present subjunctive represents that the informers may make trouble continuously. The aorist subjunctives refer to momentary actions. **6.** καί before πᾶσαν intensifies it, *even;* in next line before ἄλλο τι, it is *also.*

8. ἔασον αὐτὸ χαίρειν, *dismiss it,* that is, this anxiety. Literally, 'suffer it to say χαῖρε,' or bid farewell. **14.** μήτε . . . φοβοῦ is resumed (after all the grounds for fear have in the meantime been shown to be baseless) by μήτε φοβούμενος of l. 25, after which comes the corresponding μήτε in l. 26. **18.** ἐπ' αὐτούς, *so far as they are concerned.* In Xen. *Mem.* II. 9, 1 we are told that Crito had been harassed by frivolous lawsuits, the bringers of which he had bought off in order to avoid trouble. — σοί by its position is very emphatic, implying that for Socrates Crito is ready to expend all he has. **22.** καὶ κεκόμικεν, *has actually brought.* Simmias and Cebes, both Thebans, appear prominently in the *Phaedo.* **25.** μήτε . . . ἀποκάμῃς, *neither hesitate,* literally, ' grow weary,' not as though Socrates had already made efforts to escape, which is absurd and besides would call for a participle instead of the infinitive σῶσαι, but in the sense of a strong demand for earnest action. GMT. 903, 3. (App. III.) **27.** ὅ τι χρῷο σαυτῷ, *what to do with yourself.* The reference here is to what Socrates said in *Apol.* XXVII. 32 ff. χρῷο represents the subjunctive of deliberation in direct discourse. H. 866, 3 and 932, 2; G. 1358 and 1490; GMT. 186; B. 673; Go. 661. **28.** καὶ ἄλλοσε, *elsewhere too* as well as here. The idea of motion in what follows reverts and gives form to ἄλλοσε.

V. *If you refuse, you will destroy yourself and neglect your children and lay us open to the charge of cowardice.*

2. σαυτὸν προδοῦναι is epexegetical of πρᾶγμα. — ἐξὸν σωθῆναι, acc. abs. See note on *Apol.* XII. 5.

8. οἰχήσει καταλιπών, *you will go and abandon.* — **τὸ σὸν μέρος**, *pro tua parte, quod ad te attinet.* H. 718, c; G. 1058; B. 336; Go. 540. — With **τύχωσι** supply **πράττοντες. 9. τοῦτο** is used adverbially with **πράξουσιν**, as often are **εὖ** and **κακῶς** with **πράττειν.** Also see **ἀγαθόν** in *Apol.* XXXI. 29. — **11. γάρ** gives the reason of **τοὺς υἱεῖς . . . δοκεῖς προδιδόναι**, l. 6. **15. φάσκοντά γε δή** *especially when you assert.* By supplying **σέ**, rather than **τινά**, as the subject of **αἱρεῖσθαι**, with which **φάσκοντα** agrees, the argument is brought to bear directly on Socrates, and that is what Crito intends. **γέ** by intensifying **φάσκοντα** suggests that the assertion needs to be accompanied by the appropriate action. **δή** expresses what follows *a fortiori, above all, especially.* **17. μή** because the idea of fear is implied in **αἰσχύνομαι. 18. ἅπαν τὸ πρᾶγμα** has in apposition with it as parts, **ἡ εἴσοδος, ὁ ἀγών**, and **τὸ τελευταῖον. 20. ἐξὸν μὴ εἰσελθεῖν**: Socrates, according to a law mentioned by Lysias (X. 17), might have gone into voluntary exile, or perhaps Crito and his friends might have kept the case out of court by raising legal technicalities. **21. ὁ ἀγών**, *the conduct* of the trial as it came off, literally, 'the struggle.' **22. ὥσπερ κατάγελως τῆς πράξεως**, *like a farcical conclusion of the whole matter.* It seems absurd to Crito that Socrates should go on and die when in his opinion it would be so easy to have avoided it. **23. διαπεφευγέναι ἡμᾶς δοκεῖν**: two constructions are suggested: (1) That these words are in epexegetical apposition to **τὸ τελευταῖον, ἡμᾶς** being the subject of **δοκεῖν**, and **διαπεφευγέναι** having **κίνδυνον** (to be supplied) as its object, in which case

there is no change of structure in the sentence, and (2) that **δοκεῖν** repeats the **δόξῃ** of l. 17, but is assimilated to the near infinitive, **ἡμᾶς** being the object of **διαπεφευγέναι**. In this case the anacoluthon, arising from agitation of feeling, must occur after **κατάγελως**, or it would be in the accusative. The latter of the two explanations gives a better meaning to **τὸ τελευταῖον**, viz. the ending of the trial in Socrates' death, and also accounts for the repetition of **ἀνανδρίᾳ τῇ ἡμετέρᾳ. 25. εἴ τι . . . ὄφελος ἦν.** See *Apol.* XVI. 16. **29. βεβουλεῦσθαι**, *to have decided.* GMT. 109. **30. εἰ . . . περιμενοῦμεν**: in future conditions **εἰ** with the future is still more vivid than **ἐάν** with the subjunctive, and is used in threats and warnings. See *Apol.* XVII. 75 and XXIII. 30.

Here ends the first episode or second act of the dialogue considered as a drama.

VI.–X. SOCRATES JUSTIFIES HIS REFUSAL

VI. We ought to consider not what will happen to us, but what it is right to do, and so the opinion of the best men.

2. ἀξία: supply **ἐστίν.** The opt. **εἴη** in the condition expresses almost a wish, 'if only it were.' **5. τοιοῦτος**: supply **εἰμί.** The copula is rarely omitted except in the third person. For **οἷος** with infinitive, see note on *Apol.* XVIII. 36. **6. τῶν ἐμῶν**, *that pertains to me*, literally, 'of mine,' including all his faculties as well as external conditions. **10. τοὺς αὐτοὺς . . . οὕσπερ καί**, *the very same as.* **-περ** strengthening **οὕς** expresses that the serious danger he is in does not influence Socrates to deviate one iota from the fixed principles of his whole life, and to which Crito has always given hearty assent. **13. οὐ μή** with the subjunctive (Plato always uses ξυγχωρήσομαι for the future) is most emphatic negation. See note on *Apol.* XVII. 43. — πλείω ... ἡμᾶς μορμολύττηται, *frighten us with more bugbears* (lit. *Mormos*). πλείω is a cognate acc. of neut. adjective. Μορμώ was a hideous she-monster used by nurses to frighten children with. **15. θανάτους**: in the plural denoting *violent death.* **18. ὃν σὺ λέγεις** refers to what Crito has said in III. 4–11 and V. 17–26. **22. ἄρα,** *of course,* is ironical, as is also the preceding question. — ἄλλως : otherwise than it should be, *to no purpose.* **26. ὧδε**: that is, in danger of death. **28. νῦν δή,** *just now.* **29. ἅς** is cognate acc. **30. δέοι**: opt. in orat. obliqua. **32. ὅσα γε τἀνθρώπεια,** *in all human probability.* The antecedent (to be supplied) of ὅσα is an acc. of specification. **33. αὔριον** is strange, as it is not in accord with the conviction wrought by his dream in Socrates' mind. **37. οὐδὲ ... τῶν δ' οὔ.** See App. III. **45. πῶς δ' οὔ;** how can it but be, *it must be so.*

The chapters which follow furnish an example of the inductive method of which Aristotle says that Socrates was the discoverer. From what is generally admitted as to the body he arrives at the desired truth in regard to the soul. The *Apology* and the *Crito,* owing to the nature of their subject matter, do not contain as frequent examples of this inductive method as do many other of the Dialogues of Plato (Int. 19).

VII. *The opinion of the one who knows ought to be regarded, not that of the many.*

1. αὖ, *again.* The substance of another conversation follows. **2. τοῦτο πράττων** indicates that the man is exercising carefully in accordance with the rules of the art and not casually. **5. ἰατρός** has to do with ἐδεστέον γε καὶ ποτέον, l. 12, παιδοτρίβης with πρακτέον καὶ γυμναστέον, l. 11. **12. γέ** in a series of words indicates the beginning of a new class different from what has gone before, *yes and.* **18. μηδέν** not οὐδέν because the participle ἐπαϊόντων (with which the article before πολλῶν is also to be taken) has the force of a conditional relative clause, *and of whoever does not know.* H. 1025, a; G. 1612; B. 431; Go. 486. **26. καὶ δὴ καί,** *and in particular also,* introduces the point with which the induction is to end. Notice the double chiastic arrangement of the adjectives which follow. **34. ἐγίγνετο** and ἀπώλλυτο are in the imperfect to indicate the result of previous discussions. This is sometimes called the philosophic imperfect. They are really equivalent to γίγνεσθαι and ἀπόλλυσθαι ἐλέγετο. H. 833; GMT. 40; B. 527, note.

VIII. *Life is not worth living with the soul ruined as it will be if we give heed to anything but the truth. That the many can kill us does not alter this fact.*

3. The position of μή suggests a clause not expressed, ἀλλὰ τῇ τῶν μὴ ἐπαϊόντων δόξῃ. The negation is in this way emphasized. **4. ἆρα βιωτὸν ... ἐστιν,** *is life worth the living?* **10. ἀλλὰ ... ἄρα,** *Well then.* The inference is from the less to the greater. The negative answer is overwhelmingly implied. **11.** ᾧ though in construction conformed to λωβᾶται belongs also to ὀνίνησιν. **13.** ὅ τι ποτ᾽ ἐστί: it (the ψυχή) was not mentioned above (VII. 30), and is left for each one to supply here. **18.** ἄρα introduces the conclusion with which this inductive process ends. — οὕτω, *so* as Crito has suggested. **19.** τί, ὅ τι: this change to the indefinite relative in an ind. question is not unusual in Plato. **21.** ἡ ἀλήθεια: the truth is regarded as ὁ ἐπαΐων who tells, as the result of careful inquiry, what course is the best, or most just as it is termed in what follows. **25.** οἷοί τε . . . ἀποκτεινύναι: in order to hasten the progress of the argument Socrates here introduces the very strongest objection (which Crito has already mentioned, III. 18 and 19) to doing what the truth directs, and claims that it does not affect the case. The principle abides, nevertheless. **26.** καί, *too*, indicates that in Crito's mind there are other objections beside this. See chap. IV. (App. III.) **29.** ἔτι μένει: it had been agreed in some former talk, here merely alluded to, that the just life alone was worth living. This is the subject of discussion in the *Protagoras*. **33.** τὸ δὲ εὖ . . . ταὐτόν ἐστιν: the distinction here made is necessary because εὖ ζῆν is ambiguous, as in our expression 'to live well.'

IX. *What the truth or justice bids in regard to my escaping from prison is what we ought to do, and that alone. Either refute this or admit it and act accordingly.*

4. εἰ δὲ μή after ἐὰν μέν merely as a formula of contrast and without reference to anything else. H. 906, a; G. 1417; B. 616, 3; Go. 656, c. **5.** τὰς

σκέψεις is the antecedent but it is drawn into the relative clause which comes first. The article in such cases generally falls away. The corresponding demonstrative ταῦτα is attracted into the gender of its predicate. **7.** μὴ . . . ᾖ: the subjunctive with μή expresses a cautious assertion, *I suspect these may prove to be considerations.* This is a milder way of saying ταῦτα σκέμματά ἐστιν, strengthened by ὡς ἀληθῶς. See *Apol.* XXIX. 33. **8.** καὶ ἀναβιωσκομένων γ᾽ ἄν, *yes! and would bring to life again.* γέ emphasizing the preceding word shows the entire capriciousness of the multitude. ἀναβιώσκω is usually intransitive. ἄν with ἀναβιωσκομένων forms the apodosis. GMT. 479, 3. **9.** τούτων τῶν πολλῶν, standing at the close in apposition, has a sort of contemptuous force. **10.** ὁ λόγος . . . αἱρεῖ, *reason thus determines, ratio evincit.* This is through the technical use of αἱρεῖν, 'to convict.' This expression is in strong contrast with οὐδενὶ ξὺν νῷ, l. 9. **13.** αὐτοί: the intensive brings out clearly that both Crito and Socrates would do wrong as well as those hired. **20.** τί δρῶμεν, *what can we do?* The subjunctive of appeal. H. 866, 3; G. 1358; B. 577; Go. 471. Crito, although he assents to Socrates' reasoning, cannot bring his mind to accept the situation. πολλάκις λέγων, l. 23, shows that Socrates understands that Crito by this question is still clinging to the thought that in some way Socrates must be got out of prison. **26.** πείσας σε has its antithesis in ἀλλὰ μὴ ἄκοντος, *but not if you are unwilling.* — ταῦτα refers to the course Socrates proposes to pursue. **27.** τῆς σκέψεως τὴν ἀρχήν, *the principle which* *underlies our inquiry.* See X. 42.— ἐάν here comes indefinitely near to introducing an indirect question, but see H. 1016, c; G. 1491; GMT. 680 and 493; B. 613; Go. 655.

X. *Justice tells us it is never right to do wrong to any one, not even to retaliate, especially if it involve the violation of an agreement.*

1. ἑκόντας might have been in the dat., agreeing with ὑμῖν to be supplied as dat. of agent after ἀδικητέον εἶναι, in place of which we should expect ἀδικεῖν δεῖν, with the subject of which ἑκόντας here agrees. H. 991, a; G. 1597; GMT. 926; B. 666, note. 5. ὅπερ . . . ἐλέγετο is bracketed because just this has not been lately said. These words were probably added by a later hand.— ἢ πᾶσαι . . . ἐκκεχυμέναι εἰσίν: this repeated use of the disjunctive question (each alternative depending on the preceding clause) indicates that Crito delays to answer. Not till φαμέν, l. 16, does he speak, and then as briefly as possible. The metaphor in ἐκκεχυμέναι is as of water ' poured out ' on the ground and gone to waste; translate, *spoken in vain.* 8. τηλικοίδε, repeated in γέροντες, emphasizes the antithesis with παίδων. 13. εἴ τε καὶ πραότερα, *or even milder.* This anticlimax is to emphasize the thought that the consequences, whatever they are, do not affect a principle or our duty. 21. οὐ φαίνεται, *apparently not,* just as οὔ φημι means 'I say no' or ' deny.' 22. κακουργεῖν, as well as κακῶς ποιεῖν, l. 27, is introduced as equivalent in meaning to ἀδικεῖν and more generally used than it. 23. δήπου indicates hesitation on Crito's part, which δή would not. 30. οὔτε ἄρα ἀνταδικεῖν: this

sentiment found its highest positive expression in the words of Christ in the Sermon on the Mount. *Matt.* v. 44. 31. πάσχῃ in the third person shows that τινὰ is the subject of the preceding infinitives, the statement being a general one. 39. ἀρχώμεθα is the subj. of deliberation. See note on IX. 20. — ὡς οὐδέποτε . . . ἔχοντος is epexegetical of ἐντεῦθεν = ἐκ τούτου τοῦ λόγου. Translate, *taking it never to be right.* 42. τῆς ἀρχῆς, *this first principle.* Compare ἀρχώμεθα ἐντεῦθεν, l. 39. 48. τὸ μετὰ τοῦτο, *that which comes next,* denoting not logical sequence (as ἐκ τούτου would), but temporal. It is given in the question which follows. 49. τῷ: the indefinite here is important as representing in this case the Laws soon to be introduced. 50. ποιητέον, though a passive verbal, governs the antecedent of ἅ (ταῦτα to be supplied). H. 990; G. 1597; B. 665; Go. 596, b.— ἢ ἐξαπατητέον, Socrates says, instead of simply ἢ οὐ ποιητέον, with reference to the foregoing ἃ ἄν τις ὁμολογήσῃ τῳ, since such an agreement includes the obligation to act accordingly. Translate, *or may one deceive* (him, in those things). ἐξαπατᾶν may take an acc. of the person, here to be supplied from τῷ, and an acc. of the thing, here the antecedent of ἅ.

With the introduction of the new *dialogi persona,* the Laws or embodied state, begins the third episode or fourth act of the dialectic drama.

XI.–XVI. THE LAWS ENFORCE THE ARGUMENT OF SOCRATES

XI. *The Laws might claim that by escaping you are trying to destroy them and the city.*

1. **ἐκ τούτων**: Socrates now proceeds to apply to the case in hand the general principles just established. **4. οἷς** is assimilated to the object of ἐμμένομεν, since ὡμολογήσαμεν takes the acc. See X. 49. **7. οὐ γὰρ ἐννοῶ**: Crito's inability to understand and reply seems to rise from his fear of what will follow if he does. This answer of Crito's gives occasion to Socrates to pass over to a new treatment of the matter. **8. ἡμῖν** is to be taken with ἐπιστάντες, l. 11. **9.** Since ἀποδιδράσκειν was generally used of runaway slaves and so might be obnoxious to Crito, the expression is softened by the clause which follows. **10. τὸ κοινὸν τῆς πόλεως**, *the common-wealth*, 'the community of the city.' **11. ὦ Σώκρατες**: this change from ἡμῖν, l. 8, indicates that Socrates feels that he is individually responsible, mainly, in this matter. **12. ἄλλο τι ἤ**: for this interrogative expression, which distinctly expects the answer *yes*, see note on *Apol.* XII. 1. **14. τὸ σὸν μέρος** = καθ᾽ ὅσον δύνασαι, XII. 33, *so far as you can*. **15. ἔτι . . . εἶναι**, *longer to exist*. The sure ruin of a city in which the laws are disregarded is brought out by this positive statement of it, followed by the negative. **19. ἄλλως τε καὶ ῥήτωρ**: by these words Socrates hints that he has not the gifts or training in public speaking of professional orators, — and his opponents he includes in that class (*Apol.* I.). The tricks of public speech he may not have had, but the argument he is now making is consummately put. **20. ὑπὲρ τούτου . . . ἀπολλυμένου**, *in behalf of this law which is threatened with destruction*. The pres. and imper. of ἀπόλλυμι have

often this idea of threatened action. In Athens if any one proposed to change or repeal a law, it was the custom to appoint advocates (συνήγοροι) to defend it. **22. ὅτι** introduces here direct discourse, and is equivalent to quotation marks. See note on *Apol.* XVI. 14. — ἠδίκει: see App. III. — **γάρ**, *yes, for*. Assent is here implied to the accusation made above, and a reason is advanced for it.

XII. *But the Laws are our benefactors and we must not retaliate when we think they are wronging us, any more than we should upon parents.*

2. ταῦτα refers to the idea contained in the answer just given, that if we think the city is treating us wrongly, we in turn may wrong it. **3. ἐμμένειν** is the subject of ὡμολόγητο to be repeated in thought. **6. ἐπειδὴ καί**: Socrates represents the Laws as pursuing his own method in argument. (Int. 21.) **11. τούτοις** is to be taken with μέμφει. **13. ἀλλά** introduces a second consideration, and is instead of an ἔπειτα δέ answering to πρῶτον μέν, l. 8. **17. ἐν μουσικῇ καὶ γυμναστικῇ**: μουσική in its broader sense included elementary studies (γράμματα), music in the stricter sense, and a knowledge of the poets; in a word, all the branches of a liberal education. γυμναστική was the whole system of exercise and diet by which bodily well-being was promoted. (Int. 7.) **21. δοῦλος** connotes the entire and unquestioning obedience as of a slave to a master, involving a certain loss of individual freedom, which in Socrates' view the citizen is bound to yield in order that the state may exist. — αὐτός, πρόγονοι, in epexegetical apposition to the subject of ἦσθα, press

the obligation home more emphatically.
25. ἄρα has an ironical force. It is
repeated in the adversative clause,
l. 30, because in that clause the inconsistency comes to view. **28. οὔτε . . .
οὔτε**: in our idiom we should expect
τέ . . . τέ. The negatives are under
the influence of οὐκ ἐξ ἴσου ἦν, but
cannot be introduced in translation.
ἀντιλέγειν and ἀντιτύπτειν are explanatory of ἀντιποιεῖν. — **κακῶς ἀκούοντα** is equivalent to λοιδορούμενον.
35. ὁ . . . ἐπιμελόμενος, added in emphasis and irony, which is expressed
again in οὔτως, l. 36. **39. ἐν μείζονι
μοίρᾳ**, *in higher estimation;* literally,
' in a greater portion ' of respect due.
Connect closely with παρά. **40. σέβεσθαι**: the subject is τινά, to be supplied. **44. ἐάν τε τύπτεσθαι ἐάν τε
δεῖσθαι**: the infinitives depend on προστάττῃ and are explanatory of παθεῖν.
— ἐάν τε κτλ. in l. 45 brings in the
idea of military service, in which entire obedience is requisite, leading up
to the claim in ἐν δικαστηρίῳ, l. 48,
that there likewise the state demands
entire obedience. **46. ποιητέον ταῦτα**,
like σέβεσθαι δεῖ, l. 40, brings back the
sentence again, after the specification
of intervening details, to its connection
with ὥστε λεληθέν σε, l. 36. See note
on X. 50. **50. πείθειν**: supply δεῖ, the
idea of which is contained in the preceding verbals in -τέον, and so it is not
written. GMT. 925.

XIII. *Moreover, when you became
a citizen, you virtually agreed to do
whatsoever the Laws might command.*
3. δίκαια: predicate after ἅ . . . ἐπιχειρεῖς. **6. ὅμως**: it might be thought
that the city had already done enough
to establish its claim upon the obedience of the citizen, but *nevertheless.*

7. προαγορεύομεν τῷ . . . πεποιηκέναι,
*we publicly proclaim by giving per-
mission.* Upon προαγορεύομεν depends
ἐξεῖναι . . . ἀπιέναι, l. 10, ἐξεῖναι repeating the idea of ἐξουσίαν. **8. ἐπειδὰν
δοκιμασθῇ**, *when he shall have passed
the* (δοκιμασία or) *examination,* especially in regard to his Athenian parent-
age, which at the completion of his
eighteenth year a young man had to
pass before he could have his name
entered on the register of his deme
(ληξιαρχικὸν γραμματεῖον) and become
an Athenian citizen. **10. ἐξεῖναι . . .
ἀπιέναι** is the conclusion, the conditions of which are in δοκιμασθῇ
(and ἴδῃ), ἀρέσκωμεν, and βούληται.
11. οὐδεὶς . . . ἀπαγορεύει: by repeating the statement of the preceding sentence in this negative form, the freedom
of the young man in becoming enrolled
as a citizen is emphasized. **13. εἰς
ἀποικίαν . . . μετοικεῖν**: the Athenian
who went to an Athenian colony, as
to Thurii or Amphipolis, became a
citizen there; but a μέτοικος resided
as an alien in the city he chose to settle
in. — εἰ μὴ ἀρέσκοιμεν: the optative
implies the improbability that Athens
would not be pleasing. **22. πείθεσθαι**
rather than πείσεσθαι, although after a
verb of a future signification (see ποιήσειν, l. 19), because here it is implied
that the obedience begins at the very
moment of the agreement. GMT. 136.
24. προτιθέντων ἡμῶν: supply from
the context ἢ πείθεσθαι ἢ πείθειν,
which is equivalent to αἵρεσιν, *although
we set before him the choice.* Socrates
uses every form of statement to emphasize the entire freedom with which the
citizen has covenanted to obey the Laws.

XIV. *You, Socrates, most of all
agreed to this, because more than any*

one else you have liked the city and remained in it, and that for seventy years.

1. καὶ σέ, *you in particular.* καί introduces a particular instance. The last chapter was general; this is the special application of the general truth to the case in hand, which is aggravated by several circumstances. **2. ταῖς αἰτίαις ἐνέξεσθαι,** *will make yourself liable to these charges.* **3. ἐν τοῖς μά-λιστα :** see I. 33. **10. ἄν . . . ἐπε-δήμεις :** the sentence begins as a conditional one, but as it advances (in ἐξῆλθες, l. 12, ἐποιήσω, l. 15, and ἔλα-βεν, l. 16) the force of ἄν disappears and the statements become positive. **12. ἐπὶ θεωρίαν,** *to be a spectator of the public games,* namely, the Olym-pian, Pythian, Isthmian, and Nemean, to which men went from all parts of Greece. **13. ὅ τι μή,** *except.* The verb is not expressed. GMT. 550. See App. III. **14. στρατευσόμενος :** for Socrates' military campaigns, see Int. 5 and 9. **17. εἰδέναι,** added epexegetically, makes the gen. πόλεως seem prolep-tic. **20. καὶ . . . ἐποιήσω** is no longer dependent on ὡμολόγεις, but starts im-mediately from τά τε ἄλλα. **21. ἐξῆν :** for ἄν omitted in this conclusion, see H. 897; G. 1400; B. 567, 1; Go. 460. So also in l. 41. Socrates might have proposed exile instead of a fine of thirty minae. *Apol.* XXVIII. 23. **24. ἐκαλλωπίζου,** *you prided yourself,* lit. ' made the face beautiful.' — **ὡς οὐκ ἀγανακτῶν,** *on not caring, as you claimed.* ὡς shows that the claim is the assertion of Socrates. The context implies that the Laws regard the claim as insincere. GMT. 864 and 865. **34. φῶμεν** is subj. of deliberation or appeal, as is also ὁμολογῶμεν in l. 35.

35. ἄλλο τι ἤ distinctly expects the answer yes. So also in l. 37. See note on *Apol.* XII. 1 and *Crito* XI. 12. **38. πρὸς ἡμᾶς αὐτούς,** *between us.* **44. ὡς δὴ ἑκάστοτε :** in the writings of Plato (*Repub.* 544 and *Protag.* 342), Socrates is represented as speaking well of the discipline of these two states, both Doric in origin. So in Xenophon (*Mem.* III. 5 and IV. 4) Socrates expresses admiration for Lacedaemon on account of the strict observance of the laws by its citizens. **46. ἐλάττω . . . ἀπεδήμησας :** in the *Phaedrus,* 230 C, Socrates appears to be entirely ignorant of the suburbs of his own city, and when Phaedrus chides him with this, saying, οὕτως ἐκ τοῦ ἄστεως οὔτ' εἰς τὴν ὑπερορίαν ἀπο-δημεῖς οὔτ' ἔξω τείχους ἔμοιγε δοκεῖς τὸ παράπαν ἐξιέναι, Socrates replies, συγγίγνωσκέ μοι, ὦ ἄριστε, φιλομαθὴς γάρ εἰμι· τὰ μὲν οὖν χωρία καὶ τὰ δένδρα οὐδέν μ' ἐθέλει διδάσκειν, οἱ δ' ἐν τῷ ἄστει ἄνθρωποι. **49. δῆλον ὅτι,** *evidently,* lit. ' it is clear that.' These words particularly emphasize καὶ ἡμεῖς οἱ νόμοι, since it is the laws that are chiefly in question. (App. III.) **51. ἐὰν ἡμῖν γε πείθῃ,** *yes, if you will obey us.*

XV. *If now you violate your cove-nant with us, and leave the city, wher-ever you go you will be an object of reproach and ridicule.*

1. ταῦτα παραβὰς καὶ ἐξαμαρτάνων τι τούτων : ταῦτα and τί are cognate acc. after the participles. The aorist refers to the one act of violating his covenant in breaking jail, the present to the continuing false position he will be in ever after. **6. πρῶτον μέν** finds its adversative in ἀλλά, l. 23. Cities near and more remote are contrasted. Compare XII. 13. **8. εὐνομοῦνται**

γάρ : in Thebes, before and during the Peloponnesian war, there existed a moderate oligarchy (ὀλιγαρχία ἰσό-νομος, different from the δυναστεία ὀλίγων at the time of the Persian war), which had an inclination towards Sparta; also Megara had an oligar-chical government, and since the bat-tle of Coronea (447) stood on the side of Sparta. **10.** ὑποβλέψονται, *will regard you with suspicion*, like the Homeric ὑπόδρα ἰδών. **12.** δοκεῖν may be active ('think') or passive ('be thought'), according as δόξαν is regarded as meaning 'decision' or 'reputation.' The latter accords better with what follows. **20.** ἤ : the disjunctive introduces a direct ques-tion following a general question and suggesting the answer thereto. **22.** The fut. infin. φανεῖσθαι with ἄν represents the fut. indic. with ἄν in direct discourse (GMT. 208). — τὸ τοῦ Σωκράτους πρᾶγμα, *this matter of Socrates*, meaning Socrates himself in the plight in which he would have put himself. **25.** ἐκεῖ γάρ : the Thes-salian nobles were rich and hospitable, but bore the reputation also of being licentious and violent. Their political character is indicated by Demosthenes in *Olynth.* I. 22, τὰ τῶν Θετταλῶν . . . ἄπιστα μὲν ἦν δήπου φύσει καὶ ἀεὶ πᾶσιν ἀνθρώποις. **28.** σκευήν τέ τινα, *some disguise*, is co-ordinate with καὶ τὸ σχῆμα, l. 30, σκευή denoting attire, often of an actor, which conceals the true personality, — here explained by ἢ διφθέραν . . . ἢ ἄλλα, while σχῆμα refers to any other changes in form or person. **34.** οὐδεὶς ὅς : ἔσται is omitted. The omission of the copula occurs more often with the present. **35.** εἰ δὲ μή, *otherwise*, is equivalent

to ἄν δέ τινα λυπῇς. We might have expected εἰ δέ after the preceding neg-ative. H. 906, b; G. 1417; B. 616, 3; Go. 656, c. — ἀκούσει : ἀκούειν is here used as the passive of λέγειν. Com-pare XII. 28. The Greek inserts a καί between πολλά and ἀνάξια, which is not reproduced in our idiom. **36.** ὑπερχόμενος . . . καὶ δουλεύων, *cringing to all men and their slave.* This is one of the distasteful things Socrates will hear said. **39.** εἰς Θετ-ταλίαν : there is a reproach in this repetition. So far for so little. (App. III.) **41.** ἀλλὰ δή, *well then*, intro-duces a new objection in order to re-fute it by anticipation. **44.** ἀπολαύ-σωσιν, *may get the good of*, in irony, for the Greeks thought exile from their country a punishment. (App. III.) — τοῦτο refers to the preceding clause. **46.** θρέψονται and παιδεύ-σονται are used as futures passive. H. 496; G. 1248; B. 515, 1. **50.** γέ, *yes.*

XVI. *If you violate us, what defense can you make when you stand before our brothers, the Laws in Hades?*

4. πάντα ταῦτα ἀπολογήσασθαι, *to offer all this in your defense.* **7.** οὐδὲ ἄλλῳ τῶν σῶν : the Laws say this to imply that Crito has felt the weight of their argument and yielded. **8.** νῦν implies that Socrates will not accede to Crito's proposal.

Here, dramatically, the fourth act or third episode ends. What follows is a brief epilogue.

XVII. CONCLUSION. *I cannot dis-regard the arguments of the Laws.*

1. ὦ φίλε ἑταῖρε Κρίτων : the espe-cial tenderness of this address is to soften the positiveness of his refusal. **2. οἱ κορυβαντιῶντες :** the Corybantes were priests of the Phrygian Cybele, whose wild and enthusiastic rites were attended with furious dances and deafening music. κορυβαντιᾶν signifies here, to be *in the Corybantic phrenzy*, which continued when the music had ceased and was only imagined, just as now no one could hear the voice of the Laws. Nothing could convey a better idea of the effect produced on Socrates' mind and whole being by these solemn and searching words of the Laws, than this expressive metaphor. **4. βομβεῖ,** *resounds*. **5. ὅσα γε . . . δοκοῦντα,** *at least as it seems to me now*. This, too, is to soften the assertion. **10. ταύτῃ ὁ θεὸς ὑφηγεῖται :** compare *Apol.* II. 45 and *Crito*, II. 2 for similar expressions of trust in the divine guidance.

NOTES ON THE PHAEDO

The circumstances under which this dialogue took place are explained in Int. 37.

Title, ΦΑΙΔΩΝ. See on the sub-title to the *Crito*, p. 150.

[ἢ περὶ ψυχῆς, ἠθικός] See on the title to the *Apology*, p. 117.

Of the *dialogi personae* observe that Apollodorus does not speak anywhere in the dialogue, and Simmias and Cebes do not in the chapters here given.

This Dialogue differs from the *Crito* in that the conversation is not given directly, but is narrated. An excuse for so reporting it is given by the fact that Plato, owing to illness (II. 46), was not present, and an advantage is that in this form many details are given which in a direct conversation cannot be naturally introduced, but which a reader needs to know.

The first three chapters are part of the dramatic prologue.

I.–III. Part of the INTRODUCTION

Incidents at Phlius, and others in prison on the morning of the day on which Socrates died, before the main conversation begins.

I. *What were the circumstances attending Socrates' death, and how came he to live on in prison for thirty days?*

1. αὐτός is in contrast with ἄλλου του, l. 3. Echecrates wishes to ascertain whether Phaedo was himself a witness of what took place on the day of Socrates' death. **2. τὸ φάρμακον :** Diogenes Laertius (II. 35) calls this τὸ κώνειον. **5. ὁ ἀνήρ** as ἀνήρ in II. 21, is simply the equivalent of the personal pronoun. **7. Φλειασίων** is in apposition to τῶν πολιτῶν for greater definiteness. Compare *Apol.* XX. 9. The article is omitted as is Plato's habit before the name of a country or of the inhabitants of a country or city. **8. τὰ νῦν :** we know of nothing just after Socrates' death which would have interrupted communication between Athens and Phlius. (Int. 37.) — Ἀθήναζε after the idea of motion implied in ἐπιχωριάζει as in LXV. 1, ἀνίστατο εἰς οἴκημα. **14. ὃν τρόπον ἐγένετο** is explanatory of τὰ περὶ τῆς δίκης. **16. πολλῷ ὕστερον** : thirty days. See Xen. *Mem.* IV. 8, 2, ἀνάγκη μὲν γὰρ ἐγένετο αὐτῷ μετὰ τὴν κρίσιν τριάκοντα ἡμέρας βιῶναι διὰ τὸ Δήλια μὲν ἐκείνου τοῦ μηνὸς εἶναι. (Int. 34.) **21. ἐστεμμένη**, with wreaths of laurel, the tree sacred to Apollo. Delos was the place of his birth. **24. τὸ πλοῖον** : Plutarch, in *Theseus*, 23, says that this ship was in existence until the time of Demetrius the Phalerian (d. 282 B.C.). **25. ἐν ᾧ Θησεύς** : Plutarch tells us in *Theseus*, 15 ff., that Minos, king of Crete, once threatening Athens with destruction, was induced to withdraw by the Athenians agreeing to send seven youths and as many maidens every nine years to be offered to the Minotaur in the Labyrinth. As the tribute was brought the third time Theseus slew the monster. The yearly festival in honor of this deliverance was called the Delian. **30. πέμπουσιν** : the present here expresses a customary action. H. 824, a; G. 1253, 1; GMT. 24; B. 520, 1; Go. 454, e. **34. δεῦρο** : Plato, as an Athenian, uses this word as if the speaker was in Athens. **35. ἀπολαβόντες** is the usual word to denote the detention of ships by contrary winds. — **αὐτούς** refers to τοὺς πλέοντας, suggested by τὸ πλοῖον, l. 33. **38. τῇ προτεραίᾳ** : for the time of year, see Int. 5, note 1.

II. *On the day of Socrates' death his serene spirit so influenced us, his friends, that as he talked we almost forgot our grief.*

4. οἱ ἄρχοντες, as in *Apol.* XXXI. 3, the same as οἱ ἕνδεκα mentioned in *Apol.* XXVII. 20. **6. καὶ πολλοί γε**

corrects the idea of paucity implied in the indefinite τινές, *indeed, quite a number.* **9. ἡμῖν** indicates that there were others with Echecrates ready to listen. See I. 10 and 15. **16. τοιούτους ἑτέρους**, *others of the same disposition.* **19. οὔτε** has οὔτε αὖ, l. 27, in contrast with it. — **παρόντα με … ἔλεος εἰσῄει** : Here the acc. follows the verb, but in l. 26 we find the dative. **21. τοῦ τρόπου**, gen. of cause, as in *Crito*, I. 20. **22. ὡς … ἐτελεύτα** is epexegetical of εὐδαίμων. ὡς is equivalent to ὅτι οὕτως. GMT. 580. **23. παρίστασθαι**, *it occurred to me that.* The subject is ἐκεῖνον … ἰέναι. — **μηδέ**, *not even* in death did the favor and direction of the gods, which his disciples believed had attended Socrates in his life, fail him. For μοῖρα in the sense of 'divine allotment,' see, also, *Apol.* XXII. 9. **24. ἰέναι** and **πράξειν** are in the future because, in this indirect discourse, they represent the future in the direct. H. 855, a; G. 1276; GMT. 135; B. 548; Go. 577, a. **25. εἴ περ … ἄλλος** emphasizes ἐκεῖνον, l. 23. **27. παρόντι πένθει** is equivalent to εἴ τις παρείη πένθει. — **ἐν φιλοσοφίᾳ**, *engaged in philosophic conversation.* **29. τοιοῦτοι** refers to φιλοσοφίᾳ. **33. οὕτω**, referring to what has just been said, is still further explained by ὁτὲ μὲν γελῶντες … δακρύοντες. **35. Ἀπολλόδωρος**, termed ὁ μανικός, in *Sympos.* 173, D, on account of his excitability, is mentioned again in LXVI. 30. **42. ὁ Κριτόβουλος καὶ ὁ πατήρ** : for the father Crito, see Int. 34 and 37. They are both mentioned in *Apol.* XXII. Critobulus was famous for his beauty. **43. Ἑρμογένης**, like Socrates, was poor, although his father Hipponicus and his brother Callias were very rich. — Of Ἐπιγένης we know only that he was the son of Antiphon of the deme Cephisia. *Apol.* XXII. 25. **44.** Αἰσχίνης was the son of Lysanias (see note on *Apol.* XXII. 24), and is said to have written seven Dialogues, conversations of Socrates. —'Ἀντισθένης became the founder of the Cynics. — ἦν repeats παρῆν of l. 42, as often the simple verb stands after the compound. **45.** Μενέξενος is the same whose name is given to one of the Dialogues of Plato. Ctesippus was his cousin. **46.** Πλάτων δέ, οἶμαι, ἠσθένει. Plato˙ must surely have known whether he was ill or not, so, Wohlrab suggests, the οἶμαι indicates that his being ill and absent is merely a fiction to account for the fact that he says nothing. He could not well play the part of a dumb listener, but he does not introduce himself as speaking in any Dialogue. Others, taking ἠσθένει seriously, think that it is implied that the trial and imprisonment of his master had made Plato ill. **48.** Σιμμίας . . . Κέβης were both young. They take important parts in the conversation which follows. In the *Crito* (IV. 21–24) they are represented as ready to use their property for the benefit of their master. **49.** Φαιδωνίδης also was a Theban, of whom we know nothing else. — Εὐκλείδης became the head of the Megarian branch of the Socratic school. Of Terpsion we know nothing more. **51.** Ἀρίστιππος καὶ Κλεόμβροτος: their absence at this time is mentioned as a reproach. From so near a point they should have come to Athens to be with Socrates in his last moments. So ἐλέγοντο, l. 53, may imply that they were not in close communication with the other friends of Socrates. Aris-

tippus was the founder of the Cyrenaic school.

III. *Entering the prison early in the morning, we found Xanthippe and their youngest child there, after whose dismissal the conversation began.*

5. πλησίον γὰρ ἦν: most of the courtrooms were near the agora, and so the general location of the prison is indicated. **16.** ὑπακούειν, as in *Crito,* I. 7. **19.** παραγγέλλουσιν in the sense of 'are giving orders' is followed by ὅπως ἄν with the subjunctive denoting the purpose, *to the end that.* **23.** γάρ gives the reason of an implied 'I do not need to tell you who she is.' **24.** τὸ παιδίον: their youngest son Menexenus. **25.** ἀνευφήμησε: on this word Stallbaum says: *εὐφημεῖν et ἀνευφημεῖν proprie dicuntur de verbis et vocibus faustis ac bene ominatis. Sed κατ' ἀντίφρασιν significant etiam lamentari, vociferare, eiulare.* **29.** ἀπαγέτω τις αὐτήν: Plato in the *Phaedo* avoids dwelling on the family circumstances of Socrates. He evidently wishes to represent only the philosopher in his intercourse with his disciples, and to avoid all outbreaks of feeling. So Socrates rebukes Apollodorus (LXVI. 34) for driving the other disciples to tears by his weeping and loud lamentation. Xanthippe returns for a final farewell, in LXV. 10. **31.** τινὲς . . . Κρίτωνος: as a rich man, Crito always had a large following of servants about him. **33.** ἐξέτριψε: the force of ἐξ in the compound verb is that he rubbed until he no longer felt pain. **34.** ἅμα generally stands before the participle to which it belongs. — "ὡς ἄτοπον" ἔφη: it might have been expected that on meeting his friends Socrates' first reference would have been to his having to die on that day, instead of which he acts as unconcernedly as on other days. **35. ὡς . . . πέφυκε,** *how wonderfully it is related.* **37. τὸ . . . μὴ ἐθέλειν :** the article may be translated, *in that.* Notice the use of ἐθέλειν with inanimate things as if they were persons. **41. Αἴσωπος :** by this reference to Aesop, Cebes (in the following chapter) is reminded that Euenus was anxious to know what the object of Socrates was in versifying the fables of Aesop. After answering this question Socrates (V.) sends a kindly message to Euenus and bids him follow him to Hades as quickly as possible. The surprise of Simmias at this message draws from Socrates an expression of his belief that the true philosopher will meet death gladly, and in support of this opinion the whole argument which occupies the rest of the Dialogue is evolved.

After showing why the true philosopher will meet death gladly, in reply to a question from Cebes (XIV.) Socrates gives several reasons for his belief in a future existence. Simmias and Cebes raise objections (XXXVI.) which Socrates refutes in several arguments, and closes (LVIII.) with a myth containing a theory of the life after death and the happy fate in it of the good, especially philosophers.

The last four chapters are dramatically the Epilogue.

LXIV.–LXVII. LAST MOMENTS AND DEATH OF SOCRATES

LXIV. *Socrates converses with Crito in regard to his burial.* At the close of the last chapter Socrates has said that it will be better for him to bathe before drinking the poison, so as to spare the women the trouble of washing the body after he is dead.

3. ἐπιστέλλεις : this verb is frequently used of the last requests of the dying. **6. οὐδὲν καινότερον,** *nothing very new.* In this absolute use of the comparative its specific force has almost entirely disappeared. — **ὑμῶν αὐτῶν ἐπιμελούμενοι :** see *Apol.* XVII. 51, τῆς ψυχῆς, ὅπως ὡς βελτίστη ἔσται. **10. ὥσπερ κατ' ἴχνη,** *as though following footprints,* emphasizes κατὰ τὰ . . . εἰρημένα. **12. οὐδὲν πλέον ποιήσετε,** *will you effect anything.* πλέον here means 'more than if you do not.' **14. τίνα τρόπον :** by burning or by interment. See l. 32. **28. οὗτος . . . ἠγγυᾶτο :** ἠγγυᾶτο here may be the conative imper., *offered to give* (H. 832; G. 1255; B. 527; Go. 459, a), as the penalty of a money fine (*Apol.* XXVIII. 23) was not accepted by the dicasts. Socrates then would indicate by παραμενεῖν, l. 29, that what the dicasts feared was that he would run away without paying his fine. Another more probable explanation of the whole passage is that Crito had actually offered surety to the court that Socrates would appear at the appointed time. **34. προτίθεται :** it is here suggested that Crito, who had been so thoughtful a friend of Socrates while he lived, would also perform for him the last offices. **37. εἰ αὐτὸ τοῦτο :** an incorrect expression is an offense *in itself.* — **κακόν τι :** it may, for instance, lead us to think that the body is all that exists of a man. **39. τοὐμὸν σῶμα** is emphatically opposed to Σωκράτη, l. 35. — The first θάπτειν depends on φάναι, but the second is better taken with χρή.

LXV. *After Socrates has bathed and has bidden good-by to his wife and children, the officer of the Eleven testifies as to Socrates' conduct in prison.*

1. ἀνίστατο εἰς οἴκημα, *got up* (and went) *into a room*. See I. 8. **9. τὰ παιδία:** see *Apol.* XXII. 19. **10. οἰκεῖαι γυναῖκες**, among whom of course was Xanthippe. **18. οὐ καταγνώσομαι σου,** *I shall not have the complaint to make of you* that I do of others. **22. ἐν τούτῳ τῷ χρόνῳ:** in the month which he had spent in prison. **26. ἀλλὰ ἐκείνοις:** the man, although he appreciates Socrates' nobility so far as he himself is concerned, cannot conceive of his bearing no ill will toward those who were really the cause of his death. See *Apol.* XXXIII. 10. **27. ἀγγέλλων:** the future is not necessary. Compare ἀγγελίαν φέρων, *Crito,* I. 30. **33. προσῄει,** *used to come,* indicates that these visits were frequent, because of his liking for Socrates. **36. εἰ τέτριπται:** the poison was obtained by bruising in a mortar the seeds of the poison hemlock, which is not a tree, but a plant. **38. ἐπὶ τοῖς ὄρεσιν:** a line of mountains lies to the east and north of Athens, — the ranges of Hymettus and Pentelicus. **45. κερδαίνειν:** the future would be more natural, but the manuscript authority is for the present. **49. φειδόμενος ... ἐνόντος,** *being thrifty when there is no longer anything left* is a proverbial expression. **50. πιθοῦ, ποίει:** compare *Crito,* IV. 11.

LXVI. *The execution and Socrates' dying words.*

6. γάρ introduces the reason of the question which follows. **9. αὐτὸ ποιήσει,** *it will work of itself.* **12. τοῦ χρώματος:** the genitive is partitive, and

depends upon an οὐδέν to be supplied. **13. ταυρηδὸν ὑποβλέψας** describes the fixed piercing gaze habitual to Socrates. **15. ἀποσπεῖσαί τινι:** it was the custom, especially at banquets, before drinking wine to pour a little upon the ground as a libation to the gods. **18. μετοίκησιν ... ἐνθένδε:** compare *Apol.* XXXII. 6. **21. ἐπισχόμενος:** notice the force of the middle voice. **23. κατέχειν τὸ μὴ δακρύειν:** the negative is redundant. H. 1029; G. 1615; GMT. 811; B. 434; Go. 572. In l. 29 we have κατέχειν τὰ δάκρυα. **26. γάρ** gives the reason of ἐμαυτόν, which is the object of ἀπέκλαιον. **27. οἷον,** *in that ... of such.* With οἷος used in this way we have to supply an idea of 'thinking' or 'considering.' Compare ὡς ... ἐτελεύτα, II. 22. **32. οὐδένα ὅντινα οὐ,** *every one.* H. 1003, a; G. 1035; B. 485, note 1; Go. 614, b. **37. ἀκήκοα ὅτι ἐν εὐφημίᾳ:** Olympiodorus says that this was a precept of Pythagoras. **48. πηγνύτο:** contracted for πηγνύοιτο. — αὐτός, *himself.* Socrates curiously observes his own dissolution. His ruling passion is strong even in death. **51. ἐνεκεκάλυπτο:** it was the custom for those about to die to cover the face with their robes. After these last words Socrates again covered himself, as is seen from ἐξεκάλυψεν, l. 58. **53. τῷ Ἀσκληπιῷ ὀφείλομεν ἀλεκτρυόνα:** on recovering from illness it was the custom to offer a thank-offering to this god of healing. Socrates would imply that his life in the body was a malady from which death was a recovery. Professor Geddes quotes Timon of Athens, V. 1, " My long sickness of health and living now begins to mend." **57. ἐκινήθη** refers to the last convulsive movement in dying. **58.** ὅς is demonstrative and refers to Socrates.

LXVII. *Phaedo's estimate of Socrates.* As chapters I. and II. are an introduction to the Introduction (I.– VIII.), this last chapter, in bringing us back from the prison at Athens to Phlius, is a conclusion to the Conclusion (LXIV.–LXVII.).

3. τῶν τότε : Grote (*Plato*, II. p. 152) suggests that it is here implied that Socrates belonged to the past generation. The Dialogue begins as if it had taken place just after Socrates' death, but the τότε unconsciously indicates that a considerable time had elapsed. See Int. 2. — ὧν ἐπειράθημεν : notice the studied modesty and restraint of this closing sentence. — καὶ ἄλλως signifies that, without the preceding limitations, Socrates excelled in φρόνησις and δικαιοσύνη.

APPENDIX

VARIOUS readings of the text are found in many passages in the different editions of Plato. These variations arise from differences in the manuscripts, and from the conjectures and emendations of different editors. This appendix contains a brief account of the manuscripts, a list of some of the notable editions, and of some of the more important variations in the text of the *Apology*, the *Crito*, and the *Phaedo*, together with some of the more important authorities for each variation.

I. THE MANUSCRIPTS OF PLATO

The manuscripts of Plato, of which there are many in existence, are all based on the arrangement of the Dialogues made by Thrasyllus (Int. 3) into nine tetralogies, and so, for their source, do not go back of the first century after Christ. Any other arrangements which may previously have existed were driven out by this one. The archetype of these manuscripts probably consisted of two volumes, of which the first contained tetralogies I.–VII.; the second, tetralogies VIII. and IX., the Definitions, and the spurious Dialogues. (Martin Schanz, *Studien zur Geschichte des Platonischen Textes*, 1874, pp. 11–20.)

The best manuscript we have, the Codex Clarkianus or Bodleianus (referred to by Schanz by the letter B; by Wohlrab, after Bekker and Stallbaum, by the letter 𝔄), contains only tetralogies I.–VI., and is, for them, the highest authority. It is named after Edward Daniel Clarke, who discovered it in 1801 in a monastery on the island of Patmos. It is also called Oxoniensis and Bodleianus, from being in the Bodleian library at Oxford. It was written on parchment in a most exquisite character, in 895 A.D., by the scribe John, for Arethas deacon of Patras, who afterward became archbishop of Caesarea. (Martin Schanz, *Novae Commentationes Platonicae*, 1871, pp. 105–118.)

The Codex Venetus (referred to by Schanz by the letter T; by Wohlrab, after Bekker and Stallbaum, by t), now in the Library of St. Mark's at Venice, contains the seven tetralogies of Book I. of the archetype, and so is especially valuable in the seventh tetralogy which is lacking in Codex Clarkianus. The oldest portion of this manuscript dates from the twelfth century, or earlier according to Schanz; the later portions from the fifteenth and sixteenth centuries.

For the literature on the manuscripts of Plato, their history, and their classification in the first six tetralogies, see Wohlrab's article: *Die Platonhandschriften und ihre gegenseitige Beziehungen*, in *Fleckeisen's Jahrbücher*, Fünfzehnter Supplementband, 1887.

II. EDITIONS OF PLATO'S WORKS

1. The editions of the complete works, which mark the progress of the critical study of Plato, are as follows:

a. *Platonis Opera quae extant omnia*, John Serranus, 3 folio vols., Paris, 1578. What was most valuable in this edition was the work of the printer and scholar, Henricus Stephanus (Henri Estienne). The excellence of this edition made it for a long time the vulgate. Its pages and page divisions, (a) b, c, d, e, are noted in the margin of modern editions, and are the accepted standard of reference.

b. *Platonis Dialogi* (*Gr. et Lat.*), Immanuel Bekker, 8 vols., Berlin, 1816–23. This editor, by his systematic collation of manuscripts, laid the foundation for the present critical study of the text of Plato. His work was especially important as demonstrating that, in establishing that text, there was little need of conjecture.

c. *Platonis Opera Omnia*, Gottfried Stallbaum, 10 vols., Teubner, Leipzig, 1835–, is the best complete edition with exegetical commentary.

d. *Platonis Opera quae feruntur omnia*, Martin Schanz, Tauchnitz, Leipzig, 1875–87. This contains the most full and exact critical apparatus.

e. *Platonis Dialogi*, Martin Wohlrab after C. F. Hermann, 6 vols., Teubner, Leipzig (Vol. I., 1886), is a convenient text edition with a brief critical commentary.

2. Important editions of the Apology and Crito and of the Phaedo.

a. *Platonis Apologia Socratis et Crito*, Martin Wohlrab, 1877, being Vol. I. Sect. 1 of Stallbaum's complete Plato referred to above in c.

b. *The Apology of Plato*, James Riddell, Oxford, 1867.

c. *Platons Verteidigungsrede des Sokrates und Kriton*, Christian Cron, 8th edition, Teubner, Leipzig, 1882.

d. *Apologia* (1893) and *Krito* (1888), being the third and second volumes in *Sammlung ausgewählter Dialoge Platos*, Martin Schanz, Tauchnitz, Leipzig.

e. *Verteidigungsrede des Sokrates und Kriton*, Christian Cron, bearbeitet von Heinrich Uhle, Teubner, Leipzig, 1895.

f. *The Phaedo of Plato*, R. D. Archer-Hind, Cambridge, England, 1883.

g. *Platons Phaidon*, Martin Wohlrab, Teubner, Leipzig, 1895, being part 6 of *Platons ausgewählte Schriften für den Schulgebrauch erklärt*.

III. CRITICAL COMMENTARY

The first reading given is that which is adopted in this edition, and is generally that of Wohlrab in his revision of the text of Hermann (see above, II. 1, e). Whenever Wohlrab's reading is departed from (except in the matter of punctuation, in regard to which see Preface), it is given and referred to by the letter W. B refers to the Codex Bodleianus; T to the Codex Venetus; S to the critical edition of Schanz (II. 1, d); SA and SC respectively to the separate editions by Schanz of the *Apology* and *Crito* referred to above (II. 2, d); C to Cron's eighth edition of the *Apology* and *Crito* (II. 2, c); CU to Uhle's recension of Cron (II. 2, e); A-H to Archer-Hind's *Phaedo* (II. 2, f); and Bem. to Cron's *Kritische und exegetische Bemerkungen zu Platons Apologie*, etc., *Fleckeisen's Jahrbücher*, Fünfter Supplementband.

APOLOGY

ἀπολογία σωκράτους · ἠθικός B, but ἠθικός seems added by a later hand.

17 A, I. 1 (and throughout this book). ὅ τι as also S and CU — ὅτι W and SA. Cron in Bem. argues that ὅτι should be the form always, leaving it to the reader to determine in each case whether it means 'what' or 'that.' For the history of the usage see Kühner-Blass, *Grammatik der Gr. Sprache*, § 93.

17 A, I. 7. χρή. B has χρῆν, which SA quotes Rieckher as saying could only have been used at the end of the trial if there had been acquittal. With χρῆν we should have expected the optative ἐξαπατηθεῖτε instead of the subjunctive.

17 B, I. 15. οὖν B followed by S, SA, C, and CU — γοῦν B (the later hand) and inferior manuscripts.

17 C, I. 21. ἃ λέγω S — ἂν λέγω SA "in order to retain the reference to the future," but it refers to the present also.

17 D, I. 32. ἑβδομήκοντα B — πλείω ἑβδομήκοντα Hermann and Riddell. Wohlrab (II. 2, a) quotes from Stallbaum: *ad vim oratoriam* πλείω *utique requiri videbatur*, but adds: *At Socrates non erat orator*.

18 A, II. 3. ψευδῆ S and SA bracket as unnecessary.

18 B, II. 11. ἐμοῦ οὐδὲν ἀληθές SA — ἐμοῦ μᾶλλον οὐδὲν ἀληθές B — ἐμοῦ μὰ τόν — οὐδὲν ἀληθές S — ἐμοῦ Hermann. The conjecture of Schanz, which is an attempt to keep near to the best tradition, he himself gives up in SA.

18 B, II. 12. φροντιστής SA brackets on the ground that it separates two closely connected ideas, μετέωρα and τὰ ὑπὸ γῆς, and suggests that it was interpolated under the influence of the *Clouds* of Aristophanes, "in which the word φροντιστής, which perhaps was first coined by Aristophanes, is used to characterize Socrates."

18 D, II. 24. κωμῳδιοποιός with B and S — κωμῳδοποιός SA as being the true Attic form.

18 D, II. 27. πάντες S, SA, and CU — πάντων W.

19, C. III. 15. — ἐστιν · μή . . . ὑπὸ Μελήτου . . . φύγοιμι · S brackets μή . . . φύγοιμι · — ἐστιν · μή . . . ὑπὸ Μελήτων . . . φύγοιμι · SA and CU as, in their view, at last giving a satisfactory sense to the expression.

19 C, III. 18. αὐτοὺς ὑμῶν τοὺς πολλούς S and CU with B — αὐτῶν ὑμῶν πολλούς SA.

19 D, IV. 1. οὐδέν ἐστιν SA and CU — οὐδέν (ἐστιν) S. Perhaps οὐδὲν ἔστιν should be read.

19 E, IV. 8. οἷός τ᾽ ἐστίν S brackets but SA reinstates, following it with a colon and supplying παιδεύειν ἀνθρώπους, so that ἰὼν κτλ. follows as explanatory without connective, and there is no anacoluthon.

20 A, IV. 13. Πάριος SA brackets as anticipating the question ποδαπός of l. 28.

20 A, IV. 20. καλώ τε καὶ ἀγαθώ S with B — καλώ τε κἀγαθώ SA and CU.

20 B, IV. 31. ἔχοι SA with B — ἔχει W and S. διδάσκει S and CU with B — διδάσκοι SA. See Bem., p. 86.

20 E, V. 27. ἴστε που S and CU — ᾖστέ που SA.

20 E, V. 27. ἐμός τε ἑταῖρος ἦν . . . ἑταῖρός τε καί CU with tradition — ἐμός τε ἑταῖρος ἦν S. SA has ἐμὸς ἑταῖρός τε ἦν, and brackets ἑταῖρός τε καί as an interpolation which disturbs the sense.

21 C, VI. 16. καὶ διαλεγόμενος αὐτῷ S and SA bracket as a gloss on διασκοπῶν τοῦτον. But see Bem., p. 89.

21 E, VII. 2. καί before λυπούμενος S and SA bracket with Cobet, thus rendering the construction more difficult and losing the fine gradation.

22 A, VII. 13. ἵνα μοι — ἵνα μή μοι Stephanus, Madwig, S, and SA, which spoils the author's meaning, which is that the oracle is true and must prove to be so. The ironical tone is already present in ὥσπερ πόνους τινὰς πονοῦντος.

22 A, VII. 13. Hermann's conjecture κἂν ἐλεγκτός, like the preceding, misses the author's thought.

22 C, VII. 34. τῷ αὐτῷ C and CU — τὸ αὐτό B — τῷ αὐτῷ αὐτῶν S and SA with Bekker following inferior manuscripts. Schanz says that the sharp contrast with καὶ τῶν πολιτικῶν makes the αὐτῶν necessary.

23 A, IX. 10. τοῦτ' οὐ F. A. Wolf, Riddell, S, SA, and CU — τοῦτο inferior manuscripts and Stallbaum, whom Cron approves in Bem., p. 90 — τοῦτον B.

23 B, IX. 12. εἰ εἴποι Stephanus, S, SA, C, and CU — εἴποι B.

23 C, X. 9. αὐτοῖς B and T followed by S, SA, C, CU, and Riddell — αὑτοῖς W with Hermann and inferior manuscripts.

23 D, X. 12. ἀγνοοῦσιν C and CU — ἀπορῦσιν Ast — ἀμφιγνοοῦσιν S and SA with the mistaken idea that ἔχουσιν οὐδὲν εἰπεῖν means the same as ἀγνοοῦσιν, whereas it expresses the result of their not knowing, so ἀλλά is quite right.

23 E, X. 20. ξυντεταγμένως B followed by C, Bem., p. 92 — ξυντεταμένως S, SA, and CU with Hermann following inferior manuscripts.

23 E, X. 25. καὶ τῶν πολιτικῶν C, Bem., p. 92 — [καὶ τῶν πολιτικῶν] S, SA (where the argument for striking out these words is well presented), and CU.

24 A, X. 32. τοῖς αὐτοῖς. SA adds τούτοις, which gives explicitness but is not necessary.

25 A, XII. 23. οἱ ἐκκλησιασταί S brackets with Hirschig and Cobet, but SA again inserts. Bem., p. 93.

25 C, XIII. 1. ὦ πρὸς Διός, Μέλητε CU — ὦ πρὸς Διὸς Μέλητε W, S, and C.

25 C, XIII. 2. πότερόν ἐστιν B and CU — πότερον ἔστιν S, W, and C with Bekker.

25 C, XIII. 3. ὦ τάν S, SA, and CU — ὦ τὰν B — ὦταν C — ὦ τᾶν T and W. See Kühner-Blass, *Grammatik der Gr. Sprache,* § 141.

25 E, XIII. 20. ἀπ' αὐτοῦ B, S, C, and CU — ὑπ' αὐτοῦ SA following T, but source, and not necessarily agency, is all that is implied.

26 A, XIII. 23. ἢ εἰ διαφθείρω, ἄκων C and CU — ἢ διαφθείρω ἄκων S and SA following Stephanus.

26 A, XIII. 25. καὶ ἀκουσίων S and SA bracket. Cron (Bem., p. 94) explains ἀκουσίων as a 'pure rhetorical pleonasm,' to make distinct to the ear that which without it is perfectly clear to the understanding. The καί, he says, is not redundant as often with πολύς (e.g. 22 C, πολλὰ καὶ καλά), because ἀκουσίων adds nothing, being exactly identical with τοιούτων.

26 A, XIII. 28. ὅ C — ου S, SA, and CU — ὅ . . . ποιῶ, ποιῶν Heindorf.

26 D, XIV. 24. S and SA bracket Ἀναξαγόρου, and would supply ἐμοῦ from the context as better suiting οἴει κατηγορεῖν. With Ἀναξαγόρου, S argues, we should have κατηγορεῖς.

26 E, XIV. 33. δοκῶ S brackets, and instead of νομίζειν reads νομίζω with B. SA restoring νομίζειν conjectures that perhaps σοὶ δοκεῖν . . . νομίζω is the true reading.

27 E, XV. 35. [ἢ] καὶ ὄνων, τοὺς ἡμιόνους with S, SA, and CU — ἢ [καὶ] ὄνων [τοὺς ἡμιόνους] C and W. See Bem., p. 95.

27 E, XV. 37. S and SA bracket ταῦτα on the ground that it is a gloss added to explain ἀποπειρώμενος. W, with Hermann, brackets τὴν γραφὴν ταυτήν.

27 E, XV. 40. οὐ with the best manuscripts — [οὐ] C. Bem., p. 96. SA inserts after καὶ αὖ: μήτε δαιμόνια μήτε θεῖα καὶ δαίμονας καὶ θεοὺς καὶ αὖ, and brackets the second τοῦ αὐτοῦ.

27 E, XV. 42. μήτε ἥρωας is bracketed by S and SA.

28 A, XVI. 9. καὶ ἄλλους C and CU — καλούς S — καὶ ἄλλους ἀγαθούς.

28 C, XVI. 25. ὦ παῖ T and in margin of B. S and SA omit.

29 B, XVII. 23. τούτῳ SA brackets as a gloss to ἐνταῦθα.

30, D, XVIII. 15. **ἀποκτεινύναι.** This is the correct form. See Meyer, *Griechische Grammatik*, § 494. — ἀποκτιννύναι W and others. So also in *Crito*, VIII. 25, IX. 8, and *Phaedo*, I. 32.

30 E, XVIII. 22. **ὑπὸ τοῦ θεοῦ** S, SA, and C bracket. Bem., p. 99. CU retains these words.

31 B, XVIII. 44. **εἶχον** B, SA, C, and CU — εἶχεν S with Wex. Bem., p. 101.

31 C, XIX. 3. **πολυπραγμονῶ** C and CU with better manuscripts. πολυπραγμονῶν S and SA.

31 D, XIX. 9. After **ἀρξάμενον** S and SA have a comma which hinders the proper connection, τοῦτ᾽ ἔστιν . . . φωνή τις.

32 A, XIX. 21. **μαχούμενον** S, C, and CU — μαχόμενον SA.

32 A, XX. 5. **ἅμα κἄν** Riddell, SA, and CU — ἅμα καὶ ἄμ᾽ ἄν B. — ἅμα C and S — ἄμ᾽ ἄν καί W.

32 B, XX. 9. **['Αντιοχίς]** S, SA, and CU. W retains. C retains but discredits. Bem., p. 104.

32 B, XX. 13. **ἠναντιώθην** C, CU, S, and SA with B — ἠναντιώθην ὑμῖν W. Bem., p. 104. The object of the verb is contained in ποιεῖν.

32 B, XX. 14. **καὶ ἐναντία ἐψηφισάμην** S, SA, and C bracket. CU retains. Bem., p. 105.

33 A, XXI. 13. **ἐπιθυμοῖ** SA and CU — ἐπιθυμεῖ C, S, and W.

33 D, XXII. 20. **καὶ τιμωρεῖσθαι** C, CU, and Riddell with the better manuscripts. S and W bracket. SA omits entirely. The two infinitives are equivalent to μνησικακεῖν. By retaining these words at the end of the sentence the idea of taking vengeance is emphasized.

34 E, XXIII. 29. **τὸ Σωκράτη** SA, C, CU, and manuscripts. B has τῷ Σωκράτει with interlinear correction. S has the dative, which Riddell also contends for.

35 B, XXIII. 43. **ὑμᾶς** Riddell and C with B — ἡμᾶς W, SA, and CU.

35 D, XXIV. 12. **πάντως** C, CU, and Riddell — [πάντως] W, S, and SA.

36 A, XXV. 8. **τριάκοντα** B and other manuscripts, with which modern editors all agree. Bem., p. 108.

36 A, XXV. 9. **ἀπεπεφεύγη** SA and CU — ἀποπεφεύγη B, S, C, W, and Riddell.

36 B, XXVI. 4. ἀποτεῖσαι. This form is determined by inscriptions. See Meisterhans, *Grammatik der Attischen Inschriften*, p. 144. — ἀποτῖσαι W and others.

36 B, XXVI. 5. οἱ πολλοί — οἱ πολλοὶ οὔ SA, on the ground that to supply ἐπιμελοῦνται would be extraordinary.

36 C, XXVI. 12. ἰών C and CU — [ἰών] S and SA.

37 C, XXVII. 20. τοῖς ἕνδεκα S brackets but SA retains. CU says that these words are perhaps a foreign addition, and that ἡ ἀεὶ καθισταμένη ἀρχή is better understood of the frequent changes which in later years the government had undergone.

37, C, XXVII. 21, 23. ἐκτείσω as determined by inscriptions. See Meisterhans, *Grammatik der Attischen Inschriften*, p. 144 — ἐκτίσω W and others. So also ἐκτείσειν, XXVIII. 17 instead of ἐκτίσειν in W, and ἐκτεῖσαι, XXVIII. 19 and 20 instead of ἐκτῖσαι in W.

37 D, XXVII. 28. καὶ τοὺς λόγους SA brackets because the feminine follows.

39 B, XXIX. 39. ὄφλων B, T, S, and C — ὀφλών SA and CU with Cobet. Thus accented this form is to be regarded as a present. See Kühner-Blass, *Grammatik der Gr. Sprache*, § 141, but compare Goodwin's *Greek Grammar*, p. 395.

39 C, XXX. 8. εἴργασθε οἰόμενοι — εἰργάσασθε οἰόμενοι μέν SA, CU with Hermann on the ground of traces of erasure in B — εἰργάσασθέ με οἰόμενοι S.

41 B, XXXII. 39. ἀηδές S, C with B — ἀηδής W, SA, and CU with T.

CRITO

43 D, I. 39. [τῶν ἀγγέλων] S, SA, C, and CU — τῶν ἀγγελιῶν W. Bem., p. 115.

44 B, II. 18. ἄτοπον B and S — ὡς ἄτοπον SC and CU.

44 B, III. 4. τοῦ ἐστερῆσθαι S, SC, and CU — σοῦ ἐστερῆσθαι Hermann with B and other manuscripts. But the infinitive depending on a preposition must have the article.

44 B, III. 5. ἔτι δέ CU — ἔτι SC dropping δέ because there is no coördinate adversative. Madwig meets the difficulty at the other end by writing χωρὶς μὲν σοῦ ἐστερήσομαι — ἔτι δή S.

44 C, III. 15. ὥσπερ ἂν πραχθῇ — ὥσπερ δὴ ἐπράχθη SC, but the subjv. is better, since the events referred to are still in the future.

44 D, III. 17. δῆλα S, C, and CU — δηλοῖ SC.

45 B, IV. 21.   ξένοι οὗτοι with the manuscripts and C. Bem., p. 116
— ξένοι (οὗτοι) S — ξένοι αὖ τοι CU — ξένοι τοι SC — ξένοι ἔτι W.
See *Fleckeisen's Jahrb.*, 1877, p. 222.

45 B, IV. 25.   S reads ἀποκνῇς, but SC has ἀποκάμῃς with B and
other manuscripts.

47 A, VI. 37.   οὐδὲ . . . τῶν δ' οὔ; these words are not in B, but are
added in the margin by an old hand. S and SC omit them.

47 C, VII. 23.   διόλλυσι B as corrected, SC and CU — διολλύει S
and W.

48 B, VIII. 26.   **ΚΡ. Δῆλα δὴ καὶ ταῦτα.** W following Buttmann gives
these words to Socrates. S and SC bracket φαίη γὰρ ἄν, and give
the following ἀληθῆ λέγεις to Crito.

48 E, IX. 26.   πείσας σε S, SC, and CU — πεῖσαί σε the manuscripts.

50 B, XI. 22.   ἠδίκει S, C, and CU — ἀδικεῖ SC with Heindorf.

51 A, XII. 36.   ἢ with the manuscripts — ᾗ SC and CU. Schanz suggests that in B the first hand may have written ἤ.

51 B, XII. 42.   ἢ πείθειν SC brackets.

51 D, XIII. 13.   ἀρέσκοιμεν C and CU with B — ἀρέσκομεν S and SC
with Madwig.

51 E, XIII. 22.   πείθεσθαι C and CU with B — πείσεσθαι S and SC
with Buttmann.

52 B, XIV. 13.   [ὅ τι μὴ ὅπαξ εἰς Ἰσθμόν] is not in the text of B, but is
supplied by a later hand in the margin. S and SC omit the words
entirely. Bem., p. 121.

53 A, XIV. 49.   δῆλον . . . νόμων S and SC bracket.

53 C, XV. 20.   ἢ S and SC — ᾗ B.

53 C, XV. 22.   ἄσχημον ἂν φανεῖσθαι S and CU with B — ἄσχημον
φανεῖσθαι SC.

53 E, XV. 33.   αἰσχρῶς S with B (with γλι by a later hand in margin)
— γλισχρῶς CU and SC.

53 E, XV. 38.   ἐν Θετταλίᾳ S brackets, but SC reinserts and gives
examples of similar repetition.

54 A, XV. 44.   τοῦτο ἀπολαύσωσιν. B has σου in the margin, which
adds to the sharpness of the reproach.

54 A, XV. 47.   SC brackets ἐπιμελήσονται αὐτῶν as superfluous. —
[ἐπιμελήσονται] S.

54 B, XVI. 1.   πειθόμενος ἡμῖν. After these words Meiser would introduce τοῖς σοῖς γεννηταῖς, referring to XIII. 21.

Phaedo

φαίδων ἢ περὶ ψυχῆς· ἠθικός B, but ἠθικός seems added by a later hand.

57 A, I. 7.   **Φλειασίων.**   This form of the word is determined by inscriptions.   See Meisterhans, *Grammatik der Att. Inschriften*, p. 41 — Φλιασίων W with others.

58 B, I. 33.   **Δῆλόν τε** S and A-H after Bekker — Δῆλον B.

58 C, II. 2.   **τί.**   B has τίνα, but as a correction in the space which would be filled with τί.

58 E, II. 21.   **ἀνήρ** S and A-H after Bekker — ἀνήρ B.

59 B, II. 43.   **[Κρίτων].**   S and A-H omit the word.   It is in B, but in a later hand.

59 D, III. 12.   **ἡμέρᾳ** — [ἡμέρᾳ] S and A-H after Hermann as spurious.

60 B, III. 37.   **τὸ . . . μὴ ἐθέλειν** B followed by S and A-H — τῷ . . . μὴ ἐθέλειν W.

60 C, III. 47.   **[πρότερον].**   S omits the word which is added in the margin of B.

116 B, LXV. 11.   **ἐκείναις ἐναντίον** — ἐναντίον ἐκεῖναι B.   S and A-H bracket ἐκεῖναι.

116 C, LXV. 27.   **ἀγγέλλων** A-H with B — ἀγγελῶν S after Bekker.

116 D, LXV. 46.   S brackets εἰκότως as spurious.

117 B, LXVI. 14.   **πώματος** S and A-H after Stallbaum — πόματος B.

118 A, LXVI. 48.   **πηγνῦτο** S — πήγνυτο B.

GREEK INDEX

ὅσα γε, C. vi. 32; xvii. 5.
ὅσοι δέ with correlative μέν omitted, Ap. ii. 26.
ὅτι introducing direct discourse, Ap. vi. 12; x. 14; xvi. 14; xvii. 41; C. xi. 22.
ὅ τι μαθών, Ap. xxvi. 4.
ὅ τι μή, C. xiv. 13.
οὐ with infinitive, Ap. xiv. 27.
οὐ superfluous, Ap. xv. 40.
οὐ μή with subjv. or future, Ap. xvii. 43, 74; C. iii. 5; vi. 13.
οὐ φαίνεσθαι, C. x. 21.
οὐ φάναι, Ap. xii. 38.
οὐδεὶς ὅστις οὐ, Ph. lxvi. 32.
οὔτε, οὐδέ, Ap. iv. 1.
οὗτοι, referring to what follows, Ap. xxii. 25.
οὗτοι repeated, Ap. xxiii. 41.
ὄφελος, Ap. xvi. 16; C. v. 25.
ὀφλισκάνειν, Ap. xxv. 13; with ὑπό, Ap. xxix. 39.

παθεῖν ἢ ἀποτεῖσαι, Ap. xxvi. 4.
πάλαι, Ap. ii. 5; xix. 15.
πάντως, Ap. xxii. 20; xxiv. 12.
παραβαίνειν, C. xv. 1.
παραγγέλλειν, Ph. iii. 19.
παραλαμβάνειν, Ap. ii. 10.
παραμένειν, Ph. lxiv. 28.
παρανόμως, Ap. xx. 11.
παραχωρεῖν, Ap. xxii. 36.
πάσχειν ὑπό, Ap. i. 2.
πείθεσθαι, C. xiii. 22.
πειρᾶσθαι, Ap. (ἀπό) xv. 37; (διά) xiv. 41.
πειραστικοί, 24.
πέμπειν, Ph. i. 30.
πένης, Ap. xxvi. 23.
πέρι, Ap. iii. 13.
περιεργάζεσθαι, Ap. iii. 6.
περιττότερον, Ap. v. 4.
περιφέρεσθαι, Ap. iii. 11.
πηγνῦτο, Ph. lxvi. 48.

πηνίκα, C. i. 4.
πλάττειν λόγους, Ap. i. 23.
πλέον ποιεῖν, Ap. ii. 42; Ph. lxiv. 12.
πλῆθος, Ap. v. 28; xix. 3, 19.
πλημμέλεια, Ap. viii. 11.
πλημμελές, C. i. 23.
πλὴν ἤ, Ap. xxxiii. 25.
πλοῖον, C. i. 34; Ph. i. 24.
ποιεῖν with two accusatives, Ap. xxiii. 42.
ποιητέον, C. x. 50.
ποιητής, Ap. vii. 15.
πολιτικοί, οἱ, Ap. vi. 15; x. 22.
πολλοί, οἱ, Ap. ii. 9; iii. 18; xxvi. 5; C. iii. 24; ix. 9.
πολλοῦ δεῖν, Ap. xxvii. 13.
πολυπραγμονεῖν, Ap. xix. 3.
πονεῖν πόνους, Ap. vii. 13.
πρᾶγμα, Ap. v. 2; xxxiii. 8; C. v. 18; xv. 22.
πράττειν ἀγαθόν, Ap. xxxi. 29.
πράττειν τὰ ἐμαυτοῦ, Ap. xxi. 13.
πρίασθαι, Ap. xiv. 29.
πρό, Ap. xvi. 39; xvii. 26.
προαγορεύειν, C. xiii. 7.
προβουλεύματα, Ap. xx. 8.
πρός, Ap. ii. 2; vi. 22; xi. 2.
προσειδέναι, Ap. iv. 12.
προσκαθίζειν, Ap. xviii. 28.
προσκεῖσθαι, Ap. xviii. 21.
πρόσωπα τοῦ διαλόγου, Ap. p. 117.
προτιθέναι, C. xiii. 24.
προτίθεσθαι, Ph. lxiv. 34.
πρόχειρα, Ap. x. 14.
πρυτάνεις, Ap. xx. 8, 14.
πρῶτον μέν, ἀλλά, C. xii. 13; xv. 6.
Πυθία, ἡ, Ap. v. 34.

ῥήματα καὶ ὀνόματα, Ap. i. 17.
ῥήτωρ, Ap. xx. 15; C. xi. 19.

σκευή, C. xv. 28.
σκέψεις, C. ix. 5.
σκιαμαχεῖν, Ap. ii. 30.

ENGLISH INDEX

The numerals refer to the introduction and similar matter by page, to the notes by chapter and line.

A Grammar of Attic and Ionic Greek

By FRANK COLE BABBITT, Ph.D. (Harvard)

Professor of the Greek Language and Literature, Trinity College, Hartford; formerly Fellow of the American School of Classical Studies at Athens.

PRICE, $1.50

THIS grammar states the essential facts and principles of the Greek language in concise form, with only so much discussion as may reasonably be demanded for a clear understanding of the subject. It therefore meets the wants of secondary schools and at the same time is sufficient for all ordinary demands of the college course.

A Modern Grammar.—The book incorporates the results of the more recent philological studies, and includes many departures from conventional presentation. Due regard is paid to the fact that analogy plays an important part in language, and that the context is often more important than grammatical rules in determining the exact significance of mode or tense.

Treatment of Cases.—The treatment of cases is thoroughly logical and clear. The true genitive and the ablative genitive are distinguished from each other and considered separately; likewise the true dative, the locative dative, and the instrumental dative. In this way much confusion is avoided.

Rules of Agreement.—The general rules of agreement are first given in a preliminary paragraph and are then followed by a general statement regarding attraction and *constructio ad sensum*, and its application to substantives, adjectives, verbs, etc.

Treatment of Modes.—The general significance of each mode is summarized briefly at the beginning, with its uses grouped and treated under the head of statements, questions, wishes, commands, etc. The various forms of statement are taken up and contrasted, thus allowing the student to perceive at a glance their similarities and differences.

Classes of Verbs.—While every portion of grammar has been simplified as much as possible, the notice of teachers is directed especially to the fact that the verbs have been reduced to five classes. In spite of this, however, nothing has been sacrificed in the process.

Indirect Discourse.—The subject of indirect discourse is put at the end of syntax, and the principles have been fully stated in their proper places. The general principles are clearly enunciated, followed by the details with numerous examples.

Syntactical Usage.—Tables of syntactical usage for reference are included to make it possible for the pupil to perceive the normal usage at a glance.

AMERICAN BOOK COMPANY, Publishers.

SYNTAX OF CLASSICAL GREEK

FROM HOMER TO DEMOSTHENES

Part 1.   The Syntax of the Simple Sentence, $1.50

BY

BASIL LANNEAU GILDERSLEEVE

WITH THE CÖOPERATION OF

CHARLES WILLIAM EMIL MILLER

OF THE JOHNS HOPKINS UNIVERSITY

GILDERSLEEVE'S Syntax of Classical Greek is a Syntax of Style from one point of view, and from another an Historical Syntax of Greek Literature. This unique feature of the work is due to the fact that, in the first place, the collection of examples it contains is in the truest sense of the word representative of all the various departments of the literature, and in the second place, special attention has been given in the text itself to historical evolution.

In the presentation, ease of consultation has everywhere been aimed at, hence only a single topic has been treated in each section, and examples illustrating different categories have not been mixed. The special point treated in each section is briefly indicated by small capitals. Then follows the author's statement in regard to the particular construction involved. The standard use under each head is in most cases illustrated by a translation. Thereupon follow the examples, which are added for purposes of minuter study.

The utmost care has been exercised in the verification of the passages, and the exact text has been studiously maintained. An attempt has been made to preserve also the exact setting of the passage, as it were, by uniformly marking every omission, even the slightest; while everywhere the critical warrant for the readings given has been kept in view.

AMERICAN BOOK COMPANY